BLUE MITCHELL

TWO BOOKS

by

William A. Luckey

ALONG CHICO CREEK

and

FAST HORSES

ALONG CHICO CREEK & FAST HORSES

ALONG CHICO CREEK

by

William A. Luckey

William A. Luckey
(Belinda E. Perry)

ALONG CHICO CREEK & FAST HORSES

for my grandchildren, Nash, Pierce, and Peyton
and with thanks to Lindsay Garcia

Published in 2010. The author may be reached at
waluckey@cybermesa.com

ALONG CHICO CREEK

After the Civil War, men drifted west intent on creating new lives. Some were quite successful, even if their substantial fortunes were based on lies or outright theft.

One such gentleman was Stephen Dorsey, who moved into the northeastern part of the New Mexico territory and made claims to large amounts of land. He married, became a senator, and was involved in railroad schemes and land grant fraud. Mr. Dorsey was tried twice for misuse of postal funds, without a guilty verdict.

During the later years he planned a grandiose Victorian castle attached to the two-story log structure that had initially housed his family. He built near what is known as Mountain or Chico Springs, to the east of Springer, New Mexico, which in itself was named after the lawyer who dealt with breaking up the Maxwell Land Grant.

When driving on the back roads that wander through northeast New Mexico, just above what is now the Kiowa National Grasslands, the vistas are of flat distances, volcanic cones, a few washes, low trees; nothing to excite the imagination of the occasional tourist.

Then the road brings the driver to a crossing on one of the east-west dirt tracks and there sits the Dorsey Mansion, resting against undulating ridges. The mansion is rightfully on the National Register of Historic Houses, and to some people it is haunted, beginning with the supposed burial of a worker in the foundation walls.

To imagine a simple cowboy in the early 1890s riding those distances and finding that mansion literally in the middle of nowhere is strong inducement to tell a story with the outrageous house as part of the cast of characters.

As with any book of fiction, places are not exact, springs and creek beds and swamps are imaginary or have changed over the intervening years.

CHAPTER ONE

He stood on a narrow ridge, where he cast an elongated shadow softened by the new light. A single ray touched his closed eyes, his lips moved but he made no sound. Thin grass underfoot shook in a light breeze. Birds circled in the pale sky.

Then he opened his eyes and the moving sun highlighted their vivid blue-green color. His fingers went through the mass of tangled blond hair, shaggy and beginning to curl along his neck. He'd had a hair cut a few months back while he was unconscious and a doctor needed to sew up the terrible scalp damage. Only now was the hair growing back, marking the length of time he'd been laid up and useless.

Another badge of his chosen life; working with the rough string, teaching manners to reluctant colts. Only this last time he'd saddled a well-mannered killer and had almost been the stallion's victim.

That the owner shot the horse meant no one else would have to try and ride the son, nor would the stallion pass on his fierce temper, but the animal's death had not erased Blue's fear. He rubbed the still-tender scar gently and told himself he'd come back to his old form soon enough.

Blue Mitchell stood on the ridge top, quiet and waiting, shaken by what he'd just done.

They had camped near a stream - a rare pleasure in the high plains of southeastern Colorado, and when Blue woke in the chilled dawn air, he called to his friend and there was no answer. He stood up, walked to his friend's bedroll and pushed at the exposed shoulder. Damp flesh rolled under his hand and then lay slack. Blue knelt and listened at the half-opened mouth and there was no breath; he touched the side of the neck and found no pulse. He rocked back on his heels as it settled in his mind: his friend was dead.

Needing to know, Blue rolled the body out of its canvas and blanket wrapping and searched for any swelling on hand or belly, maybe near the eyes, meaning a snake had killed him. But he knew it was too cold for snakes and the man's face was peaceful, showing no signs of pain, nothing to explain the death. A few deep scratches on the ground near the body, and dried earth on the fingers of one hand, told of a brief struggle before dying.

Behind the bedrolls and remains of a fire, two horses stood hobbled, heads hanging, ears flickering enough to tell Blue that they were paying attention. As usual the sorrel packhorse was off by himself, grazing peaceably and uninterested in any activity.

To Blue's way of thinking, there was no point in taking the body into a town. Nothing had happened, no one got killed. It was straight fact that a good man had died.

The ground was sandy and loosened from recent rains, so Blue rolled the cooling flesh into the stiff canvas, piled in the few personal belongings and dragged the body down a shallow ridge near the streambed. Using a cottonwood branch, he jerked and pulled at the sand until part of the banking collapsed and his friend was buried. It was a temporary burial; soon enough water and scavenging animals would reduce Peter Charley's body to scattered bones, a fitting end for the lapsed Christian-schooled Indian.

The urgent need to be alone with his thoughts drew Mitchell to stand on the high ridge, where the sun burned into him until his eyes watered and his head ached. He stood motionless, not in remembrance or respect but from blank confusion. The sun finally came straight at him, hitting Blue's eyes and moving him to finish the inevitable chores, get saddled and ride somewhere. He and Peter Charley had been looking for a horse race; now it didn't seem to matter.

Blue had been drifting for ten years, working the wild stock and accepting the sudden brutality of life. For a brief time he'd shared that life with one man and now that man was nothing but food for coyotes, insects, and birds.

Near the horses, Blue picked up the dead man's rig and wondered where a Christian-raised Jicarilla Apache in Colorado got his hands on a Texas trail saddle with a tied-down Mochilla, double-rigged, well-made and barely used. The hand-woven fine leather bridle and reins, and a saddle blanket thick to the fingers and brightly colored, were more ordinary.

Blue put his own ragged blanket over the saddle, tied everything at the top of a lone juniper, and smoothed the colorful saddle blanket over the brown mustang's back. It wouldn't take long for another drifter to find the gear, read the sign of no recent camp and take his unexpected prize out of the tree. Blue hoped foolishly that whoever took the gear was a decent man.

The chores were easy, his hands knowing what to do while his mind sorted out what might have happened. Blue packed what he could onto the sorrel's back, had his mustang bitted and ready, and only then did he look at the black pony who'd been his friend's prized possession. The animal was too short for Blue; the shared joke had been that Blue's heels would click under the pony's belly. Peter Charley had been compact and quiet, while Blue stood loose-limbed and half-wild. He undid the hobbles and dropped them, walked from the black pony to his own horse. He mounted the brown mustang and swung the horse south, away from the broken ridge, the remains of a fire, the empty matted grass.

The black pony took a few steps, intending to follow the sorrel and the brown out of habit. Then as if realizing nothing held him, the black pony stopped, arched his neck, whinnied loudly and spun around. There was a moment when the brown mustang reared and the sorrel pack horse trotted toward the loose pony, but once Blue got the mustang settled, there was only blowing dust to mark the pony's disappearance.

Blue headed south, the sorrel packhorse reluctantly trailing him. He rode down a small, brush-lined canyon that would bring him out to the endless grasslands of northern New Mexico. Eventually he came across what appeared to be a well-used trail through a side canyon. The trail narrowed, then split and Blue followed the unevenly worn track, marked with cattle and horse prints and even the flat lines of thin wagon wheels. Instead of finding himself in New Mexico territory and a small town, he rode into the chaos of a homestead.

The first thing Blue saw was a corralled horse, then a small man headed toward the animal. It always surprised him, the variety of individuals who took up living in such rough and isolated land. This particular man had a fine high-colored colt securely penned and he had a parcel of noisy children circling him as he walked toward the colt. Blue sat quietly on his mustang and watched the children spread across the small ranch yard. They took no notice of him.

He studied the horse in the pen closely; behind those crazy streaks on the colt's hide, and the two-color mane and tail, there was a good horse, maybe even a great one; stout, a decent chest, wide-sprung ribcage, and the right length to the hind leg. The eyes were large, well set, a dark brown with no white showing, even as the colt was being stalked by the small man.

It appeared to Blue that the colt's owner, the small man crowded by tow-headed kids all talking too quickly, had decided to geld the colt. Blue's entrance in the small yard, even with the loose-trailing sorrel packhorse, did not stop the man from approaching the corral, one hand holding a knife, the other a rope.

Once the man stepped inside the corral, the children swarmed back past Blue to settle with little shoving or pushing on the front verandah of the crude cabin. The oldest child, a girl, moved deliberately and took the time to study Blue as she passed. She nodded once, smiled, then joined the rest of the brood to settle down and watch their papa.

Inside the corral, the man hesitated, then spoke back over his shoulder; "Be with you a minute, mister, got me a discussion with this here colt to finish." He lifted the knife as if the gesture was enough to describe his intentions. Blue shuddered, patted the mustang's neck and tried not to focus on what the man was about to do.

This morning he'd buried his friend; right now he was lost and it was of little consequence. The young ones, all ages and sizes, standing or sitting on the cabin's front steps, didn't seem to mind that they lived in a place with no name. They watched their papa, and one mid-sized boy held the hand of the smallest girl, who seemed ready to cry.

That oldest girl was staring openly at Blue now, without blushing when he turned to look at the grouped children. He remained on the steady brown mustang, hands folded on the saddle horn. Peace, his attitude said; he carried no knife, rifle, or side arm. He'd watch and wait; there was no need to hurry on his account. The girl smiled again and Blue's gut turned. She was pretty.

Inside the corral, the brood's father stepped close to the horse; the paint colt reared and struck out. The man stood his ground, still holding the knife. It would be tough for any red-blooded male to watch cutting future life from the handsome colt. Blue shuddered; he knew that geldings were easier to work with and that folks had a prejudice against high-color horses, even though this paint was mostly bay, with white streaks starting at the top of his hindquarters and down his legs. White showed in the black mane and tail, and there was a white streak down one side of his neck.

A woman, who had to be the brood's mother, came close to Blue and cocked her head. Beside her another light-headed little girl tried to get behind her mother and watch Blue at the same time. "Ma'am." Blue nodded; she smiled, waiting. He asked; "I'd like to water the horses. And maybe rest the night for chores, if that's all right with you and the mister."

All those light-colored heads watched the corral and paid no attention to Blue's talking, except for the girl. She was almost a woman Blue realized; light hair sun-streaked, wearing a too-small man's shirt and men's pants. She eyed Blue, shook her head again and disappeared into the house.

Blue found himself studying the children, appreciating their enthusiasm, until someone yelled; "Pa, don't". The children's pa had flipped the rope over the colt's head, tugged on it until the colt reared. Then he seemed to study the knife, looked again at the colt, and let go of the line. Blue wouldn't blame any man for changing his mind. The colt had prospects to make his owner some good money.

The man left the corral and walked toward Blue. Two of the bigger boys closed in behind their pa. Inside the corral, the colt reared and pawed at the rope hanging in front of him, snorting and trembling but willing to fight. The man stopped clear of Blue and looked up at him. No greeting, no manners, only the bluntness Blue preferred; "Mister, you know 'bout horses."

That was a jump, Blue thought. He knew the signs were there, in his well-mannered horses, his own ease in the saddle. But a man had to know what he was seeing before making such a statement. He nodded; "Yes sir, I've rode a bronc or two." Never brag. He'd learned that a good while ago, which in his short life was maybe six months past when that damned fancy-papered stallion nearly killed him. The man interrupted Blue's remembering.

"I surely can't make up my mind. Maybe you can help us, now that colt he's a pistol but ain't none of us here can ride him. He's hell to catch and pure misery to saddle." The man looked around as the children stared at their pa in horror. "Well he is a devil." Their pa grinned at Blue as his children looked to their ma, who didn't flinch at the swearing. The children let out a common sigh as their father continued. "You look like you can straddle that youngster and maybe put some manners on him. Meals and a five dollar piece for your trying." The man laughed; "And we'll bury you with kind words if it comes to that."

The last statement rubbed against Peter Charley's early morning death. Blue nodded and stepped down from the mustang.

After studying Blue briefly, the woman was of a mind to feed him a small meal before he worked the colt, and she was a fine cook. She had level eyes and a quick mind, an equal match for her husband who had that way of staring at Blue and nodding, as if counting scars and marks and coming out ahead. She served up eggs, beans, side meat and fresh-boiled coffee and Blue was hungry enough to eat even though he knew it wasn't smart. Hunger did that to a man, ruined his sensibilities.

When he looked up to thank her, she was watching him. He knew what he saw, a beat-up face and wild blue eyes that seemed to draw out other folks' bad temper. His hair was almost the light color of her brood. He wasn't much to look at but he could ride a horse, give it manners and a decent handle, and usually that was enough.

Blue wondered where that oldest daughter had gone. There was no sight or sound of her and he took a sip of coffee, thought on her; she'd been a pretty thing. He returned his attention to the older woman.

"Thank you, ma'am. It's been a while since I've eaten this good." She was studying him again, and Blue thought he could see in her eyes that look said she hoped he didn't stay long. The littlest girl, with white-blond hair and bright eyes, was sitting on her ma's lap. The child smiled at him and when Blue smiled back, she hid her face against her mother's bosom and the gesture embarrassed both her mother and Blue. He stood, nodded and went outside.

The colt wasn't mean; Blue entered the pen and the colt watched as Blue walk to him. The colt put his head down into Blue's cupped hands and they stood a moment. When Blue picked up the dangling rope, turned it over the colt's nose and tugged, asking for a proper step forward, the colt went straight up, pawing wildly and squealing. Blue hung on until the colt had to come down.

Immediately Blue asked for that step forward again. The colt bolted, which Blue had figured on and he dug in his heels, leaned back on the rope and the colt's head was yanked to the side, his body forced into a small circle. When the colt came around, Blue threw the end of the rope at the colt's haunches and the colt jumped forward.

In jerks, stops, and rears, the colt learned to listen to Blue's voice and keep an eye on him. Blue asked that the colt go in different directions at the end of the lead, until the youngster began to breathe hard, sweat showing on the neck, chest, and loins. When the colt was moving easy, Blue asked him to whoa and the youngster was more than willing to do what this crazy cowboy wanted.

Horse and human stood together. The only sound was the colt's harsh breathing. They studied each other, the rope hanging loose between them.

Blue left the colt to think things over while he got his gear off the brown and dragged it inside the corral. He used his hands to smooth the drying saddle blanket over the paint's back while he spoke calmly and the colt turned his head, one eye staring at Blue. When he raised the saddle, the horse flinched but a sharp word from Blue and the colt steadied.

He did try once to bite as Blue did up the cinch, and Blue's voice was enough to stop the threat. He tugged the cinch and the colt turned his head, one large brown eye staring at Blue but there was no threat.

Stepping into the saddle was easy enough. The paint stood quiet but the black-tipped ears never settled; moving sideways, back, pricked forward, then a head shake. There was no buck yet, no fight even as Blue found the off stirrup and let his weight drop gently. He picked up the reins, touched the colt's mouth through the heavy leather. It was a light bit, no curb, nothing to scare the colt. It was always Blue's choice in starting a horse.

Then the colt sat down and Blue almost slid out of the saddle backwards. He laughed, put the side of his spurred boots against the colt's ribs and they went up and into a bucking fit. He rode it, mostly, until the colt tripped over himself and they both went down. Blue hit the ground hard but was clear of the wreck. He sat up, tasting blood in his mouth.

After a few deep breaths, Blue spat out dirt and a small piece of fresh manure and got up, found the colt beginning to stand, and climbed aboard before the colt was steady on all four legs.

The colt stood quiet and Blue almost relaxed as the painted head came around and sniffed at the boot toe, licked the leather, then raised his upper lip, taking in scent, sorting through all the stories. Then without any change in the calm eye, the horse bolted, hit the fence, skidded to the right and went into some high-flying bucks. Along the fence the bucks were more forward leaps than anything sideways or fancy. Every time the colt started to slow, Blue egged him on with the lightest touch of his spurs until the bucks leveled out into an easy lope.

If the colt put that gait into his offspring, a man could make a fortune, Blue thought. He drew the colt into a trot, taking a rein in each hand to get a feel of the bronc's mouth. At first it was head high and leaning to the inside, so Blue raised his hands and kept the colt's head up there, until the colt chewed on the bit and the loosening neck muscles told Blue the colt was thinking about giving so he brought his hands down. The colt sighed and dropped his head, taking a long rein but keeping to the trot.

Then came a wild buck with the head low, hind end twisting, no chance to find a rhythm and Blue slammed into the fence, dropped and rolled into a ball as the colt squealed and tore around the pen.

Finally the colt pulled himself to a stop by catching a rein around a foreleg. Outside the pen the children were babbling, distant sounds that Blue ignored. He got up, feeling a torn shirt flap along his side where he'd scraped the fence. He knew nothing was broke but his pride so he pushed aside his sorry thoughts. The colt was all that mattered.

He approached the paint, who snorted but couldn't get his head up to bolt, rear, or strike back. Blue knelt down to unwrap the rein and then quickly stepped into the stirrup and was on the colt's back, a good hold on the wet mouth. He asked the colt to move forward and got a head shaking but no response so he thought – 'to hell with it' - and put both spurs against the sweaty bay hide. The colt wanted to buck but Blue kept the reins tight until all that was left for the colt was to go forward.

It was a deliberate three times around the pen in each direction before Blue stopped the colt, asked him to back and the colt took two steps before he quit. Blue stepped down, quickly unsaddled the paint, slipped the bridle off and walked away. It took all the discipline he had left to manage these simple chores, but he wasn't going to admit to those watching how much he wanted to fall to his knees and throw up that meal he'd eaten before saddling the bronc. He took a cup of water from the missus and drank gratefully.

Standing in the doorway of the house was the oldest daughter, face set, eyes wide. She wore a pretty flowered dress that had been made for someone smaller, and Blue nodded to her. Then he grinned and wiped his face, took off his hat and ran his fingers through the damp blond hair; for some reason these gestures usually made the girls smile.

He rode the colt twice the next day, got thrown three times and was right back in the saddle. The following morning, the colt didn't offer to buck but Blue didn't trust what he was feeling through the lines. He told the head of the clan what he thought, that even if he gelded the colt, he'd never be much of a horse for a family. The small man agreed, he'd been watching and studying and figured on the same thing. He made a decent offer to Blue, a trade for that easy-going sorrel he used as a packhorse, a trade across the board for the paint colt. Five bucks thrown in for the entertainment of watching him and the colt battle it out, and some provisions the missus had put up for

Blue; stew, biscuits, canned fruit, things a drifting man would truly appreciate.

When Blue got ready to leave, the sorrel now tucked into the pen with good hay, the mustang burdened with packs and supplies, the children came in around their parents, making a tight group that watched him. The paint colt was saddled and standing quiet for the moment, and Blue held one rein to the bridle, with a low-port curb in the colt's mouth. He'd put a thin bosal under the headstall and had the south end of the line tucked into his back pocket, so if he and the colt parted company, Blue wouldn't be left on foot.

He'd only learned the family name this morning, when the pa gave him the five dollars and put out his hand. "Name's Orton Hubert. My folks they come along the Santa Fe Trail from Kansas and here's where my pa stopped." Blue accepted the handshake; "Blue Mitchell." The two men grinned. Names hadn't been needed while Blue worked the paint colt.

Now he thought to move on when the youngest of the brood, that little girl with the pale blond head of hair, came running to him, sending the colt back two or three steps until he felt the bosal's pinch and remembered his new schooling. The colt stood quiet even as the child held out her arms and spoke Blue's name.

He bent down and she hugged him, pushing her face close to his. She smelled of soap and breakfast as Blue took a deep breath and thanked her. She said nothing but his name again and ran back to her mother to hide.

He guessed there was a first time for everything and he'd never thought a child's hug felt like this. Blue shook his head and climbed on the colt, who tried spooking sideways until he moved into a well-placed spur. The family called out 'bye' and 'so-long' and a little voice called his name again as he rode from the small ranch in the middle of nowhere.

He was several miles down the trail and out of sight of the isolated ranch before he realized that the older girl hadn't reappeared or ever spoken to him. He could only guess at the sound of her voice, or why she put on that pretty dress. For some reason his look, even though he was a no 'count drifter, seemed to bring out the flirt in females.

The colt shied at a bird cackling in the branches of a low piñon and Blue laughed; another girl waited some other place. It was a given, along with more broncs, fights, hunger and rain. It was his chosen life and despite the hardships, he wouldn't change whatever happened to him.

CHAPTER TWO

The trail emptied abruptly into grasslands, offering a glimpse of beauty that satisfied Blue. Towns and cities held nothing for him; what lay spread out for miles was where he belonged. Blue dropped the brown's lead but he couldn't trust the colt to stand loose. He kept a feel of the wet mouth as he tried by his weight deep in the saddle, the utter stillness of his own body, to teach the colt patience.

No one could teach a horse to enjoy beauty. Well maybe the brown mustang understood, for the once-wild horse remained motionless; head low, ears pricked forward, not immediately grazing or trying to move on, but standing, looking out where Blue himself was staring. It could be that memories of an earlier life ran wild through the mustang's brain.

The hills were not quite pointed at the top and colored pale green sprinkled with red chunks of rock. They created a soft world filled with distance and clouds and nothing to ease a man's soul but the rare light of color and shadow. Blue shook his head. Such thoughts didn't put food in a man's belly even as the sights eased his constant restlessness.

He wouldn't camp here. The land was rough ground and offered graze that was more thorn than grass. It was truly land that deliberately teased a man, appearing soft at the base of those hills and in the miles of open range, but Blue wouldn't make that mistake. It was all things that bit into a man's flesh even as they appeared sweet and beckoning. Like some women, Blue thought, and laughed, a sound harsh enough that the paint colt tensed and the mustang shifted his weight, preparing for whatever had caught Blue's attention.

It was a lesson no sensible horseman forgot; the ground was hard, getting thrown hurt. He studied the land a few minutes more, feeling the colt begin to relax under him. Then Blue leaned sideways to pick up the brown's lead. The colt felt the shift of balance and bucked forward into Blue's hand.

"Damn." He cursed out loud when he slipped against the saddle, lost the brown's lead as he concentrated on finding the colt's rhythm, picking up the reins and without brutality, throwing the colt off balance until the paint had to walk on, sigh and throw his head but finally listen. Blue pushed the colt with his leg, no spur this time, and the paint graciously stepped sideways.

The brown swung his head, putting the lead near Blue's grasping fingers. He laughed again as he picked up the line, remembering when the mustang was a spooky youngster like this paint only not so pretty and not handled from a baby. The brown was running wild until Blue caught him in a freak throw from a tired palomino. He figured his boss at the time owned the horse but the man saw only the brown's poor condition, the tangled mane, burrs knotting the tail, feet chipped and flattened. Blue lost respect for the man since he couldn't see past the outside to the big heart and temperament of the rough bronc.

Blue quit the job and gladly took the mustang as partial pay; the brown could outrun almost anything and his single-foot gait was easy on a man's backside while covering the miles. The periodic demotion to packhorse had been rough at first; the mustang didn't want all that junk piled on him but patience worked as usual, and now the brown waited on the colt's foolishness as if the older horse understood the need for rebellion.

Still they weren't stopping here to camp. Blue wanted to find water, something like decent grass, a bit of dried wood for a fire. As horses and rider moved on, the land changed and changed again; cut deep into gullies and washes banked with dry grasses, then the edge of a soft arroyo interrupted with staghorn cactus and yellowed brush. There were no defined trails, only the faint lines of deer and wild horse tracks, which Blue followed knowing they would always lead to water.

It was a week of dry camps, slow water, a sore backside from the colt's uneven temper and hands raw from leading the brown as he tried to steady the paint. Blue found that he was drifting west as he attempted to ride south, following the land as it offered sluggish creeks, a short rain twice in three days, and sparse grass that kept the horses moving with full bellies.

These were good conditions for the paint colt to learn the important lessons. It wasn't all corrals and grain and sun-cured hay or watered grass, but miles of rock and sand for traveling. At the end of the week, Blue considered the colt might become a decent mount.

The colt grunted with each stride as they climbed another steep hill. Ahead were trees, the wind shook dried leaves that turned in the late sun, glinting like the gold of a false treasure. Blue grinned as he felt the tired colt perk up, the brown step with a livelier gait. Trees meant water, which meant grass and wood, broke-off branches and dead leaves for starting a fire. Trees meant a decent camp and Blue knew the two horses had earned the rest.

The place was obviously well-used by travelers and thankfully empty. Blue stepped from the colt, who was too tired to object when it was done from the off side, another piece of the colt's education. A narrow creek threaded between sandy banks, starting where a spring bubbled up. Trees were thick around the edges and in a curve of the stream bed, a pool had formed that was deep enough Blue intended to soak in it. As he studied the place, pleased with himself for finding it, he realized the water level was low; dried grasses and roots hung above the water but not touching it. He'd not realized the land was this dry.

He'd wait until the horses were watered and hobbled, turned loose to graze. Then he'd eat a few strips of jerked venison washed down with mouthfuls of cold clear water. When all those simple needs were cared for, only then would he wade into the clear pool and let himself sink to the bottom, knees drawn up, head back. Maybe when he surfaced, the promise of a quarter moon would rise and he'd float a while, cleansing himself from the past few weeks.

He woke once before midnight to see the white streaks of the paint colt and the mustang's darker shadow; they stood hobbled, close together, heads low, tails barely moving. Just before he settled back to sleep, Blue heard a grunt, then a thump and he grinned. The brown knew how to lie down and get up with hobbles; the colt hadn't learned that trick yet.

They rode out well after sunrise, both horses rested and moving with easy strides, no longer snapping at the scattered stalks of high grass. Blue followed the bank of a dry wash in a general west and south direction. At one point the colt stumbled and almost went to his knees. Blue leaned back and kept the horse upright, then let the colt take a step before he studied the ground.

There was the dark rounded shape of a pipe barely free of covering dirt. Blue followed what could be more of the pipeline with his eyes and realized when he turned the colt to look back at where they'd camped, he could see a simple humped trail; more pipe that had stayed buried. The spring had been tapped and whoever had done the work, they'd kill the source soon enough. Blue shook his head. Water was riches out here, and someone was almighty greedy.

At one point the creek bent back on itself so he crossed a long patch of thin grass and came around the point of a ridge, a collection of hills and gullies that seemed to run on endlessly.

He grunted then, as tired as the colt and as bored as the brown mustang. He'd gotten them into this mess and now it was time to find them flat land that didn't take so much out of both horses and their tired rider.

It was enough of a surprise to stop the colt who allowed the brown to bump him, this time without protest. Blue figured his own jaw dropped six inches. Looking down from the ridge top, even at this odd angle, there it was, a goddamn log cabin set up next to a fancy stone house like they wanted to be related. The roof tiles overlapped, metal gullies spanned the edges to carry whatever rain fell to a long gully emptying into a man-made pond.

He turned his head slowly, noting the stone and wood out-buildings and that in a separate canyon there was another set of houses, small and large, seeming to be connected with covered runs and wood walkways. Whoever did the building in this part of the grassland had their own idea of what they wanted and the money to get it done.

It was the fanciest house he'd ever seen and he had been in cities like Denver and Tucson. The building was constructed of local sandstone and logs hauled from a long distance, with two stories of a high-pitched roof, a long section of the house sticking out to the back. Big son of a bitch, he thought. He snorted and the colt whinnied, the brown shook his head.

A round room with a crown on it took up most of the middle of the front; stone faces glared out from under the roof. Some distance from the house, set in trees and bushes, there was a hard-edged pool holding a few inches of rusty water. The structure was big enough to be a hotel but there wasn't much traffic here, no deep ruts or well-packed trails. To the back, up against the long-sided ridge, were the corrals and barns and there wasn't enough fenced graze to feed horses or cattle. Land, yes, miles of it outside the house windows but it was thin land, holding dust, cactus, those damned red rocks and not enough for a decent bovine supper. Straight ahead from the house and pointed south were the miles of grass and softer gullies, streams that ran only after rains. Nothing lived on much water out here.

The pipe coming out of that spring maybe six miles back brought water to the pool and the odd statue that spouted drops through an upturned mouth. The fancy system would offer the lady of the house a constant supply of water, for no man living alone built like this. There was always a woman around when a man had to show off.

Blue reined the colt around, headed up the side of the ridge to ride behind the house and away from its rows of windows and too many doors. He wanted no encounters with the people who would build such a place. The slope of hills that half-circled the house had their own boundaries. Blue stopped the paint to study the wall made of stone, pieces well- fitted together to keep the fancy horses and blooded cattle safe from animal or human predators. They didn't work but their design pleased a man's eye.

It took an hour or more to get out of sight from the house. All that time it felt like something hard and ugly watched from the high windows and cut stone. The notion made his back itch, taunted him with wanting to set the colt into a run, let the brown catch up as he would. It made no sense so Blue held the restless paint to a walk and damned the place behind him as if it were alive.

The colt jumped sideways almost before Blue heard the shot. It was too distant to be aimed at him, and right at the moment he didn't think anyone in particular was out for his hide. He stroked the colt's neck, eased his own breathing and picked up the reins. This time the colt liked being told what to do as Blue aimed for a distant rock. The colt almost nodded as he slipped into that easy trot to take them where Blue had pointed.

Eventually the land changed again, becoming rocky underfoot but there were trees along the creek, and a swamp coming up to his left, ringed with high grass that he knew too well would cut a horse's mouth; thick matted grass that sank as a horse tried to cross what looked to be solid ground. Swamp all right and in the middle of the desert. Blue laughed.

The rich greens were pretty though, until birds flew up ahead of him and the two broncs. There were twitters and chirps from the smaller ones, then a growing number of larger, darker birds that Blue instantly disliked. There were no signs of human life except narrow wheel ruts high-sided with drying mud. The tracks were reasonably fresh and made by a team of draft horses, for the prints were of good-sized hooves traveling at speed. Good, he thought, and rubbed the colt's damp neck. Good. There wasn't company waiting on him. He preferred riding alone.

The bay paint bogged his head and let out a buck then went sideways and continued in a series of small bucking leaps as if to run away from something terrible. Blue's body swayed dangerously but he found his balance and guided the paint in a circle till they returned to the point where the son of a bitch had started the foolishness.

The stop was abrupt and stiff as Blue was jammed into the saddle swell, then sat back. He took the time to wipe his mouth, rub at a rib that'd been hit by the horn, giving the colt time to quiet. Then he saw what had spooked the horse and a chill ran down his neck. The brown mustang stood his ground and shook his head, unimpressed with the youngster's bucking. Then the brown snorted and shivered as his nostrils widened to take in a terrible scent.

It was a buckboard, the trim fresh and the wheels outlined in bright colors. The team of sorrels stood quiet, legs sunk above the fetlocks in bent grass and mud. Occasionally one horse would stretch down to search for tender fodder, then raise its head, a strand of saw-edged grass hanging from its teeth. The team's driver still held the lines, each hand crumpled around the leather. Blood had darkened down his back, soaked into the leather-covered seat, blood that crawled with shimmering, greedy flies. There was no doubt the man was dead, and it was a recent kill.

24

Blue Mitchell had witnessed death but he'd never seen this much fresh blood. The sorrel team had to be saints for standing, or maybe they were worn-out. The flesh was bled out, stinking, flies crawling over the man's back, around the fist-sized hole that showed through the dark coat.

The dead man wasn't a rancher or the usual storekeeper from a nearby town. Blue'd rarely seen clothes like the corpse wore. The coat was long enough the sides were bunched on the seat, and silver lines cut through the heavy black material. The corpse looked like an undertaker or a banker and not someone to be back-shot and left in the brush.

It came to Blue that the man could live in that house he'd passed a while back, but there hadn't been tracks that would fit with this wagon's wheels, or hoof prints the size of the team. The sorrels were draft horses and not a fine-stepping fancy pair of well-bred and matched geldings as would suit a gentleman's life.

He finally convinced the skittish paint colt to walk forward, as the team's presence seemed to ease the colt's nerves. The man's front was messy against the bibbed white shirt with one of those fly-away collars half undone, a gray vest covered in a faded pattern, and suspenders spattered with more blood. Something tall and black lay at the man's feet, sideways and tipped so Blue couldn't really see the shape, but it hadn't moved yet so he ignored it.

He couldn't leave a body to rot; the horses would starve in harness or take flight and cause one hell of a wreck. It would be shameful if a dead man came flying into his home ranch or house where someone waited for his return.

Blue looked up, finally seeing what would have told him if he'd been paying attention. Birds in growing numbers circled the sky above him, too far away to see feathers or colors but any man with sense knew they were buzzards keen to a fresh kill. Now they would stay away; the presence of Blue and the horses meant there was life below mixed in with the scent of death. Blue wanted to curse them, but they were doing their job, waiting to pick clean new death and rid the land of stench and sickness.

That prompted Blue into action. If he untangled the lines from those lifeless hands, or more'n likely cut the leathers close to the pale flesh, then he could drag the team onto decent ground and follow them till they got within seeing distance of home. Then he'd tie up the sorrels and go on ahead to warn anyone to the house.

It was a gruesome plan but the best he could do, since he wasn't up to sharing a buckboard seat with that much blood, and the staring eyes, the terrible hole through the body. There was a ring on one hand, a fine watch chain dangled from the vest pocket. All in all the man was a true gentleman even out of his element, and extremely dead.

He stepped off the colt and tied him to a distant bush. The white-eyed youngster pulled back and pawed the ground. The brown grazed, keeping one eye alert to Blue's action. Blue patted the colt's soaked neck and swore under his breath.

As he walked toward the team and buckboard, the colt whinnied after him, and the sorrels took up the call. There were horses bouncing and fussing in front of him and at his back. Blue made sure he had a knife in hand as he got near the team. The off sorrel, the one closest to him, rolled its eyes and lifted a threatening hind leg.

He spoke to the sorrels and the team settled finally, tails down, all four legs, or eight if he was to count right, on the ground, waiting for their promised freedom.

The indistinct shape turned out to be nothing but a hat, black and tall, rounded brim, no good in the hot sun but what he'd seen in towns on bankers and such. It was an item worn only by the better class of folks, so he'd been told too many times.

Here and now he knew that class didn't matter, dead was dead. The man wore that fancy long coat and all the rest, even the boots were laced and short, not meant for riding or work. It was a lesson learned too late; killing didn't care about a man's social standing.

Damn, Blue said out loud. Damn. Chances were he'd be the first suspect in this death and the law would have to search him, find his pistol wrapped in an old shirt, his rifle with spiders living in it. Like it or not, shooting wasn't the way he made his living, or robbing folks for that matter. But he knew how the law saw him and he'd too often had the privilege of being locked up for defending himself. Blue shrugged; at least he wasn't back-shot and dead.

First he tried sliding the reins through the soft fingers and it wasn't easy since he refused to touch the pulpy flesh. He pulled sideways, sawed back and then forward and nothing really moved excepting the loose hands with those miserable curled fingers.

He finally sliced the fine leather reins while ignoring what held to the lines. Despite his hard years, all the scrapes and fights and wrecks, cutting close to a dead man's hands, smelling the stink of blood and unmentionable fluids, seeing the eyes still open, the jaw hanging, flies going in and out – it was enough that Blue had to turn and take gulps of fresh air before he could finish the chore.

The sorrel team sighed. Blue took the off sorrel by the bit, pushed the near sorrel's nose and gently backed the pair, then drew them out of the low marsh where they'd been stranded. It didn't take long for the pair to move as he let go. When they stepped into a good walk, Blue hurried to the colt who was trying to circle and call out to the team. Blue grabbed onto a rein and for a brief moment the colt stood immobile as Blue steadied him.

Blue barely slipped his boot into the stirrup as the colt lined out toward the buckboard. He landed lightly in the saddle while reaching for the reins. They were immediately air-born as the colt fought to get his head. Blue leaned forward, touched the colt's withers and eased him back onto the ground. They compromised, with the colt going into a long trot and Blue standing in the stirrups. He didn't want to push the team but to let them find their way home without being hurried.

The brown mustang came along at his own speed, stopping at the good places for a nip of lush grass. The horse was a master at taking care of himself. Those memories were almost enough for Blue to grin briefly, for the brown had gotten him in and out of some bad places and made him what little cash he had stuffed deep in his pocket.

It was an odd way to backtrack a life; the team thought together and when they came to a turn in the road, they went at an angle across the deeper tracks to a thin double line that wound through brush and a few flowering cactus. There must have been a late rain for it was coming winter and yet the cactus stubbornly bloomed. They were strange things, Blue decided, ungainly forms each wearing a crown of pink flowers. As the team picked up speed, swinging the buckboard and bouncing the dead driver, there was Blue, following along like one of the vultures while grinning at the sight of cactus flowers.

The team almost caught the side of a wheel when they managed too sharp a turn, and Blue saw past the wagon to where they were headed. The track led into a deep valley backed by low hills, where buildings, pens, and catch corrals were built close to the hills' protection.

The house was white wood sided with clapboards, unlike the usual low ranch house. It even had pillars across the front; Blue matched those against the black top hat and long coat and figured he was bringing a southern gentleman home. There would be some unhappy folks down there when the team arrived, so he gigged the colt and came up alongside the buckboard.

Naturally the near sorrel tried to bite the colt who, being young and entire, was more than willing to fight back and Blue had to convince the two of them that charging downhill toward a ranch house while dueling wasn't sensible. He was able to haul in the team, close enough to a low cottonwood that he could dismount and tie them by the shortened reins before proceeding to the house.

CHAPTER THREE

The corpse had fallen sideways and at first glance the buckboard looked empty. That suited Blue, as folks were beginning to appear and he didn't want to be accused before he got to explain. The brown stayed back, tearing into a particularly fine patch of graze.

Blue couldn't stomach knowing the corpse was jammed under the buckboard seat, limbs stretched in ugly, useless poses. He went back, knotted the colt's reins to the back of the wagon and struggled with the corpse until it lay on its side, arms folded, one boot sticking up from a bent knee. He rubbed his face, spat, and untied his bedroll, took out the worn canvas that Peter Charley had used as a ground sheet, and covered the leaking body.

Then he led the unwilling colt away from the team, walking slowly, giving those watching him plenty of time to read his intentions. He deliberately kept his hands slightly in front of him. There was no handgun strapped to his hip, the saddle gun rested unused in its scabbard.

One man came out of a low shed; another stepped down from a bronc in the corral and tied it to the fence before slipping through the rails. Blue could understand these men, deal with them on a common ground. It was the woman under the verandah, dainty feet in pretty shoes, flesh tightened into a flowered dress that was bright but not as pretty as the cactus. This was a lady and not a ranch women, a fine lady who stood and watched him; her arms rested gracefully at her side, her face was shadowed by the verandah roof but he could see the motion of her head, turned slightly away from him as if to listen for what was missing.

He had the oddest sense of that pretty girl at the Hubert ranch, and the way her dress fitted her young body. This woman in front of him was formal, that girl had something else on her mind.

Blue's mouth went dry, he slowed his walk, his fingers loosened enough on the reins that the colt thought he was free and pulled back, sat down and then reared, pawing at Blue, who took a light hold of one rein, turned the colt and brought him down. "Mind your manners, son. There's folks watching." The colt seemed to bend around Blue, touching his nose briefly to Blue's shirt, then snorted, finally willing to stand.

The man from the shed came at Blue, stopped ten feet away and Blue sighed. Here it was, those hard range eyes judging him with a deepening scowl. Blue stood quiet, hands at his side, the paint colt standing with him, occasionally pushing at Blue's elbow. The man in the corral, slight and dark haired, had disappeared; gone to find the others, Blue figured. The first words out of the man facing him were what Blue expected. Some things never changed.

"Mister, you get off this place. There ain't no room here for you and that stud you're riding." Crude but to the point and Blue grinned, knowing it was the wrong choice but the man was so damned easy. He was wondering when the man would get roaring mad 'bout the brown cropping his grass. The round face turned into a ball of etched lines as the man patted his empty thigh, where the outline of a holster was shaded into the striped wool pants. He seemed surprised that no pistol appeared by magic into his searching hand.

The woman's voice was delicate and soft, yet her words were clear across the ranch yard. "Sir, if you would. Please. Come speak to me. I run this ranch when my husband is not available." Pure iron, he thought, as the man glaring at him went red in the face, the wrinkles slackened and fell into the heavy jowls. The man took a reluctant half-step back. This was a woman who would allow no man other than her own to protect her.

Blue knew that the dead man lying halfway inside the buckboard was her absent husband. Walking toward the woman, keeping a tight hold on both his temper and the fractious colt, he studied her face and manner much as she was judging him. He was no different from her, he thought, making up what he already believed about her before he and the lady entered into any exchange.

She was a neat figure, corseted tight enough that she breathed in silent gasps, proper and lady-like and absolutely helpless for any useful work. Blue couldn't imagine her in a kitchen. She studied him with quick sideways glances, and Blue grunted, too familiar with this behavior.

It was for her to ask the questions, keeping in mind that Madison would call the approaching man a drifter. The term was more 'western', he said, more in keeping with their new surroundings. He did not approve of 'bum' or 'bummer', taken from Sherman's men who marched through the South and foraged for their provisions. Madison had never forgiven the North for their treatment of Atlanta and the surrounding lands, although none of his family's holdings had been affected. She in turn spoke of such callers as gentlemen of leisure, not wishing to give in to the more western terminology. She felt that the appellation of 'drifter' was far too unpleasant.

This particular man was intriguing even as she accepted he was bringing bad news, for their homestead was placed deliberately off the road, intended to be difficult to find. He knew to stop a number of feet from the verandah and remove his hat. "Morning, ma'am." He dropped his head briefly, then looked up at her with the oddest eyes. Almost a blue green, like certain stones she had seen worn by some of the native men. This man's eyes were of that brilliant color, astonishing against the sun-darkened skin. And the exposed hair was of a streaked blond such as young women pined for. The ragged hair curled at the neck and over the ears, hanging close to his eyes when he shook his head. He was indeed peculiar.

"Mrs. Tremont," she said, as she took a short breath and thought of the rare times when she was not bound into this hated corset. Only then did she find the breath to speak again. "Sir." He smiled, a grimace formed out of politeness. "Yes, ma'am, Mrs. Tremont. The name's Blue Mitchell. I come. . . ." Then his easy face went hard and those eyes turned a darker blue as he glanced away and returned to look at her. He was here about her beloved Madison.

She resisted the most southern of female gestures, one hand to the throat, a slight gasp, a tremble of the head and blinking eyes. Instead she invited the gentleman up onto the verandah. He refused politely, explaining that he could not trust the colt to stand, tied or untied. Perhaps she would walk with him?

Melinda agreed, knowing she had shed a southern nicety but this unusual visitor had words obviously meant for her ears alone. Mr. Cook stood near the corrals, feet spread wide, ample belly pushed forward, scowling she would imagine. Mr. Cook often scowled when she had any influence on ranch matters. She noted briefly that a brown horse carrying a balanced pack load grazed on the flowers she had planted to decorate the rock-lined pathway.

It was second nature to raise the hem of her skirt as she descended the three steps and that gesture seemed to frighten the lovely young horse Mr. Mitchell was leading. The colt, for he was entire, and Melinda knew enough of such matters to recognize the colt's lack of maturity, went high on his hind legs and tried to pull away. It was then that Melinda Tremont learned all she needed to know about their uninvited visitor. He held to the reins, neither jerking nor hauling but holding quiet, legs spread to keep his balance, and as he lightly shook the leather, he spoke to the colt whose ears came forward as the front end came down, bouncing lightly on delicate hooves.

Despite his wild looks and disheveled manner, the man was kind. She needed to rely on this one fact.

The colt came with them, head low, ears loose, minding the slightest touch on those reins Mr. Mitchell held in one rather large and scarred hand. She could not get used to the manner in which a westerner was injured and recovered, most often with little nursing or care. They simply washed off the worst of the bleeding, wrapped a torn bit of cloth over the wound and went about the endless chores and hard work.

It was then that she truly heard Mr. Mitchell's voice and realized she had been tending to her own thoughts so she would not acknowledge what he came to tell her. As for Mr. Mitchell, he could not rationally know she was the correct person who needed to hear his news, and yet he'd had the sensibility to draw her away from any onlookers. With this unexpected gesture, he was telling her that whatever news he intended to impart was of a disastrous nature.

He stopped and faced her, the colt swung around him and almost pushed into Melinda. Mitchell guided the colt into his proper place. "Ma'am." The pain in his voice was magnified by the beating of her heart. "Ma'am. You are married, and moved here with your husband?" She nodded, not wanting to risk her voice breaking on an answer. He kept on, implacable yet with kindness in his choice of words.

"He is about my height, a bit heavier, with dark hair and a moustache?" Here Mr. Mitchell lost the ability to keep the truth from his neutral inquisition. "He had brown eyes, light maybe, but brown." A statement, not a question, and he'd spoken in the past tense. She did not approve of the gasp that quickly formed and escape from her throat without permission. The odd man looked into her tearing eyes and put out a hand as if willing to hold her. It was an intimacy she could not bear.

Melinda Tremont stepped back, sighed and held her breath from the pinch at her rib. "Yes, that sounds like my husband. He is in trouble?" A foolish ploy and one that did not stop Mr. Mitchell's horrible words; "He is dead, ma'am. Do you know anyone who'd shoot him?"

There it was. Implacable death brought to her by a stranger, a truth unbearable and yet real. "No one hated Tremont enough to kill him." Those were words she wished she believed. The tremble was there despite her efforts and its betrayal angered her. Melinda cleared her throat, turning away from this man as she did so. His hand touched her elbow and she withdrew quickly.

"Ma'am, I don't mean to hurt you." The several meanings to those words surprised her and she thought to explain her gesture until Mr. Cook came up hurriedly as if to save the boss's wife. She put out a hand, palm first, and Mr. Cook showed unusual intelligence by stopping, eyes watchful but awaiting her disposition as to what might have occurred without his knowledge.

"Mr. Cook, this gentleman has news for me. Please, sir, see to harnessing the bay mare to my runabout, while. . . ." Her composure slipped, only for a moment, but the man interceded on her behalf. While he did not offer his hand, he nodded and spoke quite carefully to Cook as if he'd recognized that the foreman possessed a slow mind.

"The lady and I, we've got private business. When she wants you to know, she'll tell you. I ain't here to do nothing but give her some news." Bland enough, she thought, close to admiring the man for his awkward diplomacy. The words were neither threatening nor bragging while trying to leave Cook some dignity, a task which she might explain to Mr. Mitchell later had no meaning at all, for Cook was without redeeming character except that he was willing, on occasion, to do his work.

The new hand, who'd started work a month earlier, came up behind Cook. He stood quietly and said nothing; Melinda noticed that Mr. Mitchell studied that particular man rather than focusing on Ira Cook. In a small part of her mind, she began to admire Mitchell's instincts.

She quickly interceded, wishing to spare further violence to either man; "Mr. Cook, this gentleman was offering me information, not attacking me. I thank you for the rescue but it is not necessary." She wasn't prepared to tell Cook anything of what Mitchell had imparted for she had yet to see the corpse and verify it was indeed her husband. Until that task was accomplished, she could keep up a pretense of lesser news.

"Mr. Cook." The woman's voice was iron, not a hint of fear or concern. "Please see that. . . ." Here she hesitated again and Blue came to her aid. "You got a place the colt'll be safe and not cause trouble? The lady and I have some business."

Blue studied the dark-haired man. There were a few scars and some wrinkles on the face, not of age but sunlight and long miles. Blue'd seen him step down from that bronc in the pen and disappear. Now he was backing up Cook. He was familiar, not in knowing his name but in what he was.

The man extended his fist and Blue handed over the colt's reins. The silent man nodded at Blue without lifting his eyes, then tugged gently on the reins. The colt hesitated and the wrangler made a chirping noise that seemed to soothe the colt's initial worry. Horse and man walked away and for once Blue had no concerns about the colt rebelling or being mistreated.

Blue noted that no one yet had said a word about the brown mustang, who raised his head as the paint colt was led past him. A flower hung from the brown's mouth, giving him the look of a fool. Blue knew better, yet the outward shape of the brown, like Blue himself, was both commonplace and peculiar. He nodded absently toward the mustang, who'd gone back to eating the sweet flowers.

The woman took no notice of the destruction, so Blue followed her to the house. Seen through the opened front door, the interior of the house was what he expected; filled with heavy furniture and enough gewgaws to please a high-quality woman. He stopped at the front door, for she was too polite to suggest he go around to the back entrance. He spent a lot of time scrubbing the bottoms of his boots on a wire rack. Even then, the stench of rank sweat and miles traveled was overpowering.

The new widow frowned when Blue told her it was unseemly for him to enter her fine house. He replaced his hat as he spoke, wanting to maintain his manners yet he was determined not to go inside. He meant to be kind but the words were blunt and he choked on them; "Ma'am, I don't know anyone here, and no one knows me so it's only proper I stay outside."

He took two steps back and leaned on a wood slat chair. He studied her even as she glared at him. Then it seemed to go through her, the knowledge of what his being on her verandah meant. She glided, he thought, she didn't walk like most folks but slid across the painted wood floor to sit gracefully in the chair that Blue guessed he'd been holding steady for her.

He found another chair like hers only with arms. He finally sat down very carefully as he knew from experience that these rocking chair could throw a man if he got too rowdy settling in.

"Well," she said. She was barely looking at him, spending her time studying the white gate, the low fence around her small yard, and past that fence to where the brown was still munching flowers. He understood how deeply she was hurt when she did not complain about the brown's assault.

It was a rough start; "I was just riding through and found your. . .a man slumped over in a buckboard." Her eyes widened briefly; "What color. . . I mean the buckboard?"

As he named off the colors, he understood her reasoning. Most buckboards out here were scrubbed brown or gray by blown sand and harsh winters. The dead man's buckboard was one of a kind. Her head began to shake as each color was named and Blue quit, hating to hurt someone with simple words. Right now hitting a man alongside his jaw or deep into the belly would feel good, and it might get rid of the anger building inside his gut.

He heard a whinny, the screech of dry wheels, and then silence, guessing that the angry red-eyed man was standing close and trying to listen. Blue half-stood, said to the woman;

"Ma'am, you sure you want to do this?" She nodded, opened her mouth and then shut it. For the first time the woman wasn't pretty. All her fear and worry showed in the eyes and brightly colored mouth, harsh against pure white skin. He stood up, careful about the chair; "I'll get my horse."

Her voice was a struggle; "No, sir. You will drive me." She allowed him no uncertainty as to what must be done, but he didn't like the idea. "I'll need to unsaddle the colt, put him in a pen by himself, and catch up the brown, he's almost done with your flowers." She was angry now; "You do that. I have little time to waste." Then she turned her back to him, expecting him to get off the verandah, get to his chores and then drive her to whatever horror was waiting.

Then, as if his last words had penetrated wherever it was she'd retreated from the truth, she turned to him and her face eased, her mouth opened the slightest and she brought up a hand to shade her eyes. Her voice, so different from the earlier tone, was soft, breathy, a pleasure to Blue's ear.

"I do hope, sir, that your horse has enjoyed eating those flowers as much as I have enjoyed sitting here in the past, drawing in their scent and their fragile beauty." She belatedly realized that her complaint, voiced in a most polite manner, spoke even more to the fact that her life now would never be the same. And it most certainly was not Mr. Mitchell's fault. "Sir, thank you for your consideration."

Blue picked up the brown's lead and walked toward the corral, he shook his head and muttered to himself. Women were creatures he didn't understand. And from the feel of things around here, he'd be glad when this was done and he could ride out.

The colt had pawed at the dirt where he was tied, making a steep hole for himself. The paint stood butt to the sky, black and white tail thrashing, ears pinned back. As Blue untied the colt and started toward an empty pen, the red-faced man laughed. "Not much on manners is he." "'Bout as well behaved as you are, mister." Hell, Blue thought, knowing he'd be better of keeping his mouth shut, if the son couldn't see the colt was nothing but a three-year-old and fresh branded, then the man didn't know horses.

One small pen was set by itself. Most good ranches had a pen like this to hold sick horses or a visitor's less than sociable mount. Blue checked and there was fairly clean water in a wood tub, and remnants of fresh hay, a luxury that surprised him. The hay would keep the colt and the mustang entertained while his rider ventured out to deal with a dead husband.

He turned the brown loose in the pen after stripping off his gear, and when the colt was set free, he strutted to the mustang, arched his neck, pawed the ground and the brown walked past the colt toward the piled hay. The colt sagged, his head went down and he followed the wiser mustang.

When Blue left the corral, there was the woman, seated primly in the runabout, and Ira Cook was holding the mare's bridle, occasionally jerking on the bit when the mare tried to rub against him.

She would have to speak to Madison about. . .oh dear. Mr. Mitchell walked toward her, studying the ground rather than looking up and she was not used to being ignored by any man. At home she had been considered a beauty and men paid tribute to that vision with proper manner and much flirting. Here, as Madison had warned her, such niceties would not be observed. On occasion, she still missed the attention.

Mr. Mitchell was quickly in the seat, picked up the reins, lines she amended, hearing Madison's voice chide her oh so softly on the correct terminology. She felt the instant tears; his was a voice she would not hear again.

As she suspected, the bay mare responded to Mr. Mitchell's hands on those 'lines' with a smooth forward walk instead of the usual pull and jerk that she gave to Melinda. After all, Melinda drove only rarely by herself because of her unfamiliarity with both the art of driving and the land surrounding the ranch. She would not choose to be lost in such a brittle and ugly place.

Her mind refused to dwell on what awaited her. There were so many different sides to her beloved Madison, so much behind their marriage, that she could lose herself in dreaming and briefly keep reality at bay.

A horse whinnied and Melinda's head jerked up from staring at her ungloved hands. There was Madison's team tied by their reins, an act she had been forbidden to do. There were dried white marks on their coats, and fresh piles of manure at the back ends; details that a true lady would neither notice nor comment upon.

She and Madison had so many plans. She choked yet absolutely refused to cry. These plans would not happen and the knowledge was unbearable. "Ma'am, let me walk you to the horses." This kind and unexpected sentiment from an uncouth stranger was disturbing. He had stopped the mare some distance away from the remarkable wagon. Its carefully chosen vivid colors had been Madison's playful way of announcing their entrance into this backward society.

Now Mr. Mitchell did not want her to look directly at the bulky object covered in the buckboard. But she knew. She rested her hand on his arm. "Please, Mr. Mitchell." He responded as a true gentleman, stepping down first, steadying the mare with his voice, and then reaching up for Melinda Tremont, offering whatever assistance she chose to accept.

The more he studied this woman, the more he was certain she was older than her husband, which might be why they lived out from nowhere. He didn't much care himself, but with her being so close, leaning against his arms, he could see the faint lines, the loosening skin. Her eyes closed suddenly. They'd been staring at him, deep brown eyes flat with unexpected pain so he saw nothing in them. Not even tears.

The body lay on its side, still covered with Peter Charley's canvas to keep birds and such from pecking or

39

chewing at puffed flesh. Arms and legs were displayed in a mockery of life, knees drawn, backside sticking out, hands folded across the body as Blue had positioned the corpse. In an hour or so it would a long time before the man could be unfolded

The woman walked holding tightly to his forearm, taking even steps with no uncertainty. They stopped at the edge of the buckboard where Blue made her let go. Her fingers had pressed hard into his arm, the only sign of her distress.

He removed her hand, placed it on the buckboard's edge and as he pulled back the blanket, he spoke to the team, readying them for almost any reaction from the woman. It came as the slightest cry, a blink of those huge eyes and the face went pale, lips bloodless, but nothing more. He held the blanket away from the sticky flesh, let her see fully, then replaced the stiffened canvas over the open mouth and staring eyes.

Mrs. Tremont turned away from the messy tangle of clothing, blood, and swelling flesh. Her legs barely wobbled as she returned to the buggy and Blue was caught between admiration and dislike. It couldn't have been much of a marriage for her to take the brutal sight of her man's death without tears.

The eyes were muddy but not wet as she leaned on him to be helped into the buggy. Blue shook his head as she settled. "Do not judge me, Mr. Mitchell. I am grieving. I have been grieving since you walked into the ranch yard for I could see it in your face. You do not know me, nor did you know Mr. Tremont and our life together. It is not possible for you to tell me what I must feel."

Blue hesitated, lectured and made to feel like a boy in trouble at school again. The woman was straight; he had no business making judgments. He'd always damned the world for its judgment of him and now he was the idiot who saw without seeing.

"Ma'am, I 'pologize." She almost smiled, that mouth pulling up, then quickly thinned. "Neither of us need to explain,

Mr. Mitchell. I will drive the mare back. You will follow with the team and. . . ." Here was a quickstep in her voice before she continued, not allowing Blue any chance for sympathy. "You bring in the buckboard and team, for those poor animals must be thirsty and tired."

She added the one word that demanded Blue do her bidding; "Please."

CHAPTER FOUR

Ira Cook was mad clear through. That damned drifter came trotting Mr. Tremont's sorrels into the yard, passing the runabout where Mrs. Tremont struggled with the usually quiet bay mare. The man had no business here, not bothering the missus, and certainly not driving the sorrel team.

Finally it occurred to Ira that there wasn't no sign of Mr. Tremont and that bothered him even more. There had to be something bad going on between these two, the drifter and the missus, for she never took kindly to just anyone coming to the ranch house. The woman was fussy about folks taking up her husband's time, Mr. Tremont had once told him. Ira shook his head and stepped out to the oncoming team, wanting to catch them at the bit and stop that goddamn drifter.

The son knew what Ira had in mind for he directed the team in a quick dodge and only then did the ranch foreman get a look-see at what lay bundled on the wagon bed, the fist of one hand showed and as quickly was covered by a badly stained canvas.

He swallowed hard. No man should take a woman to see a body like this. The dead man had to be Mr. Tremont. Damn that drifter for not knowing how to treat a lady. He didn't look like a shooter, more like a fighter and horse breaker, seeing as how that colt was quality despite his color. The bronc wasn't a horse most men would ride; hot, uncut, probably dangerous yet the horse breaker handled the colt like it was a child's mount.

Ira Cook already disliked the man but wouldn't have thought he was a killer.

He stepped to the missus in her fine buggy, runabout Mr. Tremont would have corrected him. This time Ira grabbed the mare's bit and turned her so she stopped, jerking the buggy but the woman didn't seem to notice. Maybe she'd been in on this. Maybe she already knew when the blond-haired son of a bitch came to the ranch that the killing was done. Now it was time for the law to get here.

The bay mare bit Cook's hand and he slapped her and the woman had the nerve to look at him as she spoke her mind. Ira realized there were no more checks on the woman, she would have her way without Mr. Tremont to stop her.

"Mister Cook you will not hit the mare. You have scared her and she is only defending herself." Mrs. Tremont's voice showed no grief or weakness and Ira thought it strange for a woman who'd just lost her husband to say nothing 'bout his death while taking on about a goddamn horse like it was made of glass.

He was wise enough not to argue but nodded his head. "Yes, ma'am. Let me take her for you. 'Pears to me you got some matters need settling." There, Cook thought, he'd told her in his own way he was suspicious of the goings-on. She frowned some, bit her lip like she often did and Ira knew to get out of the way.

When a woman like this one got to thinking, Cook found himself doing things he'd never done before. He wouldn't have thought he could hoe down a vegetable row or hang up them cloths in the living room. 'Draperies' she called them, not drapes or curtains. He'd got a lecture on what they were called while he hung from a ladder too close to a large glass window and struggled to put in nails and then those cross rods to hang her fancies. Women like this one were a peculiar lot.

If he stayed around too long and tended to the mare and listened to the woman's instructions, then hell, Mrs. Tremont might expect him to lay out the body. If he spoke up quick, he could get word to the law. "Ma'am, I seen. . .I'll send a man into town. The law needs to know. Ma'am." He stopped there, seeing her eyes darken, then get wet and her mouth pulled tight. "Sorry, ma'am, sorry for you losing. . . ." It was all he could say. He sure didn't want to hear the words said out loud.

He'd need to find a new job. It'd been hard enough finding this one, he knew he wasn't too smart and thankfully these eastern folks hadn't known the difference. Now it was back to ranch hand or riding the grub line.

Ira called out; "Ridge!" and spooked the mare, which had the woman open her mouth in warning. He called out again, "Ridge", and the son of a bitch showed, hat shoved wrong on his head but hurrying like being called meant something. That too would end; most of these cowboys wouldn't last with another boss or new owners.

"You catch up that dun, get down to Abbott. We need the sheriff or some kind of law." Ridge didn't ask anything but went to rope and saddle the bronc he'd just put away. The son was a hard-headed mustang with mule ears but it could run. That speed was why the Tremonts kept the sorry horse, so when they needed something real fast. . .thinking too much, Ira said to himself, he was thinking too much.

Behind Ridge, the woman picked up the lines, shook her head when her foreman offered to lead the mare. "No, Mr. Cook, I am quite capable of guiding her from here to the barn. You may take her then, if you promise to be gentle." She drove a few steps, then halted the mare and looked back at him. Her confidence in her husband's choice of foreman had surfaced and was bitter to Ira Cook's mind. "Mr. Cook, please have the men bring Mr. Tremont's body to the house. I will lay him out with Priscilla's help. Thank you."

Blue had the sorrel team unharnessed, the gear hung where he found an empty line of pegs and he'd scrubbed down each horse, got rid of the itchy salt, smoothed their coats and talked to them. As he worked on the horses, he kept his eyes off the wagon box. He was conscious of time and the rising heat. They needed to get the dead body inside the house, washed and laid out best they could. Pretty soon it would be impossible to move the limbs or flatten the body.

He and the small rider, the quiet one with watchful eyes, had stood a moment face to face inside the barn. Neither man spoke as they studied each other. Each then nodded and went on with their business.

The red-faced man led in the fine bay mare and grunted at Blue, pushed him aside and stripped the mare, spanked her into a straight stall and turned quickly to glare at Blue. The smaller man had led an ugly dun horse outside and Blue could hear the hoof beats disappear at a growing speed.

Cook stood directly in front of Blue, legs wide, arms crossed over his belly. "I sent a man to town just now. You want to start running, here's your chance. I just as soon have you gone." Strange words, Blue thought as he studied the face too close to him. Then the offer made sense; "You think I had something to do with that killing?" He couldn't keep the surprise from his voice and the resulting smirk on the stupid face told him the truth. Blue laughed. It might be the wrong thing to do given a dead man in the buckboard, but from too much experience, Blue understood that the dead didn't mind such matters.

The red-faced son of a bitch shoved a big hand on Blue's chest. Blue leaned into the hand, took a step closer, looked into the tight eyes and shook his head. "Now mister if I'm the killer you ain't being too smart, and if I ain't, what's the point? You think on it."

He was careful to step back, let the man have some room for the dignity he clearly lacked, give him a chance to change his mind. Blue hated fighting and this time it was over a dead man he'd hardly seen and sure as hell didn't know.

The woman's voice from somewhere back of the two men settled the matter; "Mr. Cook, as I have already asked, please do bring my. . . ." There was that break again in her voice, barely noticeable but Blue had already learned her pattern of speech and it was clear to him she was struggling.

"Have my husband's body brought to the house."

Priscilla watched the activity in the ranch yard through the kitchen side window. The woman had demanded more windows be put into the house walls, even though it made the summers hotter and a cold draft came blowing through in the winter until those heavy curtains had been put up. They made the difference but they also blocked the sunlight. It surely was a lot of fuss over nothing, Priscilla thought, but her thoughts and ideas weren't why she'd been hired.

It was worth working for Mrs. Tremont, for it meant she and Turner were making good money, which they intended to put it away for the ranch he'd always wanted. She and Turner, they'd been married six months now, all the time working here even though they'd met first in town. No one spoke of what she'd been doing since the men were scared of Turner's fists. He was the only married cowhand and the newly-weds had themselves a room of their own that Turner had built with Mr. Tremont's permission.

What if she'd been working in a saloon, and was two years older than Turner. He wasn't no boy despite that round face and simple smile and she wasn't as old as Mrs. Tremont was to her husband, not at all. Her Turner's face was sweet enough, with that soft look around the mouth and the thick hair hanging over his eyes unless she pushed it back when she held on to him. She loved her husband as best she could. He didn't hit her, was kind in those moments, shy there too but learning and he never held it against her that she knew more'n he did about men and women together. He seemed to like the learning, and it eased what was left of her conscience to finally not be ashamed.

She had already figured that Turner's promises didn't mean shit. A cowhand and a house girl, they couldn't earn enough to buy much of nothing. As for homesteading like her folks had done, most of that good land was gone. It took water to raise cattle here and only the rich could afford those fancy windmills to bring up enough water.

If nothing else, Priscilla knew the realities of life and this hard work might feed and bed a couple but it was no way to buy a homestead.

With the mister gone, laid out on that shiny table in the dining room, with him gone now, even the ranch job might slide away. Then she and Turner would be out on their own, homeless and drifting again. The thought scared her since she'd always been afraid of having no place to call home, even if it was a single room in a fancy house.

Mrs. Tremont called and Priscilla pushed at her hair, sighed and shook her head.

Melinda would work with the girl; female and married as she was, together they could remove Mr. Tremont's clothes and with the discretionary use of a torn sheet he would remain decent even as they washed away all signs of his killing. Or at least removed the drying blood, she amended, for the holes in his flesh would never heal, never draw together with reborn skin.

After the rider went for the law, Melinda overheard Mr. Cook telling the strange man who brought Madison home that now was his chance to run if he were indeed the killer. She had let out a breath at the man's response. It had inexplicably pleased her when the man barely shook his head and said that if he'd been the killer, he wouldn't have brought Madison's body to the ranch, which was simple logic and far beyond Cook's ability to comprehend.

Perhaps fate had presented her with an ally in the midst of strangers and those in her service. She would need to temper her imperious tone with Mr. Mitchell for he obviously would not take orders. Clever words and demure looks were better weapons with which to ensnare him. Despite his rough demeanor, he had acted as a gentleman throughout the discovery and delivery of her once-beloved Madison.

It took three men to bring Madison's body into the house. The flesh had begun to stiffen. Arms and legs had to be pushed and physically maneuvered, as if his last act was one of defiance against the mortal world.

She had been surprised at the gentleness of those men, Mr. Mitchell included, as they laid Madison on the table, drawing down the cramped legs, rolling the head to lie upright, setting the arms next to his ribs, fingers curled near the hip. Mr. Cook had not participated after placing Mr. Tremont on the table. It was Mitchell, and the usually sullen Turner, who pulled and stroked the flesh only beginning to swell. It was time now to wash and dress Madison before he became completely unmanageable.

She stood a moment, lost inside her own house. Then the girl made a noise, not abrupt or even a word but a distraction that moved Melinda into looking up, clearing her eyes and her mind. "We must wash him. . .his corpse." She would not use euphemisms. She would speak clearly, one of the few freedoms she earned in the unholy move from her beloved South.

Madison Tremont's abandoned physical manifestation was laid directly on the top of her prized mahogany table with its carved legs and ability to seat fourteen people with the use of the leaves. These extensions to the table were stored in a closet, wrapped in soft flannel to avoid disfiguring scratches. She should have thought to spread a blanket or quilt on the table top, for protection and sanitary issues, and to offer the body some vague remnant of comfort. Foolish, she knew, but it was in her mind.

Priscilla held out a wadded cloth. "Ma'am, I'd be pleased if we could roll this under him. It makes me nervous. . .well you know." Then as an after thought, as if it finally occurred to the girl that her request might sound foolish, she spoke firmly; "That is, ma'am, if you agree." It had taken several months and a number of scoldings to force the word 'ma'am' out of the girl's mouth. Melinda shook herself, an internal shiver to jar her thoughts loose and tend to business.

"Good. Yes. Thank you, Priscilla. Help me roll him onto his side." She persisted in calling the inert flesh him and he, refusing to use the more proper and dehumanizing it. This was still her Madison. Until he was washed and wrapped and laid carefully in the ground, he was her husband.

The flesh was soft enough that, as they pushed and rolled with delicate fingers, a faintly sweet odor was released. Melinda glanced at the girl, who had closed her eyes and tightened her mouth. But together they had him on his side and Priscilla held him still while Melinda laid out the quilt, pushing it up against the loosened back and buttocks, deep into the falling thigh muscle and along the calves.

Then they rolled him back, almost to the other side, and this time, while Melinda held onto Madison's ribs and shoulder, the girl pulled and flattened out the quilt. Allowing gravity to do its job, Melinda felt the flesh dent against her fingers before it rolled away. She heard the softened thud, saw the impression of her fingers linger in the flaccid muscle at his shoulder and upper arm.

A brutal taste soured her mouth. "Priscilla, please get us each a glass of lemonade." Lemons were a luxury when available, brought in from Clayton where most of their provisions were purchased. Madison always made the effort to have them in the house. Now she would share their familiar tart flavor with the girl. The work they were tending to was the ugly chore of all women. Melinda could not refuse anyone a taste of the exotic to mask death's flavor.

While the girl went to make up two glasses of lemonade, reminded to only use a half teaspoon each of sugar lest the drink become cloying, Melinda studied the task she had self-assigned. It was quite simple, to unbutton the ruined shirt.

The shirt was one she had hand-stitched for her betrothed before their union. It had frayed at the cuffs and

48

collar and she had meant to turn both. Letting her fingers rest on an unstained section of the shirt front brought back different times; the material was a fine lawn from a tailor in Atlanta who knew exactly what quality Melinda and her aunt and mama preferred.

Droplets stained the fine lawn; Melinda wiped one hand against her eyes, then across her mouth, and continued to unbutton the shirt. The blood would not give at the last buttonhole and she tore the pale blue lawn, shredding it as the button flew past her head. Good, she thought, he's free now. Her fingers grazed the undergarment that Madison wore except in their most intimate moments. It was puckered cotton knit, light to the skin but sticking where the blood glued fabric to flesh.

She did not roll him over; she could not bear to see the wound where it had first killed him. His chest, smeared in drying blood, hid the exit of a tired bullet. It would be the larger hole, not what would meet her eyes when she cleaned his back. That hole would be the smaller entry, signaling the start of death.

She might be fooling herself but she could not bear the shattered skin, the hint of bone showing under her blind fingers. It would be for Priscilla to wash the back, to remove the soaked cloth and then together they could ready Madison for his burial.

Blue found a corner in the barn. The paint colt was hollering and snorting outside but he wasn't going to chide the colt for his poor manners. Not now, not with what he guessed lay ahead. The brown mustang wisely ignored the colt's antics, picking his way through some stemmy hay.

He could feel her hands on the damp flesh, he could smell the death. It lay outside his own scarred body, where too many times he had escaped dying. The intimate memories made him ask questions to which he had no answers. How long had Tremont been dead, it couldn't have been too long for the flesh was still soft. Who and why didn't interest him as much, but he did remember the paint colt jumping at a gunshot. The law would be here soon, then Blue could ask questions as well as give his few answers.

It was a strange connection to the grieving widow, one he would not share. But he knew what dying felt like; those cold hands wiping his skin and he could hear voices at a distance from his flesh, talking about him even though he was a stranger. Guessing, touching old wounds and wondering about his life. They thought him dead, and he barely remembered their faces as he struggled to find breath.

Using common sense, Blue found the slab-sided shed typical of most ranches out behind the barn. Off to the right, sitting in a clearing and surrounded by trimmed cactus stood a tin tub. He'd seen one before, had a bath on a few occasions, usually after he'd had a shearing. A damned bath tub. Rusted from lack of use, probably had mice living inside, thinking they'd found a home fancy as that monster back a few miles. Blue shook his head; some folks were odd.

As he used the outhouse, Blue thought about the woman, the lady in her house with shiny wood floors and thick rugs; she would not have the luxury of feeling her husband breathe again. Blue shook his head, let his fingers rise to touch the healed flesh under his shirt.

He returned to the barn and was settling down for a moment's rest when Ira Cook, the stupid one who figured Blue might be the murderer, he stuck his head inside and rattled Blue. "You, get out here. We got the law wanting to talk." Hell Blue thought, he must have slept or something for any nearby town had to be more miles than a man could ride and return this fast.

He came out of the barn slowly, eyes blinking into the sun. There was a sight waiting for him, a small man, downright skinny if that counted, a star pinned on a collarless shirt, light glinting against the polished metal, hat pushed back over thinning pale hair. The man was perched on a long-legged bay roan, slab-sided and lean like his rider. Built for speed, Blue decided, not for cow work. Then again a lawman had no need to tie hard on an escaping steer. Catching a running man would be different.

The law was studying Blue as he appeared. The face wasn't too old; adorned with a heavy mustache that probably weighed more than the man himself, he had suspicious eyes, knotted hands, and the smallest of bellies under a frayed shirt, showing what town life could do to a lawman.

"You the one brought him in?" Question with a head nod toward the house and Blue nodded in return. "Tell me where and when. How come you knew to bring him here?" The man climbed down from his roan, more like sliding than stepping off. Passable horse, thought Blue, sixteen hands with short cannon bone, narrow in the rib and chest, decent neck and a calm, mildly curious nature but not excited about a sudden grouping of men shoving in around him.

As he always did, Hale Patton took quick mental notes; study the clothes, the hands, the ease in the slow walk, the fire in those damned eyes. He knew this one, had heard about him from the law in Cimarron and a deputy up near Trinidad. He'd been warned about not judging too quickly. Wait they each said. Find out for yourself, this one's rare.

It was best he listened, Patton thought. And damned better for the horseman that Patton knew something of his reputation. On looks alone he'd put the son in jail, anyone come out of a stranger's barn, head cocked, hands loose, no weapon but those goddamned eyes and that wild set to his whole manner and a decent lawman would go for his pistol, dig out handcuffs from his saddlebags and set them around those wrists, careful to ignore any hatred coming from the peculiar eyes.

It was a fact, that life and death was all in how you studied on it. Patton nodded to the man; "Let me get this horse seen to." He turned to the foreman; "Here Cook, you take him, watch out he's been known to bite." This was said just fast enough that Cook had time to duck when Hawk snapped at his arm and that made Patton grin. He and Hawk had been doing this to unsuspecting folks a long time now. "Thanks, Cook. I'll listen to his story. You take good care of Hawk, you hear!"

Patton held quiet as he looked carefully around him. The few men who worked for the brand were stepping away, cautious around the badge even pinned to a slight chest on a short man. Patton grinned as there were heads shaking, eyes looking down. Men were easy to read, men like this bunch. They all had something in their life they didn't want the law to know.

Picking at Mitchell would give him a hint, though the man's rep did not include violence without cause or anything the law would jail him for. Fighting a drunk, more likely hitting a man mean to a bronc, those actions Patton understood without being told. It rode the same with most horsemen he'd known; horses meant more than people, a feeling that as a lawman Patton could understand.

He took a step toward Mitchell who in turn held his ground. Patton studied the man as he was studied in return. The boy wasn't that old except for lines at his eyes and a fresh scar to the side of his head. He glanced down to the browned hands and shook his head. The man chose a hard life and it seemed to agree with him for when Patton looked up into the long face and those fiery eyes, the man was grinning and Patton grinned too. Getting a straight answer from this one might be rough, but the talk surely would entertain the listener.

"We best set ourselves to the verandah, Mitchell. You got some things I need to know." The son shook his head and Patton thought he might have to revise his early opinion. But Mitchell spoke carefully and Patton understood. "She's in that house with her man, laying him out for the burying." Silence, Patton looked to the ground and nodded at the man's common sense. Mitchell continued; "It's best we sit on that log. It ain't much for comfort but it's far from the house and I won't speak where she can hear me."

Son of a bitch had him a brain. Patton rubbed the side of his jaw. "Well now you'd think I'd done this often enough to know better. Thanks, Mitchell." There was silence as they walked across the yard to where logs were dumped, ready to be bucked into winter fuel.

Blue sat at one end of a dried-out pine brought in from the distant mountains, the law put his backside down very carefully at the other end of the trunk. Both men stared at the dirt yard. Blue spoke, not looking at the law. "You know my name." He glanced at Patten then; there was a moment's wait, then that almost delicate hand rubbed at the beardless jaw.

Patton figured it was his turn. "Collier in Cimarron, he told me 'bout you and that chestnut stallion." Blue rubbed his own jaw, wishing he could rub away the memories and grief that easily. He shuddered quickly; the friend he'd buried only weeks ago was from that time. Blue studied the lawman, wondered if he should talk about what had happened that morning, about Peter Charley's death.

"Mitchell, you found Mr. Tremont and brought him in though I'd wish you'd let him be. I'll need to read tracks, check the area, see if maybe there was a trail to follow." Blue accepted the scolding, for despite the polite words he'd known the law would be annoyed. He offered a tidbit; "That team had run themselves tired from the shooting. They had to leave a good trail since they jammed themselves into a sawgrass swamp at top speed."

He wiped at his eyes, forcing them shut hard enough that light flickered behind the lids and wiped out a terrible picture. "No man in good conscience could leave a body like that." His voice was ragged, giving his sensibilities away. Blue saw the blood, smelled it, heard the flies rising, felt them sticking to his face and shirt, his hands, while he had fought to cover the corpse. He drew in a deep breath, nodded twice, and the law began to ask endless questions.

CHAPTER FIVE

Patton's understanding of Mitchell's character was a culmination of hearsay, direct tales from other lawmen and his own careful study as the man spoke. Words didn't come easy from Mitchell for he needed time to find how to say things right, voice raw, sometimes too low. Patton didn't demand, but leaned forward to hear better and Mitchell recognized the gesture, tried then to speak up.

"That colt I was riding, he's a pistol so I wasn't paying attention to where I was, just how I planned on staying aboard. The brown, that one's no trouble. The colt went high and wide and I couldn't see a reason until he came down, me still setting on top out of luck and prayer and then I saw the tail end of a wagon. Fancy wheels, bright colors; the brown whinnied and when that team hollered back, the colt went into a repeat performance and I clung on, madder'n hell till we landed and I saw. . . ." Here the story quit, all the colorful terminology wasted.

"You know, mister, you work with death everywhere, all kinds. Me I buried a good friend not too long ago." Patton put that comment on hold. He'd maybe go back and ask when Tremont's death was solved. And he'd bet it would be a tale. Mitchell kept going, checking though on whether or not Patton had paid attention; "This dead man, he ain't mine, I just happened on him."

Patton nodded, cocked his head, willing to ignore the cowhand's wanting to get shut of the mess. Couldn't blame him, still he'd brought in a dead man and the matter had to be cleared. Patton waited, face composed, seeing what silence would dig out.

Mitchell spoke slowly; "Whoever shot her husband was long gone by the time I chanced by. I told you that team ran a good mile. It's easy enough to ride the trail backward."

The man stood up and Patton was careful to watch without reacting much. He shifted his backside on the hard log, let the motion move his pistol closer to his hand without it being a deliberate act. Mitchell looked down at him and there was the slightest hint of a grin. "Good move, Mr. Lawman." Hale stood up, put out his hand; "Name's Patton, Hale Patton. Guess we didn't get to formal introductions." Mitchell accepted the handshake, and Patton noted his grip was neither light nor aggressive.

Mitchell headed to his gear stacked close to a pen. Inside the high fence, the colt and the brown mustang stood head to tail, sweeping flies off each other. The colt skidded back at Mitchell's appearance; the brown sighed and didn't bother. Mitchell pulled out his saddle gun, and untied his saddlebags and Patton thought for a moment he'd misjudged the man.

Then he was given the rifle, the opened bags. "Look here, you tell me." The unexpected move was clever, putting Patton at a disadvantage but he deliberately broke open the rifle and knew it hadn't been fired, and it was the same with the pistol and rig dug out of the bags.

Mitchell's voice softened; "I don't shoot much, I just ain't good at it. I don't know these folks, never have hired out for killings, don't have the temper for it." The two men studied each other. Mitchell switched to studying the dirt between his boots and spoke without looking direct at Patton. "Now you mistreat a horse, or something weaker'n you and I'll fight you anyway I can. I don't hate enough to kill, ain't greedy enough to need the dollars and sure am a poor shot especially when I'm mad." Patton grunted.

He would learn, in his own good time, where each man had been when Mr. Tremont was killed. He wouldn't ask the few men working for Tremont direct, not like he'd asked Mitchell; he would slide certain questions in with other comments, and watch the face, study the hands, the eyes, as each man answered.

For now Patton was satisfied that Mr. Mitchell had chanced upon trouble not of his own making. But he needed the man to stay put until all the facts were gleaned and sifted.

She could not bear to watch them, nor could she retreat into the parlor, which even with the door closed held Madison's body on the other side, in the center of the dining room where she would not take a meal again. He was cleaned, washed so that the skin briefly had turned pink from rubbing, scouring off dried blood, and with that brief pink tinge to his flesh, a foolish hope crowded into her mouth and behind her eyes that he was alive.

Then as they stopped scrubbing the pink disappeared, and that pale ugly gray, not the color of flesh but of doves' wings and her mother's morning dresses and the hide of her father's favorite team, that color resurfaced taking her fantasies, her deepest wishes, and drowned them within its spoiling hue.

The hole in his chest was much larger than the one in his back. That simple fact was enough to make her quite ill. His killer had not had the courage to face a good man as he was murdered.

Death was gray, felt with the tips of her fingers and once, when Priscilla had gone to the kitchen to heat up water and fill the bowl, tear more fresh rags, gray was the taste of her dead husband's mouth.

When she had the chance, Priscilla came out the back steps of the kitchen and told her husband what she and the missus had done, that they'd washed that flesh, soft and damp and ugly and there was more to be done to his backside and Turner knew exactly what his wife was doing. He'd shot him animals, deer mostly, a few steers when no one was looking. He'd never seen a dead man, not up close but he could see the torn flesh of the living things he'd killed to eat, to keep him alive. He never could shoot a man that way.

His wife was crying, a hard woman who'd seen more of life than Turner ever would but she loved him and let him play on her and she played back. He guessed that was love. It was the only kind he'd ever known.

She had to go into the house she said, they weren't done on Mr. Tremont's body. She got three steps away from him and turned, ran to him. No women ever run to him before. She was soft up against him not wanting patting or rubbing, not even a kiss. 'Hold me' was what she breathed into his chest and he obliged, gentle as he could for Turner was a strong man who'd been blamed for hurting things he hadn't meant to. He let her cry against him until his shirt was wet and she was gasping and he let his hands rest at the small of her back to offer what comfort a man such as Turner Burbank could manage.

She pulled herself away; spoke softly as if Turner wasn't there. "I didn't know the holes would be so. . .big, like I could see into his heart, it was cut, a mass of. . .we're ugly inside, just like the animals my pa used to gut and clean." Her voice rose; "Turner!" His arms cradled her back, felt her flesh and bone tremble and he wanted to take that fear away.

"Mr. Mitchell, you saddle up and we'll ride back . . . ." A hand gesture toward the house and Blue nodded. While Patton got his wind, Mitchell went to the brown mustang and slipped a simple bit in the ugly son's mouth. The horse sighed, probably Mitchell did too. Man and horse turned to walk away, leaving a dark bay paint stud colt to find out he was alone.

It was a quick saddling while Patton tightened the cinch to his old centerfire rig. Cowboys now, they sometimes used a three-quarter rigging but Patton as a lawman didn't have much cause to hard-tie on a 700 pound steer so he kept to the old rig, liked its comfort and the stirrups that were well-turned to carry his weight.

He had one question for Mitchell before they rode out, and it should have been asked long before this; "When do you think Mr. Tremont died?" The roan rubbed his long head on Patton's shoulder and he pushed the horse away. Mitchell seemed to have trouble suddenly doing up the cinch on the brown. The man's balance shifted, his shoulders tightened as he turned to Patton.

"I don't know 'bout humans, but more than two hours before I came on the body, there was a shot. It was far from me and my horses, but it sure spooked the colt. I figured it was a hunter." Both men studied those words. Mitchell finished; "Deer hunting, why the body stiffens after a few hours, I can't see that a man would be much different."

Patton climbed on his good roan and eased his sore behind into the two dents his butt had made over the years. He sighed, didn't touch the reins as he watched Mitchell swing up on the brown. Mitchell looked over at him and those eyes, well Patton had that urge to hit the son of a. . .but he knew better, it was a late reaction to death and not particular to this man.

"Why'd you saddle the brown, he don't look like much." Not maybe the best way to get the man talking, but Patton was tired, and fretting from the chore ahead. It had been luck he was in Abbott and not over to Clayton or even Raton. Mitchell's answer was short and left no room for small talk.

"He rides easier than the colt, and he don't tire so fast." Then a big breath, a hand across that mouth, those eyes lowered to the ground but their glint left a warning for Hale. This wasn't a man to fool with. He studied, thought, considered things. Listening would be the smartest course a lawman could take with Mitchell. Hale settled himself deeper in the old saddle; "Let's do it."

A mile at a quick trot made Patton's gut turn over and had him grabbing the saddle swell, trying to raise his nether parts from the hard seat and take his weight in his feet. Damn that brown moved quick, at a smooth gait that Mitchell rode standing, leaned forward. He was younger than Hale, and a better horseman but Hale wasn't jealous except for the man's obvious ease. Now he understood now why the rider chose the homely brown.

Mitchell eased the mustang into a walk where Hale's roan jarred on its front legs and he cursed, first under his breath and then out loud; "Damn." The blood trail was immediately evident, soaked into shallow earth like a line drawn clear enough for a child to follow.

Patton waited as Mitchell tried to explain; "I cut them loose before here and that blood leaked from under the seat. See, here the team was trotting, then they slowed, got tired I guess. I caught them just before they hit the ranch." In the too-long silence, Hale cocked his head as if waiting. Mitchell gulped, then continued; "I surely didn't want the team with their passenger to run into the middle of a home. It wouldn't have been right." Mitchell wiped his mouth again, eyes shut, then he sighed. "I found them where they'd got stuck from no one driving them. It was the only way I knew to find out where the body belonged. Horses know the way home."

Hale let out a snort, wiped his mouth; sentimental words from a hard man, and to Hale's mind close-enough proof Mitchell wasn't the killer. They rode at a slow gait to where the team had been stopped. The mud told everything; churned and drying at the edges, sawgrass tromped or tore down. Blue folded his hands on the saddle horn and waited.

The law let his horse make a tight circle, then again to the other direction. The man's eyes were set on the ground, barely lifting as the horse turned. Then the roan stopped, let out a sigh. "What do you think happened here, Mitchell?"

Blue only stared at the man. "I'm not the law so what I think don't count." "Hmmm." Then a long silence until Hale cocked his head and Mitchell picked up the silent command to keep explaining. "The team ran themselves into the swamp and got stuck. There's nothing says the killer or killers came up to the wagon at all. All that's here is the end of a fast run and the team stuck in that damned grass. Mr. Tremont, he was shot long before the team got to this point. There isn't that much blood, excepting what pooled at his feet."

Mitchell's burned eyes never left Hale's face, so in return Hale offered his own suggestion; "We can check the back trail." Mitchell nodded once, wiped at his face. "That's exactly what a smart man'd do." Patton turned the roan, the horse immediately got high-headed and anxious. Blue angled the brown mustang up near the roan and they stepped into a trot as if they were a team.

The back trail of the panicking draft horses was wide and deep, showing the labored strides of the startled animals. Eventually the erratic line led back to the soft dust of the road and the teams' strides were shorter, more organized, obviously under guidance.

That the shot had come unexpected, without signal or confrontation, was easily read by the great digging leaps at one point on the road. Blood had instantly spilled from the wagon. At first it was a few droplets, then a dark red-soaked line as Madison Tremont's life poured from him.

Wordlessly the two men rode past where the team had dug in, one man riding the left side, one on the right of the dirt track. Both men were able to see the small differences of bent grasses or a broken twig, anything that might show a man on horseback had come this way and where the rider had gone.

Blue found a spot with several piles of manure, a bare place where a horse had pawed, boot prints crossed on each other. He called out for the law, who rode to the edge of the low clearing. Blue looked down, the law dismounted and tied his roan, stepped wide around the trampled ground and came in next to Blue.

They were still, studying what they could see, forming their own ideas of what might have happened right here. Patton spoke first; "A few boot prints is all. We don't know what he was thinking, or even if he was waiting on Tremont. Waiting all right, but it could have been on a pronghorn or mule deer."

Blue backed his horse, turned away; "You stand there, I'll go 'round, then pick up your line of sight, see if I can find what's on the other side." He crossed the track, noting that right here the sorrel teams' prints were regular and even. Then he stopped the brown and saw exactly where within two strides the team had bolted. When Blue shook his head, Patton called out;

"There?" Blue nodded, stepped the brown into the brush, glancing back once to see Patton's shape.

He slid from the brown and tied him, then carefully parted brush, low trees, even touched some of the high grasses. There had been a disturbance, a man had waited here not long ago. Blue shook his head.

He then knelt down where a darker stain told him what his nose already knew; the man had pissed while standing here. The boot prints were spread across the small clearing, and the edges were scuffed, as if the person had trouble balancing. The watcher must have had a full bladder and he wasn't much of a hunter, to leave a strong scent. If he was waiting on an ambush, then the urine scent wouldn't matter. The facts told him it was a planned murder.

Blue stood slowly, glanced at the road and turned slightly to watch the law. Between them lay the track and if he stood along the same line as the team had traveled, he could see exactly where the horses had lurched themselves into a panicked run. There were no shells left behind that he could find, no way to know if it was one clean shot or more fired in haste until Tremont was killed

The brush was thick, bent in places but still partly hiding the road, which meant there was no way of knowing whether or not the bullet had been intended for Madison Tremont or someone or something else. A man could claim shooting at game, the brush was thick enough. But a decent hunter would hear the team coming and lift the rifle barrel to wait as the team passed safely. Any game would be gone, but no one would have been killed.

Or he'd already shot once and the sound echoed so that he could not hear the team. Blue shook his head, knelt and let one finger trace the boot prints. Big boots, definitely a large man, yet underneath were smaller prints. It was impossible to tell when either set of prints were made. The edges were blurred, the rolled dirt, still in clumps, was from the bigger, newer print. The urine stain had already dried but that meant little in the high desert.

Hale Patton pushed through the brush and spoke slowly, head cocked as if to hear the past. "It had to be a man without much sense to be shooting along a road." It was a long thought, a pause where Blue chewed on the words. "Or a man bent on deliberately killing a particular person of some routine in his daily habits." Blue pointed to a single toe print below the width of a huge boot heel. "Those are different, I can't tell. . .don't know." He didn't mention the stain, for already Patton's nose had twitched and the man poked at the urine with a stick. "Hmmm." Blue nodded.

Patton squatted and studied the awkward prints. The man had nothing to say. Then he stood carefully; "Guess I best check out a few rifles at the Tremont place. Might could be a man there would have a hate for Mr. Tremont. He seems not to have been a forgiving man. And he surely hired himself a ragged bunch."

The load of information, the quiet voice without challenge or insult, let Blue know he was no longer a suspect. He wanted to laugh at the foolishness of his brief career as a killer but it would be wrong. A man was dead, whether it was careless or planned, and laughter out of relief was no excuse.

Once mounted, with horses turned toward the Tremont spread, the brown knew where they were headed and picked up the pace until Patton's long-legged roan had to lope. Patton rode stiff against the horse's rough gait and Blue wanted to offer a suggestion but figured the man's dignity would object, and the roan seemed to be willing enough to carry the object bouncing on his back if it meant getting to the ranch and a good feed of hay.

Blue took the roan's bridle and put the lanky son in a stall in the barn. He stripped off the gear, made sure there was hay in the manger before he tied the horse snug by a halter and then slipped a rope behind his quarters. When he got outside to put up the brown, the mustang was standing in the lady's flowers again. As Blue approached, the horse side-stepped, caught a trailing rein in a small plant and the ugly head was jerked by the pull. Blue unexpectedly laughed, since the large purple flower hanging from the brown's mouth was a startling contrast to the animal's boney nose and long ears.

It was that voice, already too familiar, a sound that tore into him. "Sir, there is something that draws laughter from you even on such a day?" He winced from the unintended reminder. He had not meant for anyone to hear him. "Ma'am." He nodded to her, a shadow under the verandah roof, then he caught the brown and gently removed the crushed flower from the horse's teeth.

He wasn't watching but felt the edge of her movement; a hand quick to her face, the slightest cough. "That is indeed silly, Mr. Mitchell." Then she paused. Even when he wanted to lead the brown to the corral, Blue felt the woman hold him.

She spoke carefully, almost in a whisper; "Thank you, Mr. Mitchell." He waited. "You have reminded me the world will go on despite all that has happened."

Hale Patton walked into the bunkhouse where a man sat cleaning a rifle. He studied the seated man, whose hand, with a grease-soaked wad of cloth stuck to it, remained in mid air. Hale's badge did that to folks, made them stop what they were doing and wonder what he expected.

Now why would a cowhand sit on the edge of his bunk in mid-day and clean a rifle when it needed to be kept to a saddle rig ready for mountain lions or a horse with a broke leg. Because he'd been shooting lately was the only reason. And since it didn't look like this outfit was short on rations, deer hunting for sport was most likely. Or the man was a cold-blooded murderer without common sense.

The man's face was flushed despite the easy work. Hale thought he might lean on a wall and ask the cowhand a few questions.

His name was Turner, Hale didn't catch the last name, and he'd hired on when the Tremonts bought the old Lord place. They'd turned that rough cabin into a fancy house and made friends with all those nearby who had money, all the social fancy folk they was. Didn't pay top dollar for wages, Turner admitted, but then again they didn't ask much and the hands ate well 'cause Turner's wife knew how to cook. It seemed to the man that the Tremonts were ranching to say they were ranchers, not to make a living from the land and cattle. Fine cattle too the man said, some kind of eastern type that did well on the thin grass and calved out real easy.

All this was interesting and Hale filed away some useful facts but the man so far hadn't answered why he was cleaning a rifle instead of riding fence or doctoring a cow with screwworms, or rasping down a chipped hoof on his best night horse.

Hale pushed away from the wall and rubbed his jaw; "Mr. Turner, now I asked polite-like and you haven't given a direct answer. Why are you here cleaning that rifle when there is work to be done?"

The man looked up, his face flushed, drops of water falling from the crooked nose. "Mr. ah Patton I come in 'cause Cook he can't give us nothing to do. He got his orders from the mister and well. . . ." The deep-set eyes blinked hard. "I got me a deer couple of days past, was caught in the fence line and I shot it clean through the head. Drug it home and skinned it and now I got the time to clean out this here rifle. I don't want trouble, Mr. Patton. Let me show you."

The man put down the rifle and stood and his size was impressive, until Hale studied the small hands, looked into the deep-set eyes that skidded away from his gaze. Something most definitely was out of line in the story, but for now he would follow Turner to whatever it was the man wanted to show him.

Turner wandered and Hale kept a certain distance as the man had a rank air. It had been a while since Hale last enjoyed a good meal, and Turner with no last name did not add to the fragrance of the Colorado air, nor did his aroma soothe Hale's hungry belly.

Turner eventually brought the law to the backside of the barn where a small shed stood lopsided and windowless. 'In there,' was Turner's entire contribution to the unanswered earlier questions. Hale prompted the man with a gentle shove to the ribs and Turner growled but got the message to move aside.

The shed was dark and stinking. Even Turner's ripeness faded against the heated stench. Indeed there was a deer hide, fleshed out and hanging on a wall and strips of meat hooked over the remains of a fire. Turner mumbled; "I like deer jerky when I'm riding herd."

Hale nodded, then touched a hand lightly on an edge of the hide; stiff and definitely stinking. For now he would accept Turner's labored explanation of why he was cleaning his rifle the day his boss was found back shot.

CHAPTER SIX

Madison's body was rolled and wrapped in tidy folds of fine sheeting. It was the last of the wedding linens embroidered with their intertwined initials, given as a reluctant present by Melinda's great-aunt Roberta Cross. Melinda understood the symbolic nature of wrapping the remains of her marriage with her deceased husband; to her family it would be quite fitting. They had never accepted Madison and now the family name and heritage would be forever entangled with his rotting corpse even as they chided Melinda for her mistake.

These were harsh thoughts for a southern lady, a woman schooled in the delicate arts of embroidery and water colors, tatting linens and arranging flowers in a most becoming manner. When the killer fired a shot into Madison's back, her life was over. She had a ranch to run, a ranch that Madison had allowed to deteriorate as he hired Ira Cook and left the man to his own decisions with only the bare bones of Madison's orders, which were few and generally unproductive.

She would tend to Ira Cook, a most disrespectful and disrespected man. Cook always spoke the words as coming from Mr. Tremont but indeed Madison had not cared and Cook's outdated ideas had almost brought them to ruin. Their impending bankruptcy, despite a fine appearance, was similar to their good friends the Dorseys, who had finished their elegant European home in time to run out of funds and the approval of their neighbors.

Of course the rumors of Mr. Dorsey's less than stellar reputation, enlarged by that party held at the ranch house while he was on trial in the country's capitol for fraud with the US Post Office as his adversary, did not support trust in the man's honesty. Melinda had been slightly reluctant to befriend these people, but where the Dorseys lived was the center of the small universe here in the grasslands, and they set a decent table, held glorious gatherings and were more than willing to become friends with the transplanted southerners. There could not help but be some suspicion as to why Madison Tremont, of fine breeding and high education, chose such a remote area in which to settle. She believed that the same family concerns could be voiced for Stephen Dorsey and his lovely wife Helen.

Melinda gasped slightly, and succumbed to that timeworn gesture of putting her hand to her throat. Oh dear, Helen and Stephen Dorsey. She must get word to them, for Mr. Dorsey and Tremont had several business ventures together and Madison's death would be of serious concern to the man. She knew also that Madison's affairs lately had been doubtful, investing in several schemes of Mr. Dorsey's that had not come to expected fruition. Now it would be she who must stand up to the redoubtable Mr. Dorsey and refuse payment owed until Madison's estate could be settled and all monies accounted for.

And, she admitted to herself, it would be of some comfort to speak intimately with Helen. Although the young woman was from a fine Ohio family, she too had confessed to feeling terrified by the wilderness in which they now lived. Helen's husband was charming, much like Madison, and he had made a career in this strangely empty and sometimes beautiful land. But it most definitely was at the social cost of neighbors and parties and dear visits from friends.

It would be necessary to send a rider to the mansion, to deliver the devastating news.

The law was following Turner, looking like a terrier chasing an escaped steer, and the foreman, Mr. Ira Cook, was yelling at the rider who'd gone for the law. The foreman wasn't giving orders, telling the man to check a pasture or a fence line but yelling that he was a good-for-nothing lazy bum. It seemed to Blue that tomorrow the ranch could be minus a decent hand.

He'd leave now if he could, but without saying so, the law wanted him to stay and Blue figured it wasn't worth the argument. More'n likely he could get a meal from the house, a decent night's sleep in the barn and a bait of grain for the paint colt and the brown mustang. They'd earned a rest and decent feed.

If he admitted the truth to himself, he had no particular direction in mind but riding miles to put manners on the colt. Then he'd sell the paint stud to some rancher who fancied being a horse breeder. With no special place to be, Blue had no excuse to turn down anything asked of him. He'd seen her eyes, felt her tremble; Mrs. Tremont might need someone who could be trusted. Far as Blue could figure, everyone on the ranch except the law and himself was a suspect.

The female from the kitchen came into the barn while Blue sat reworking a string to the saddle skirt. He'd cut one off a few hundred miles back, needing it for a quick tie on a broken rein. He had carefully sliced down a long piece of rawhide, kept in his saddlebags for such repairs, and punched holes in the string to rethread it to the saddle. Then he over-braided the repair to the rein. His next chore was cleaning off the matted underside of Peter Charley's saddle blanket. He'd already taken the stiffened, crusted canvas out back of the barn to roll up and throw into an arroyo. When it rained next, the damned canvas would be destroyed.

There were black hairs woven into the blanket alongside the brown's hair, and now the two colors, red bay and white, from the painted colt. It was a good time to clean all his gear.

The woman's loud voice interrupted his chores; "You come to the house. The missus she has something needs tending to. Asked for you, I said you was to the barn doing nothing." Blue set down the half-done repair, slipped the knife into its leather pocket on his hip and stood, nodded to the woman who turned and walked away.

She might be disgusted with him, or with all men, but there was invitation in the walk that Blue studied. This woman knew too much about men. It was all in the hips, a slow easy roll that told him she'd been a member of an old profession that once practiced wasn't ever forgotten.

The baby-faced man who was her husband wouldn't have any way of handling this female. She was hell and damnation rolled into a kitchen girl working for day wages and a warm bed.

Blue slowed up, uneasy being too close to the woman's deliberate invitation. When he headed to the back door, the woman shook her head without looking around; "She said to meet her at the front." Her voice faded as she went around the edge of the extended kitchen. As directed, Blue went toward the verandah.

"Mr. Mitchell." Soft command, words unspoken that any man knew to respect. "Yes, ma'am." Blue nodded as he took the first of the three front steps. "Mr. Mitchell. Sir." He was already in trouble for he could not say no to whatever it was she intended to ask. He looked up and she stepped back, drawing him onto the verandah floor. "Sir." It was a gentle voice now; "I have a note I wish you to deliver. Perhaps Mr. Cook can saddle you a fresh horse. I would greatly appreciate it being delivered quickly." Here the voice faltered before using that word; "Please."

She had too quickly learned his soft underside; a lady, any woman for that matter, who said 'please' with such gentleness, could not be dismissed. It was a common failing in cowhands and drifters since they were lonesome by nature and easy pickings for a woman of the right look and manner. "Yes, ma'am?" He smiled and saw her shoulders relax, her hands opened even as her eyes eased.

He saddled the colt this time, who wasn't delighted with the activity and Blue had to cuff the colt as he bit down on Blue's arm. The colt backed up while Blue fitted the saddle to his humped back until his hindquarters hit the fence and when the colt tried to jump forward, Blue steadied him with a pull on one rein and the command to 'whoa'.

He rode up to the long verandah for orders. "It is three miles north and east of here, Mr. Mitchell. Simply follow the creek going north. You cannot miss it. The house is multi-storied and ornate. Fancy, you might call it." He nodded, looked away from her and she seemed to be angry. "Sir, I am giving you directions to a place you have not visited. Please do me the kindness of paying attention."

Blue didn't bother to explain that once a drifter rode past that castle, he'd never forget it. And there wouldn't be two of them in this country or any place other than a distant city.

She didn't deserve his annoyance so he held out a hand to acknowledge the reprimand, and the simple gesture spooked the paint colt who whirled and spun until Blue had to dismount and take one step up, wait for the woman to approach him again.

She gave him the note and he didn't look at it but felt its weight. Something raised on the envelope's backside was smooth under his callused thumb, and he smiled at her. Such formality was to be expected. Then he climbed aboard and it was easy to spin the colt in a half circle, ride out a short buck, slip the reins and let the colt run.

She settled with some discomfort in the rocking chair. Its jutting arms were meant for a man, Mama had taught her. A woman's chair had no arms, allowing her voluminous skirts and petticoats to be easily spread around the seat to form a beguiling picture.

Already Melinda had ventured into a new realm, having removed all but one of the crinoline layers demanded of a woman in polite society. These layers of starched and reinforced materials maddened Priscilla as Melinda stood beside her and told her in detail exactly how to iron and shape them.

Out here, suddenly without a husband and no need to encumber herself with layers upon layers of crinoline, Melinda Broadus Tremont felt the size and shape of her own flesh settle in a wood-seated chair without all the intervening layers. She was not quite bold enough to give up the last crinoline but her body was close to indecent, or it would be seen so in her family's eyes, as she enjoyed her first act of an unwanted freedom.

The sensation she experienced would mean nothing to a woman brought up out here, where a simple dress, knickers or one petticoat, an apron, lisle stockings and boots, were worn as a companion to her man's wool pants and collarless shirt. A few of the braver women actually wore pants and rode astride. These hard-working people wore practical clothes in a world that demanded practicality to ensure survival.

Melinda watched the retreat of the peculiar horseman, who had been an unwitting catalyst to the stunning devastation of her domestic life. The prettily marked colt seemed to twist and slide and leap too high and yet its rider remained in the middle of the horse's back. No spurring or spanking, no yells or curses; he rode with a hand wrapped around the split reins and his body loosely balanced. To watch the rider and horse was almost as beautiful as being entertained by a dancer on stage.

Then the colt came down from a vertical protest and stepped into a lope. She waited as horse and rider became smaller and wished for that amount of confidence and ability, and the freedom to ride out and simply disappear.

Blue began to wonder about the colt. The youngster still had too much buck to him even after the weeks of traveling. Maybe the colt was better off cut and maybe this time Blue had a mount he couldn't handle.

His head ached from the bucking; he'd taken a bite out of his tongue and the familiar spill of blood annoyed him. He pushed the colt into a slow gallop, figuring a mile or three might exhaust the colt's need to fight.

It was easy to keep to the creek bed like the woman told him. He remembered following it south and west. This time he wondered about the people he'd gotten involved with. He suspected the woman handing him the note had ideas he wouldn't much like if she spoke them, something about taming him to fit into her husband's shoes.

It could be his own self-importance gave him these notions, but it had been tried before. Women liked it, that Blue was as contrary and full of buck as the paint colt he rode. They thought they saw the possibilities of redemption in taming a half-broke man. He'd meant to ask one of these women, did they earn something extra by taking away a man's freedom.

He was able to retrace the colt's tracks to where he'd come down off the ridge, skirting around the grand house. This time, with the colt finally walking on a loose rein, Blue eased up and had the colt stand and wait while he studied the house. Earlier he'd been spooked by the round tower and stone figures and too many windows looking out onto plains with not even one cow or a single horse to break up the distance.

The damned place looked like a prison, he thought, all windows and stonework and heads stuck to high walls. He let his legs touch the colt's sides and laughed as the youngster tried to bolt. He wanted a proper walk up to this proper house. It wasn't old, he could tell that by the raw land close around it, but the money must have dried up along with the hard-edged pools, the silent fountains and the lack of activity. Even the scrub trees and bent flowers planted in front looked as poor as the land. From the few prints, there was probably only one horse and it was missing. There were buggy tracks, thin metal rims easy to follow. They looked to be several days' old with no return. Blue hoped he hadn't ridden here on an empty errand.

The front had a rounded entrance, same fuss and fancy as the massive stone tower rising above it, shaded by a long verandah with one step up to the wood flooring and the huge front door. Blue grunted for there was no place nearby to tie a horse. He dismounted, stood a moment with the colt, playing with the youngster's chin whiskers and lips, letting the colt nibble until he relaxed and Blue led him up the step and onto the verandah floor.

For a moment he thought there might be an argument as the wood planks shifted and the colt's hooves struck hard notes, so using common sense, he held the reins close to the bit as he knocked on the door. It was a massive son of a bitch with hammered black metal hinges, a small window with lead around the glass right at eye level. Blue grinned and nodded to whoever might be looking out at him. The colt pulled back at the knocking and Blue let the reins slide six inches, then held and the colt stopped, stared down at a stalk of grass just out of reach.

Blue knocked again, began to turn away in the silence until he heard a voice, a woman's voice, barely an echo inside what had to be a large room. He waited, felt the colt stiffen when the dulled brass doorknob began to turn. He stepped back expecting disaster.

When the door opened, his first thought was uncharitable. Mrs. Dorsey might be younger than Mrs. Tremont but she had the same style and manner designed to torment any man. That soft sweet voice, a head turned slightly, eyes barely making contact, looking away quickly. "Yes?" These women were dangerous.

Blue wanted to kick something, to tug at his hair or rub his jaw but both hands were full, one holding the paint's reins, the other wrapped around a pale cream envelope now decorated with fingerprints and sweat. "Here." It was all he could think of to say but she did not take the envelope. Then he remembered; "Ma'am."

"Sir." They were the same, these two women, made of soft voices and beautiful eyes, genteel manners and laced clothing. They belonged to a world with no place for the likes of Blue Mitchell. She continued, and he waited to correct her; "Sir, my husband is indisposed at the moment and our servant." She hesitated, caught between a lie he could see coming and the truth that would lessen her stature in a worthless stranger's eyes. He wondered what made him important enough that a decent woman would consider lying.

"Ma'am, it ain't smart to tell a stranger you're alone." Here he too hesitated, thought over the words. "I take it he ain't in, or even around the backside of this place. It might be all your hands are gone too. Strangers out here can be kind or helpful but you can just as easy have opened the door to a killer. Ma'am."

Her smile was as sweet as her face and manner; "Sir, you have come to hand me a note from Mrs. Tremont. That's her monogram on the envelope. I sincerely doubt that she would have sent along a killer to make such a delightful delivery." He realized she was looking for an invite, not a death notice. His impulse was to get the hell away from this empty place.

"Mister, ah?" She tilted her head and gave him one of those smiles. Blue was beginning to get a handle on these ladies, how they led a man to say what they wanted to hear. He waited, then spoke; "My name is Blue Mitchell, Mrs. Dorsey. Mrs. Tremont asked me to hand-deliver this." He held out the envelope; there, he thought, it's done. Then he took a step back, felt the colt push up against him. The verandah was level with the inside of the house and the colt had thought to walk inside.

Blue laughed gently, put a hand on the colt's chest and tugged on one rein. An eye rolled toward him, but the colt gave in and for once minded his manners.

Now where had Melinda found such an unusual personage as this gentleman? There was a certain lack of interesting residents in the desolate land both women occupied at the request of their husbands.

At first Helen had been nervous about coming to the door. Stephen was away trying to raise funds, although he denied that they were in financial difficulties. And why would he think she did not know? He had let the housekeeper go, fired all but one man who took care of the single horse. The hands were gone, along with much of the vast acreage. Did her beloved husband believe she was so blinded by the fragility of her sex that she could not understand the necessity for these changes? The man amused her at times, despite the fear that lack of money inspired.

This one, he did not seem daunted by his obvious poverty. In fact he was smiling, grinning perhaps was a better word. Insolent, Stephen would call him. Those beautiful eyes and that blond hair; Helen shook her head. She was after all a married woman and must not be observed watching another man.

Then again, there was no one in the house or grounds to criticize her behavior. It was a strange sensation, not in keeping with her usual life. If it weren't for her son, Clayton, and the woman hired to care for him, Helen would be alone.

His voice surprised her; "Ma'am, you best read that letter. If you want, I can take a note to Missus Tremont." That brought her back to the visit from Melinda's odd messenger.

While this horseman would own nothing of value, it was a distinct pleasure to study his face and form. His voice, however, directed her otherwise, and as she had been trained early in feminine compliance, Helen Dorsey did as he suggested.

She opened the fine velum paper folded properly as to hide its words from a casual observer. She read quickly, then dropped the note and put both hands to her mouth. She swayed dangerously and the sunlight hurt her eyes before she hid behind her hands.

The horseman, Melinda's valiant cowboy, braced himself and held her shoulders, accepting the burden of her slight frame as the world spun; Madison Tremont was dead, callously slaughtered. And he had been one of Mr. Dorsey's major supporters, a promise of funds given verbally. Now their downfall would happen sooner. Stephen would be most angry.

She righted herself. It was horrible to be thinking of finances when it was Melinda Tremont in dire pain. Helen swept a loose wisp of hair from her face; "Please harness a horse for me, mister. . . ." Oh dear she'd forgotten his name if she ever knew it.

"Ma'am, the colt I rode ain't harness broke, barely broke to saddle as it is. You got a good sensible horse to the corrals? I didn't read any such sign when I came up to your place."

He was indeed an observant man who seemed to know too much too quickly. He spoke before she could form a reply; "I'll take your answer to Mrs. Tremont and she'll send a buggy for you." Helen sighed and shook her head. "Sir, I have ridden to hounds back east and would not suspect that any animal here could throw me." She glanced down at his boots and Blue shuddered, knowing what was going through the woman's mind.

"Ma'am, while I admire your willingness to risk your life for friendship, the walk won't do my feet much good and the colt ain't broke near well enough to handle a woman on his back." He hesitated, and she was curious as to what would stop this man from speaking his thoughts. But it was a simple, practical matter. "Ma'am, you ride and I lead but that colt won't accept a woman's petticoats against his sides. It's no answer to the problem." Then he dared to grin at her and while the image was enticing, his words infuriated her. "Unless of course, ma'am, you would put on a pair of your husband's britches.

She glared at him, eyes flashing, hands on hips, head turned and mouth tight. His suggestion was totally unacceptable. She was a woman used to having her own way and yet he resisted; "Ma'am, I'll have a buggy come back for you. Mrs. Tremont will understand." She stamped her foot as he backed from the door and the paint colt reared high, came down sideways and kicked out, hit one of the fancy posts and scared himself, leaped forward then stopped and held up the hind leg. Blue backed the colt and sighed.

The woman said a few words with Blue paying no attention. He checked the colt's cinch, stepped into the stirrup and before he could land the colt bolted, which is what Blue figured he'd do. This time it was all right, he didn't want more dealings with a woman who thought because she jumped a few fences on a quiet hack that she could handle the paint colt.

Three lurching strides and the colt was solid on that hind leg and they went flying down the dirt track alongside the creek, headed home as far as the colt was concerned. Blue let him run since it took out some of his own temper. This was a mess he'd come into without one bit of wrongdoing and now folks were ordering him one place or another as if he'd hired on to work without pay.

CHAPTER SEVEN

Hale Patton let on that he had no particular thought in mind as he looked through the barn and the sheds out back, poked some along the fence near to the grasslands and even sat down a moment under a good sized tree and remembered how he'd been told there was a spring nearby, some called it Mountain Springs, other stuck to the old name of Chico.

He'd found a couple of things that disturbed him. The hide that the homely cowboy said was from a deer a few days back, it was too fresh, had been tanned too fast and there were no cut marks from a wire fence. He could still smell the brains used to tan that hide, and the hidden scent of rot that such a hurried job would leave.

No decent hunter left a rifle that long without a good cleaning. Of course Turner wasn't the smartest man Hale'd come across. In fact most criminals and killers were downright stupid, leaving behind a spur with their brand on it or riding a high-colored horse with one blue eye.

Turner was first on his suspect list except for why the man would kill his boss and lose a good job. Turner had a willing woman and a place of their own, and that was a lot for an indifferent cowhand. Those facts made it senseless for Turner to be the killer but for the odd evidence.

There were other men he hadn't talked with yet. That small one, the quiet, watchful horse breaker, it wasn't that he'd run or was mean, it wasn't even that he didn't look a man straight for his eyes drifted down most of the time. His face had one healed cut below the left ear, and the hands were sprung, large knuckles, a bad scar, looked like an old rope burn, across the left palm. Nothing unusual in the man's chosen line of work. There was something about the quiet hesitation, even when the son rode into the small town of Abbott and caught Hale in his office for once. Even then the son had an off way of acting. It might be interesting when he talked to the rider but for now it would have to wait.

Natural curiosity brought him to the corral fence as the wild-eyed son, well named by his ma or pa, came in on the sweaty paint colt. That quality of horse, despite his coloring, couldn't be bought on the law's wages, but Hale knew that the long-legged rider would put manners on the colt and sell him high-dollar. Not a bad life if you had the skill and patience, and such a calling was about as dangerous as wearing a star. Horses were natural outlaws, resisting the harsh reins of humankind.

Hale cocked his head, rubbed at his jaw and laughed at himself. By god he'd had a thought about the quality of a man's life as compared to a rank mustang's education. Both could fight back, but it was the majority of commonplace laws that inevitably won.

Mitchell nodded to him as he stepped off the colt, who immediately stretched his head and neck down and sighed in relief. Mitchell patted the colt on the shoulder. "A few more miles and he'll figure it out."

Patton took a step back and another close look at this particular rider. He'd gone from suspecting him of murder to valuing his opinion, and he wasn't sure why except that the man was no fool, since only a fool would bring in the body of a man he'd just killed.

Mitchell stood quiet, allowing Hale to study him. He didn't make much of a picture, he was dusty, mouth rimmed with dirt, a growth of light whiskers softened his long jaw. There was age in the vivid eyes and face, even though he couldn't be thirty, and a quiet sadness. An unknown man's death had gotten to him, Patton would bet, and that made Mitchell even less of a suspect. Right now it would be difficult for Mitchell to refuse Mrs. Tremont anything she asked.

"Son, you look like a rank sidewinder been rode hard and put up wet." Mitchell grinned, Hale grinned back, liking the man for the effort. "Mr. Patton, I surely would value a cup of coffee 'bout now, but these ladies, well. . . ." The man shook his head; "Mrs. Dorsey's alone, ain't got no horse to pull a buggy. I figure Mrs. Tremont, she needs a neighbor." He shook his head again, that blond hair moving dust from itself onto the man's shirt collar.

Turner took that moment to slip through the barn door and Mitchell grabbed him. Not by his shirt collar or arm, but by his voice. "You, hitch up a good horse to bring a lady to your missus here. Right now, don't go asking her if you have to but get a horse and harness it proper to a buggy suitable for the ladies."

Turner stopped quick enough to send up more dust. The man studied Hale, then looked again at the tall rider and back to Hale, shook his head once and nodded. Even spoke up real polite; "Yes sir."

Hale sighed; "Mr. Mitchell, you can drive, I'll tag along, if you don't mind the company." Blue answered; "You drive, Mr. Patton, I'll be glad to go 'long as a guard. It'll give Paint here another chance to learn how a good horse does his job." They both knew it was an opportunity to learn what the other thought. There wasn't anything Blue liked about the whole damned mess, except maybe the company of Hale Patton.

Turner drew out a solid sorrel, not one of the team and nothing like the light-footed bay mare he'd harnessed for his boss's wife. It was a wide-chested, medium-boned horse that could plow a furrow or herd cattle. Turner harnessed the sorrel to a decent rig with a fringed top. That the sorrel wasn't the buggy's regular hack was obvious by Turner trying to even up the traces, but the quiet horse was a good choice.

Hale Patton took the lines from Turner as Blue loosened the paint's cinch, lift the saddle for a bit of fresh hair on the hot hide and the colt half-reared and kicked out. Blue got the colt down and the cinch drawn up again. He mounted smoothly as Hale struggled into the buggy seat and touched the sorrel with a light whip. The horse leaned into the soft breast collar and eased the rig forward.

Blue stood in the saddle, one hand tucked under the swell. His nether parts and his temper had done enough today so he would cheat and let the colt trot out. Eventually Blue guided the colt alongside Patton and looked over to study the man.

For a small size and a hard job, Hale Patton had a gentle touch on the lines and got a decent trot out of the sorrel. It would be hard-going to talk though, the wheels needed greasing and the ground was rough, sending Patton up and down out of step with the sorrel's efforts. As the harnessed horse found his stride, Blue gave up and pushed the colt into a lope, a gait easier on his backside and allowing him time to think.

Mitchell rode that rank colt like it was a rocking chair and damn but Hale wished he could ride that way. He'd counted on talking to the man, but with the noise and dust, and Mitchell paying close attention to the colt's mind, talk wasn't going to happen.

The colt boogered unexpectedly, went up and sideways and spun quick, sitting almost on his tail, head against the bit, ears pinned and then from almost sitting the damned horse bolted into a lurching run and Hale drew in the sorrel, felt trembling in his hands down the lines to the sorrel's mouth so he made himself relax and watched the show.

It looked like the colt was about to quit when he took a sideways leap and went down, face flat to the ground, knees bent under him, then the body went over, damned colt more'n likely broke his neck in the fall. Hale called out, surprised by his dismay; "You all right?" As Mitchell pitched forward half-under the colt, the man turned toward Hale with a peculiar glow to the eyes, then coiled up and lay still.

It took a moment but as the dust settled, Mitchell reappeared, bent over but no blood dripped off his face or hands. He went to the colt, who was finally untangled from his own legs, and with Mitchell's encouragement the animal stood, shook off dust and grass, then rubbed his face on an extended leg. Hale waited patiently through all the fuss, until Mitchell led the colt up to him. "Think I might ride with you a while, give this 'un a chance to sort himself out."

Mitchell's weight shifting the buggy woke the sorrel, who turned its head and cocked an ear. Hale picked up the lines and the horse pulled forward, following the faint tracks that had to be Mitchell's from his earlier ride. The colt lunged sideways, then walked forward, limping on the off fore.

Mitchell said nothing but held the reins and stared straight ahead. There was no grimacing or fuss despite a thin scratch that left a bloody line on his jaw. Hale kept his hands steady on the lines and the sorrel trotted up, pulling the colt along until the paint moved without any limp.

Patton considered his first words carefully; "What spooked him?" It was an easy-enough question that provoked a string of oddly-matched answers; "I don't know, he's young, been coddled all his three years and he thinks the bigger world's out to get him." Mitchell rubbed the scratch on his face, smearing the fresh blood. "He sure is quick though. I like that in a working horse." Hale thought it a peculiar take on what could have been a bad spill.

Then Patton asked his passenger; "You got any idea who done the shooting?" Mitchell let out a long sigh; "It's not like there was folks lining up to kill the man. Dorsey's traveling somewhere and he's got one old man to his place. Ira Cook ain't got the brains, plus he's out of a job now. Turner, he's got some rough places but he's not much of a hand and with a wife, he'll have trouble finding another riding job and I can't see him working in a dry goods store."

Both men were quiet, then Mitchell spoke what Patton was thinking; "I don't think that other man, can't remember his name, he only wants to ride his horses and keep to himself. I know the breed well."

Hale glanced quickly at his companion, "That still leaves us with a dead man." He was thinking as he spoke that Mitchell had been describing himself with those last words. Mitchell shook his head; "Those tracks near the shooting area, they covered other tracks and left little proof of when they were made." Mitchell made a rough noise; "Too much depends on the wind."

Hale shook his head as he encouraged the sorrel to pick up a faster trot. Mitchell rubbed his face again but didn't turn his head; "Mr. Patton, it occurred to me while I was rolling under that paint, that you asking me if I was all right wasn't a question I could answer at the particular moment." Hale swallowed as he considered the intent of those words. Mitchell continued; "Seems to me it'd be more useful if you held off asking till the dust cleared and I knew for certain I was mostly in one piece." He hesitated, as if giving great thought to what he would say next. "Ain't much sense in asking a man how he's doing while he's being rolled and kicked. You might wait till the ruckus is finished."

Hale pulled up the sorrel, who sighed and lowered his head. The paint colt seemed glad to be standing still. Hale turned and studied his traveling companion; "Mr. Mitchell, I do believe you are absolutely correct. I will not make that mistake again."

She watched from the grand library, where the window went floor to ceiling and most of the books from those layers of shelves had been sold. Even the absent fine paintings had left their shadows high on the wall. They too had been sold to pay the paltry bills that returned each month. Her husband spoke well of his grand ideas, but had yet to guarantee her safety in their flamboyant life.

Now she would journey to comfort a dear friend in her terrible moment. That Melinda Tremont was older than her husband had never been discussed in their meetings; it had been mostly conversations of music and paintings and the infrequent beauty of desert flowers. However, Helen was quite certain that the Tremonts' presence in this barren part of the world had behind it the specter of family dissension.

Without moving the drapery, aware that she did not wish anyone to know of her interest, she studied the vehicle as it approached. There were two men in the single seated buggy, and one led a horse. It was that pretty colt, the one not steady enough for a woman. She snorted, pushed back her hair, aware that the noise she made was unladylike. But the horseman's insistence on her being unable to handle the paint colt had rubbed against her vanity, a fault that Stephen was not lax in mentioning at certain times.

She again brushed her hair into place and patted the waist of her dark-colored silk dress. While she was not wearing black, she had changed into a more suitable dress for the heart-wrenching errand. She had spoken to the nanny, and to her son, stressing that one must go to the aid of friends in need. Clayton seemed to understand.

The buggy was driven up to the door and halted smartly, the lines held by a small man she did not recognize except for the star pinned to his shirt. The single horse he drove had once belonged to her husband, lost in a poker game to a high roller out of Santa Fe. The sorrel had a peculiarly crooked blaze and a rather sweet temper. The two men had chosen well, although she hoped their choice had not been made out of spite, but then they could not know the sorrel's origins, unless Miss Melinda had thought to tell them.

The cowboy climbed off the buggy seat, and seemed lame as he dragged the colt up the step to knock once again on the front door. He was polite, if not a gentleman. His mama had taught him well.

When she opened the door, of course the colt pulled back and the man had been ready, hand near the bit and he turned the colt's head, keeping him close and easing his fear.

There had been an accident of sorts, the rider's face was marred with bruising and he seemed bent slightly to one side. Since he did not seem uncomfortable, she made no mention of his appearance. The reason for the journey was enough for her to accept. He was slow to pick up her valise, struggling with it for a moment, then he backed the colt as she walked to the buggy.

The driver stepped down, removed his hat and bowed; "Ma'am. The name's Hale Patton, it's a good thing you're doing, going to Mrs. Tremont's aid." The lawman's face was correctly somber, and Helen barely nodded as she accepted his hand as an assist into the buggy seat. The cowboy handed up the valise, which seemed to terrify his horse. She could not believe it, but despite the foolishness of the young horse, the man was indeed smiling.

He made the colt stand a moment. The youngster stuck out his nose, stretched his neck and touched the valise's leather hide. Then it was done, the colt licked the leather and the man pulled the colt's pretty head away. "Ma'am." He nodded to her as if thanking her for some invisible aid. She watched closely as he stepped up into the saddle.

With an escort on a paint colt and a driver of some reputation in the territory, Helen Dorsey was transported to the home of her friend, to console and commiserate with the new widow.

The colt was tiring, walking now on a loose rein, head low, stride remarkably even and long but still Blue felt the colt's slow response to rein or leg.

He looked to the buggy, saw the lawman's head bent to listen, heard sound from the woman but none of it made sense and he was glad. He'd had enough of talk, questions and demands and orders and back and forth to that strange house. No rest, no time, and the ugliness behind the errands made him uneasy. Somewhere in the close scrub trees, high grasses and the thin water of Chico Creek, there was a killer who'd destroyed a man's life and a woman's love.

He shook his head and the colt stopped, sighed deeply, stretched out to piss and Blue stood in the stirrups. In all the weeks of riding, it was the first time the colt had done this, marking that he'd learned a bit of trust and manners. It wasn't sign of an important lesson of skill or direction but a change of attitude. The paint might be growing up.

Blue folded his arms on the saddle horn and when the colt was done, horse and rider stood quiet, watching the buggy and the sorrel horse trot away from them and the colt didn't seem to care about being left behind. A light touch of Blue's leg and the colt walked on, another touch and the colt stepped into a lope to bring them alongside the buggy seat.

The law nodded to Blue, interrupting the woman's flow of talk; "He's learning ain't he." Not a question but an acknowledgement. Blue nodded.

Now it was her turn. Melinda pulled back the drapery, allowing her fingers to stroke the heavy velvet. They were a luxury, and unnecessary here, collecting dust and darkening the rooms, but the green color and thick soft texture delighted her, and Madison always vowed he would do anything within his power to make her happy.

Her fingers stroked the velvet and she remembered how their ranch foreman had complained about standing on a mahogany step stool, originally designed to remove a gentleman's high boots after a day's fox-hunting, how he complained about having to put up the draperies to her direction. The stool had come west with them from Madison's family, who were noted foxhunters throughout the South. She would have to write them of Madison's tragic death.

Now she could slide the pleated drapery back on the polished wood pole, watching sunlight glint off the metal rings, and think of better times, home, her husband, other men she might have married.

It would be a comfort to have Helen with her. She hoped the young woman brought the necessities to spend the night, those few items which a lady carried with her but did not discuss.

There he was, that uncouth rider, stepping down from the colt, walking away from Mrs. Dorsey and the lawman, she couldn't remember his name. The rider stumbled once, catching himself on the colt's saddle and the colt didn't shy or rear.

It finally occurred to Mrs. Tremont that perhaps the bearer of her bad news had been in constant motion throughout the day and might be hungry.

She spoke without turning her head, sensing that the girl was there behind her; "Priscilla, see that mister. . . ." She hesitated and the girl filled in for her; "It's Blue Mitchell, Mr. Mitchell." How rude of the girl to offer corrections, but Melinda remained gracious, true to her upbringing; "Yes, thank you. Please fix a decent meal for the man. And ask your husband to make certain his two horses have plenty of good hay and water. The man has done. . . ." Her manners failed and Melinda Tremont shuddered. "He has worked hard for us today despite not knowing who we are. It is a most admirable and generous trait."

The girl disrupted her watching out the window; "Ma'am, do I feed the lawman and Mitchell to the house, or do they eat with the hands to the cook shack like most of these drifters do?"

The words were almost insulting in a trying day. Melinda inhaled, let out her breath in short puffs to ease her temper. "Set a place in the kitchen for the law as well as Mr. Mitchell, please, Priscilla. They have been busy on our account." She could hear the heavy footsteps out of the parlor and knew once again she had ruffled the girl's sensibility. The two of them, Priscilla and her idiot of a husband, were necessary on the ranch but did not suit Melinda's taste in servants.

Blue had stripped the colt, scrubbed him clean, tuned him back with the brown and set his gear in a safe place before the law returned from delivering Mrs. Dorsey to the grieving widow.

The words and gestures, hugs and gentle kisses on the cheek, might be kind but he had a feeling that the loss of a husband was more practical than passionate for both women. They were a type he did not understand, for there was the sense of being directed by these women without ever being asked. He would be glad to ride out tomorrow.

After a few minutes' rest, Blue planned to go investigate smells and sounds that led him to believe a meal was being readied. There was a crew of sorts and someone needed to feed them. He didn't figure that anyone would mind his presence. He'd done a chore for them they would not have chosen for themselves. No one would speak to him, but at least he'd get vittles he didn't have to cook.

He sat down against a hard post, took in the smells of a barn; clean smells that were always the best of his memories. His head nodded, his chin hit his chest and he slept.

CHAPTER EIGHT

The barn interior smelled of offal and stale urine mixed with sweet hay; Hale Patton took a deep breath and his nose itched, he raised a hand to scratch and saw movement to his right. He dropped that hand to his pistol and then nodded to himself. It was the rider, Mitchell, legs stretched out, head propped on the cradling softness of a wood beam. Hale eased closer, the scattered hay and damp dirt floor softened his footsteps. He watched the man twitch, throw an arm out and bring it back but he never woke up.

All the stories making the rounds about this one were less than truthful, for they didn't mention endurance or kindness, or go far enough in talking of his way with a spoiled bronc. Hale cocked his head, wanting to squat down but knew being that close would wake the man.

Hale grinned, kicked the bottom of the worn boot closest to him and Mitchell came awake, quickly but without moving, eyes half-opened, hands clenched, an indrawn breath, a slow turn of the head. Then the eyes opened fully and stared up at Hale; "Damn it mister, I was finally getting death out of my head."

Those words brought back the long day and Hale shuddered. "We got us an invite to supper, to the main house mind you, the back door if I'm right. Those women, well those ladies, they'll feed the likes of us but not visit unless it's to answer official questions."

He hesitated, studied Mitchell as the man gathered himself and stood, straightening to a good six inches taller than

Hale; "You ain't offended?" Mitchell grinned; "Hell no, not if supper's involved. I ate a strip of deer jerky this morning before sun-up, drank me a belly full of good water and that's about how I've traveled these past weeks."

As Hale's granpap would say, the man was pure quill. Hale rubbed his jaw in silent agreement. "Let's eat."

She had Priscilla set out a clean tablecloth and decent silver utensils on the crude kitchen table. Helen was a blessing, taking charge, directing Priscilla as to the obvious choice for the gentlemen's meal. They were hard-working cowhands, and she was of the opinion that this particular lawman fitted within the category, and consequently they were in need of good solid food. A lesser cut of steak, potatoes fried with a few wild onions, carrots out of the pitiful garden, and biscuits, lots of biscuits. There was always coffee kept to the back of the stove, and Priscilla seemed to have a genius hand at not burning the dark bitter version of this essentially elegant drink.

Only when the table was set and delicious smells emanated from the kitchen into the parlor where Helen and Melinda were sitting, a tea service on the table in front of them, cups empty, tea pot cold, that Melinda recognized the single flaw in her planning.

She would never eat from that dining room table again. Tonight's reason was physical; Madison was laid out waiting for tomorrow's burial. Word had been sent for a preacher, and to a few friends who might find comfort in attending the simple graveside service.

She was unaccountably hungry. From emotion, she suspected, and the afternoon's brutal activity. Melinda glanced at her guest, who was busy patting her hair and staring through the delicate lawn curtaining to the stark and empty ranch yard. "Helen." She kept her voice low and it took a moment's brief hesitation before Helen Dorsey remembered where she was and why.

"Yes, dear friend?" A most appropriate and sweet response, which in turn firmed Melinda's radical idea; "We cannot eat in the. . .there. We shall have to join the gentlemen in the kitchen. Would you be so kind as to have Priscilla set two more places. Use the second-best china of course."

The woman was a fool. Priscilla brushed at her hair, spat onto her hand and wiped it over the offending strands until they stayed in place. If she didn't, the woman would insist on her wearing a hairnet, which she had sent from her 'home' in the South and Priscilla hated the fool things. She cooked hot, picked out whatever fell into the food and it'd always been good enough.

It'd be quieter now that husband was gone. Washing his body, laying him proper-like, was another damned fool thing. They was burying him tomorrow, setting him in a dirt hole, maybe surrounded by a wood coffin, maybe not. Most folks hereabout got wrapped in a sheet, not one usually with initials sewn into it, that was kind of pretty, she thought. But not worth putting all that work into a piece of cloth covering a dead man.

Tomorrow morning Turner would dig a grave wherever the missus said, and it would take him less time than two other men digging together. Priscilla flipped a slab of meat over in the pan, flipped the second one, then the Dorsey lady she come and told her that the 'ladies' would be sharing the meal with the guests. Priscilla shook her head and forked two more slabs of meat onto the blackened skillet.

She then sliced a corner out of the lard bucket and let it sizzle under the meat. Biscuits were cooking, something green boiled in a pot with those damned carrots, potatoes were yet to be sliced and cooked in the same lard. The onions the lady insisted on using smelled hot and raw and Priscilla's eyes ran when she chopped them.

Then again the food was better'n she'd ever had before, and even Turner said it felt like her teeth were steadying in her mouth when he kissed her. Now that was Turner, all practical when a woman wanted sweet words and petting.

It made her grin though, thinking 'bout what she was teaching Turner that came after those kisses. Guess her rough education was paying off in keeping a man of her own.

The whole damned evening was a blur of barely remembered manners, polite words and meat that was tougher to cut than an old sow Blue'd once shot out of desperation. It wouldn't be easy for anyone to do this to good beef. Blue eyed the law as the man struggled with the meat without splashing juice or sending burnt muscle flying into the ladies' laps. The struggle had its good points, though, taking care of having to talk while they sawed away. Being polite as a man struggled with food was different; that was the only way Blue could explain the situation to himself.

Blue finally quit trying, hungry as he was, and ate three biscuits, had real butter on them too. And then he cautiously attacked the green and orange vegetables handed around in fine china bowls with flowers painted on the edge. The vegetables tasted good, almost good enough to make up for the missing beef.

Two scoops of the potatoes and he was filled up. Missed having a good steak though, but it wouldn't be polite to mention the trouble. Then Mrs. Tremont spoke; "Mr. Mitchell?"

He was caught, mouth filled with potato and no place to spit and he couldn't swallow. "Mr. Mitchell, where were you headed?" She swallowed the rest of the question; Blue coughed and the whole wad went down hard. "Ma'am?"

Even the other lady, Mrs. Dorsey, looked upset at the question. It would have been better to leave the subject alone. "Nowhere. Ma'am." Mrs. Tremont looked at him oddly and he figured she'd forgotten what she had asked him. "Riding no place in particular, just putting miles on the colt." Her face went still, then a strange look bunched her features. "You have always had that freedom, to ride where you choose?"

Ah, he thought. A woman bound by family and marriage, now single and unsure. He glanced around the room, a big enough kitchen, painted and shiny, and needing a better cook as he thought on the meat still clinging to the plate.

"Yes ma'am, I've been on my own half my life. Work when I need to, ride where I choose. Ain't much of a life but it suits my temper." She would not take his easy talk. "I would like to consider such a life, Mr. Mitchell. Do you have any suggestions?"

It was a real struggle for Hale Patten not to burst into laughter. Now this ought to be a real dustup. The drifter explaining to the well-born lady just how she needed to stay home in safety and comfort and not consider running away from her new duties.

Hale made another stab at sawing through the meat, which had to be a haunch from the oldest damned cow in the West, and Blue seemed to be watching as Hale put the small corner he'd extracted from the main carcass into his mouth, chewing with some delicacy to prevent unintended tooth removal. Mitchell cocked his head and it looked like he might be grinning but Patton didn't pay attention. Instead he nearly choked over the son of a bitch's words.

"Ma'am, first you need a good pack horse, and a saddle horse worth his salt. Not a quiet lady-broke mount but one's got some fire and heart to him. You'll need it, bad weather and you're in a gully, you need a horse that'll go straight up the wall for you. And you don't want a good-looking horse 'cause someone'll try to steal it, and it's always hard killing a man."

Mitchell took a deep breath and Hale hoped the man had sense enough to quit but then he laughed to himself. He already knew Mitchell had no people sense. It was why being around the man was an experience.

"Now me, I'll ride the colt till he's steady and sell him to some rancher wants good breeding stock." Mitchell didn't even duck his head or blush when he spoke of such matters. "I usually take hard cash and a rough-string horse the hands won't

91

ride." Mitchell grinned and wiped his mouth careful-like with the white napkin provided by the ladies.

"You need only a few things. Most of what you have here you can leave behind. Take a warm coat, a good oilskin too. They're heavy but they keep you almost dry in a storm. Fry pan of course, coffee pot and beans and I usually try to keep the same rock along to crush the beans. A line rider can't always count on finding a rock when it's needed." He paused here, took a sip of cooled coffee; "They do seem to show, rocks that is, when a rider gets bucked off, and it's bound to happen once or twice."

Both women sat absolutely still, probably it was the first time in their lives they weren't the center of the talk. Mitchell went on like he had no idea how his words struck each listener.

"It's best if your mount is barefoot but it ain't always possible. Now that brown I ride, he got caught in wire and tore into a front hoof so I keep him shod. I considered selling him, and once I thought of eating him, but he's a good horse and I won a lot of races on him so it's worth keeping shoes on him." The women had gasped at the mention of eating the horse. Mitchell's face twitched even as he kept talking.

"I carry a rasp, a good knife, extra shoes if the horse is shod. Can't always find a town with a decent smith if the horse throws a shoe. Now that's another thing, learn how to keep a sharp edge to any knife or tool. It can mean your life, owning a sharp knife. I got caught in a rope one time, man on the other end was bound to drag me. Might well have cut me up some, but I had a knife and by god. . . ." Here he did stop a moment, thinking on the cruelty of his words, then plunged on and Hale was beginning to truly appreciate the show.

Simply telling Melinda Tremont she could not do something would more'n likely force her decision. Mitchell in his rough way was brilliant as he mocked himself and the life he led, telling tales that would scare a working cowhand nevermind a well-born lady, telling them as if they were commonplace and what every line-rider experienced.

"The knife had a good edge and went through that rope like this here butter you put down for the biscuits. That blade went through the rawhide and the owner got mad there for a bit, but a clunk on the head from my fry pan simmered him down." This was getting quite funny, and horrifying, at the same time. Hale was enjoying the performance as Mitchell continued; "I'd always thought a fry pan was a woman's weapon but since the son had spilled out my possibles, I grabbed whatever might work, and by god that pan did the trick."

Mitchell pushed back from the table and the glint in those peculiar eyes pleased Hale. No mercy, not from this son. "Good boots help, but when they wear down you can wrap them with uncured hide and they snug up real good. Smell some, but since there ain't no one around it don't matter." The poor manner of speaking was beginning to be too much, but Hale studied the women's faces and decided that the crude speech was having its desired effect.

"Always keep a good supply of bullets, and extra rawhide, I cut the hide in thin strips. You can use them for tying up torn clothing or fix a saddle stirrup, even plait a rein if your bronc breaks one. Best thing is to think first of your horses. Without them, you got nothing. And ma'am, you're a right pretty woman so you need to let your hair grow long and greasy, don't bathe too often and sure as hell don't wear nothing fits real good. Men are rank when they're alone. You best learn to shoot dead center and know you have to do it. Life's bad enough for a man on his own, a woman, well. Don't listen, don't ask or talk learned like you do. Manners don't count out there. You shoot the son of a bitch and then find out his intentions."

It was enough and Mitchell knew it. "Ma'am, I thank you for the meal. Ma'am." He looked past Mrs. Tremont to the woman done the cooking, smiling at her. "Them biscuits saved my life. You know the secret, all I'd add would be some homemade jam, strawberry if you had it. Hell I'd even pick them for you, if I could find a patch. Thank you."

The drifter and self-styled horse breaker stepped around the kitchen woman, who had leaned back against a cupboard, eyes wide, mouth wet. Now damn if Mitchell hadn't charmed her too. The man was gone, nodding once to the Dorsey woman and leaving Hale to deal with the wreckage.

Hale had to fight to keep his seat; he wanted to shake Mitchell's hand and slap his shoulder and tell the son it had been a brave and clever performance. But the ladies were quiet in a way Hale didn't trust. Then Mrs. Tremont gathered herself and spoke calmly to the serving woman with great effort; "Priscilla, you have a peach cobbler for us. Please serve Mr. Patton first. I am certain he will enjoy the treat." Then her face tightened; "It is too bad that Mr. Mitchell did not remain with us for dessert. Priscilla makes an excellent cobbler."

The woman was a marvel. Hale studied her for too long, knowing it wasn't good manners but she had him baffled. Her husband died a gruesome and ugly death only this morning, and despite being a high-born lady, she had washed his body and laid him out. Now she was sharing a meal with a drifter and a lawman, and even the reassuring presence of a friend did not normally allow the bereaved such confidence.

All this made Hale suspicious; her composure wasn't what a usual woman showed on the death of her man. He wanted reddened eyes and a white face, mouth drawn in sorrow, not politeness and curiosity about a free life lived by a wild man. None of this was right and Hale knew it. Still a woman of her quality did not kill a valued husband.

They were all fools and Priscilla said exactly that to her husband after he was done and rolled off her. It was a comfort, his wide body atop her, his face buried in her neck, licking her, wanting her and not just any woman or place he could leave his seed. Made her wonder sometimes how come they hadn't produced a child.

"Turner, there they sat, the lot of them, listening while that man with the crazy eyes talked about how he lived and cruel happenings and he didn't keep nothing back, didn't remember she was a lady. At least she's always telling me how a 'lady' does things and that's how I'm to do them. Pure damned foolishness."

Then Turner rolled up closer to her, put his hand in a place she bet he'd never really looked at but he liked his hand there, when they were done. She squeezed her thighs together and kept talking.

"I can't help thinking we need to get that man gone. The law, he don't worry me much. He plays it regular like he's supposed to but this fella, he don't follow no rules." Then it came to her; "I think Cook wants Mr. Tremont's place, running the ranch and the house and the woman. If you say something to him, why Cook'll have him a plan. He'll know how to get rid of this trouble."

She knew it was deceitful and unfair to her husband but sometimes Turner needed prodding to get him thinking her way. And Cook, well she stayed away from him much as she could, the man had an evil eye and thoughts to match. Oh well, words spoke into Turner's mind would get spread to Cook and she'd not be any part of what happened.

He stroked her belly and she felt him prodding her; her man had a need that in her previous profession would not have been a pleasure. Now it belonged to her and despite her indifference to the act, she hugged Turner and murmured into his ear.

Ira Cook figured things out; it took him all night but he had the answer come morning. He knew the drifter slept to the barn. At least that much was done proper. But him eating with the lady and Mrs. Dorsey for the evening meal, that wasn't right no matter what the son of a bitch had done yesterday. Now Ira, if he found that body, he would cover it decent and drive the team into the yard, call for help and not gotten her all upset dealing with the remains. Not right and proper at all.

The man could do nothing wrong, riding that flash-colored colt no respectable rancher would saddle, and staying on the bucking fits, well that made the ladies think he was a hero.

Ira had thoughts on how to change their way of seeing this son of a bitch. Right now Mitchell, he was still asleep in the barn, nested in the good hay wrapped in sour blankets and his boots hung from the rafters, his saddle and gear closer to the horses' outside pen. Right in a place where a man could stick a burr in that bottom thick blanket, where the multi-colored matted hairs told Ike the blanket needed a good cleaning and the man was in no hurry to do the chore.

He found one of them pointy little cactus, nasty things that got in a man's pant legs or socks and made life pure misery. The sticker was small enough he could work it in to the wool and he'd bet Mr. Blue Mitchell wouldn't see or feel it when it came time to saddle the colt.

It was a pleasure to force the cactus into that matting, making sure the bigger points were turned out and down, waiting to meet that streaked bay hide, tender from yesterday's runs. The colt would come out stiff, needing a light workout to keep him sound. Mitchell was enough of a horseman to tend to the colt's needs.

And the law, Hale Patton, he was coming in now, riding that leggy roan and grinning a good morning. He asked the question Ira was waiting to hear; "You seen Mitchell, I got a place I need him to study." Ira grinned; "He's sleeping, Mr. Patton. Be 'long directly I wake him."

CHAPTER NINE

Voices woke him and he stretched and coughed as hay tickled his nose. The he sat up listening, making out a few words. It was the law interrupting a perfectly good sleep.

96

The horses needed to be feed. Blue got up, tucked in his shirt, shucked into his boots with a struggle, damn even his feet were sore. He went outside with a bare nod to Patton, a grunt for Cook, and scattered a pile of hay into the pen. Damn Cook and the men working for him for none of them had thought to feed the brown and the colt. They weren't horsemen if they couldn't feed out a stranger's stock.

"Mitchell, I got something I want you to see." Blue didn't look up, but he let the lawman know how he felt. "I need coffee and some privacy if you don't mind. I do have certain standards. . . ." He heard Patton snort, along with a bark from Cook and he went to the backside of the barn, where the stinking outhouse waited. And that bath tub, by its lonesome; he'd have to ask about the tub sometime.

Blue finished up and headed to a pump, ducked his head and washed out the hay stalks, scrubbed his hands, then went to the kitchen door. Patton and Cook were already there, each holding a steaming tin cup.

The woman was clever even if she wasn't much of a cook and the coffee was hot, laced this time with canned milk. Blue thanked her and she smiled, then he took two long swallows and waited a bit before turning to study his companions.

Cook was neatly shaved, in a clean shirt, wearing a fine-tooled belt and smelled something like you'd find in a cathouse. Patton was the same as he'd been yesterday, only more whiskers and a different wrinkled shirt but the eyes were lively and watchful. The man was more awake than Blue and in some kind of hurry.

"A minute, Patton, and I'll saddle up. Breakfast can wait, I've got more of that jerky to my saddle bags." The three of them walked to the barn and corrals.

Cook found he was holding his breath. Time got slowed down by hope and a tinge of fear for he'd guess that Mitchell would come straight for him if he found the burr. But the man was hurried too, just woke up, not enough coffee yet to make a difference. Cook turned away while Mitchell caught the colt for it wasn't smart to look interested. In fact another cup of coffee began to sound like a good idea.

Turner's wife laughed at him as she handed over the tin cup. "You been catting, Mr. Cook, or just headed out now?" She was not polite and had no respect for his position on the ranch, but he drank the coffee and kept quiet, his back deliberately turned from Patton, the horse pen, and Mitchell's paint colt.

The colt was stiff, but not as stiff as the brown. Blue held the mustang's nose with his other hand on the poll, and walked the horse a few steps, then he knelt and felt the brown's tendons, even his hooves. Nothing bad, no swelling or heat but a stiffness that said the running around yesterday, after easy weeks on the trail with that colt to teach, was enough for the horse. So he turned to the paint, who was young and in need of learning the hard life of a riding horse.

He had to rope him first, snug a little on the noose to get the paint's attention, then the colt remembered and let his head drop as Blue walked to him. Behind the fence, Patton was fretting and fussing but Blue paid him no mind.

He tied up the colt, dragged his gear out and saddled up. As he put the blanket on the colt's back, he made note to give it a good currying since he didn't want to scald the colt's hide but when he pressed down along the spine, the colt didn't flinch or reach around to bite him.

When he took up the cinch slow, the colt grunted and lashed his tail. He untied the colt, pulled down on his hat, stepped up into the saddle easy and light. He groaned softly, feeling the pull of his own sore muscles, and he had more respect for both of his horses.

The colt walked over to Patton and his roan, the two horses met up, sniffed and squealed, the colt arched his neck and pawed twice, then Hale Patton reined his horse around, motioned to Blue. "I saw more footprints, like the ones underneath what we saw first. Saw 'em in a different place. They make no sense and I want you to take a look."

Patton got that big roan half-turned out of the ranch yard and Blue asked the colt to move up so he could listen while Patton talked.

The paint went from three steps at the walk to an explosion of straight up then bucking sideways, hitting Patton's horse at the ribs and both horses went down. The colt came up out of the spill kicking, Blue was spread across Patton's roan and as he raised himself the colt's hoof caught him above the right eye. He was rolled back and tangled in the roan's thrashing legs. The colt took off bucking and squalling and all the ranch hands came running. The door to the house opened up, the women emerged, long skirts and loose hair, fearful of what they might see.

The colt disappeared straight into the brush, the roan sat, then stood, Patton remained in the saddle, bewildered, without his hat. Dirt smeared the left side of his face.

Only Mitchell was quiet; arms and legs plowed into the dirt, blood seeping from his face, blond hair slowly turning red.

There would be a funeral this afternoon, she said. There wasn't room for Mr. Mitchell in the house as Madison was laid out in the dining room and they could not accommodate another body. He wasn't dead, Hale Patton kept telling her but she shook her head and insisted that one body in the house was sufficient.

The law directed Turner and that quiet man, said again that his name was Ridge, to carry Blue inside the house, put him in a spare room. Once they laid Mitchell out on a short bed, Patton stood over Mitchell and studied the rider. The hands were loose, the mouth relaxed and the only sign of trouble was the cut over his eye that no longer bled. It crossed an older scar. Son of a bitch had him some bad times with the broncs.

Patton directed Turner's woman, he couldn't remember her name. She was to keep a wet towel on the cut and if he woke and wanted anything, Hale would be on the front porch talking to the missus. The two men, Turner and that Ridge, they backed out real silent and quick. Hale didn't blame them, he wanted out of the house and the whole damned mess, but it wasn't done yet.

Mitchell's spill from that colt was a good reminder that life never warned you what was coming next.

'No,' he yelled. 'NO! Not again. I can't see.' It was a too-familiar war; his flesh needed to live again, roaring its command into a damaged mind that desperately wanted unconscious peace.

Blue sat up, felt something wet slide from his face and there was light blinking at him, he turned to it – outside, through a window half open, a damn piece of material flapping in a wind. He gave a sigh that turned into a cough and it hurt like blazes but he could see.

Footsteps, boots on hard wood, the clatter enough to split Blue's head but he could almost focus on the face coming through the doorway. The law, wasn't sure of his name, saying something about a killing but Blue didn't remember. The man's face was twisted, muddy on one side, he kind of walk bent sideways too. And his question made no sense, words not finished, not complete. Blue could hear sound out of order.

Patton was direct; "What's wrong, why're you yelling?" Blue tried to sit up, found he wanted his head resting on that soft pillow. It hurt to speak; "What noise?" His voice had an echo.

Patton didn't let up; "You yelled 'no'. The woman here was washing your face, trying to keep you comfortable." Then Blue remembered and his mouth got dry, heart bumping so he could hear it inside his skull. Blind, helpless, ah hell.

The law's face told him he needed to explain. "I got kicked there before." Patton nodded; "I figured you'd been pretty bad hurt." Blue said the single word; "Blind." He took in a hard breath. "Close to dying." The lawman did it again; "I know." Blue wanted to strike out, no one knew, not any man even one who'd been shot or trampled or half dead himself. Each man's time close to death was his and no one else's.

Blue shook his head. "No."

Ridgeway Johns knew that after the burying he'd put in his time. Cook was a fool, Mr. Madison had had some business sense but a roving eye, and the woman was strict, no humor at all and he wasn't wasting what years he had left in such miserable company.

Ridge stood close to the corral fence, took a deep breath to rid himself of the smells in that house. He'd been surprised that the law was a decent man, but with his past, Ridge needed to stay invisible while Patton hung around.

Ridge knew he was nothing but a petty thief. It'd been one steer, and if he admitted it, there'd been a half-starved bronc too. Ridge used the steer for his survival that winter, gorging on the barely cooked meat. Come spring he'd caught up the horse and found decent work with a ranch north of Taos. He wasn't even sure the law still wanted him, or had ever wanted him. It was his own sorry conscience that made him wary of Hale Patton.

He hadn't backed out or run off when he was told to pick up the unconscious rider's legs and help get him into the house. Running right then would have set off the law's alarm. Ridge didn't know if they was born with it or it got issued with the star, but Ridge never fancied himself a gambler so he didn't want to find out.

The law set the rules and Ira Cook gave the orders. Ridge was to find and bring in that hot-tempered paint colt and later Mr. Patton would see to the horse, check him over for any signs of what prompted the fit. For it had been an unexpected explosion from a tired three-year-old ridden by a decent horse breaker. Colts ridden this way don't come unglued so fast without good reason.

Ridge had seen everything and was stunned into doing nothing, amazed when that long-legged ugly roan the law rode went down and lay flat, legs still running, the law still in the saddle even as Mitchell was pinned by the violence. Everyone watched as the colt kicked and bucked into the brush and cactus and kept going through the worst of the thorns.

Then the roan horse sat up and the law was still in the saddle and it was almost funny if a man hadn't been down.

Ridge had pulled the legs, hands hard around the high-topped boots, pulled them straight back out of the way so the roan could stand without stepping on Mitchell. Then he'd knelt down and wiped Mitchell's nose and mouth, pushing away clods of peeled dirt. The body jumped and scared the hell out of Ridge, then lay back but Mitchell's chest moved up and down finally and Ridge figured he might have saved a life.

Being the first man to see what was happening and do something about it brought Ridge to the law's attention but then the women saved him by flying from the house in screams and cries and Patton went to calm them, quickly telling Ridge and Turner to bring Mitchell inside over the lady of the house's unreasonable protests.

Ridge saddled a buckskin gelding he'd been bringing along. The horse was more than decent, had cow sense and an easy gait. The buckskin's ability was wasted here, for Cook's orders had the men doing little cow work and the few chores were mostly time-wasters like fencing around the house and making things pretty. It wasn't exactly how Ridge figured on spending his days.

It wasn't more than a theory, but he'd lived thirty rough years and it was why he felt kin to Mitchell. They were horse breakers, though he'd heard about Mitchell, folks talked about those damnable eyes and how he sat a horse. Ridge had no such skill but he'd made a fair life for himself, other than that one early spring when his judgment was off and he stole from another man.

The fact stayed with him but he didn't even know who he could find to say his apology. Helping a man like Mitchell, now that was one path to redemption. No one else cared, and he sure as hell wasn't going to tell the law, but it made Ridge feel better inside.

He checked the buckskin's legs, slipped in the light bit, cinched up and walked the horse, cinched up again until the saddle didn't slide on the rounded back. The horse wasn't much in the withers and high in the quarters but made up for the faults by being quick and good-minded, and Ridge sometimes wished he really was in the horse-stealing business.

It was easy to follow the colt's path of broke spines, bent grass, tracks digging through hell in the thick brush. The buckskin pinned his ears as he kept to the ugly trail. Ridge promised he'd go over the horse and pick out every damned spine when they returned to the barn.

The high whinny brought the buckskin up quick; Ridge listened, heard it again, thankfully it sounded like the colt had pushed through the tangle and was nearby, caught in his reins or maybe just downright lonesome.

Ah hell he thought, as he saw the colt standing three-legged with the near hind lifted. The colt trembled, whinnying louder until the buckskin whinnied back and Ridge lifted on the reins to remind the horse of his manners.

He slipped off his horse, dropped the reins, took a moment to touch the buckskin's muzzle, then walked closer, shaking his head, knowing the truth already. Bone showed through the hide above the fetlock. It was purely a damned shame.

Ridge stopped, rubbed his mouth. A man worth his salt always carried a good knife and a saddle gun. Ridge had both but there wasn't a choice. The buckskin wasn't gun-broke yet and this wasn't the time to start, not with the bloody killing of a good horse. It had to be the knife and he was glad he kept his sharp.

Ridge was methodical. He first stripped the saddle and blankets off the colt, rubbing the horse's neck to comfort them both. Then he slit the colt's throat, feeling the knife blade catch briefly on the windpipe and then glide through. Ridge stepped back as the colt struggled, eyes blazing as he bled out. The paint went down on bent knees, falling sideways, groaning, then silent. The slaughter took less than five minutes.

Only then did the buckskin whinny and back up until a trailing rein slapped his leg to remind him and he stood, shaking at the smell of death but obedient to Ridge's careful training.

It was a brief thought and he didn't say it out loud; not even on his lonesome would it feel right to mourn a horse, but Ridge let his arm slip over the buckskin's neck and he took heart from the horse rubbing his head on Ridge's belly. It wasn't much, only a bit of time to honor a death. That's all, and about what Ridge would get when he himself died.

He hefted Mitchell's saddle and studied it. There was no nameplate, nothing burned into the thick leather to tell its maker. Home done, he figured. He wondered if Mitchell made it. Could be, the man seemed to have the skills. The blanket was thick enough for good padding under a saddle but it was matted and woven with hair. Ridge shrugged.

The bridle had a broken-mouth bit with no shank, and the headstall was rawhide braided across the forehead with twists of horsehair, reins with thick slobber straps before the thin leather. Split of course. Mitchell had taken parts of wherever he'd worked and used what suited him. Ridge admired that in a man, to know his own mind.

He tied the bridle and blanket behind the cantle with the strings, and it made an awkward load as he climbed on the buckskin while holding to Mitchell's gear. The horse skidded sideways and Ridge guessed he didn't blame him but still a working bronc had to mind his manners.

The buckskin stopped at the brush and cactus and Ridge agreed to go wide and around and back on the normal trail used to ride this part of the ranch. He considered who would tell Mitchell, for losing that colt meant money lost. Then again, the man had that roman-headed brown mustang so at least he wasn't on foot.

Ridge got to the barn and stepped down, placed the gear on the dirt and Cook of all people grabbed up the saddle, said he would hang it in the barn and Ridge considered the man's behavior strange. It took a while until he remembered what had been going on and damn the two days of hell and this whole place was wrong and he wanted shut of it.

He took the buckskin to a pen, shed the blanket and saddle, and knelt to each leg, finding spines in the damndest places. His skin got pricked as his fingers tried to grab even the smallest spine.

"Get that bronc put away, Ridge. There's more needs doing than picking through his legs like a momma hen." It was Cook of course, so Ridge didn't look up or answer. He kept finding spines, even up near the buckskin's tail, along one hip, one so damned close to the right eye it scared Ridge on what he'd done forcing the horse through that mess. Then he squeezed his own eyes shut and saw the colt, the ruined leg, felt that warm flesh giving under his knife hand and smelled hot blood. Ridge shivered as he pinched the spine, even felt the touch of the buckskin's eye lashes as the horse flinched.

A buggy came in the yard; the driver wore a black suit and a flat-rimmed hat. It had to be the preacher and Ridge remembered there was a dead man to the house. Madison Tremont was a man he never liked but he'd taken the offered wages. Ridge stood up, patted the buckskin one more time and slipped the bridle off the clean gold head. The horse stood a moment, rubbed his head on Ridge's arm, then walked away tail going, no hurry, just curious to see if there was any hay waiting.

Sitting made Blue sick and he threw up all over himself like a drunk in an alley. He wanted to clean his own mess but the woman tending to him told him to quit, he was making it worse. His head ached and he knew a man couldn't keep getting his skull cracked and expect to walk away in a straight line.

Blue tried to remember something important, something that he'd seen. He knew not to rub the ache over his right eye, but it itched and that was a good sign. Maybe someone had taken a few stitches in the torn flesh. He was tired of deep scars, they turned red first, then white, then burned in the sun or went hard and ugly. They told the world too much about a man's failures.

It was always about a horse. Blue could smell the sweaty hide, feel the animal's muscle and then the brief sense of hoof striking bone. He closed his eyes and couldn't seem to breathe. It was always about a horse. He lived this time because he hadn't bothered to shoe the colt.

The burial was short. The two women stood at the grave, both wrapped in black; netting, dresses, boots, hats. Ridge wondered if when a woman married she bought such garments in hope or simple practicality.

The preacher was a decent man with a strong voice so no one could miss the sermon, the pleading to a righteous god, the sorrow and the glory of one man's dying. Ridge couldn't rightly see how such words would help the widow, but she had quit crying and leaned against her friend, a beautiful young woman who he knew came with a husband full-bellied and proud.

It was Turner who'd dug the hole, backed up to a thin tree, about the only one not caught up in marsh or along a stream bed or arroyo. These arroyos were no place to bury a man. One good rain, which happened on occasion here so Ridge had been told, and water in the arroyos ran hard enough to take trees and boulders and the odd hidden corpse or two downstream.

The small tree would grow with its new companion. Madison Tremont was buried wrapped in a fine ivory linen sheet, laid with reverence and kindness in a deep hole, and dirt carefully dropped back on him, making a thump in the beginning, then as each man took his turn, the sound was softer, quieter, slowing with the women's sobs until there was nothing but a faint sweep, like a raven too close overhead, drawing a man to look up, see the black of those wings and know the sound was leaving as the bird disappeared.

CHAPTER TEN

If he were in his office, he'd pour out a cup of thick coffee, set in that carved-out wood chair that bent back on some kind of spring, put his feet up on the desk and cogitate. But he couldn't leave the ranch, couldn't tell the woman he had no ideas and ride on out leaving no one with any hint as to who killed Madison Tremont. Fancy name, he thought, high-toned and fancy and it did nothing to keep the man from death.

Instead Hale set on a stump at the end of the log where he'd first talked with Mitchell. It seemed forever ago but it was yesterday. Too much had happened. Mr. Tremont was buried, the women were back in the house with those heavy curtains pulled so no sunlight could reach them, and in a back room lay the stunned horseman.

Mitchell could sit up now, even walk without much help, get himself to the outhouse and back, sit in a chair on the verandah and look at a man when he talked but Hale knew better. He saw distance in those eyes that he didn't like. He had no idea how to help or what would help, maybe time would be the answer. No one'd told Mitchell yet about the paint. Then it came to Hale, he'd send Ridge to do the telling. Maybe have the rider describe what happened to the colt and the words would stir the man's mind, bring life back into the startling eyes.

That was one problem looked at and fixed; now he had to figure out who was the killer. He'd spoke with Ridge, Cook, and Turner and while he still didn't think much of Turner's explanation about the deer hide and the cleaned rifle, he also didn't think the man was capable of cold-blooded murder.

That was another reason he wanted Mitchell's mind in one piece. Those footprints that bothered him, they were still there, blown now, their outlines softening from light winds against the sandy soil, but there was enough left he wanted Mitchell to inspect them, then they could talk and Hale could use Mitchell's unusual way of thinking and seeing to maybe find a clue. That's what he needed, a clue.

He got off the stump, walked to the pen where Ridge was unsaddling a mealy bay that Hale himself wouldn't take as a gift. Pig-eyed and close in front.

"Ridge." Hale spoke soft, no law voice to startle the bronc and unnerve the man. For inside Ridgeway Johns, Hale recognized a secret ate at the man, and while it might be in the law's interest to know the cause, for now Hale wanted help with Mitchell, and the two horse breakers had recognized each other, not in name or place but in shared instinct.

Ridge tugged at the latigo; "What do you want?" His voice was clear as he kept to the task. Hale spoke quietly; "Ridge, I need you to do me a favor." That brought the man's face around. "I can't leave this colt yet, he ain't much and I don't trust him. Let me finish here first." Hale grinned; the man was blunt like Mitchell. Guess it took a certain mind to fool with a rank horse and get him working proper.

"Okay. I'll wait." Hale leaned on the corral fence to watch. And he saw what he expected; Ridge's hands got uncertain, the bay twitched and backed up, Ridge gave a yank to the bridle rein and then Hale learned a whole lot more about the man.

Ridge stopped, went absolutely still and the mealy bay fussed around some, chewing on that bit, shaking its ugly head and yet Ridge stood waiting. The horse finally settled and the man stroked its neck, lowered his own head and finished undoing the saddle. Ridge dropped the rig on its fork and was careful in picking up the blanket, laying it so not a corner or edge touched the ground. Then he slipped off the bridle and turned to face Hale.

A quick nod and the small man picked up the heavy rig like it was nothing. Hale got the gate, Ridge nodded polite as could be and went into the barn. Hale took his time latching the gate and when he arrived in the barn, the man was waiting for him, leaning up against a post near where Mitchell had slept last night.

"Well?" That was one more word than Hale expected out of the puncher. He found his own post and leaned against it, crossed his arms. "You know Mitchell ain't right in the head." Ridge nodded in that sharp manner he had. Hale continued; "I've got something to help him, but I need you." There was no change in the mild face and those eyes still hadn't looked straight at Hale. It wasn't right, the man was capable and honest to his work. Hale tried again; "I want you to go tell Mitchell what happened to his colt. A clean description of what you did, straight to him, no howdy or setting and visiting. You speak your piece and come tell me what happens."

The eyes came up then, steadied on Hale's face. The voice was harsh; "That's cruel." Judgmental but Hale understood. "It's meant to be, it might be the way to unlock Mitchell's head. Something has to jar him loose." Silence, a long breath, then; "You're right, Mr. Patton." Ridge left him, didn't stop to question or ask how, he just lifted his hat to smooth back his hair and walked out into sunlight.

It was a complex and troubling situation and yet the rider needed no definite orders. He took in the thought, rolled it around briefly and said yes. Hale Patton would like to be there, to eavesdrop or simply sit and listen, but the idea was plumb foolish. Those two were kin; he was the law. They wouldn't say a useful word with him nearby.

Ridge nodded once to himself as he got halfway across the yard and could see the length of leg that had to belong to Mitchell, setting there up on that verandah the ladies called it. Mitchell being outside and away from the back room meant they could talk where both men were comfortable.

He kept to a slow walk as he wanted to give the man's scrambled mind time to sort through who was coming at him.

Ridge knew how a hard blow to the head put some strange and fearful pictures inside the brain, like dreams while you were awake, colors sometimes, sounds and visions that didn't make sense. Thoughts lost, time missing.

He put one foot on the step to the verandah, stopped, hand on the rail, and looked at the figure stretched out in a rocking chair. He was polite in asking; "You mind company?" Mitchell's head turned toward him and even in the deep shadows, Ridge could see those eyes widened, then half close. The voice cracked; "Your company's fine."

It was easy enough to climb the steps, find a chair and drag it close in to where Mitchell sat. Ridge found that the chair seat, some kind of braided straw, was damned uncomfortable on his backside, like being scratched through his britches, and he wasn't surprised. Chairs meant for visiting or thinking were easy to set in; these were more for show. He glanced down, took in the painted wood floor, kind of a pretty soft green, and then noted that Mitchell's feet were bare naked; ugly bent things that made Ridge want to laugh.

Mitchell didn't particularly look at Ridge but kept his head at an angle. There was a white cloth wound around his skull, the blond hair was loose and dirty, the faintest red stained some of the whiter strands. In a land where a horse thief was marked by a cropped ear and a need to hide it, an honest man naturally wouldn't choose long hair and yet Mitchell did exactly that and to hell with them. Ridge guessed that the gesture told him what he'd figured earlier; the man didn't give a damn how others saw him.

They sat quietly; Mitchell rocked slow and easy. Then Ridge guessed he needed to find the words; "Your colt's dead." The chair kept rocking. Mitchell's words were brief; "Figured that." And a long silence as Ridge chewed on the words. "How?" Mitchell very carefully shook his head; "The colt never came back. That brown mustang was the only friend he had." Ridge understood; even in the horse world a friend could mean life or death.

110

Mitchell let the chair ease to a stop; "Why?" This was the tough part. Ridge took in a deep breath. "He'd broke that near hind above the fetlock. Nothing. . . ." Mitchell looked away. "I saw you on that buckskin when I rode in. He's a youngster and you ain't done teaching him." Another moment, both men staring straight ahead. Mitchell had to speak; "You cut the colt's throat. That's rough on a man. It don't matter to the horse, he don't feel much past that first draw but the man doing it, if he's got a soul." Silence again, and Ridge felt a punch in his heart, an extra beat as if he might have known pity or sadness

Once again Mitchell surprised him; "Thank you." Odd, Ridge thought, being thanked for killing a man's horse. Mitchell continued; "It's wrong, whatever happened to that colt. He was high-tempered and young, and beginning to understand." The words made Ridge wonder too, why had the colt bucked so hard and then bolted into hell. It didn't make sense. Like Tremont's murder didn't make sense.

Mitchell finally leaned forward in the slowed chair, rested his elbows on his knees and very carefully turned his shoulders so he could look straight into Ridge. Ridge winced before he could stop himself. My god how had the man survive? The whole side of his face, eye and forehead and down his check was black with swollen flesh. The skin was darker above the bandage with a few small drops of red soaked through the white cloth. The son of a bitch was tough to be up and about after that kicking.

His words were repeated back to him, more amazing since he hadn't said them out loud; "Why'd the colt buck like that? It don't make sense, he'd been ridden hard these past weeks, and hell we made trips out and back like I can't keep track of. Shouldn't of been anything left of a buck inside that youngster."

Then the man rubbed his jaw and scared Ridge. "Was that yesterday or today? I can't quite get around it in my mind." They both looked out then, to the yard and the long shadows that came at dusk, the soft light, sun barely showing through low brush to the west, hidden soon enough by the distant mountains.

"Mr. Mitchell." The man almost shook his head, then held up a hand. "You're Ridge, I'm Blue. We ain't misters, we're horse breakers, it's all that suits either you or me." Okay, Ridge thought. "Blue, it's today, this morning was when the colt kicked you and I went hunting him. You were out 'bout an hour, then came to yelling. I guess that's what got to all of us. You yelling like that."

Rough, Ridge thought, not liking himself at the moment, but it was part of what Mitchell needed to remember. Ridge looked straight into Mitchell's eyes and that wasn't easy. He'd gotten used to looking away, anywhere except into a face that might see and accuse him. Mitchell grinned. Damn the man for his gut strength.

"What'd you do to yourself, Ridge?"

Blue's head ached. There was a reason a man went unconscious, it kept him from suffering the real pain of getting his skull cracked by a rank horse. He wanted to shut his eyes, go lie down in that soft, beckoning bed even though he knew better. Sleep wouldn't help him; working his mind, reading the signs, thinking things through, all that would put together whatever was knocked sideways in his brain.

Now this ranny with the good hands and bad temper and a sense of horses and how to train them, he had a hole in him like Blue's own private hell. Blue's hole was running from an old man and a lost childhood, running from anyone wanting to come in close. Ridge, now, his broken place seemed deeper, more something he'd done than what had been done to him.

Blue studied the lean face, watching dark eyes that skittered away. Blue's eyes got him into trouble, he'd learned that. Something inside showed, a 'go to hell' sense that got him in and out of fights, and kept him riding lonesome. Ridge didn't look straight at a man but glanced sideways, head bent down, carrying a weight too heavy to share.

Blue had to ask; "What'd you do that makes you hate yourself?" Ridge stood and went back down the steps and across the yard with Blue watching him at first, until the headache got to him and he closed his eyes. He'd spoken wrong, he knew. He spoke too close and too soon. Each man had his own devils, and Ridge wanted to keep his quiet, fearing that they might swallow him if he spoke out loud. Blue regretted his hasty question but there was no taking it back.

It took a moment finding where he could set his head it didn't hurt so much, then Blue stood, let go of the rocker arm that held him upright, managed one step, then another, until he was back inside the house and through that parlor and down a hall to the room where he'd been laid out. Poor choice of words, he thought, remembering the widow and her loss, but they had pushed him down on a bed and pulled his boots and left him there.

Earlier he hadn't been able to lean over and get the boots back on and he sure as hell wasn't going to ask for help doing the chore. He wasn't used to looking down and seeing bare toes. He almost shook his head but stopped himself. A man without all his clothes was a peculiar object.

That woman came in to the room just then with no knock, no voice warning him, just pushed open the door and stood there, hands on her hips, mouth pulled tight like he had done something wrong. "You got no business out walking 'round, with bare feet of all things." He didn't bother with her but sat quiet, let the bed hold him, let his feet rest easy on the rug braided from torn clothes to cover the wood floor.

This was the woman who washed his face while he lay flat on the bed, she'd unbutton the waist of his pants, opened his shirt, tried to wash out the blood from his hair. He thought then, that maybe the widow'd come into the room, he remembered voices and they was both female so it was only these two women. Then he thought of the friend, the woman he went to get yesterday, with the law along to ask him questions.

It was an odd jumble of memories but in there was an edge, a sense that he did not like this woman's hands on him. He recognized it wasn't fair. She'd nursed him, what all women did when a man was injured. They were good at the job, starting with wiping a baby's bottom, holding a child's hand, pulling out splinters, suffering a man's death and burying him, doing his work the next day.

This woman, though, Blue wasn't sure. She had eyes that studied places on a man no decent woman would acknowledge. She offered to help him with the outhouse chore even as he was able to stand. She laughed at him and his fumbling attempts to find his boots. Barefoot outside was hurtful but better than her look of pleasure at any weakness.

She was bitter and sour, offering a hint of honey but not enough to cover the bad taste. Like the herbed medicines his own mama gave him, with a promise it wouldn't taste bad and he'd wanted to spit out the liquid but her smile stopped him. This woman was that medicine. He didn't like it but he knew well enough that not everything about every woman was good.

The law wasn't near the barn so Ridge waited a moment, looking around but he couldn't raise sign or movement to help him. Then there it was, behind the half-closed barn doors, a sound he recognized; a man walking, hard boots to packed earth. Ridge went to the doorway and stopped. The late sun's deepening light colored the skies like fire and water mixed, creating shadows out of human forms.

Inside the barn was gray and black, mostly smells and sounds, a horse chewing, birds squawking over where each one got to roost on a particular rafter. And a man, too round and thick to be anyone but Ira Cook, was fiddling with gear tossed on a stall rail, picking at the saddle blanket, digging with his fingers.

Ridge didn't say nothing, he didn't think Cook wanted to be seen playing with Mitchell's gear. He watched as Cook's thick fingers yanked and mangled the woven wool, sending mats of hair in all direction. Cook spat once or twice, cursed low all the time he kept digging with those dirty hands, nails blackened with weeks of filth, barely callused along the base of each finger.

Whatever was hiding in the saddle blanket, it couldn't be much if Cook still hadn't found it. Then the man brought his hand to his face, seemed please by what he saw and flicked away whatever it was, stuck the finger in his mouth and sucked on it, which made Ridge's gut roll over. He didn't like what he was seeing so he backed out, turned and walked to that old log and the stump where he sat down and waited and Cook never appeared. The foreman must have gone out the back, which meant he didn't want to be seen. It had to mean something, but Ridge couldn't put the pieces together.

"What'd he have to say?" The voice was soft and too close. Ridge held on to the log and didn't allow fear to move him. He answered quiet as he could; "Mitchell said he already knew." Ridge stopped, rubbed his jaw. "His feet were bare. I ain't never seen a man walking 'round with no boots on. Indians yes but a cowhand ain't nothing without his boots." There, he figured he'd covered his fear with nonsense.

"How's his head?" Patton wouldn't let it go. Ridge sighed; "Bandaged, and his face is terrible. But his eyes, they look clear into you." Ridge couldn't forget the question he'd walked away from.

Then Patton said it; "How'd he know?" Ridge grinned for it had taken him a moment too. "Common sense, he said. The paint didn't come back to the brown mustang so he had to be dead." Patton shook his head, mostly noticeable by the movement of his eyes. It was getting late, Ridge thought, time he found supper and a bed. He wondered briefly if he should tell Patton about Cook's behavior, then said to hell with it. It was none of his business until he was asked the right question.

"Was he confused or did he know where he was?" Patton had asked the wrong question but Ridge had an answer. "Well I figure the bare feet came from not wanting to bend over and pull on his boots. Can't blame him, his face, that colt kicked him pretty bad."

"That's not what I asked," said Patton abruptly. Sure, thought Ridge, bully me like most lawmen do and they know it. But Patton surprised him. "I ain't trying to push you, Johns. Ridge they call you. It's that I like the man, even under the circumstances. And I heard 'bout his being kicked before, up to Cimarron." That made sense to Ridge

"Me too. He's good at reading folks well as horses." Ridge surprised himself by saying it. "He knew without my telling him, both about the colt dying, and that I hadn't shot him but used my knife." He took in a deep breath. "He knew how that felt too. He even thanked me. Son of a bitch that was strange, but his mind's there. Most of the time."

He'd tried to eat, then tried to sleep; neither worked so Blue went back outside, slower, more careful in the dark 'cause he didn't like splinters in his feet and didn't fancy bending down yet to pull on his boots.

The women were there, quiet, not rocking those chairs or talking, staring as if they'd talked and cried and felt enough and needed time to do nothing. He stopped, hit a toe and muttered and the lady, Mrs. Tremont, spoke very carefully; "Mr. Mitchell, please join us. We are taking the air, letting the past days' events dissipate. I still cannot. . . ." There she quit and anyway he knew what she meant.

He found a chair separate from where he'd sat talking with Ridge. He was oddly pleased that the chairs were pulled together; in fact the Dorsey woman on occasion would reach over and pat her friend's hand in a rightful female gesture, a wordless understanding. Women had a special feel that way, owning a nature finer than most men.

The widow's voice was gentle; "Mr. Mitchell, you were yelling at us. Why? What could we have done that frightened you?" Well it was one hell of a question to ask a man who'd had his brains almost knocked out of his skull. Mrs. Dorsey sat back and folded her arms across her waist. It made a pretty picture, these two ladies, now that the chairs were moving slightly, as if blown by a breeze. Blue wished the same wind would take the question with it.

"Mrs. Tremont, ma'am." He nodded to both of them. "I got kicked a year or so back." He wasn't clear on the time, hours and days and years didn't matter much. "Blinded me right off, and I was down for too long. Scared the. . . ." He quit, coughed, wiped his mouth and in the gray evening he saw the Dorsey woman smile. Her voice was lovely; "Mr. Mitchell, we gave up being hot-house females when we moved here with our husbands. Please, tell us what happened to you."

He could see her, when his eyes finally opened and he remembered the past, the callused hands that had cared for him, he saw the face that had once bent down and kissed him. He remembered death stalking him and her kiss had been a reminder of the living. It wasn't the Dorsey woman, or the new widow he was seeing, it was the past come back to him.

He gave his present company a brief description of the accident, the days that followed, but offered little mention of the homely woman who had so lovingly tended him. That was a piece of himself he would not share, knowing she had loved him to no point, no possibility but compassion for a dying creature.

Finally he'd talked enough and he could hear the restless breaths of the two women. "Ladies, my feet're cold, guess I'll go in." Both of them laughed, a small pleasure in the middle of terrible times. As if suddenly aware she was laughing, Mrs. Tremont covered her mouth, but the glimpse of pleasure remained in her eyes. Blue went in to bed, relieved to lie down on the easy comfort of the mattress and fall asleep without dreams.

CHAPTER ELEVEN

Although there had been no further mention of Madison's appalling death, it was present in each word spoken to her, a fractional hesitation before stating the simplest of things. Even as Priscilla announced a light supper, that short breath came before the words. Helen, her dearest friend here, had taken on the same annoying habit.

No one could be blamed for such laxity in manner; it was not taught in any finishing school that Melinda was aware of, no classes given in how to deal with a sudden death or killing. Funerals, yes, the correct clothes to wear, the length of time a family member must wear certain items, when a widow may begin to return color into her wardrobe. These were very specific dates and times for each step returning her to society's whims, an awful education to give young women intending to marry well and bear the correct number of attractive, intelligent children.

But there were no such teachings or structures out here, no manner in which anyone could be forced to accept that she well knew her husband was dead and that each hesitation in speech or glances only rubbed in the knowledge as soap or salt stung a wound.

She had loved Tremont enough to run away with him, but it had been love born from loneliness, not from needing one special man or wanting children. Now Tremont was dead and she grieved him but would not stay alone. She did not wish to retreat to her family home, where she would be a spinster again. They would place her in a corner despite her good mind, her practicality and newfound abilities. They would give her pity and light duties to pretend she was useful, but they would not allow her another love unless the match would enhance the family.

First she would fire Ira Cook and then hire on that man who had found Tremont and returned him to her. Mr. Mitchell, despite his unusual deportmant and his youth, was a man of sense and substance and she needed such a man if her radical ideas on how to run a ranch were to be even marginally successful.

Helen patted her arm and Melinda reached over with her other hand, to acknowledge her friend's gesture. "Melinda, he certainly is an interesting specimen. I suspect you have ideas that he could implement. Both Turner and that Ridge, and even the law, they all like him. And Mr. Cook cannot abide his presence in the house, which in itself is an excellent indication of the man's qualities." Helen then crossed a line; "But my dear, he's even younger than your late husband. . .Madison."

Melinda Tremont would have laughed but for laughter's inappropriateness under the circumstances.

He managed his boots this time; he even found that Mrs. Tremont had left him clean socks and a few shirts. The shirts almost fit, tight across the shoulders, short in the arm, but the socks suited him, knit with even stitches and no lumps. It felt good to pull on his boots over their cushioned wool.

Only when he stood up, in a clean shirt and new socks, did he remember that yesterday he couldn't even put on the holey socks he did own. One hand went to his head and he realized the bandage was gone. There was a good scab that his fingers tentatively brushed. The touch hurt but was bearable.

That woman was in the kitchen. She turned and smiled at him, hands on her hips as usual. Once again she seemed to be exhibiting herself. The habit made him want to shake his head but that still wasn't a good idea. 'Mornin' ma'am' was enough and she turned back, poured out a cup filled with black coffee, almost to the edge and he had to walk it careful to the table. A good sip made room for canned milk and Blue took one more sip, let out a sigh and thanked the woman again.

It was full morning and no offer came for breakfast but there were biscuits on the table so he pocketed two in the clean shirt and made his way out to the verandah. One chair held the coffee while he sat down.

The biscuits were still warm and sweetened with sugar and something else on the browned top. He bit into one, took a long drink of coffee, repeated the pattern and found himself smiling for the first time in a few days. Then he remembered why he was sitting here and what happened. He took another bite, more sips of the coffee and let the sadness roll away. The man was dead and buried, the law was still trying to find the killer, and Blue was unexpectedly alive.

Feeling steadied from the sparse meal, Blue headed to the barn. The colt's gear was sideways on a stall rail, headstall and bit hanging, saddle blanket folded back on itself, matted and frayed in one place. He took the blanket outside, sat on that damned log and started picking at the clumped hairs, remembering the colt and only then did it come to him he needed a second horse.

The colt had been money to get him through the winter. His fingers felt through the wool, pulled at the hairs, and the mindless activity gave him too much time to think on where he was now.

The log shifted under him and he kept picking at the blanket. There seemed to be a widening in some of the twisted wool and he knew the Indian woman who made this blanket would never leave an open weave. It could have come from the spill, but that didn't fit with what Blue remembered.

"What'd you find there, Mitchell?" It was Hale Patton of course. Blue answered too quickly, not sure what his thoughts meant. "There's someone been digging at the blanket. Not meaning to help me by taking off those mats I needed to have done long before this, but pulling the weave apart. It wasn't like this when I saddled the colt."

Patton must have moved for the log shifted again. Blue's restless fingers had found something, so he ran the soft side of his left thumb across the surface, felt the lightest of pricks. He removed a small barb, broke off from one of those damned round cactus grew out of the tiny white flowers and made a man

120

ignore them with their prettiness. They hurt like hell if you stepped down on one.

"Here." He held out the broke spine; balanced on his thumb it looked powerless but Blue and the law knew what that particular cactus could do. Blue muttered, as much to himself as to Patton; "I don't drop my gear. I know better, it can make a killer bucking horse out of a tired colt. A rider's weight would drive one of these things in deep." Blue flicked the small barb with his fingers; the two men looked at each other.

Patton acknowledged Blue's sentiments; "I've seen you care for your gear. Not like this." Both men nodded, Patton kept talking. "Now if a man was deliberate in wanting you hurt, why that cactus burr would unglue your colt, any decent horse would do the same."

Blue kept fingering the blanket. "I don't know these folks and they don't know me well enough to hate me." He wouldn't look at the law but played with the blankets and worried some on the problem.

Patton fretted too; "You cut a wide trail bringing in Tremont's body. Any man figuring to be the head honcho, he could take exception to your good deed." Blue looked at Patton, letting his confusion show. Patton didn't disappoint him; "Hell Mitchell, you ain't that dumb, just not book educated. You know what I'm saying. Someone with big ideas might not like you bringing in the news and the proof. Could be he done the killing so he could take over. It's which 'he' are we talking 'bout that's the question."

Blue spoke his mind; "There are two choices, or maybe three. Count Ridge out, he don't want nothing but for folks to not see him." Hale agreed, lifting an eyebrow; "But?" Blue felt he'd stepped in it, might as well give the man what he wanted. "Turner's dumb enough he does what his wife says. I can't see that he'd kill his boss and she wouldn't want to lose their job and place. She knows and he might not, that finding a job like this at a decent spread is scarce." Saying it out loud made Blue wonder if her treatment of him had anything to do with looking for a replacement. Maybe the woman had figured out Turner wasn't much of a bargain.

"And Cook?" Hale was beginning to enjoy hearing what Mitchell had to say. The rider'd had time to watch and learn and most folks wouldn't be so careful around him, not with the head wound and a funeral. The law, well everyone, innocent or not, kept away from him.

Mitchell hesitated; Hale thought maybe the fear had gotten to him too. He was wrong. "Cook makes no sense to me, Patton. He don't run a ranch decent enough to keep the fences tight or the cattle watered. I rode over and around this land getting here and it's been eaten too close in places, not close enough in others. Some of the water holes're stopped up with weeds and those fancy windmills. . .hell the man's no decent foreman. He's got no feel for the land."

Hale kept pushing; "If you had to guess, Mitchell, who'd you pick for the killing?" Mitchell laid the double blanket across his legs, smoothed the underside, picked off more hair. Then he raised his eyes slowly and studied the light pattern of hair as the wind took some strands, left others to fall.

"Hell, mister law. I thought you gentlemen galloped around on your mounts and threatened folks with guns and pistol whippings until you got your killer. Asking a gent like me, well you must be short on answers." Hale got angry, started to lift himself off the log until he heard the low sound and knew he was being laughed at so he settled down.

"Mitchell, I bet you get yourself in a lot of fights, you talk to most folks like that." The laughter grew louder, and Hale joined in. "There's no bet in that and you know it," Mitchell responded. There was a long silence, then; "I can't see any of these men for the killing, Patton. It had to be someone with a grudge. Most of these people needed Tremont alive more than dead. Even Mrs. Dorsey's husband had nothing to do with it. I gather Mr. Tremont had promised the man money." Hale found himself nodding his head at each word. Mitchell's thoughts echoed his own and he was no closer to the killer than finding excuses for those who didn't kill the dead man.

Blue rose slowly, feeling lightheaded from too much talk, knowing he needed to see to the brown mustang. He first took the cleaned saddle blanket back to lay it over his saddle. Absently, thinking of the past few days, he checked the strength of the bridle ties, the reins and slobber straps, even bent down and tugged on the latigo, felt along the sheepskin lining to the saddle itself. He sure didn't want a wreck off of the brown. He knew how that one could buck, unless these past two years had erased that particular ability.

He went out to the pen where a solitary horse stood nose deep in sweet hay. A shadow moved across a distant pen and it was Ridge Johns, easy to know by the head tilt and the stiff walk. He wanted to thank the man for feeding the brown, but Ridge shrugged, just enough Blue could see, and kept going toward that narrow shack behind the barn. No point in stopping a man with such business on his mind.

He was moving around all right now, dizzy at times but doing chores, walking and thinking and talking so he had no right to stay in the widow's house. He returned to the house standing on its slight rise, around to the back door to knock and heard the woman's command to enter. Her voice was hard; Blue had a sudden pity for Turner.

"I just came for my things, ma'am." Blue offered her the same courtesies he'd offer any woman. She responded by glaring at him; "I don't own this place, I ain't the one to tell. And I ain't her messenger, you go speak to Mrs. Tremont, leave me to my work." He wasn't sure of what set off the temper but it was time to get out of the kitchen.

Mrs. Tremont was in the parlor, and the doors to the dining room were still pulled closed, one of those fancy paired doors that was stuck in the wall and slid out with fingers put in a brass hole. Practical Blue thought, taking up less room but useful only if the carpenter was skilled.

123

"Mr. Mitchell, please sit a moment." Blue studied his boots, the hair on his pants' legs, more filth on his hands. He spoke the truth; "Ma'am, I ain't fit. . . ." She waved a hand. "Sit, Mr. Mitchell. I know how you look. It's only furniture, nothing that Priscilla can't clean." Now he had two women telling him what to do. It wasn't what he liked but he sat down. She'd been kind enough to him, and he knew to be gentle around her, although the pale flowered dress wasn't what most new widows wore.

"I wish to hire you, Mr. Mitchell. I have known for several months that Mr. Cook was a less than acceptable ranch manager, but Madison. . . ." Here she sighed but he thought it was for show and not what she really felt. "Madison trusted the man and I could not go against my husband."

In an odd way, Blue recognized that the woman had just given him a reason for her being the killer. It rattled him, to consider that a woman could be cold-blooded.

"Ma'am." He spoke the one word gently She put up her hand. "No, not yet. You have not taken enough time to think about this. It will be a fine salary and a cabin of your own and I will promise you the best horses money can buy." She certainly knew his weakness.

But that bribe made no difference; "Ma'am. No." "Why, Mr. Mitchell?" Blue recognize that her insistence meant he did not need to honor any sympathy for the woman's loss. Gentleness wouldn't work with Mrs. Tremont. "Ma'am, I don't ever want a boss or a job or walls around me. Good horses are easy for me to find and what you're offering is a prison. No thanks."

She caught him off balance when she threw her head back and laughed like a western woman, strong, clear laughter and none of that mannered titter. Then she put her hand over her mouth as if she'd shocked herself.

"Mr. Mitchell, I mourn my husband and his loss, but I am not foolish enough to have the vapors, you know what that means, and to think that life stops because he is gone. I must try everything possible to keep this place running, for I will not give up what freedom the land offers me and go home to disapproval and dismissal. Do you understand?"

Uncomfortable at such revelations, Blue stood and turned away from the woman, seeing that other woman watching from a doorway. "Ma'am, thanks for the offer. I'll be gone in a day or two. I only came in to get my things."

She never looked back at him, never said another word, just sat rigid in the single chair near the window and he got the hell out of there, the parlor, the tough female in the kitchen, to the remote comfort of the back room. He took his clothes, left the shirts but kept the socks, grabbed what little gear they'd brought in to the house with him. He knew where the hay could be shaped into a bed, knew where the outhouse was, the pump handle for cold water, and knew that the wound on his head was halfway to healing.

The law was there of course, waiting for him with that look and Blue shook his head briefly, touched the skin above the cut and winced and Patton nodded, went 'round the barn and Blue figured he was gone after Ridge instead. For a moment he felt sorry for the man. But more questions, more damn talk, was a burden Blue would not take.

He accepted doing the few chores he could not shrug off. The brown mustang needed tending to, a good grooming, a short ride to loosen his muscles. The horse wasn't used to confinement and neither was Blue, and it was time to get out for a gallop, a run at the freedom momentarily denied them.

The woman they brought over from that mansion a few miles north of the ranch, she needed to go home. He'd seen it in their faces last night and again this morning. Mrs. Dorsey had done what she could, and Blue was uncertain but awed by Mrs. Tremont's determination. Admiration was one thing, staying in one place went against his religion.

He put his bits of clothing and such near the saddle, picked up the bridle and found a stiff brush in his saddlebags. Habit forced him outside to the pen; he stood a moment, suddenly uncertain. Watching the brown mustang circle in the pen, he remembered past rides on the horse, remembered too well flying off the brown's back, landing hard, losing air and lying there while the horse bucked around him.

A shudder of fear brought the memories too close. He froze, it was hard to breathe and then that horse breaker Ridge came by, slowed and walked in close to Blue but didn't look at him, and Blue knew not to expect anything more than a few words. Ridge surprised him; "That brown's a good-looking son of a gun even with that head. He's a tough one, good feet and bone to him." Blue nodded.

Ridge kept quiet a bit, head down as usual, studying the dirt, then glancing sideways at the mustang, who'd come to their side of the pen, nose stuck over the high railing. The horse blew hard, wet hay flew from his mouth. Then he spun around and kicked out and Blue flinched.

Ridge started it; "Just thought I'd ask. I surely would like to ride that son. I want to see what kind of handle you put on your horses." Blue recognized what the man was doing and appreciated being left some dignity while not having to admit the truth.

Blue answered quickly; "He rides smooth for all his flaws, and he sure can run." Ridge grinned; "Now I got to ride him. You want to set that buckskin, he's decent, probably too quiet for what you like but I'd admire to hear what you think of him." It was spoken of as an even deal; Blue almost smiled.

Each man brushed their own horse, and the mustang kept pushing at Blue, even nipping at his arm. Bending down to see to the hooves or brush the lower legs wasn't a good idea Blue discovered, so he did the front feet and quit.

Ridge brought over his saddle and blanket and laid them on the brown's hide. The brown grunted and snapped at the man when he did up the cinch. Blue tugged on the rein to remind the brown of his manners. "He got a name?" Ridge's voice was easy, the question mostly nonsense. "I don't name my horses," Blue answered. There was silence, both men thinking along the same lines of what could and did happen to good horses. "But I've had this son a while now and call him Keno if I ain't rightfully calling him 'son of a bitch.'"

Blue took the reins to the buckskin, who was already saddled with his gear. Along the neck and chest were drying salt marks saying the horse had been ridden recently and hard. There wasn't much to say until Ridge gave away his motives; "I've watched, Mitchell, and you do something to these horses I don't understand. I figure riding with you might teach me. I hear 'bout you too often when I ask for work."

Blue ducked his head into his saddle on the buckskin; those words, the sentiment, they were almost a compliment and he didn't know how to answer, so he tugged that last notch in the latigo and stepped onto the buckskin. The colt bowed his neck to Blue's hands light on the reins.

Ridge getting on the brown mustang, now that was a show; the man took too long setting his boot to the stirrup, took up the reins too tight and Blue opened his mouth to warn him when the brown uncorked and went high, sideways, down and up again. Ridge managed to find the off stirrup but it was close. The brown completed a full circle, Blue and the buckskin in the center, and eventually Ridge found the brown's rhythm and even had time to pick off his hat and wave it.

When the brown snorted and quit, Ridge was still in the saddle and they had an audience. The law was there, and Turner, with Cook holding back, not wanting to be too close. Even the women had come out and were curious, hands to their mouths as the horse kicked higher. It was easy to see that Ridge was pleased putting on his own show.

Cook spoke up from a good distance. "Guess we know who's the better man with the horses, Mitchell. That there brown still bucks, and Ridge's buckskin, hell man you're setting there quiet as can be. Ridge sure can set up a bronc." Blue laughed, the law had that look to his eyes that he was laughing too. Turner's wife finally came out onto the verandah and shook her head, went back inside.

Blue reined the buckskin around and headed out along the ranch road. The horse had an easy swing to its trot and Blue stood in the stirrups, hand to the swell. Each step hit inside his head but he wasn't going to let it show.

Ridge caught up to him, letting the brown run on a few strides. "Damn that was fun. If he runs like he fights, hell you could live off of your winnings." Blue kept his eyes on the buckskin's ears, noting that they flicked back and sideways and then were pinned to the gold neck and Blue touched one side of the colt's ribcage with his spur, signaling that any fuss with the brown alongside would bring about instant correction. The black-tipped ears went forward and Blue grinned as he patted the neck.

Out of sight from the ranch, he sat deep and brought the horse to a walk. When Ridge came in too close, both horses laid back their ears and Blue nudged the buckskin ribs again.

"Ridge, these two don't know each other, how 'bout you ride off a ways. Keno there has a temper even if you just rode him down." Ridge reined the brown hard and the mustang spun a full circle. When Ridge straightened himself out, his face was white and Blue had to laugh.

"How you put such a spin on this son? He's rank sure enough but man I breathe and he goes." Ridge was enjoying his ride. They talked then, about horses and light hands and a touch of a leg, what to do with leaning and balance, all about the world both men inhabited, horses broke to ride not by strength but from an instinctive sense of each animal.

Abruptly Blue reined in the buckskin. He stared at the ground and Ridge picked up what Blue was seeing. Footprints again, sized like those under the bigger boot prints near the site of the murder. Blue wondered if this was what Hale Patton had wanted him to see. And if someone to the ranch had planted that burr under the colt's blankets to keep him from getting out here to read sign.

That didn't make sense. It would be easier and less risky to ride out and push a horse back and over those tracks till they

128

were wiped out. None of this damned mess made sense. Blue stepped off the buckskin, knelt down slowly and studied the prints. Heeled, narrow toe, about the length of his hand, fingers spread. The prints had to come from a lady's boot. He shook his head. That didn't make sense either. A woman had walked out here and it wasn't near where Tremont was killed.

Blue learned that standing up too quick didn't make sense either. His head went bucking on its own and he almost fell but Ridge grabbed an arm and kept him standing. The brown snorted and pushed his nose into Blue's gut, the buckskin pulled back out of fear and Blue stood in the middle, barely able to see. His face itched; he rubbed it, drew blood and cursed.

"I've got to tell Hale what we've found," he said. "You stand here, Ridge, I'll go back and get him. He needs to see these, they're important but I don't know how." Blue glanced up, expecting Ridge to be looking somewhere else but the man's eyes were steady on Blue's face. "You all right, Mitchell? That there cut's bleeding again."

Blue shrugged and stepped back on the buckskin, who skidded around Blue, wanting already to run. He settled in, held the reins, bringing the buckskin's head to his left knee, then to his right until finally the colt stood still. Then he nodded to Ridge; "You wait here", and directed the buckskin back the way they'd come.

CHAPTER TWELVE

The entire visit had been disquieting. Of course Mr. Tremont's death was a terrible occurrence, and the loss was there in every move of Melinda's face or hands, and especially in her eyes. Helen felt she was of little comfort now as Melinda spoke of her plans to expand the ranch, at the very time Helen's husband was dividing their land and searching for financial backing. Helen even understood that Mr. Dorsey had accepted assistance from Mr. Tremont verbally, and the dismissal of that funding could finalize losing their home.

At one point after breakfast, with a cup of that terrible coffee sitting on a low table on the verandah, Helen had tried gently to mention the promise made to Mr. Dorsey, and ask her friend what she intended to do about the loan. Melinda had stiffened, dropped her shoulders and leaned forward with a straight back to pick up her half-full cup. "I will of course honor all of Mr. Tremont's debts." There had been no further discussion.

Helen was now a traitor, to her husband for being on the Tremont property, and disloyal to Melinda during her time of need. It was impossible and quite uncomfortable to remain within the rather simple home Mr. Tremont had built for his wife, and Helen often wondered how Melinda could stand living in such confines. However, it was no longer an issue; she would ask to be driven to her castle where despite its architectural oddities, she felt secure. Her remaining child was well-tended by his nanny, but still there was the pull of motherhood. She was certain Melinda would understand without any mention of children, for it was a forbidden subject.

Helen spoke briefly to Melinda, who accepted Helen's wishes, and said she would find a man to drive her home. A quick view of the ranch yard made it obvious only two choices remained, neither of which pleased the women. Ira Cook was fumbling with some broken leather straps in the barn, and Turner had managed to waste time putting in a new fence post when, to Melinda's knowledge, he needed to be checking on a clogged water hole that she'd seen recently and had mentioned to Mr. Cook.

Melinda saw this act as further proof of Ira Cook's ineffectiveness. Of course the law was still hanging around but Melinda did not think it appropriate to engage the man in such a domestic excursion again.

Then Mr. Mitchell appeared, on Ridge's favored buckskin, and the problem was settled. She would ask later why Mitchell rode the horse, and where his brown mustang had gone. But since Ridge had also disappeared, the answer should be obvious.

As she approached across the ranch yard, Melinda thought to revise her demand. The peculiar range rider, drifter, horse breaker and savior of the deceased was himself worn down. The cut over his eye had opened through the poor stitching and blood was dried on his face, but his eyes were a shaded blue quite unlike the hot turquoise color when he'd first appeared. His skin tone was grey, his mouth thinned. Riding was not the correct activity for one so recently injured.

He nodded to her, tipped his hat but remained on the buckskin. Melinda made her needs known; "Mr. Mitchell, Mrs. Dorsey needs to be driven home. I would greatly appreciate it." His eyes stopped her, weary in the drawn face and yet he smiled. "Ma'am, I've got a small deal going with Ridge and Mr. Patton. When we're done, I'd be pleased to help you. Ma'am."

It was the most polite dismissal of a request she had ever received. And she could not help but return his smile. In his own way, Mr. Mitchell was a distinct if highly individual gentleman.

Blue moved his weight in the saddle, turned his head and the quick buckskin shifted under him, headed toward the barn where Hale Patton had appeared. He reined in the horse, climbed down, stiff and with a head that ached, but it was nothing more than he expected.

Patton only stared. Blue spoke up; "Seems to me we was headed toward some prints you wanted me to study when that colt came apart." He stopped, took a breath and resisted wiping at the itch on his face. Patton grunted. Blue found the next words; "Ridge and me we found prints, maybe the ones you wanted to talk over. Catch yourself up that monster you ride and we'll go back where Ridge is waiting over them." Hale turned away, Blue finished a thought that been coming to him. "Ridge is riding down the brown for me, and he took the buck out of this here colt too. He's a good man."

It took Patton less than ten minutes to saddle and ride. Blue sat on that damnable log, held the buckskin's reins, closed his eyes and tried not to think. Whatever mess he'd gotten into this time, he saw only more confusion and trouble coming at him.

It was wasted time setting on the restless mustang doing nothing. Those prints weren't going to disappear and the day was clean, with that sun sliding in and out of clouds. Now those clouds they could be a problem, a five-minute rain would wipe out the prints, which were important to Mitchell and the law. And there was nothing Ridge could do to stop a washout. His slicker was back at the bunkhouse, his shirt wouldn't ward off bird spit.

He had a good horse under him, a horse that took the bit, chewed on it lightly, flex his head and even at the walk, Ridge could feel the hindquarters working, long strides pushing the body forward, easily covering a lot of ground.

Mitchell had bragged of the horse's speed, and the brown was rested, ready to go. Why the hell not. Ridge could see for miles to the north and west along the waving bend of trees that bordered the creek bed. It made for a nice smooth track.

He let the brown move into a walk, then studied a point at a good distance along the creek. There were a few easy turns, no trees excepting those old cottonwoods deep into the banking; Ridge grinned as he eased the brown in a lope, then leaned forward and squeezed lightly with his heels. He was right, that Mitchell knew how to cue a horse for the brown jumped from a slow-traveling lope to a flat-out bottom-down run and after Ridge found his breath he hollered and let the horse take it.

It took Ridge a good mile to slow the brown, who pulled through the bit, tossed his head, half-reared in the middle of the run and scared the hell out of Ridge but eventually the horse gave in so that Ridge could circle him as the brown came to an easy trot, then into that long, sweeping walk again.

A good distance from where he'd been standing guard over faint boot prints, Ridge was startled to see a man he couldn't recognize. Ridge immediately kicked the brown into a run but the man saw him and disappeared into the brush behind the prints. Ridge hurried the brown but the man had gotten deep into the thicket and Ridge didn't want to leave the prints unguarded again.

He stepped down from the mustang, tied the reins to a scrub tree and walked the area, seeing the marks of where the man had damaged the prints until Ridge appeared to stop their total destruction. Damn, he thought, hunkered on his heels, staring at the disturbed ground. Damn if he'd been here, no one would have tried to wipe out the prints. Or then again, he could be dead, lying sprawled across them damnable tracks.

Ridge wished he knew who the man was; he could follow the fresh tracks but he best stay where he was and wait on Mitchell and Hale Patton. He needed to do something right, even if it was helping the law.

He was leaned back against the scrub tree, the brown half asleep standing over him; lip hanging, hind leg cocked, the horse was almost snoring. Looking up was a peculiar sight, that big mouth, the bright pink inside of the curled edge. Hell, the horse even had a decent mustache on his upper lip.

The brown horse twitched an ear, straightened out the hind leg, arched his neck. Ridge didn't hear anything but he trusted the horse's instincts. One real good point to riding a mustang was their ability to smell, sense, and hear what might be coming up on a man.

He stood, untied the brown, checked the cinch. Whatever was coming might not be the law and Mitchell, it might be that unknown man returning. Ridge asked the brown to step back three strides, for no reason other than his own nerves.

The shot hit the squat tree, took out one limb, puny thing it was but it was sliced off clean and the brown went back fast enough he almost jerked Ridge off his feet. Ridge kept a hard grip on the reins, ducked down trying to make himself smaller. Whoever was shooting had to be a bad shot to miss clear out in the open. Or maybe the shooter wasn't trying too hard.

The hoof beats were Mitchell and the law, coming in fast, the law with a handgun tight in his fist, "You all right?" Mitchell's voice was raw as he slid the buckskin to a quick stop. Patton's long roan took more time and bounced hard. The look to the law's face almost made Ridge laugh except that some son of a bitch was taking shots at him.

It was quiet, too quiet. No birds called, nothing flew or squawked. Ridge nodded, "I'm right fine, now that the coward's gone. He must of seen you come up. He's not much of a shot 'cause I was standing and he missed the horse too. Makes me think he wasn't keen on hitting nothing." Now he was scared, he could hear it in his own voice, the words thick on his tongue. But damn someone taking shots at a man could make him nervous. He felt better seeing the law and that was the first time in several years Ridge could say such a thing. But he wouldn't be saying it out loud, not in this company

With the fuss and churning, maybe the two wouldn't see how someone had tried to brush out the prints. Mitchell climbed down real slow and handed the buckskin's reins to Ridge. He walked to the mustang, and patted the brown's neck, let the horse nose his shirtfront. "Runs fast, don't he." No question, no anger, just stating a fact. Ridge found he could move enough muscles to grin; "Yeah."

The law stayed aboard his roan, and it was Mitchell who found the prints, knelt down, touched a finger to the edge of something and looked back at Ridge. "He got to them, didn't he." It was another statement, not a question. Ridge was shamed; "Yeah." Mitchell looked over to the law. "These what you meant before?" As if Ridge hadn't done wrong by leaving the prints unguarded.

Hale Patton watched the words and thoughts go between the two men and guessed that Ridge was beating on himself for something he hadn't done like he'd been asked. The small man had a conscience after all. Ridge turned his head as Mitchell answered a question that hadn't been asked; "There's enough left, and a man's boot over them, pulled across on the edge, got a worn place where the stirrup rubbed and the leather's been patched. I figure the man wouldn't think on such a thing betraying him."

Patton interrupted with a shrug; "Most cowhands have patched boots." Mitchell nodded back; "Yeah well we know it ain't a woman. Even a big-footed one." Patton lifted one shoulder. His words were abrupt; "We still don't know who it is, or who they're covering for by wiping out the tracks." Mitchell stood, very carefully, and Hale could guess at the ache in his head. "No but I can tell you Mrs. Dorsey didn't make these tracks, or the ones we found near where Tremont was killed." The blunt statement felt odd, and the law and Ridge glanced at each other. It was almost sinful to be talking about women connected with a brutal killing.

Ridge opened his mouth; "I seen Mrs. Tremont and she wears those high topped lace boots but they got a flat bottom, nothing to leave much of a print." Patton agreed, then offered more; "We ain't seen all of her shoes, just what she wears on the ranch. Riding boots, maybe they're different." He looked directly at Ridge; "Does she. . .ah, did she ride out much by herself?"

Ridge lifted his head, stood straighter, shoulders back. Being asked his opinion on what he'd seen and thought was new for Ridge, close to being respectable. "She rides, usually side-saddle, and she's got that bay mare she drives to a buggy, the mare's good tempered and tolerates the rig. I'll have to think on it, I've seen the bottom of her riding boots, can't quite remember. . . ." Hale Patton agreed; "Don't push it, son. You let me know. Or Mitchell here. Keep all this to yourself. Our suspicions ain't based on much. Yet."

As he talked to the nervous cowhand, Patton kept an eye on Mitchell, who was too slow getting back on the buckskin. He knew well enough now that the man was chewing on something. Not ready to talk on it, but thinking. And he wondered if maybe the horse breaker was tired of getting tossed up into the sky and might consider a safer, saner job as a deputy in the law. He knew the answer to that question and didn't bother to ask.

Blue tried pulling his hat down over his eyes but it rested on the opened wound. He couldn't ride with his eyes closed, even on the good buckskin and he needed to remember to thank Ridge for taking the buck out of Keno.

Blue accepted that naming a horse was never a good idea but the little mustang deserved more than horse, or brownie. That didn't help his pounding head though. He heard a noise behind him, looked back to see the law on that post-legged horse he rode, trying to rein the horse to the side, ride up close to Blue and as he fell or slid out of his own saddle, cinched onto the wrong colored horse though, Blue hoped like hell that gangly roan didn't step on him.

Lying on his belly, he found that dust tasted pretty bad but he already knew that. His eyes were open enough to see each grain of sand, the edge of a print and it clicked in his mind. Not sure why, but he knew more now than he did setting on the buckskin. Or squatting down, using his fingers instead of his eyes to understand.

Blue closed his eyes since there was no point in keeping them open. Then a hand shook his shoulder, disturbed the sand that grated in his mouth, made him spit as he hit the hand prodding him and it was Patton's voice asking, another voice joining in.

All of Blue's energy went into rolling over and opening his eyes. Two men stared at him. "You all right?" Patton's words held no worry, just curious. Ridge now, standing next to the law, he looked fearful and Blue grinned at the man, licked his teeth clean of that damned sand and spat again. Then he closed his eyes, trying to remember what he'd seen. It would come to him after he got some rest.

Between them they managed to get Mitchell on the brown, figuring he'd want to ride his own horse now that the run was out of him. The saddle didn't fit since Ridge's stirrup length came just below Mitchell's knees. The long-legged son didn't look that tall standing. Or maybe it was him being relaxed, half asleep but awake enough to croak out a word to Patton, and to Ridge, thanking both of them and that he'd figured something out but he needed to close his eyes now. Patton shook his head. What in hell would a man half out of his mind and lying in the dirt see that had any meaning?

It was a miracle that the rider stayed in the saddle as they walked to the ranch yard. His body swayed and then a hand would grab one side of the swell, or the brown would stop and let Mitchell adjust. It seemed to Hale that the brown horse and its rider had too much practice in the art of half-conscious balancing.

Patton placed his roan next to Mitchell on one side, gestured to Ridge that he ride that buckskin in on the other. They could reach out and push gently to help keep Mitchell upright.

Patton knew it was one hell of a way to enter into the yard after the past days' commotion. And sure enough the women came out, hurried again, fretful of what might have happened. Mrs. Dorsey was in a traveling outfit, a full skirt of some dark material, a jacket and hat to match, and as she picked up the hem of her skirt, Hale noted she wore laced boots that seemed to leave little imprint.

Mrs. Tremont wore one of those light flowered things, loose and looked more comfortable and when she ran, well a gentleman didn't watch such movement in a decent woman. The missus, she too had on those high-laced boots, guess women wore them out here and he'd never thought to notice before.

It wasn't right, thinking that a woman might kill; it was more reasonable to think a man would kill for a woman. Now that had been a good enough reason for several murders Hale had investigated. And then Mitchell slid off the brown, who stopped, Mitchell half hanging from the horse's neck. Mitchell leaned on the brown, seemed to be talking to the horse and the brown twitched an ear back, listening to the boss explain something Hale wished he was close enough to hear.

Blue could see now, through the haze over his eyes. There was less sun to hurt his head, his body wasn't so useless, legs almost held him.

The women were all skirts and colors, hats with feathers. Why did white women wear feathers in their hats and yet all white people hated the Indians for wearing feathers in their hair. Blue thought he might tell the woman, not the missus who was in that flowered dress again and he wondered why she didn't wear black. He might tell these women about feathers.

He felt his knees give, nothing there to hold him; he started going backwards, landing easy, looking at the sun, then boots, legs, spurs and manure. Ah hell.

Ridge had seen it coming and caught Mitchell but the man's weight drove them both down. Ridge was smothered, and felt something leak onto his face. He could smell it; fresh blood.

It took the law and Turner, who was slow out of the barn, to pick up Mitchell and carry him belly and backside sagging, shoulders and feet in strong arms, up the verandah steps and into the house again.

The women friends clung to each other; Priscilla walked behind her husband and seemed to be cursing, which Ridge, who'd sat up and was planning on standing in a minute or two, found strange. Women, even one like Priscilla was supposed to have been, women didn't curse.

Helen rubbed her bare hands on her arms. The confusion was distressing. Melinda Dorsey no longer mentioned Madison but fretted on the wellness of the strange man who had come to fetch Helen. Helen had assumed he would of course be delivering her to her home.

Now there was no one available to even harness a horse for her departure. It was important Helen be returned safely, for Stephen was due late afternoon or on the morrow. He had promised her. She touched Melinda's arm, and the woman turned very slowly. As if Helen's request was lacking in merit.

Helen stared at her supposed friend; there was more concern in those fine eyes than was acceptable for a new widow, and over a drifter at that. Melinda dismissed her urgency; "When Turner is finished, he'll harness the mare to the runabout. I will send someone over tomorrow to pick it up. The mare is very even tempered and you should have no trouble driving her home." Helen knew it was the ending of a minor friendship, despite her willingness to come running at Melinda's summons.

"Helen, dear." The women studied each other. Melinda continued; "Thank you for your kindness. Now, please excuse me." There, dismissed and for an absolutely worthless rider. Hmmm, she would have something to speak to Stephen about when he returned.

Priscilla watched the two women, real ladies with their fine clothes and manners, and then studied on what to do with the man stuck in that back room again. He wasn't much of a nuisance, but she didn't like having him so close while she worked in the house. She didn't trust those eyes that seemed to know her.

Now it was fetch and clean for him again, while the mistress of the house sat in a chair in his room and worried 'bout a man not her husband. She knew his kind, they were quick and charming and left town without goodbye. Not like her Turner, not like him at all.

Someone had taken his clothes and left him buck naked under a thin sheet and blanket. Sleep. He didn't want to wake this time. He knew something, saw it lying while he was stretched flat on the ground, surprised his mind could hold a thought as his body quit.

A nail hammered into a broken edge of a boot. Not uncommon but certainly leaving its individual mark on the ground wherever the boot, and the man wearing it, happened to travel. Blue wanted to get out of the damned bed now so he sat up, swung his feet over the edge, felt that braided rug under his toes and wondered just how he planned to drift unnoticed through the house and back outside, to study the ground and know that what he'd seen was real.

Out here a buck-naked man wouldn't get far. And there were no clothes piled on a chair waiting for him. The boots were there, set on a folded cloth, bits of dried mud stuck in small clumps to the worn leather. He stood, unsteady at first, then feeling stronger as he walked to a bureau, opened a drawer, found nothing, opened the next drawer and there was a shirt, some long johns, a pile of socks. All he needed was pants. A tall cupboard stood against a wall, what his ma would have called a chifferobe, so he angled himself toward it, twisted and pulled at the knob and one side opened.

On a hook, barely showing under a long coat, was a pair of those banker's pants, black with the silver stripe. Blue laughed, he would be a sight wandering in the yard but nothing would keep him in here.

The pants were short, and big at the waist, so he tucked the legs into his high boots and shrugged into one of the fancy shirts. He felt like a gambler on hard times, guessed in a way that's what he was. And it came to him that the lack of clothes was meant to keep him in the small room where he couldn't get in more trouble.

At least they left the boots but no socks; he looked in the drawers again, found thin socks of a light feel to them so he put two on each foot. They felt good on his skin but wouldn't be much protection from a day's work.

Oddly dressed but decently covered, Blue walked from the back room and almost immediately ran into the widowed Mrs. Tremont. He couldn't look at her as she studied him. He heard her though, that delicate gasp saying she recognized the clothing. Without looking, he tried to apologize. "Ma'am, there wasn't nothing else for me." Blue shrugged and gave up.

Her first thought was how dare he and she immediately knew the foolishness of those words. Priscilla had taken the man's filthy clothes to wash them and no one thought to search his saddlebags to see if there were replacements. He had done well, looking almost civilized in the banded shirt and dark pants, ruining the effect only slightly by tucking the legs into his high boots. He was a good four inches taller than her husband, than Madison had been. Tears flooded from her eyes and she turned her head away to not embarrass Mr. Mitchell.

He was a gentleman, for he put a hand on her arm, lightly so as to not be offensive but to tell her he understood. She smiled, wanting desperately to have him hold her but that was impossible. It was there, in his eyes, knowledge and refusal mixed together. He was one man she could neither entice nor command.

"Ma'am. I knew it'd be hard but I have a fact that Hale Patton needs to know something I remember. Be obliged, ma'am, if you'd let me pass." He moved gracefully in his escape despite his rather pitiful condition of wild hair, bruised face, lean body contained by the oddly formal clothes.

She watched him ease down the hall into the parlor and across that floor to the outside, where he stopped a moment, taking a deep breath she imagined. He certainly was not a man to be kept house-bound or under a woman's hand.

Her tears had stopped; she felt exhausted, almost tired enough to simply sit on the floor and wait for either salvation or sleep.

CHAPTER THIRTEEN

It was Ridge who drove the lady home. He tried to bluff his way out but one glance from the law and he gave in, figuring it was safer away from Patton if Mitchell wasn't nearby to save him.

The bay mare was a sweetheart, easy to brush and harness. The woman however, she stood at the barn door, a small bag at her feet, and fussed when he took enough time to clean the mare and adjust the saddle and collar to her back the way it should have been done. When the woman spoke sharp to him, he kept his face turned away, forehead resting on the mare's neck. Ridge unbuckled the hames, then reset them to fit better.

Hames and a collar weren't needed for the lightweight runabout but Ridge had a rule he wouldn't break, that a breast collar was no way for a horse, or mare, to pull. It was hard on their windpipe, not enough for them to lean into if the buggy got stuck in sand. Out here mud wasn't usually the problem, but if a rain came, he knew that getting across an arroyo after rushing water thickened the sand was rough, and to his way of thinking no breast collar would let a horse pull decent.

He explained all this to the mare, who bent an ear and listened, nodding a few times as if agreeing. The woman made a few peculiar noises, then she stopped and Ridge hoped it was that she too listened as he spoke. He truly doubted it, these high-bred women usually didn't listen to no one but themselves and perhaps, on some occasions, their husbands or their mamas. Maybe that was the trouble, they listened too much to their mamas.

He led the mare outside and thankfully the woman had moved, taking the bag with her. She stood near the log, the bag at her feet, head high and mouth pulled tight as if Ridge had offended her. Good, he thought, she'd leave him alone on the drive. Far as he was seeing it, she wasn't much of a friend, leaving the new widow to herself after only a day.

Then again he wasn't much of a friend, the way he was taking care of Mitchell. He sat and watched them shuffle the man into that house this time, never went to check on him, never sat at his bed and talked or offered to help Mitchell any way he could.

The woman fussed with her skirts as he helped her into the runabout, and then she talked endlessly, talked on enough he could pay attention to the feel of the bay mare's mouth, remembering how he and Mitchell spoke about horses and their instincts and what a man did to them to make them listen or run.

If he had a choice, he'd run from the mouthy woman but he was better raised and kept nodding his head at those times she stopped long enough to breathe, which wasn't very often, and Ridge began to have a great respect for the woman's set of lungs. There wasn't nothing else he found admirable or even pretty about the great Stephen Dorsey's wife, and he'd heard from cowhands and barkeeps that the bride was considered a beauty.

He was mannered enough to help her down from the runabout and carry her bag through the front door of the house. He stood there, hands holding on to the valise, mouth open, eyes turned up. He'd never seen a place like it with all the doors and halls and a big room past the rounded entryway. Big flat slabs of shiny wood, carved ornaments, fancy doorways; Ridge'd never seen nothing like it.

He was almighty glad to be back in the runabout with the mare eager and headed home.

When he drove up to the scrubbed set of prints, Ridge was enjoying himself. His hands had found that feel through the lines, a whole new experience where he could tighten a finger and the mare's ear would flicker on that side, giving him the slightest bend of her neck, a willingness to turn or at least move across the dirt track. This new way of talking to a horse pleased him. He'd have to tell Mitchell when the man was up and about.

So the clearing where messing the prints had happened surprised him; his fists tightened without him thinking about it and the mare stopped, hard enough the breeching spanked her hindquarters and she squealed but held still. When his fists let go of the lines, the mare sighed and shook her head, and he laughed. Ridge had been scolded often enough that he recognized the signs, even coming from a bay mare.

He got out slowly, careful not to step where he wasn't meant to. The tracks and the visible neglect of his chore to guard them were ten feet away, ground all churned up. His face went hot, his hands got wet. Dumb fool thing to do, but racing that mustang was a pleasure. Being shot at hadn't been pleasing but the racing, well it was a glory he'd never forget.

Ridge watched where each foot got put down, taking note of where Mitchell had fallen, where the law had climbed down off that speckled mountain he rode. He studied the tracks, saw a small indentation that puzzled him, then it made sense. Now he had an offering for Mitchell and the law to make up for his carelessness.

He was hit in the back, a hard fist that punched through, drowning him as his heart quit. He was dead before he landed on his side and slowly his weight rolled him face down.

The mare tensed, snorted at the fearful scent, and then stood as she had been trained. After a few minutes, the mare took a step, stopped, moved forward again and nothing yelled or pulled so she began to trot, holding her head high and sideways to avoid the dragging reins.

Blue checked the barn and the pen before he realized several things were missing. The house was quiet so the Dorsey woman must be gone. The bay mare and the fancy runabout were missing, and when he couldn't find Ridge but saw the buckskin and that mealy bay in a pen, he figured it out. It was late in the day but not dusk, and there was still time to find the law and ask his question.

Hale Patton showed up as Blue stood fretting and unable to make a choice. Patton walked around him, came in at an angle so Blue was certain to know he was coming. Blue grinned; the man returned it with a half salute. "You feel better now, Mitchell? I'm getting tired of picking you up and putting you down. Ridge, when he gets back from an errand you could have done, he might well feel the same way."

Then the bay mare trotted alone into the ranch yard, came to a slow walk and stopped just short of Blue and Patton. The runabout seat was empty, the lines were partly wrapped around a wheel hub and the corners of the bay mare's mouth were cut. A few drops of blood dotted the settling dust. Blue took a step and touched the mare's neck. She was trembling.

The birds flew up slowly, some tripping in their attempt to fly. Hale Patton reined in first, using his hand to stop Blue and the mustang. Both men knew what attracted the birds. Blue cursed under his breath, Patton grunted.

It was Blue who stepped down, gave Keno's reins to Patton who could not look into Blue's eyes. Blue drew in clean air until he could hear his own heart beat.

True to form, the birds had gone for the easiest parts first; Ridge lay on his belly, head turned so the birds had taken one eye then widened the hole in his back, shredding his shirt and flesh, tearing small pieces exposed by the bullet. Even now those birds were only a short distance from their find, squawking and complaining that Blue and Patton had interrupted their meal.

"Back shot." Blue said the words hard, the closest birds rose a few inches off the ground, landed a foot or so farther away from Blue. "Boot prints again." No birds rose this time, they had figured out these two living humans would not bother them.

Blue had brought a length of canvas from the ranch saddle room and he untied it from the cantle, laid it next to Ridge and began to roll the form over, tidying it into the canvas, making the truth about Ridge disappear. Blue looked up at Patton; "I need your help." The law climbed down from his roan and tied both horses to a low bush.

"On your horse?" Blue nodded. "Across the saddle. I'll walk him in." The brown snorted as the two men raised the canvas bundle high enough to slide across the saddle, but as Blue spoke, Keno steadied.

Patton had little to say; "You be careful. Me, I'm going hunting." Blue nodded; "Watch your back trail, Patton." The law paused and then the two men looked into each other's faces.

Blue saw anger, a righteous fury building in the lawman. Patton read the same anger in Mitchell, fury for killing a decent man, all to cover another killing. Both men looked away; shared emotion was foreign to them.

The mustang walked easily beside Blue, no tugging on the reins to graze the high grasses, no spooking from the flapping canvas. Blue let his arm rest across the corpse as they walked, helping to balance the ugly burden.

He hated coming into the ranch yard even though there weren't many people left to notice. Ira Cook shook his head and disappeared into the barn. The woman sat on the verandah in her rocker; she abruptly stopped its slow rhythm. Turner's big shape came from behind the barn, carrying a shovel. The man glared at Blue, rested the shovel against the barn siding and disappeared.

Blue tied up the mustang and waited. He smelled her first, a light flower scent against the blood and dirt, the stench of manure and loosened bowels. "Yes, ma'am. It's Ridge. I'll bury him near to your husband." He never looked at the woman, never waited for her answer, for any response; he plain didn't care what she would tell him.

146

There'd be no white sheet with family initials for Ridge. He would stay in the canvas, placed in the ground that way. He would be mourned though, settled in the short list of men and horses that Blue admired. A few words, a sharing of knowledge about the rough string and Blue had come to see the dead man as a friend.

They didn't make friends easy, men who drifted from job to job, knowing too well they would always ride on. Blue needed to remember Peter Charley and the unexpected lingering pain of that death. It had been too quick, too easy, to let Ridge become a friend; a good man with a secret he never spoke of, a man like Blue himself, and even Hale Patton. Men who wanted to do right by their beliefs but not give in to their needs.

Blue hesitated then picked up the shovel with one hand, felt his fingers weaken and he dropped the damned thing, bent down to pick it up and almost fell over. He would dig Ridge's grave, he would bury the man. Then he would come back and settle these murders. He had more information now, and a different idea as to who was the killer.

Hale thought of himself as a decent tracker, he certainly had enough experience, but this man who'd killed slid down into an arroyo, climbed on a tied horse and rode away from any buildings, more toward the strange mansion. Then the horse's tracks mixed in with cattle and loose horses and even though Hale followed the herd for a good mile, there was no sign of a single, ridden horse leaving the trail.

It had to be Turner, no other man fitted. No reason yet that Hale could figure but it had to be Turner. The trouble with being the law, he couldn't go up to a man and say 'well now I suspect you for murder and am taking you in.' He needed a reason and proof and this time he didn't have anything but the numbers of those still alive, and the sense that Turner was a bad one.

It came to him as he climbed on the roan; he could set Mitchell on Turner, have him take fighting words to the man, prod him like a mean old bull until Turner fought back. And with Ridge's death, Hale had the gut feeling Mitchell would agree to anything that might bring down the killer.

The yard was quiet, only Ridge's buckskin paced in a pen. The brown mustang was gone and that worried Hale until Turner's thick shape came from the barn and the man told him that the mad-eyed son of a bitch had gone to dig a grave and took the dead man with him.

Then Turner looked straight at Hale and asked when he was going to figure out who was doing all the damned killing. For one moment Hale considered that Turner wasn't the man he was looking for. He didn't believe a man dumb as Turner could lie that easily, lie almost well enough to fool an old lawman. Then he heard the words, the swearing as if Turner cared. He'd shown no interest before at the death of his boss and hadn't thought much of Ridge. Why would he care now?

Turner grinned, and that was a mistake, breaking Hale's momentary doubt and reinforcing his distrust. But there wasn't proof, not even the badly-tanned deer hide and the freshly cleaned rifle could be used against Turner without more evidence and a motive.

Digging a burying hole hurt the inside of a man more than the outside. Blue's hands were hard-callused, his arms muscled, even his back strong enough to bend and dig and throw dirt from the hole. But inside the mind, the chore of digging another grave tore at a man, opening too many thoughts and memories.

He was tired, sweat dripped from his face. His arms ached while his head pounded but he expected these as a reminder that he too had come close. Although why the shooter would use a burr under the saddle to get him made no sense. No one could plan on killing a man from the back of a raging bronc. A rifle shot, now that was quick and sure and rarely by accident.

There was no sense to it, standing silent next to a wrapped corpse, readying the package to fit into the freshly-dug hole. Blue had to kneel, pushing at the feet then the shoulders, not touching the head through the stiffened canvas. Man had bled all he was going to; the canvas was ruined, making it a good coffin for a loose-footed horse breaker.

It was push and shove and then push again until the form slid into the hole, making a small thump as it hit dirt. Blue stood, wiped his face, hoping to find no fresh blood on his hands.

There wasn't much to say; "Friend, it comes to us all. You sooner than most and for that I'm sorry." He began shoveling the dirt, hating the rattle of the first clumps that scattered on the canvas. It was a sound no man ever forgot.

Patton was at the barn, scrubbing down his roan's back, taking time, talking to the horse. Waiting. Blue released the mustang in a nearby pen, spent time wiping the few stains off his gear and the brown's rump. Both men were reluctant to speak of what had just been done.

The law coughed, wiped his mouth; "You buried him?" "Yeah." Blue scrubbed at the saddle marks and the brown snaked his head. He had to tell Patton; "Near the same place as Tremont." "Hmmm. That's done right then."

There was nothing for a while, each man tending to their horse. Then Patton faced Blue; "My bet's on Turner but there's no proof." He got nothing from Mitchell. Hale tried again; "Anything you've seen makes you think the same? Got any idea why he would want to kill your friend?"

Mitchell's words were low, harsh, and exactly what Hale wanted. "No but I got an idea that'll push him." Mitchell knew by instinct; "You telling me to go ahead?"

Hale nodded; "Yes."

Turner got himself up to something and Priscilla planned to dig it out of him. Maybe that was a bad word, since she'd known Mitchell went and dug a hole for that Ridge fella's body and yesterday, only yesterday Turner had gone to that same tree and dug a hole there for Mr. Tremont.

She laughed at herself for it wasn't like her to think such foolishness, words weren't her place, doing came more natural to her. She didn't mind cooking and cleaning for the lady of the house; it kept her living a life in daylight, not something she'd had much of in the past nine years.

She would challenge Turner, which wasn't much of a fight. Again she laughed. It felt like she was getting clever as she got older, maybe it took decent food and less booze to clear her mind.

Turner's horse was in its pen. The bronc had to be a big son of a bitch to carry Turner's bulk. She always knew when Turner was checking fence or maybe even thinking to clean a water hole 'cause that big horse would be gone. Today the horse had thick dirt on its rump, old sweat and dust on its shoulders. Turner didn't clean up his horses after working them, and Priscilla recognized that at least he took better care of her.

The man didn't always think ahead, just bulled through using his strength. Sometimes, like with that devil-eyed man, Turner came up short, depending on his muscle when Mitchell could run circles 'round him only using his mind. The law too, he talked with Turner about the deer hide, and she wondered how come no one had arrested Turner.

Where the hell was her husband?

It was a day for thinking. Plans fell left and right, nothing worked. That sad, quiet man had been killed, much like her Madison. Shot in the back by an unknown assassin, a callous, cruel way to take a man's life. At least deer and other game had a chance, they could see and smell and hear their stalkers but mankind was limited, both in the senses and the ability to judge right and wrong.

Melinda allowed the rocking chair's even motion to soothe her. Life was in the process of falling apart and she had no notion of how to repair the damage. Now Mr. Mitchell had the ability and was intelligent enough to make the ranch work for her, and with patience he could become a pleasant enough companion. However the ill-considered man had so quickly and thoroughly rebuffed her suggestion that at this point all she wanted was for him and his penchant for death to move on. She would not settle for Ira Cook and his too obvious intentions as to the ranch and her own person. A clean shirt and terrible cologne liberally applied did not make a gentleman.

It was a pity about Mr. Mitchell. However, she consoled herself as she kept the rocker in motion, there was the lawman, Mr. Hale Patton, of some reputation and knowledge in the territory, and passable in his stature and manner of talk and dress. He had managed to not spend a night in the house, or in the barn or bunkhouse according to Mr. Cook. Yet he was clean, had shaved on occasion, and wore decent clothes, fresh shirts, proper whipcord pants. She believed he also might have applied some polish, or at least washed off his boots, for they carried no stench or unsightly clumps of barnyard matter.

Melinda sighed and knew she must changed her focus. She would study Mr. Patton as he continued his investigation. While he had not yet determined Madison's killer, it had only been a few days, and those days were filled with violent indecencies that were both offensive and frightening.

And, in an admission she had resisted making to herself, she did owe something to the Dorseys, even though the promise had been made between two men of questionable reputation on a handshake. It was time to go through Madison's papers and see if, perhaps, there had been a written and signed agreement after all.

Ira Cook watched her. Wearing that flowered dress, not even a plain brown or dark blue but light and flowered and my god she sure looked pretty setting up there. She had talked direct to him earlier this morning, resting a hand lightly on his arm, speaking to him as a friend and he liked hearing her voice.

"Mr. Cook." That's how she began. "I greatly appreciate your concerns for me, sir." That meant she liked his attention. "You do not have to go out of your way, or take time from your

duties, to console me. I am capable of taking care of myself."
She was a sturdy one for all her airs and beauty. "Please do not
waste your time with your best shirts and that cologne. The
scent of a man who works hard and takes good care of himself
is far superior to any manufactured smell."

He wasn't quite sure but it sounded to him that she liked
how he smelled. Pretty personal for such a woman to say to the
likes of Ira Cook, and the words made Ira grin. She was coming
'round, he would bet on that. Give her time. When she was
finally on her lonesome, she would need him.

Blue was restless and angry and Patton knew it but wouldn't let
him ride on. Instead the law had told him to finish the
investigation the way Patton himself would like to, and then
they could both get to their own business.

It was time to go hunting. He had two ideas and two sets
of tracks to follow. Some son of a bitch put a burr in the paint
colt's saddle blanket. He knew his anger was as much about the
colt's death as his own injured pride. Then he turned around
quickly to see the look on Patton's face and knew the man was
reading him so he offered his thoughts.

"Ridge would never do that to an animal. Turner
wouldn't think about it, either to put the burr in, or get it out
without someone seeing him." Blue spoke hard, then went
quiet. Eventually he finished the thought; "That leaves Ira Cook
who wants this place for his own and by god that woman won't
be taking him on as nothing more than a paid servant. But he
won't accept he's got no chance." Hale tipped his head, giving
silent agreement.

Unspoken between the two men was the notion that a
woman would never choose Ira Cook over a younger man like
Blue, or even a steady and thoughtful man like Hale Patton
himself. It would be bragging for either of them to make that
comment.

Blue nodded once. "Think I'll have me a talk with Mr.
Cook." He shivered; "Then I've got another son of a bitch whose

life needs changing." Having come to know something of the man's temper and strength, Hale Patton almost felt sorry for the two men.

Life was going to be turned upside-down and Hale kind of liked what he was doing. No proof, nothing a lawman could use, but Mitchell's temper would put the scare of hell into either man and the truth had to appear.

CHAPTER FOURTEEN

Blue could smell Cook outside the bunkhouse, stinking like a whore only whores smelled a lot better 'cause they were female. Blue slammed open the bunkhouse door, took note as he crossed the wood floor that one bunk had been pulled free of bedding, with clothing and gear dumped on it. Cook was already throwing away Ridge's life.

"Damn you." Blue grabbed Cook's neck one-handed, hard as he could. "You're the son of a bitch hurt that colt. He was worth more'n you'll ever be, you piece of garbage. I'd as soon stuff you down the outhouse seat if you'd fit. Or leave you stuck in headfirst." Way in the back of his mind, Blue felt anger take over and he didn't fight the impulse. His hands ached; the man needed killing.

Cook choked and tried to reach backwards, clawing at Blue, fighting to get out words, excuses, curses. Blue kept his hold, then shook the man's head, throwing him forward hard on his knees, making the wood floor crack. Blue waited; the man stood and turned slowly, as if bruised inside, and stared at Blue, eyes wide, mouth opening and shutting like a half-dead fish pulled out of low water.

"I didn't mean for that to happen. The colt. . . ." The man hadn't question why Blue attacked him. All the proof Blue needed was Cook's empty conscience. Blue stopped himself from murder; he was filled with rage yet unwilling to treat anything, even Cook, this badly. He had the words though, and the ability to use them.

"You're gone from here, Cook. That lady she don't want you, you're fooling yourself like you had her husband fooled. Mrs. Dorsey, when I went to get her, she talked about you and how useless Mr. Dorsey and yes, your boss, Tremont, how useless those men thought you were." Those words wounded Cook more than Blue's attempted strangling.

"You've thrown away Ridge's life, now get your own backside out of here. Head down to Las Vegas or across the pass to Trinidad. Some fool up there will hire you on, and you can ruin his ranch instead of Mrs. Tremont's. Get on the move before I lose my temper."

Blue got out of the bunkhouse, away from its stink and the bitterness of diminishing fury. Now he needed a rank horse to ride, something that could ease his anger by a good fight. There was Patton leaning on that miserable log again and Blue went around him, roped out the mealy bay that Ridge said was no good and got a halfway decent argument out of the bronc. It made his head hurt by god, and snapped his neck a few times in a climbing buck that plunged down hard but the horse had little heart and within a few minutes the mealy bay was circling, stopping, even backing on command.

Ridge had done a good job starting the horse. Blue felt anger stir again and if Ira Cook had been within reach, he would have strangled the man all over again. He knew it wasn't Cook who'd done the back-shooting, but the supposed foreman had left nothing of Ridge's belongings untouched in a tangled mass of gear and bedding. Later, when he was calm or close to it, Blue would gather up Ridge's gear and sort through what might be useable.

Sweaty and tired but more at ease, Blue climbed off the bay and unsaddled the horse, rubbed it down with some twisted hay, turned it back into a pen with hay and a full water trough. Ridge had been on the mark, the bay had no guts or stamina. But the fight made Blue feel better as it eased his ornery streak.

"You ride like that all the time, son?" It was Patton of course, leaning and watching and letting Blue ease back into a reasonable world. He had short words for Patton's observation; "Sometimes it's the only way to take it out of a horse like that bay. Me and Ridge we talked about the bronc and he was right."

"Well, Mitchell. You best wash your face 'fore we go up for supper, if the lady of the house'll have us. That bay's antics opened your cut." "Ah hell." Blue wiped at the mess and rolled the sticky blood between his fingers.

Then he heard it, a short-strided horse carrying its own weight and that of a heavy rider came out of the barn, jogged past Blue and Patton, and Patton raised his hand in a mild salute. Blue turned his back. One man gone; one left.

While Blue cleaned up, he struggled through his thoughts. Supper meant setting down at a polite table with the mistress of the house and the law, everyone on their best behavior, the woman expecting light talk and passable manners while the men struggled between hunger and burned food. All Blue needed was something to fill his belly and no talk, no questions from the woman or Hale Patton, nothing to do with folks, just food so he wouldn't starve.

He thought about it, shook his head when Patton came by to walk with him. "No sir, I ain't fit company tonight. You tell her that, in your polite way that seems to keep her happy while you look for her husband's killer. I know what I've got to do but now. . .hell Patton, I buried a good man today. I ain't up to the social niceties."

It was more than he'd thought to say, and Hale Patton let his jaw drop as Blue went on until the man's grinning eyes shut Blue's mouth. "Mr. Mitchell sometimes you surprise me. Most of the time in fact. I will share your regrets with Mrs. Tremont, and while she will be saddened at your inability to join us for the meal, I am certain she will understand."

There, Blue thought, both of them had begun to talk like the fancy folk they'd been dealing with. But it was the truth, he could not consider a polite meal, his belly would twist and turn at each word. "You have a chance, Hale, you grab me a biscuit or two. That'll be my supper."

Hale Patton walked carefully up to the main house. He found himself in an agitated state and in looking for reasons, he found that the two deaths, while unsolved and definitely weighing on his thoughts, were not the source of his fretting.

It might be, he considered, that he was about to share a meal with a most intelligent and lovely woman who happened to be a widow. It was improper, and against all that he had sworn as a lawman, but life did not always fit in with promises and regulations. Oh well, he thought, as he stopped at the edge of the steps to the verandah, it would be a pleasant meal in good company. Then Mitchell would go on the attack tomorrow and quite possibly the mystery would be over.

She was at the door, dressed in a somber gown of a heavy material that had to be uncomfortable even in the cool evening air. She was corseted, a fact he would not choose to notice but with his lawman's eye, and being male, he could not help but see the smoothed line of the dress front.

Her face barely moved as he offered Mitchell's apology for not joining them as if she already knew or was pleased to be relieved of Mitchell's company. Hale did not assume either was correct. He held her chair as she sat at the small table set up in the front parlor, and wasn't surprised as the woman, Turner's wife, removed the third chair and unused place setting without being told.

"Mr. Patton, it will be a simple meal, but at the moment I do not have much of an appetite. However Priscilla has seen to it there are seconds, and a decent pudding for dessert." Pudding, who would expect pudding, a 'decent' pudding at that, in the middle of nowhere under such circumstance, and that it would be discussed in advance amused and bothered Patton in equal proportions.

It was a meal of low words, quiet laugher, a hand touched on his wrist, a head turned to listen, eyes steady on his face as he answered any number of her questions. She was indeed a lovely woman despite her tragic circumstances, and it was easy to understand why a younger man such as Madison Tremont would marry her.

Patton left before ten with venison stew, three biscuits and a bowl of that decent pudding. Light and airy, beaten eggs and cream and a flavor he thought was vanilla but then again his tastes were fashioned by hot chile and too many refried beans, so pudding itself was a rare experience.

Mitchell was asleep inside the barn, rolled up in a grey blanket, head cushioned by a thick sheepskin coat. The man didn't snore, but a quick change in his breathing told Patton his presence was known.

"Supper", Patton said as he placed two bowls and the biscuits on an upright tree trunk where at times a smith would bang away on heated metal.

'Thanks' was what he got in return.

Cold food and the sweet made for a decent meal just at dawn. Blue wished for hot coffee, but he sat outside to the back of the barn where it faced east, and chewed the meat, swallowed the vegetables whole while noting the potatoes were soft enough, and the gravy had cooled to where fat lay white and thick across the top.

Biscuits dunked in the solid gravy were passable, and the bowl of sweet settled the rest in his belly. He sat back leaning on the barn boards, to watch the sun rise. Lines of light and heat probed through cactus and a few low trees, slid between ridges, stunning him as the sun's head appeared. He could see it move, measured against the distant cones of the northeast part of New Mexico. Eventually Blue stood, wiped at his forehead and felt the thin scab. He thought about his intentions and knew that the healed-over wound would be torn again. He didn't figure that Turner would take the accusations and turn coward as Cook had, betraying himself as he ran.

Then again, what Blue intended to put to Turner was murder, maybe two murders, and no man would back down and give in on that accusation without a battle. He sighed, wiped his mouth, spat out a lingering bitterness. He'd risk a cup of coffee boiled by Turner's wife to let the meal settle, and then he'd go after the ugly truth.

It was a pleasure to feed out the horses, check each pen for water. The mealy bay kept its distance, the buckskin came over and sniffed at Blue. This had been Ridge's favored mount and Blue had a sense about the horse, it would be a shame to waste the buckskin on this place, with no one here to value the animal or finish its training.

The brown mustang approached Blue with ears pinned back, shaking his head. Blue laughed. The son was jealous. Blue took time to rub the brown's forehead until the ears relaxed and Keno sighed and then Blue threw down the hay he'd been carrying and stayed to watch the brown lip through the pile to find the best stalks. Horses did this for him, let him laugh at himself and find distance from the rest of the miserable world.

Here that grinning bastard was, eyes too bright for the hour, already smelling of sweat and she hated having to feed these cowboys and this one in particular 'cause he didn't belong to the ranch and made her Turner nervous.

Priscilla was up because the missus said so, while Turner still lay in their bed. Ira Cook was gone and her lazy husband didn't get the idea that if he did something, almost anything on his own that could be seen and noted, then he'd be the foreman and maybe that high-toned lady would let him hire on a few men and they could all get back to ranching.

This might be the only chance she and Turner would have to run a spread. But not Turner, he only rolled over and didn't wake when she pushed him in the back and told him in her harshest voice to get his lazy backside out of the bed and show the missus he had some gumption.

In a poor temper herself, Priscilla pounded hard at the roasted beans, smashing them until bits of coffee flew around the kitchen and finally she had to laugh and grind more beans. There was nothing worse on a ranch than weak coffee.

And damned if the first one to show, not that there were a lot of men to this place anymore, never were but at least there had been some life hanging 'round; of course the first one to show was that drifter with the eyes that burned into her until she had to look away. God help Turner if this one ever went for him. Turner might be an ox, but there was something to this rider that frightened Priscilla. She poured him his cup, let him lace it with the canned milk and real sugar and he thanked her politely but she still didn't trust him.

He wandered off the back step, moving stiff and almost lame, like he was hurting someplace deep. She felt relief and no pity since with a few injuries the man would be less of a threat to her Turner.

Blue returned the cup a half hour later. He saw Turner cross behind the barn from the outhouse to the pump, and then come to the back door for some of his wife's cooking. Blue didn't think or wonder or fret or notice anything around him. He was motionless, intent on studying Turner as he approached. Turner was a big son of a bitch, thick shoulders and hands, the belly a tribute to his eating habits, the face showing little understanding of what was coming his way.

Blue slammed his shoulder into Turner hard enough the man stumbled backward and Blue caught his shirt at the throat, tightened his grip until Turner choked and spittle showed at the corners of his mouth.

"You." He hauled Turner up, looked into those deep-set eyes and read fear and confusion, which was exactly what Blue wanted to see. "Why'd you kill Mr. Tremont? That story about the deer and not getting 'round to cleaning your weapon, no man worth his salt lets a weapon sit a day or two. You know better." Blue saw confusion as Turner's mouth opened, then a fist came up and Blue twisted the filthy shirt collar until Turner dropped his arm and went to his knees.

Hale Patton appeared, drinking coffee from a dented cup. He took a second gulp, wiped his mouth, nodded to Blue and said nothing. Blue could barely hear beyond the fury inside his head. "You talk to me, Turner, or I'll kill you." He released one twist of the shirt, saw Turner's bunched fist open. The man could move his head and he spoke to the law; "You can't let him do this to me." Patton shrugged; "Hell, Turner, you answer his questions and I'll be glad to set you free. But he's crazy enough right now that I ain't going to fight him."

Turner's face was blank; the eyes flat, holding fear and anger together. "I done nothing. . . ." Blue twisted the shirt, held the man to his knees. Turner choked and Blue was of a mind to keep twisting, strangling the man until he was nothing left but dead weight meant to be thrown away. He tasted bitterness in his mouth, hated the thoughts in his head and eased up on Turner.

"You leave him be." It was the wife of course. Caught unaware and at the mercy of rage, Blue looked up and she was waving a fry pan at him and he laughed. Patton stepped in her way and with some struggle took the weapon. She glared at Blue, her face broken in angry lines, her eyes wild. "You goddamn leave him alone."

The shock of a woman swearing loosened his hand on Turner's neck. Turner's fist struck hard on that barely-healed cut. The blow put Blue down and half-senseless, knowing still to roll and he felt the sweep of Turner's boot as it skipped over his back. He kept rolling and came up standing, blood in his vision but he could see Turner's bulk and as the man swung again, Blue grabbed the fist, slid behind the man twisting that arm until Turner yelled and went quiet.

Blue coughed, spat out dirt, finally got his voice; "Hurts don't it you damn fool." Blue spoke directly into Turner's ear. Then the woman landed on his back, clawing his neck and spitting more oaths. Blue held on until Patton pulled her away.

Blue took in a deep breath; "Turner, you let this woman take care of you. Well she can't help you when you're hanging for a man's murder."

Turner was scared. He'd hit that man with all his strength and got his arm bent so it hurt every breath he took and the man wasn't quitting. The law had Priscilla who was glaring at him and Turner knew she wanted him to keep quiet about what got done on her account. But he didn't want to hang.

"I done it for her. She told me and so I done it. You can't hang a man for taking care of his wife. It ain't right. It was that Ridge looking at things wasn't none of his business. He talked to you, Mitchell, he'd tell you what. . .she didn't want no one to know."

That Patton fella he looked at Turner like he'd confessed to something terrible but it was Priscilla who had the trouble, Priscilla who needed a strong man to help her. "Can't you understand, I can't let no man hurt her, she's married to me."

Then she spoke, and Turner knew his life was gone. "I didn't ask him to do anything like what he's done. This morning he tried to hit me. He can't use me. It's wrong." The words were lies but they sounded convincing and the look to his wife's face, those eyes sad and wet, hell Turner thought, that look made him weak.

He studied her, saw the body he enjoyed gone all tight and stiff. He tried to reach to her with one hand and she pulled away. "Don't you touch me." Like she'd never come into their bed with ideas and things they could do he'd never known nothing about. Like she was disgusted by his need to touch her.

The hold on his arm loosened, he could feel Mitchell relaxing, like something had been finished. The man didn't know much, Turner decided. He hadn't said he'd killed anyone. It was Priscilla's yelling at him got everything confused.

All he'd done was to help his wife, take care of her and protect her like the preacher man said when he stood up and spoke to them, Turner and Priscilla he called them like they were all good friends. The preacher had looked straight at Turner and said that she was his to love and protect now, that he was taking on a joyous burden and that these words spoken in the presence of God meant that Turner agreed to abide by his word. That's what the preacher said.

Preacher didn't say nothing about her turning on him, or him being kind to a stranger that wanted to hurt Priscilla and half-pull Turner's arm out of his body. He swung his fist again, hitting Mitchell to the side of his skull, next to that bloody cut and the man went down, raising dust that made Turner cough and his throat hurt, raw where Mitchell had tried to choke him so he kicked Mitchell in the rib, then the back and then the law yelled at him and Turner shook his head, angry now that he was no longer the target. Damn them all. He raised his leg to kick Mitchell again.

Hale Patton shot Turner and the bullet's force slammed him backwards. Damn he wanted to kick that Mitchell again but his leg didn't work and he couldn't stand, couldn't reach Mitchell with either hand and then Priscilla walked away as if she owed him nothing.

Blue rolled over and coughed and spat out blood, watched more blood drip from the reopened cut and cursed the whole world standing over him, behind him, anywhere near him. He remembered the gunshot, knew it had most likely saved his life, and as he raised himself to standing, feeling a pull on a rib, a muscle complaining, he considered the man lumped on the ground. Too much blood poured from a small hole high in the thigh. That particular shot could bleed a man dry in minutes.

Blue looked around and Hale Patton was shaking his head as he replaced the single empty shell. The law was an efficient man, but he dismissed the fact that his prisoner would die without care.

Mrs. Tremont stood with both hands over her mouth as if the gesture would remove her from the half corpse at her feet. Turner's wife was headed to the house in no hurry so Blue

ALONG CHICO CREEK & FAST HORSES

guessed she wasn't planning to run for bandages to save her husband's pitiful life. The man cried as Blue shuck out of his shirt and knelt down, lifted the wounded leg and tied the shirt tight up into the groin. Turner swore and Blue told him to shut up, he'd live unlike the men he'd backshot and Turner's face got all bent and odd, with his lower lip hanging and his eyes wet, mouth drooling.

"I didn't mean. . . ." Blue gave an extra pull on the shirt as Turner groaned and lay back in the dirt. Blue settled on his boot heels, glad he wasn't wearing spurs. He was chilled, shaky, hands covered again in blood. At least this time it wasn't his blood pouring out, taking life with its flow.

"He won't die, not yet anyway." He spoke to no one in particular, no one was paying attention and it didn't seem to matter if Turner lived or died.

Melinda Tremont could not believe what she had witnessed. In many ways the violence was worse than the sadness of tending to Tremont's body, washing the wounds already begun to dry, touching the damp gray skin. It had been a test of will to keep her composure while working alongside Priscilla, who showed no interest or sadness at the death of the man she had worked for these past few years.

The heartless hussy; with her own husband lying on the ground, writhing in obvious pain and bleeding copiously, Priscilla walked away. As if the violence meant nothing, as if Turner's wound were a minor scratch that would heal with no treatment. The woman's extraordinary lack of compassion stunned Melinda. Even an animal in such dire condition deserved attention, if not a killing shot to relieve it of such misery.

Then there was Mr. Mitchell, shirtless now, ragged undershirt torn across his back and side, a bruise showing through the grayish fabric. The man must be cold, for it was October and the air was chilled even at this hour. It was almost eight in the morning on the day life once again changed radically.

She could not live in this land for she no longer would accept these standards of behavior. Shootings, killings, fights and bleeding bodies and yet the law, Mr. Patton, who had been so interesting and attentive last night, was only now putting his pistol back in its holster where it belonged. He had shot a man, aimed quite deliberately for she had been watching him. Shot a man and brought him down and seemed uninterested in the shooting's effect.

When she studied over the words spoken, accusations thrown around, it came to Melinda that in truth there had been no confession or revelation of truth. All Mr. Turner had said was that he defended his wife, which was only proper. But that was no explanation for either Tremont's death or that cowhand's shooting.

She looked at Mr. Patton, who nodded to her in return as if they were parting now from the friendship and pleasant exchange of last night's informal supper. "Mr. Patton, what do you intend doing with this man? He cannot travel with that wound, and I absolutely will not have him in the house." Patton seemed to smile; "Well, ma'am, I'd say we put him in his wife's bed, with handcuffs to keep him from running around. And when he's feeling up to it, we'll take a short journey into town to a decent jail where he can't escape. That's what I intend to do with him."

Mr. Patton was mocking her, with his language and the content of the words and it was extremely annoying. "Well." It was not much, but from the flinch she read in Mr. Patton's eyes, he understood her contempt. She too turned her back on the men still caught in their ineffective struggle. There was nothing she would do for them. She would return to the house and resume the meager breakfast Priscilla had laid down in front of her, as per her request.

A voice stopped her before she got started; "Ma'am, you've got another shirt I can use? This one's not. . . ." Then, as if the man needed to acknowledge without words what use had been made of the shirt she had given him, Mitchell, the drifter who had ruined life here on this lovely place, apologized by looking away, his voice softening. "Ma'am, I need the borrow of another shirt."

CHAPTER FIFTEEN

Hale made Turner get up and walk. Between Mitchell's face and ribs and Hale's need to keep a gun on the supposed killer, there wasn't anyone left to carry the son and putting him on a horse to go maybe forty feet seemed like a waste of time. The man didn't fight or curse much, except when he stumbled and put most of his weight on that bad leg.

Mitchell had saved Turner's miserable life. Hale had been studying on whether or not it was worth the effort to stop a man from bleeding out just to hang him. Mitchell's actions told Hale he'd met a better man, for there had been no hesitation as Blue shucked out of his shirt, and he knew exactly how to tie the twisted material high and hard to stop the blood flow.

However Hale needed to get Turner well enough to travel and find a place to hold him for trial. Even though the man's words hadn't been clear, those listening had the sense that Turner was the killer, and that a good talk, a few threats and the man would confess. Hale followed Mitchell and the prisoner, noting absently that there was little blood left as a trail.

Turner's woman wasn't in their room and Hale wasn't much surprised at her going back to work without a second thought for her man. Their home hung off the side of the saddle room and it had no real floor, just swept and hard-packed earth, walls covered with eastern newspapers that Mr. Tremont would have had had sent to him. A few drawings of fashionable ladies in fancy clothes were nailed up near the bed.

As for the bed itself, it was rough-shaped metal with crude flowers and vines running through the head and foot. Hale found it tough to put Turner's soulless kills with the sad attempts of a love-smitten man moved to create something beautiful for a woman.

He made Turner lie down, cuffed him with one hand to the bent metal, and then helped the man slide out of his boots. Turner yelped when Hale yanked on the wounded leg but that was all.

Mitchell's donated shirt was ruined so Hale dug out one of Turner's shirts, untied the bloody mess and watched as more blood came from the angry wound. But a few wraps with the dry shirt, a good high tie and the blood slowed, then stopped. A few flies buzzed in to circle Turner's leg. Hale left Turner lying in a mess bound to make Turner's wife even angrier if she even came back to the shared room. Her posture as she walked away had been stiff, with no sway or give to her very female body. Damn if she wasn't a hard woman.

Turner tried, using words that weren't one of Turner's talent; "I didn't do nothing but save my wife. You can't leave me here I need a doc, hell mister, I'll bleed out and die and you'll be the killer." Hale admired the effort but he wasn't going to listen.

He found Mitchell at the hand pump. Head down, cold water roaring through the matted hair; when Mitchell got enough flow, he'd let go of the handle and scrub at his face, even that widening cut. Then the pump handle slowed and Mitchell went at it again.

The man came up for air finally; head soaked, water running down his face leaving streaks through dirt. The eyes were vivid against the wet skin, wild and intemperate, as if Mitchell would strike at anything within reach. Patton backed up; "Mitchell, you can leave off having to roust a man. I can see you haven't the disposition for the law. But you've done well. Two crimes got solved. Now the law will try Turner and Mrs. Tremont may go about her life knowing her husband's death has been satisfied."

They weren't easy words for Hale Patton to speak because he knew they weren't the truth, but he wanted to keep stirring this pot, and using Mitchell's honesty against him might well fill out the facts. It was tough, for those eyes stared back at him and Hale saw disgust and disappointment and he liked the man even more. After this was settled, maybe then Hale could tell Mitchell how he'd been used. For now, it was painful to see himself in those eyes and know that a man he admired thoroughly disliked him.

Blue straightened up, ran a hand through his dripping hair to pull it off his face. He studied Patton, noted the hand too close to the holstered pistol, the head tilted, eyes steady on Blue's face as if expecting an explosion.

Blue wiped his wet hand across his mouth. Patton hadn't been paying attention or they had been in separate brawls or the man wasn't as smart as he appeared. It was clear to Blue that Turner hardly knew how his supposed confession had seemed to the rest of them. It was obvious the man did not understand he had almost confessed to at least one killing if not two.

No one was concerned about Ridge, no one talked about a horse breaker who meant no harm. And the prints weren't mentioned, the smaller boot under the large print, scuffed and almost erased. Maybe that's what Turner confessed to, not the killing.

Blue studied Patton's face, disappointed in the man's easy acceptance of Turner's few words and how simple it had been for Patton to shoot the man. A crack over the head, a gun barrel to the ribs and Turner would have stopped, for he was no more than a bully and a coward.

Blue went back to his cleaning, not yet satisfied the man's blood was gone from his hands and face. All this blood and death tore into a man; he wanted gone from the place, released from the prison of his unintended good deed.

It wasn't time to leave; he had to talk to Turner with none of these people as witnesses. Turner blustered and made himself what he wasn't if his wife was near, and Patton cowed the man. Blue figured he could look in on Turner with the explanation of wanting to check on the wound.

If the wife was there, seated on the bed near her husband, it would be a shake of the head, a 'good day to you, ma'am' for her, a slight nod to Turner with a promise in his eyes that he would be back.

That might even be enough to scare the son of a bitch into telling what he didn't know was the truth. In Turner's addled brain, everything that happened here was to take care of his wife. He probably didn't understand what his wife was telling him and everyone else, when she chose to walk away and ignore Turner's suffering.

All of this, the small things that didn't add up, these were arrows pointing to a raw deal for Turner and Hale Patton needed to step up and do what he was paid to do.

Damn, Blue thought, guessed he said it out loud as Patton flinched. "That scrubbing hurt, Mitchell?" Blue shrugged and grinned for now he had the measure of the law. The man wanted an easy answer, refusing to see what didn't fit. "Damn," Blue said again. And he meant it this time for the likes of Hale Patton.

Mitchell then had the nerve to walk away, angled toward the barn and those horse pens where his mustang stood, head hanging, ears loose. The horse was napping after a decent breakfast and yet the brown horse lifted his head and whinnied. The man had magic in him if a horse he rode every day, and rode hard, was pleased to see him.

None of it was personal or mattered to the law. Hale Patton let his hand rest on the butt of his pistol and decided he was in need of more coffee and maybe a talk in the kitchen with Turner's wife before he made the next move.

The woman barely looked up as Patton walked into the kitchen without a knock or call. She was bent over a cloth-covered board, slapping at a mound of dough and Hale wondered what treat would be waiting for the mistress of the house at noon.

He used his law voice; "Ma'am, you need to answer my questions." She didn't even turn to look at him but it seemed she hit at that bread dough even harder. This made him smile, to be able to bother people in such an obvious manner. He pushed a chair at her.

"Lady. Sit." This time she obeyed, although her face had a nasty smile as she leaned back in the chair, pulled her hair away from her face and presented all of her feminine charms. He could have leaned forward and buried himself between her breasts. No wonder Turner was so eager to protect this woman.

Hale took another chair, turned it around and straddled it. She wanted to play, well he'd do the same to her. All this nonsense might dig something useful from her by mistake.

"Ma'am, I need to know why your husband finds it necessary to shoot a man to keep you safe. What did you do that he needs to kill for you?" Lots of room for lots of different answers in those questions, he thought. Clever, giving her room to hang them both.

She leaned forward until she was sitting straight, her head tilted to one side. She must have been pretty before she was used up. Turner had to be a relief for her after those hard years.

"He ain't done nothing to help me, 'cepting in bed." She was teasing and Hale recognized the voice, the force behind the words. She was trying to give him a picture that would make him forget why he was talking to her.

"Can you handle a rifle?" He didn't know why he asked the question but it came to him and for a second she tightened, then leaned back again and laughed and he didn't know which to believe. "Mister, I can handle most anything, but a woman like me, well I don't need to use a rifle most times."

"Ma'am, why'd you walk away from Turner?" He gave her that moment, a small bit of time, to remind her he'd seen her leave Turner bleeding out on the ground. She wasn't impressed with his tactics. "Turner he had you and that madman tending to him, I was needed to the house. She's not used to being a widow yet, you know. Someone's got to take care of the missus."

She had answers for everything and he wasn't getting what he wanted. Hale smiled politely and stood up, tipped his head to her. "Ma'am." He would withdraw for now, but he wasn't yet in full retreat.

She heard voices that were unfriendly, high-pitched and barely decipherable. Melinda Tremont took exception to people speaking so vehemently within these walls. It was meant to be quiet and hushed in the house; her husband had been killed, did these loud people not understand the implications of that simple fact, how badly their raised voices excited her nerves.

The voices belonged to Priscilla, who herself needed to be sad and worried as her own husband lay wounded and handcuffed to a bed not twenty feet from the kitchen door. And of course the lawman, Mr. Patton; his voice was unforgettable for he used it as an instrument, soft and endearing, then harsh and commanding. All the varieties of his voice were cold fabrications, intended to dig out of each suspect their deepest and most personal thoughts. She wondered if she had misspoken any truths last night. It was difficult to remember, as having the full attention of a man was a pleasure she had grown used to enjoying. Once it had been her entire life although since moving here, it was Madison at his best only when Mr. Dorsey or other such questionable characters graced their table.

Helen Dorsey's visit had been a disappointment. The younger woman was bland, speaking of foolish fashion matters as if they were sisters discussing the upcoming season. Melinda had tried twice to speak of more intimate and distressing subjects but Helen proved to be adept at changing the subject.

Melinda had asked the woman to leave, almost to the moment that Helen herself said the violence and fear she experienced at the Tremont ranch was too much for her. No female should be expected to deal with death, dying, blood, or pain; at least not the class of women that Helen Dorsey aspired to become. The continuing violence that Madison's death had triggered was difficult to accept.

Melinda Tremont knew better. She had washed and cared for her dead husband, she was privy to the pain of the drifter who brought Madison home. She had seen that same man act with tenderness over another dead man. The West was unstructured and lawless, despite the sworn duties of men like Hale Patton, but there was a brutal, unforgiving reality to life here that she had not experienced in her privileged isolation back east. Unfortunately, she would not remain here, she could not.

With these warring thoughts in her mind, Melinda Tremont entered the kitchen and found it deserted.

"You bastard. Leave him alone." Hands on her hips, mouth going with the ugly words and Blue laughed, which made her even angrier. "Ma'am, I figured since you walked away, I'd come see how your man was doing. He got shot trying to kill me, there's a feeling I owe him some consideration."

He had brought a canteen of water, another soft bit of a torn shirt. He was in a stinking shirt once hand-tailored for a gentleman, now a rag pulled from his own saddlebags. Nothing had come from his asking for a fresh shirt, so he had given up and the shirt he wore smelled fierce but he wasn't going around half naked in this bunch of crazy folk.

The bleeding was stopped, and Blue was using the cloth to wash Turner's face and then he'd tie the wet cloth under the torn pants leg, over the wrinkled, deadly hole.

The woman stood at the door and yelled at him. Blue looked down into Turner's face. The man was worn to nothing and flinched each time the hellion at the door cursed.

Finally Turner raised his head, supported himself on his elbows and even that effort was too much. A stench came off him that Blue recognized; the scent of rot and sickness. It could take a man quick, since that Colt had drilled itself right on through the leg and nicked an artery.

Turner's words were ragged; "You quit me. Whatever I done, you quit me and now I don't care." Curious about what the wife would say, Blue stepped back to give them room at each other. He figured, well he hoped he was right, that he was stronger right now than either of them. She was a tough female, but Blue knew his own strength and he could wrestle a fry pan or a rifle out of her hands quick enough.

As for Turner, the man was laid flat, one hand cuffed to a fancy headboard, the other hand trembling even as it rested on the bedclothes. The man couldn't do much harm, so Blue leaned against a wall halfway between the wife and her husband and acted as if he didn't care.

There was nothing left for Priscilla to feel, only that lazy Turner lying in their bed, his blood everywhere. He smelled like a skunk trapped by hounds and by god she'd find herself another place to sleep tonight. She wasn't a nursemaid to no one, not even her husband.

The other one, that lean mad-eyed son of a bitch who'd messed with her life since he'd gotten here, that one rested himself on the wall, an ugly grin on his face, hands stained and she wasn't going to think on those stains. She'd called it right, he was a bastard child roaming the land and making trouble wherever he landed. She'd told Mrs. Tremont, moment he rode into the yard, she told her that man was nothing but trouble.

Priscilla crossed her arms and studied her enemies. Both of them sons of bitches had no idea the life a woman led out here, no sense at all of how she had to protect herself because no one, not even a sworn husband, could do the job.

Then that cowboy leaning on the wall, he began to talk without looking at her. His eyes were fixed on Turner, watching that fat face turn different colors of anger and maybe even shame. She hadn't known Turner felt much of anything except a need for food and sex, and she was caught listening and watching without paying enough attention to what was being said.

"Turner, this is how I see it." Blue kept his gaze off the woman, wanting to ignore her, make her mad enough to explode. "This woman you married, she's been lying to you. Or maybe you do know her past, picked her up out of some bordello for a night's fun and she sweet-talked you into marrying."

He'd been thinking on this, not seeing Turner as a man who killed for no particular reason. And all of Turner's loyalties were to his wife, well maybe not now after she so easily abandoned him in front of the law and the missus of the property. More than likely the man's pride was wounded along with his leg.

Blue pressed on; "You killed a man for her and she walked away. Maybe even you killed two men, good men from what I've learned. You make that square with your conscience yet? I'd hate to be living inside your head right now, with death on your hands and death coming for you."

Turner tried to roll away from Blue's gaze. He mumbled sounds Blue didn't understand, so he kept talking as if to himself, going over out loud what he'd been thinking on all night. "Now those prints; Patton and I we found the first ones in the brush, on the line of sight to where Mr. Tremont was back shot. Small prints, with a rough sole, scuffed and almost wiped out by larger prints, like a cowhand's heeled boots."

He waited then, still focused on Turner, whose head rolled on the wadded, stained pillow, his one hand picking at the rough bedding. "No." Turner lifted his head and glared at Blue, said it again; "No." The unbound wound began to seep blood and Blue held up the drying cloth, letting it swing back and forth.

"No what, Turner?" Blue grinned and felt mean doing it but the man was rattled enough to tell the truth. "No to you and those big feet of yours scuffing up the smaller prints? Now why would you do that, and how do I know it was you?" He waited then, leaning back to the wall, still not looking at the woman. He kept grinning broadly as if he had a powerful secret.

Blue opened his hand and the stiffened cloth folded on itself to lie tangled on the dirt floor. Blue bent down and hauled up one of Turner's boots, stained with Tuner's blood.

She spat at Blue with her words; "You leave Turner alone, he's hurt, maybe dying, you got no reason to pick on him." Blue laughed; "Ma'am." He drew out the word, tasting it. Then he turned back to watch Turner. "I remember what I'd seen when you knocked me down and kicked me. And before, when that colt. . . ." He couldn't go back to that moment.

Blue took a deep breath; "Funny how a man's mind will grab onto an odd detail even as some bastard's trying to kill him." Blue moved the boot closer to Turner's face, letting Turner's slow brain take in what Blue had said.

The man's voice was raspy; "What's got into you, Mitchell? I was defending my. . . ." Turner stopped, coughed, looked over at his wife and she didn't move, didn't come to him with any tears or sympathy. Blue found himself feeling sorry for the man until he remembered what had been done.

His voice was raw; "A nail's been set into that patch you've got on the outside of your foot, where the stirrup rubs. Most cowboys have that patch stitched on their boots, not many of them seal it with a nail. Handmade nail at that, you can tell from the square head. A word, Turner, if you're going to cover up a killing, or kill someone, don't wear those boots. They got your name on them."

Turner's breathing went slow, then in quick gasps and for a moment Blue thought the man would die right then. Turner's expression was thoughtful and Blue kept quiet. Turner was almost crying; "I didn't want to. . .Ridge."

Blue wasn't expecting the woman who came at him, one hand holding a knife. Not high overhead like most females or men who'd never been in a fight, but at her waist, pointed at Blue's gut and he twisted away from the knife tip and then away from Turner's reaching arm. He found himself trapped in a corner with a mad woman.

She faced him, the knife steady, a sexual smile on her face. It was violence that excited her, violence that brought her to Turner's bed. "Ma'am." The single word, respectable and out of place, startled the woman. "What?"

He kept at her; "You cut and drop me, leave me here, you leave Turner with another murder. Can't say that you love the man you married, you're so willing to use him and then throw him away." He was talking out of desperation, watching that knife, hearing noise coming from Turner, who must be trying to stand and the son was strong enough to pick up the bed frame to protect his wife. Blue laughed at the sheer stupidity of what he'd stepped into this time.

The woman yelled and lunged at him, Turner rolled out of the bed, twisting over his cuffed arm and the woman got slammed by his weight. They went down together, Turner on top of his wife, leg bleeding again, bed frame tilted and rattling, the mattress smothering both of them. The woman screamed then went quiet too sudden, and Blue guessed what had happened. He pulled the mattress off the tangled pair and Turner was dead, the knife driven into his ribs as if the woman knew exactly where to make the cut. Blue yanked her dead husband off the woman and she glared up at him, eyes filled with hate. He used her anger to find the last answers. "Why'd you have to kill Mr. Tremont? And why'd you make Turner kill Ridge? He didn't know anything about what you'd done, he saw those prints and they meant nothing to him. All Ridge wanted was to find out how fast the mustang could run. Hale and me, we were the ones who'd begun to figure it out. You killed a man for nothing."

He became aware of a form at the doorway, guessed it was Hale Patton but he kept his attention on the woman; waiting for her answer seemed to take forever. She sat up, drenched in blood, blood in her hair, on her face and clothing and Blue was tired of blood. He wanted to walk past her and out the door to clean air, a good horse, miles between him and this stinking place.

Her voice was filled with a strange pleasure. "That gentleman, Mister Tremont, he knew me from being a whore." Blue flinched. "He wanted me, said I could stay to the ranch, live married with Turner, as long as I pleased him a few nights a month. His wife was doing her duty when he asked, but she was tame and Madison he liked it rough."

These answers were more than Blue wanted to know, but he'd asked for an accounting. The woman sat up and pushed herself away from Turner's body with her feet, smearing more blood on the dirt floor. She did not seem to notice that Hale Patton stood behind her, listening to her confession.

Her voice turned dreamy, softness came across her face; "I wasn't going back to that life, I told him so and he laughed. So I let him think he'd won, and promised to meet him past the ranch at a stone hut where a sheep herder lived once. It still had a bed and two chairs inside that weren't too rat-chewed. The fool, he came from town in his fancy clothes, driving that team pulling the painted buckboard and he was something up there, all prettied and sweet-smelling just for me."

She studied Blue intently; her eyes were greedy, missing any sense of sadness, for the dead man at her feet or the story she was about to finish. "I got there and set myself in the brush, that's them prints you saw, I didn't think on them. Could only think of shooting Tremont, the son of a bitch wanted me for free. He wasn't going to pay extra or nothing. Nosir, I wasn't doing that again, not for free."

She wiped a hand across her face, pushing blood into dirt, painting her skin as if she was going to war. "It was easy shooting him. He made a good target in that fancy coat and that damned fool hat. I hit square first shot, and it was a sight to watch that hat fly up and come back down. If the team'd been moving slower, probably the hat would have fallen under their feet. I would have liked that. I never thought those chunk horses could pick up speed so fast."

He wanted to strangle this woman just as he'd scared her husband by tightening that shirt collar around his neck. Then Hale Patton cleared his throat, and the woman jumped, moving forward toward Turner where she got her hands on the knife rising from his side and slid it free, blade wavering until it found a target.

Blue had to kick the knife from her hands and as his boot connected with her wrist, he realized what she had intended; the knife blade had been pointed to her own throat.

CHAPTER SIXTEEN

The woman was a quiet prisoner. Hale used the cuffs he opened off her dead husband to clamp her arms together, and wasn't surprised that with only a small adjustment the cuffs fit. She was a sturdy woman, more muscle and meat than he'd first expected. Watching her fight Mitchell gave Hale an entirely new perspective as to the strength of females. He'd known this, simply hadn't seen it for a while. And he'd never had a female prisoner before.

He put Mitchell to work again, not listening when the man said he'd had enough of dead bodies and it was the law's work, not his. Hale refused him, shook his head that he wouldn't listen and Mitchell finally saddled up the mustang and rode around back of the tack shed and up to the door where Turner's body lay, drained of all blood, flattened and offensive.

Mitchell looped the end of his rope around Turner's two feet and set the brown backwards until Turner was skidded across the dirt. Hale turned away and felt his belly rise in protest. When he could, he studied Mitchell's face as the brown horse worked the grisly chore. The man showed Hale nothing, didn't look at him, didn't seem to be paying attention to what he'd asked his horse to do.

It was another burying, this time with Mitchell refusing to dig and since Hale was the only man left, it was his turn. It took a long time since it had to be a deep hole for the likes of Turner.

He had the woman chained to that same bed, mattress covered with an old blanket that Mrs. Tremont offered. Much to Hale's surprise, Mrs. Tremont managed to separate what Priscilla had done from having to sit on a blood-stained and rotting mattress. Hale wasn't sure what the process was in the lady's mind but he accepted the blanket with thanks, and again made his apologies for the horror of what she'd gone through. He even attempted to console her by putting out his hand, palm up, giving her the choice to accept his touch or remove herself from human contact. She pulled back, he frowned. "Yes, ma'am. I'll take this to Turner's widow."

Well old son, he thought on his way to the room hanging off the shed, you had a chance there and now it's gone. Hale shrugged, he never did think he would make much of a husband. And from what they'd all been through, no decent woman would stay on this murderous place.

As he went around the back of the barn, there was Mitchell roping out a fresh horse from the pen. It wasn't that mealy bay but the shiny gold buckskin. Hale raised a hand to Mitchell but the man pretended he didn't see. Hale couldn't blame him either. The man had been half-killed and lost a good horse, had a woman near to kill him and then had to drag her dead husband from his deathbed.

He wondered, stopping to watch Mitchell clean off the buckskin before saddling the bronc, he wondered what Mrs. Tremont intended to do with the ranch and its buildings, the poor land claimed for its stock, and the few horses with no one to ride them.

The team and the bay mare, and that steady sorrel too, she could get decent money for them. And the mealy bay wasn't worth more than turning loose to run wild. Some poor soul would catch up the horse and be surprised at how easy it was to break. Hale had taken note that Tremont's brand wasn't on any of the horses, and that was odd but then Madison Tremont had been known to be odd.

He might speak to Mrs. Tremont before he rode out tomorrow with the woman manacled to a saddle, for it would have to be the mealy bay that she rode. Hell, Hale thought, he wasn't riding with that bitch behind him on his good roan. She'd probably kill him and the horse before taking her own life.

He'd speak to Mrs. Tremont in the morning. First he had some explaining to do.

Mitchell was placing the saddle on that bright-colored wool blanket when Hale sat himself down on the near end of the log and spoke the man's name. He saw a shiver go across the man's back and guessed it was the only acknowledgement he would get. But he still needed to explain.

"Mitchell, I couldn't tell you. I needed to use your anger to get to the truth. That woman would never break if I talked to her, and I can't hit a woman, no matter what she might of done."

The cinch was drawn up, the buckskin grunted. Mitchell touched the buckskin's neck and waited, back turned. Hale picked through what he needed to say, knowing it could not be enough.

"You're right to be disgusted with me, for shooting Turner, and for telling you while she listened that the deaths were solved." He hesitated, studying the rigid back. "If she thought she was free, she would relax, and you always made her angry so I needed you. She hated you. Me, I'm this small man wearing a badge who couldn't get her to say a thing."

The bridle slipped easily over the buckskin's ears. Hale noted that it was a simple bit, no curb or chains but only a broken mouth piece. "Turner never could do what his woman had done, but he loved her enough to protect her when he found out. It was bad luck for Ridge, nothing more. Whatever the man had done in the past to make him fear me, it couldn't have been anything serious."

The shoulders went up, came down, the head turned enough that Hale could see the ruined scar, the still swollen face as the mouth worked out the thought; "Now it's done." Hale knew those few words were all he would get from Mitchell. Hale Patton stood up, nodded once; "You ride safe, Mitchell. Under different circumstances I think we could have been friends."

Blue rode the buckskin toward a windmill, another one of Tremont's eastern ideas. He could smell the cold water brought up from deep in the ground. He needed scouring, rinsing, ducking under water until all the filth of the past days were froze off him. His flesh felt alive, his skin itched even where he'd washed and scrubbed. Rinsed and washed again but it was under that damned pump where a man couldn't get truly clean.

This was new to him; he didn't mind riding for weeks, living with filthy clothes, combinations and shirts that smelled like him, but death got inside where hand-washing wasn't enough.

He still didn't know why a bath tub sat surrounded by cactus behind the Tremonts' barn. Now he'd never get to know. Blue let the buckskin pick up an easy lope and he sat quiet, enjoying the cupped sound of hooves hitting thick dirt. The horse moved smoothly, letting Blue shed worry and disgust as easily as the horse covered the short distance.

The captured water brought up by the windmill shimmered in a high-walled dirt fort; Madison Tremont's cowhands would have cursed as they dug and shape the tank to their Southern boss's expectations.

After hobbling the buckskin, Blue hopped on one foot to get the boot off, then was careful while he slid off the other boot, set the pair where they wouldn't get wet or let critters inside, and he laid his holey socks on top, protecting them as well. Then it was out of his hard-wool pants, with leather sewn down the length of his leg where he sat the horse. It saved on buying new pants too often, and helped him keep to the saddle on a high-standing bronc.

Still in shirt and combinations, Blue jumped into the dirt tank's water, and cried out as his body plunged in up to his chest. After a few minutes of life or death trying to draw in enough air, he began to float on the surface, relaxed by the fall sun overhead. It was noon, high sun telling him the hour and he couldn't believe it, wouldn't go back over what had happened in such a short time.

His shirt tails bubbled up over his lean belly, and his bare toes stuck out from the end of the combinations. Anyone watching would be studying a fool.

He'd been used, he knew it, knew it when Patton suggested Blue could bull ahead where the law was held back by the rules. It wasn't said but understood, that short of outright killing, Blue could force a confession from the suspects however it worked.

He'd been too successful. Hale Patton's apologies had helped, and changed his mind again about the man, but being used by Patton still bothered Blue. Maybe if he ran across the lawman in a year or two, he might be able to talk polite, but he was counting on never seeing Patton again.

Floating around in the water didn't get him clean so Blue stood and reached over to grab up clean sand. He saw the buckskin horse, whose gold head came up at the sight of a wet and naked cowhand hiding in the water. The horse's eyes showed white, the neck arched and the horse snorted, blew loud enough the sound traveled over the rushing water around Blue's belly and backside.

Then the horse snorted again, lowering his neck, shaking his head, and went back to grazing on the wisps of lush grass growing near the water.

Blue scrubbed around and under the clothes, whatever places he could reach that weren't too tender for sanding, until he finally felt that the water ran pale red with other folks' blood, the memory scraped off until he was clean. He stood up slowly; talking to the buckskin, then got out of the dirt tank and sat on a half-dead tree, waiting to dry.

A note was tacked to the fence of the pen where the buckskin's hay waited, when Blue and the horse got back from bathing. Blue thought he'd keep going south, or maybe turn himself around and go north again. It didn't matter. The traveling had been meant to put miles on the paint colt.

The note was simple, asking for his presence on the front verandah, at his convenience of course. And she would have provisions for him, that he might resume his journey in some comfort.

He'd been summoned for an audience with the queen. Blue laughed. One time in the quieter past, he'd swapped books with a well-read gentleman, and Blue had gotten some plays, written too long ago and using such fancy language that the reading of them was done out loud to whatever horse he had at the time.

Her note made him think of those plays, and the one night he'd shared camp with the old man. They'd talked about stars and distance, and the importance of words. The old man had been surprised that Blue could read. He took no offence; if it hadn't been for his mother, Blue would be as ignorant as most ranch hand and bronc' busters.

It took him time to brush down the buckskin and in doing so fresh dirt stuck to him, but for once it felt like his insides were clean and he could handle whatever came next.

"Please, Mr. Mitchell, sit here, next to me." She was gracious as usual. "You are indeed an unlikely knight, Mr. Mitchell, in both appearance and manner. Yet you have a finer instinct, which can be completely ignored by those with a far better education and upbringing." She flinched at her own words; "I hope I didn't insult you by my meanderings, Mr. Mitchell. My husband could never quite grasp the life you lead or its imperatives."

She was talking over her own discomfort, and he was betting that Hale Patton never told her why her husband had been killed. That was a good choice, Blue decided, and he thought better of the law.

"Mr. Mitchell, I am giving you that buckskin for two reasons." She hesitated; Blue almost grinned but felt it was wrong. "You and Ridge, you seemed to know each other. And I know he valued that horse. He'd asked Madison to find more like him, said that the ranch would be better served with good stock."

Now that was the truth, Blue thought. No one could want a mount like the mealy bay if the buckskin were close by. Even the big old plug that Cook had wandered off riding, that horse was far better than the mealy bay. "Yes, ma'am. Thank you."

Two reasons, she said. They hung in the quiet, the words she was struggling with until she coughed, raised a white handkerchief to her mouth and dabbed politely. "Mr. Mitchell, it is actually two more things I would ask of you." Good, he thought, the number'd been changed. It felt like an omen, and he sure could use the luck.

"I would like you to join me for a light supper. It will be my first time cooking in this kitchen and so please do not expect much." Her eyes were wide and Blue did grin at her this time. "Ma'am, I can make a good mess of eggs, if you've got some chile, and biscuits long as you got the flour. With bacon we'd have us a fine meal. And I'll show you some of the tricks."

Thinking on it, Blue had to laugh and she coughed again in trying to hide her own laughter; Blue Mitchell giving cooking lessons.

It was as if he'd offered to carry her somewhere she'd never been, like over the ocean to that place Europe, or to the top of a mountain no one had ever climbed. She smiled at him, without being careful or tempering the gesture. "Mr. Mitchell, what a fine offer. I noted that Mr. Patton has ridden out and that he took the bay horse you so obviously did not like. It is only the two of us here now. I hope that fact doesn't upset you."

He studied her, listening for her own fears or concerns. She smiled without anything behind it except good manners and ease.

"Ma'am, what else other than teaching you to make biscuits do you want me to do?" Her face became tight; "I have gone through Madison's papers and found a note signed in his hand promising money to Mr. Dorsey." If a woman could spit out a name, Mrs. Tremont would have launched the sound of Stephen Dorsey as far as she could.

"Mr. Dorsey's wife, you remember Helen Dorsey." It wasn't a question and he nodded, which was enough response. "She insisted that Madison had agreed to underwrite more of Mr. Dorsey's plans." Here was that firm, bitter voice again; Blue wisely held quiet.

"I want you to deliver a note from me to the Dorseys. And to see that it is signed by them. Acknowledging that I am giving over this ranch, but not the brand, to Mr. Dorsey in service of my husband's debt. I will not allow Madison's memory to be sullied by anything Stephen Dorsey or his wife might say about him not keeping a promise once made. On a handshake, mind you, as even I did not know about the note, and Dorsey had not signed it. However, I will allow nothing to ruin Madison's name."

This Blue understood, it was a matter of honor. He agreed, then changed the subject; "Yes, ma'am. Now about that supper." She smiled at him, a true gesture of delight. "Mr. Mitchell, I plan to set down on a chair in the kitchen and watch as you produce this miracle."

He slept easily for once, rolled up in a clean blanket, the ground well-padded with mounded hay, his coat making the perfect resting place for his head. The wound over the eye was healing but had added some width to the cut. It would be a spectacular mark. The scar under it was a half-moon shape, echoing the tip of the horse's front hoof, leftover from that earlier blow meant to kill him.

By remembering the past, Blue could push away all the anger and confusion of these few days. He wanted nothing more to do with people for a while, and of course the lady to the house, after watching him cook a quick and satisfying meal of eggs and side meat and light biscuits, well she wanted one more thing from him and he studied her as if amazed at her even asking.

The biscuits though, she'd made a fuss over them. And he admitted to himself they were better than usual. That came from having good flour, lard instead of drippings, and a clean place to do the work. She sat and watched as she said she would, and seemed amused by his ability to make up something so easily that tasted so good. A bit of salt, some baking powder, even rolling out and kneading the dough so the biscuits were light and high.

They sat at the small table in the kitchen, across from each other. She finally put her elbows up, held the steaming biscuit with both hands and chewed her way through while making pleased noises. Blue grinned once, and she pulled back, started to slide her elbows away, to return to proper manners and he chided her. "Ma'am. No one's looking, me I don't care. You enjoy now, it's your pleasure."

She seemed to study his face, making him conscious of his poor manners as he licked a bit of escaping honey from the corner of his mouth. It was foolish he knew, but the gesture, automatic and necessary, embarrassed him. The lady turned her head, looking away and then smiling back at him.

He told her the truth; "Ma'am, you're a nice woman to share a supper with, when you don't treat me like something you own." Instead of pulling away, or going all stiff and high-minded on him, she smiled. "Mr. Mitchell, Blue, that's the nicest thing a man has ever said to me." Then of course she told him the very last thing he needed to do for her.

He saddled the buckskin and eased the pack onto Keno, who snuffed at the load, sighed and lifted his tail. Nothing had changed, nothing murderous had happened as far as the brown mustang was concerned.

There were two papers stuffed in the saddlebags. One was a bill of sale for the buckskin, passing ownership to Blue despite the horse's fresh brand. That brand, Mrs. Tremont said, was about to go out of use unless someone would pay her extra for the privilege. She was returning to her ancestral home, rejecting the freedoms offered to a woman in the West. The bloodshed was too high a payment for ethereal practices such as speaking one's own mind or riding astride.

Unspoken between them was a question, a lack of understanding they shared. How could a woman kill in cold blood? How could that woman take a rifle belonging to the intended victim and place herself in a manner where she could shoot directly into his back, and then walk away untouched by a death she had delivered. The exact reasoning might be unknown to Mrs. Tremont, but Blue trusted his instinct that the widow knew some of the bitter details.

Blue was relieved when the second paper was handed to him and it was folded, stuffed in an envelope with initials engraved and intertwined on the back. Please, she said, in a return to the cultured tones, the stiff back and raised head that went with the voice, as if producing those particular sounds around the words demanded that posture and stiffness of jaw. Blue grinned at her, held his eyes on her a long time until she had the grace to laugh at herself. Her shoulders slumped, she asked for more coffee and maybe another one of those biscuits with honey for dessert.

Would he please, as she stuffed a biscuit into her mouth and honey slid onto two fingers and a thumb, would he take a signed deed, with her signature added as Madison's survivor, would he take the document to Mr. and Mrs. Dorsey, and then ride into Raton and see that the transfer was recorded? As a last request from her? Please. She did not wish to leave the recording of the transfer to Mr. Dorsey, as he was predisposed to changing land dimensions to suit his notion of what belonged to him.

Blue laughed and she laughed with him. It might be a peculiar way to describe a thief, but he would honor her request as it gave him a direction. He'd been north, had come from there to the eastern part of the territory. Raton was near that pass and he'd get back into Trinidad and head north and west this time.

Blue forced himself to listen. "Do this for me", she insisted, then hesitated and took a risk he imagined was a first in her life. "Blue." He touched her sticky hand. "Yes, ma'am."

As he swung up onto the buckskin's back and the horse squealed and threatened to explode, Blue felt that push inside him. A new place, two stops along the way to finish business and he'd pick a trail, find his way to a place where folks didn't shoot each other in the back. Then he laughed as the buckskin shook the reins and pinned his ears when Keno raised his head and whinnied.

EPILOGUE

Even as Blue knew what lay curved against sandstone and gullies, he was shaking his head at the foolish waste of building materials and money to create a showpiece few would see. The house was a matching of two different lives. Maybe the builder, the infamous Stephen Dorsey, meant it to be that way, to show to an indifferent world that he was indeed a success.

The fancy wagon and matched team, the high clothes and foolish hat had been Madison Tremont's statement to the world, better suited to whatever city he came from than the West that didn't care. These men thought they had the land tamed and harnessed but they'd had no idea what lay out here, miles of nothing shaped by wind and drought.

A man who had everything in the world couldn't bribe the skies to soak him to the skin. Couldn't banish snow storms, ice that froze their cattle, ears and muzzles and tails like icicles, whole herds froze and dead standing up against each other. Dead cattle leaning on a wire fence, piled three and four high in a desperate attempt to escape freezing winds. Money could do nothing against these forces.

Mr. Dorsey had arrived home just before Blue Mitchell came calling. Dorsey's fancy matched team was standing hip shot in a small corral. Poor hay was scattered at their feet, manure lay in dried piles against fresh manure. Those Dorsey hired didn't take care of the stock. Blue already didn't like him.

It was the man of the house who met Blue at the front door. Blue had to work at not grinning. Dorsey was too easy; a big belly pushing through a worn woolen suit coat open to a patterned vest.

Blue nodded to Dorsey, got a short nod in return. "Well?" "I've got papers for you from Mrs. Tremont," Blue said. Dorsey was blunt; "Give them here."

Son of a bitch wore a thick moustache and an air of grand intention that tired Blue. He let out a tight breath; "Mrs. Tremont wants me to witness you signing them, and I'm to take them to the land office in Raton to be recorded." He was glad she'd given him the words so that Mr. Dorsey couldn't use ignorance against him.

Then the wife appeared, shocked at first to see a ghost standing in her fancy hall, then remembering her manners and saying 'How nice it is to see you again, Mr. Mitchell.' She turned to her husband; "Dear, this is the gentleman who drove me over to offer my sympathies to Melinda on her tragic loss."

There was butter and molasses in her voice and no hint of the ugliness, the distance between the two women when Mrs. Dorsey was driven home. Blue kept his voice pleasant; "Ma'am."

They took him into a huge room with stuffed animal heads hanging on the walls. Blue swallowed a laugh. The table was enormous, with thick paws for legs. He gave Mr. Dorsey the papers and let the man read what he was to sign. Even an untaught cowhand knew that much.

Dorsey thought to protest; "But, but he was meant to give me. . . ." Mrs. Dorsey pressed her hand down on her husband's shoulder and the man stopped. With no more fuss he signed and had his wife sign on both sets of papers, and Blue bent down to scrawl his own name on a line that said 'witness'. Mrs. Tremont had explained the term to him and showed him where he was to sign. They had leaned close together and he grinned when she asked him if he could indeed write his own name. It was the first time he was legal in an undertaking. He hoped no one would try to find this 'witness' any time in the future.

He rode out feeling light and free, even slipped his hat and rolled it up into his hand before he asked the buckskin for a run, dropped the mustang's lead, knowing the good horse would follow on his own time.

It became a race, full speed roaring through him, whipping his hair into his eyes and mouth. There was nothing but wind and heat and the buckskin's harsh breathing, the lightness of hoof striking sand.

A small gully cut through the racecourse and the horse bellied down, took the ditch in stride before picking up greater speed. Blue yelled and behind him the brown mustang whinnied.

To read reviews of William Luckey's other books, and to follow Joe Evan and his horse as they walk from Pennsylvania to Nebraska, please go to www.waluckey-west.com

FAST HORSES

by

William A. Luckey

Published in 2010. The author may be reached at waluckey@cybermesa.com

to Mimi and Tom Sidwell,
and thanks as always to Heidi Hutchinson

1891

CHAPTER ONE

Blue Mitchell counted the years by horses; a paint colt that broke a leg and had to be killed, that was down in northern New Mexico in the fall. He'd been kicked pretty bad in the head a year, or was it six months before the paint; a time he never got straight since he'd skipped a month or two blind and unconscious. It was a chestnut stallion in Cimarron, a fancy-blooded horse that struck Blue over the right eye. Eventually he rode out of Cimarron in one piece, on the pacing brown mustang he still favored.

Time was measured through horses, rarely named, mostly remembered for one accident or another; they were how he calculated life. Each time he felt an ache, he could see the time of year, remember the horse's coat, winter coarse or slick from hot sun. Colors mingled together; bays and duns, a few paints, a number of sorrels, several good buckskins, a slow palomino and a brown pacing mustang.

Some earned him five dollars in coin for bucking them out and putting on a few manners. Others he bought and rode and then sold them a hundred miles away as trained. And they were trained. It was Blue's pride that he never sold a horse he wouldn't keep for himself.

As a kid he'd found safety with horses, away from his family and their squabbles. He had a brother and a sister, and maybe they were still alive. There had been a mother who cared, a violent father who bullied his family.

When Blue was twelve, his ma died and his pa put him on rank horses, swearing to their owners that his boy could ride anything. He got bucked off, stomped, rolled on twice, and began to figure there had to be an easier, even kinder way to deal with the scared animals.

It's what he'd sorted out on his own. He knew fear too well; his pa's raised hand, his mother's tears before her early death. Fear made him lonely and he used that knowledge to deal with frightened broncs. When he was fifteen, or so he thought, he rode out of the small ranch too far from the Lightning River in Wyoming, and never went back.

Now he was. . .Blue shook his head, it was odd. He couldn't remember his age, which had started this whole litany of horses and dates and times. He had to be almost twenty-five or older, pushing the useful life of those who thought to make a living from breaking horses.

Blue shrugged, then laughed, and the brown's ears came back and flicked forward. It was on to new pastures, different worlds, where horses waited for Blue's steady hand to train them.

He'd spent the winter in a livery stable in Colorado. A long cold miserable winter, but for the first time he didn't have the need to ride on; all he wanted was a warm place to sleep and time to heal.

The scar over his right eye filled in slowly; it had been a terrible wound but healing until the paint colt kicked him and tore a new scar over the old. The skin grew back slower this time, tender and occasionally bleeding. Now it was solid, no longer scabbed or weak.

In the beginning, he had headaches that crippled him, so he made a deal with the black-hearted and sour man who owned the livery and claimed rights to knowing all about horses and the fools who rode them. It didn't matter to Blue; a few stalls to be cleaned, throwing down fresh bedding, making a place for himself deep in the hay loft above the winter-stalled horses. The deal gave him time to sleep. What he earned cleaning the stables fed him two meals a day, and the light work kept him from stiffening up.

Eventually he rode some of the horses for Cobleigh, sanded down a few rough edges, taking more time with each horse. His own aches lessened, the head wound quit hurting and life despite Cobleigh's black heart held a few moments of ease and pleasure.

This time it had been a woman's dead husband that stopped Blue from riding deeper into New Mexico; instead he rode into a ranch yard and a crazy set of people intent on killing each other. He'd lost a paint colt and the future he'd seen, lost most of his sanity too, dealing with the widow and her flights of fancy. In turn he'd come away with a decent buckskin gelding and still had the brown mustang so he figured he wasn't that bad off.

It made Blue laugh to see himself this way, to try and understand how the world took note of his bruises and peculiarities and nodded its head, thought no more about him. The itch was back; it was time to ride away from Cobleigh and his orders and his ideas of how a man rode down and worked a horse. They hadn't seen eye to eye yet on horses, but it had been a good place to winter.

It came up quick, before Blue had the words to tell Cobleigh he was riding out. Cobleigh's voice was harsh; "Hey Mitchell, I got a rank one in last night. I'll pay you five bucks to ride him for me." Blue stretched and felt the edges of old hay stick through the blanket into his back. He woke this way near to every morning when he rolled over, trying to hold the comfort of that last bit of sleep.

He sat up, rubbed his free, careful still around the scar, and decided that he'd ride this last horse for Cobleigh. Blue owed the miserable son of a bitch for the days he hadn't been able to work.

Cobleigh demanded some kind of response so Blue sat up, shook his whole body, waited a moment before he tried to stand. "What's wrong with the bronc?"

Mitchell's question was Cobleigh's answer; yeah Mitchell would ride the horse but in his own peculiar manner and Cobleigh wasn't yet convinced it was the right way. Still, the *horses that the drifter saddled were usable in the livery string, and now and again he sold one to a rancher or townsman wanting a well-mannered ride. Cobleigh found it was good business and it was a challenge he enjoyed, to keep buying up the rough stock, seeing how far he could push before Mitchell and whatever bronc it was this time, finally parted company.*

It wasn't that Mitchell couldn't top off the rank ones, it was that he wasted time setting in the corral, watching the horse, then fiddling around with a rope and too much talking, nothing that made any sense to Cobleigh, when he had the time to watch and listen.

Business was pretty good in Rocky Ford and getting better as he paid the fancy horse-tamer with a few bucks. Cobleigh liked the arrangement and thought he might of found a shack near the town's edge where Mitchell could live permanent and keep working for him. Sleeping in the barn could give a man ideas about moving on come better weather.

Cobleigh couldn't decide if he liked Mitchell, admired his talent, or thought little of him for his drifting ways. The man had come through Cobleigh's town before, but he'd had enough money and a place to go, so he wouldn't stay and work for keep, just paid up for the night and was gone in the morning. Still, the man's reputation was talked about, and ranchers came in to Cobleigh's stable just to take a look at the wild-eye, yellow-haired bronc rider of some fame. That fact alone put money in Cobleigh's hands.

Knowing a bit about Mitchell and his ways told Cobleigh he'd best up the pay, and offer the house to keep the man hired. What he did with the rough stock purely amazed Cobleigh though he hated admitting it; the results weren't magic but close to it.

The new challenge was a big son of a bitch maybe fourteen hundred pounds and close to sixteen hands. He carried draft blood, you could see it in the feathers on his cannon bone, the lump of forehead between the wide-set and large eyes, and the heavy, divided rump with its sloping croup.

A black was always a good seller; a man with some money and wanting to be noticed liked a solid black horse. This big son, he fit the bill except no one could ride him. The cowhand that brought in the horse said the bronc fought dirty and might best get him sold to a Wild West show. It wouldn't be much of a profit but it would keep would-be horse tamers out of the hospital or an early grave. Cobleigh paid the cowhand five greasy dollars for the horse. Five bucks now for Mitchell and he could have him a fifty-dollar horse in a few days.

Mitchell moved slowly through the stables, taking with him the tin cup of bitter coffee Cobleigh had waiting. A few moments of watching the new animal and then the two men would bargain and settle.

The big horse circled a high-fenced corral, about the only thing that would hold him. Blue laughed, a man couldn't do much else. Cobleigh bought himself a monster and wanted a quick ride. Blue went back into the livery and found Cobleigh sitting in his cramped office, horseshoes piled in a corner, three bridles dumped near a chair. Feet up, hands behind his head; "What you thinking 'bout that bronc, Mitchell? Ain't he a wonder!"

Blue poured out a second cup of coffee, laced it with tinned milk and took a long swallow. Cobleigh hated to be kept waiting.

"The price goes up on him, Cobleigh. You may see shiny dollars in that black hide but there's a whole lot more to him. You look at his eyes, you study those feet. Hell man, the horse ain't worth more than a few flank steaks and a fancy cured hide to warm the floor."

Now that made Cobleigh mad. Mitchell could ride a horse, get him reining and backing and all those damned extras a cattleman wanted. Cobleigh'd been in the business a long time and no one questioned his choice when it came to judging horseflesh.

He let the chair slam to the floor, put his hands flat on the desk. Both men watched the dust fly up, slowly settle back. Cobleigh sneezed. "You ride that son of a bitch for ten dollar and then we'll talk 'bout who knows what and anything else comes to mind." There were times when he hated that face, the blond hair grown out and tied back with rawhide, the long jaw, loose body, and those heated eyes that looked straight into a man and always knew too much. He'd wanted to punch out Mitchell a couple of times this winter; one more comment about his ability to pick a good horse and the man'd have him a broke nose.

Cobleigh knew he was thinking plumb foolish; "Mitchell, you get paid to ride that horse." Mitchell didn't back down; "He ain't worth it." Flat out, no give. "High dollar?" "Can't go high enough." "I'll fire you." Mitchell shrugged. Cobleigh was getting downright mad. "You ready to saddle up and get out?" That damned smile opened the man's face and Cobleigh knew he'd lost. A shake of the head, blond hair flipped back, a shrug. The blue eyes glowed; "Any time."

Cobleigh hated being bested but he was too smart to let the man leave and lose a good business deal. "Twenty for a few day's work, don't know how you can pass that up, Mitchell. It's more'n a decent cowhand gets in two weeks."

The son of a bitch grinned, agreeing with an easy shrug. "The deal is time, you leave me to do my work, Cobleigh, no more standing outside the fence telling me where I'm going wrong." Cobleigh accepted the offer, then laughed as Mitchell left the office. He'd already begun his real money-maker, getting the locals to make bet on when Mitchell rode the bronc and a few takers on how long the man hung on before the big black tossed him.

This horse business wasn't a bad way to make a living. Cobleigh got up to pour the dregs of boiled coffee into his cup, and maybe a shot of whiskey to set everything right in his stomach.

Blue leaned against the corral rails and studied the horse. It was a big son, and stout. On that much he and Cobleigh agreed, but the stare Blue got in return from those large dark eyes, the snorting, a front hoof pawing the corral dirt; Blue had his own ideas about this one. More'n likely it was left too long a stud, probably had a year or two of running with a band and he sure wasn't going to get over the insults man did to him. Taking him from the mares, cutting him, trying to make this rank bronc behave like a regular saddle horse and the black would have none of it; no wonder the cowhand who brought the horse to Cobleigh was glad to get rid of it for whatever small amount the horse trader paid him.

Blue caught up a rope halter tied to a long line and went inside the corral. He leaned on the fence there, holding the halter as a puny weapon against the black's strength. The horse snorted and trotted to the far side of the corral, turned and studied Blue. It was a stand-off; horse as interested as human in what the opponent offered.

Blue walked toward the horse, halter and lead coiled over his left arm. One way to find out was to go straight for the head. The black side-stepped, then hesitated as Blue slowed but kept walking toward the point of the black's shoulder and the black swung his head around as Blue slid the rope end over the crested neck. The horse seemed to grow larger, lifting his massive head above Blue's reaching arm.

He grabbed the nose at the soft cartilage and pushed, released and pushed again and the horse seemed surprised, bringing his head down to sniff at Blue's hands. The halter slipped on easily, and would not reach over the black's poll to tie at the throat. Damn; he caught the rope swinging off the neck and fashioned it into a loose halter, dragging the useless one at the wrong end.

The horse wouldn't budge; Blue pushed on a shoulder, one front hoof took a half step sideways and then the horse shook its head. Blue pulled the head to him and the black tried to bite his arm. But the horse would not move. After ten minutes of push and pull but no forward steps, the black tired of the game and stood quietly while Blue tried to rub feeling back into his arm. He tugged again and this time the black followed him, head lowered, no resistance and while three men standing outside the corral cheered, Blue had the distinct sense that the horse was plotting the next attack.

He glared at the men, and one of them explained the interest; "Mitchell, bets're all over town on you and this 'un. Better get used to having an audience." Blue turned his back to the men, slid down a saddle blanket from under his saddle thrown over the top railing. Working slowly, no quick moves, he rubbed the wool over the horse, back and quarters, under the belly, front legs, over the crested neck, down to cover the ears and eyes and the horse offered nothing. Blue didn't like the attitude. He wanted some attention, some spark of anger or fear, anything but indifference.

'Think I might change my bet' came from one of the men; Blue bent down, found a rock and threw it at the gathered cowboys. There was laugher and the men scattered, with a few offhand and rank comments about Blue losing to the big horse, and the only betting was on when and how bad.

The black was a puzzle; at times he'd lead, turn, stop in a most agreeable manner, then Blue would ask for a turn to the right and the horse would rear, or strike out at Blue. Then walk on as if nothing had happened. The son of a bitch could be obliging but only on his terms.

It was going to be hell riding the horse. No way around it. Blue eased off the make-shift halter and walked away from the horse, slid out through the barely opened gate. He'd fix up a halter that fitted the black, and set out hay and water. But he would make no attempt to become friends with the horse. He would simply treat him with a respect the black had quickly earned.

Nothing ever showed in the dark, calm eye even as the horse tried to catch Blue with a massive front hoof. Blue didn't *bother spanking the horse or chasing him with the rope. The rebellion went deep, far enough into the animal that Blue doubted he could work the horse until he was safe to ride.*

Blue woke in the dark, nothing in particular to catch his attention as he lay rolled in his blankets, eyes picking out the narrow boards that framed the loft in the livery, ears hearing the differing rustles of tied horses, varmints, a mule lying down and snoring. Nothing was different from all the nights he'd slept in Cobleigh's hayloft, away from the wind and snow of a bad Colorado winter.

He woke 'cause he'd been dreaming of the black horse. He knew that horse was outside in a corral, fed and watered. Blue had groomed the black for about ten minutes and the black had obviously enjoyed the attention, whickering at Blue when he left, but Blue had no belief in the black turning mild. It was a command, a 'come brush me again' nicker and not about surrender.

Cobleigh had made him angry of course, saying the horse was ready to ride. The man purely didn't know much about a horse bad as this one. Blue had let him know; "So you're betting on an early ride and you're going to lose." He thought maybe then Cobleigh would fire him and he'd walk away in one piece but the man only tipped that damned chair back and grinned and Blue felt like cursing and didn't because his words would do nothing but please the livery owner.

Damn them all for betting on a man's life. Blue closed his eyes and in his mind the heavy body, the massive head and thick neck stood over him, a front leg pawing, telling him what was to come.

A few more hours of restless sleep and Blue got up to fumble through the dark and make coffee. He wanted to sit outside where stars and a few lights in distant houses let him see the movement of the black horse. The animal endlessly paced the corral's circle, head resting barely on the top rail, eyes glaring, nostrils opened. The black snorted when he sensed Blue's presence even as the pacing continued.

Blue settled on a flat tree stump, a place where other men sat to talk with Cobleigh, brag about the value of their own horse while they ran down Cobleigh's offering; men who enjoyed the bargaining as much as the new horse or the small profit both of them hoped to make.

He tossed out the coffee dregs and went back into the barn. The black snorted, then reared and that was Blue's final memory before he closed the flat door. A shadow, outlined against stars and the tops of trees, of a black horse carrying an indignant rage.

Cobleigh studied Mitchell as the man went about morning chores, washing up and drinking more of that fouled coffee. He nodded and stalked off toward the café and Cobleigh scratched his head. Mitchell didn't seem to have much to say and Cobleigh wanted a report, something for the bettors coming in to place their money, wanting to know each day's progress.

The whole damned town, winter-sick and ready for action, was heating up on the black and Mitchell, getting to a place Cobleigh liked where talk and a couple of drinks and some loud bragging brought in more bets. He watched as Mitchell returned from a quick meal, went to the corral with that damned outsized halter he'd rigged up, and a lead. No riding today, the man was that predictable, and Cobleigh shook his head. Damn but he wanted those bets to come in.

The horse greeted Blue with a rubbing of the head, a muzzle pushed into Blue's cupped hands and it was a simple matter to halter the animal, coil up the lead and swing onto the wide back. The black shivered, froze, then responded to Blue's legs asking for a walk.

There weren't any onlookers, which pleased Blue. Cobleigh, he was most likely staring out the filthy window from his office, mad clear through that no one was here as witness. Blue wondered who had today, early morning, as their bet. More'n likely no one, for it'd be damned foolish to ride the black so soon, and even crazier without using a saddle and a heavy bit, to most folks' opinion.

The horse was agreeable to a good walk, a slow trot, then a soft lope that surprised Blue. Horses this size were usually flat-footed and hard to balance but the black only grunted and kept to a slow stride and Blue felt himself relaxing, letting his legs hang, moving with the horse who showed no signs of fight.

Quietly, with no resistance, the black traveled both directions of the corral; stop, back, stand, move on into the lope again and Blue came to enjoy the horse, not trusting him yet, not till a saddle went on over a thick blanket, cinched and settled. But the horse had more promise than he'd first thought. He slid off the dark hide and the big head came around, as if checking who had been sitting on his back. Blue rubbed the soft nose and the dark eye was calm, the ears relaxed. Just maybe this was possible.

Cobleigh met him at the barn; "You ought'n to ride that son with no gear. It don't do much for teaching him." Mitchell cocked his head and those damnable eyes were glowing. The gaze made Cobleigh mad clear through; "He'll kill you one of those rides."

Blue wasn't fooled by the obviousness of Cobleigh's concern. He answered back, maybe not the smartest thing he could do but Cobleigh rubbed him wrong. "Mr. Cobleigh I didn't know you'd mind a good bucking death. That big a fight would bring in more bets for your pocket." They stood too close, glaring at each other, Cobleigh knowing the man would ride out soon; he'd had enough of the back talk, wouldn't have no man working for him didn't take him as the boss. Still, he recognized that Mitchell was enjoying his war with the black and wouldn't leave until the horse was riding decent. Or maybe Mitchell was crippled. Hell, Cobleigh thought, he didn't want a cripple hanging around the livery.

Then again, he liked the bets coming in and he'd wait until the fight was over. Blue grinned at him and Cobleigh wanted to punch the son of a bitch.

He knew it soon as he dragged out the saddle, and fitted a bridle to the black's head. He'd made an extra piece and cut it into the headstall so the bridle would fit, and even found a bar bit Cobleigh used on a work team to settle in the black's wide mouth. It wasn't much of a bit, but the horse would run through anything put in his mouth. Blue already knew that as a plain truth; force would do nothing to the black except make the horse fight harder.

The bridle went on, the black chewing, then holding the bit as if fine with the idea. An extra large blanket was smoothed over the broad back, saddle on, latigo let out to go 'round that massive belly. No trouble doing up the cinch, in fact the horse brought his head around and rubbed against Blue like the whole gearing up was nothing but interesting.

He climbed on, taking a moment to find the off stirrup before he shifted his backside into the deep seat. The black hardly moved his weight as Blue sat, both boots in the stirrups, hands on the split reins, a light feel to the black's mouth.

Cobleigh had gone out of town and told Blue not to ride the bronc while he was gone. Blue had shrugged, Cobleigh's timing didn't matter, he'd do what he wanted when it was right. And he knew Cobleigh had no thought but to produce more bets. It didn't matter to Cobleigh when the black got ridden, only that he had enough bets down to win either way.

One man stood near the corner of the livery, hand raised to his mouth with a smoke, eyes turned away from the corrals but he wasn't fooling Blue, he was waiting for the explosion.

The black horse finally obliged; he bogged his head with a squeal and uncorked a high-flyer buck, then straight back and up in a rear, balanced on the hindquarters, those strong legs wide and steady, Blue feeling easy up that high. He kept his weight forward, hands talking to the black, who shook his head and came down hard as Blue leaned back, kicked the ribs until the black shook, leaped high again, bogged his head and went forward and sideways, slamming them both into the corral fence which shook, the top rails barely holding.

Blue steered the bronc away from the fence, felt the horse sit back, half-rear and then hop forward like nothing he'd ridden before. Without warning, the horse leaped straight up and above the fence rail, pulled the reins through Blue's hands and kicked out and Blue leaned, pulled up on the bridle reins, threw his left arm back and the horse screamed in rage, came down hard and ran the corral fencing, kicking out and rattling more rails.

There were three men watching now; Blue damned them as he leaned on the outside rein and caught the horse's head against a post. The horse jammed to a stop, and briefly Blue had hopes until the horse reared up and went over backwards; no holding, no balancing or time to jump. The fence saved Blue as it caught the horse across the neck and held long enough Blue slid out, left foot caught in the stirrup but away from the weight as the fall slammed him on packed dirt.

He heard the fence give, saw the post buckle and then snap like a twig breaking under a man's boot, leaving nothing to hold the black's weight, which flattened into the ground, sending broken wood pieces and dust in a high cloud.

The boot twisted free, Blue crawled on his hands and knees, fell on his face, groaned but was clear. Behind him he felt and heard the flesh drop, the ground rattle. He coughed, choked, lay flat.

When he heard the shot, he knew the truth and half-raised himself, then laid his face back in the dust, not caring. Damning himself for wanting to beat the odds. And it was the black horse that paid for his poor judgment.

207

CHAPTER TWO

Cobleigh never made good on the bets; no one had thought the contest would end this bad. He had a man unconscious for two days, a horse shot in the head whose carcass pulled down the whole corral. The spill had broke both front legs. The whole match was a waste of time and horseflesh and nothing to show for it. No one to yell at for Mitchell was still at the doc's, laid out on a narrow bed in the back room, muttering at times and the doc said if he woke up soon, he'd more than likely be fine. Nothing was broke so there was nothing for the doc to fix.

Cobleigh had to give back the money and for all his hard work, he had nothing but a mound of rotting horseflesh and a bronc buster laid out costing him money. Cobleigh was mad clear through to his backbone.

His headache was the first thing he remembered, then the big horse coming back on him, the smell of rank dirt, sweat and fear, dust making him cough. Hurt like hell to cough, in his chest and rib, and inside his head. He was back where he started; flat out on a bed not sure what might happen next.

Tom Cobleigh took care of that; the stable owner came in when the doc said it was all right and looked at Blue. Shook his head; "You cost me a horse. You owe me, Mitchell. Here I give you room and work all winter and you kill a horse for your sorry hide. I take back every good thing I said 'bout you and your riding, your rep's gone, mister, I got men out spreading the word."

Blue sat up, swung his legs over the thin mattress edge, look at his bare feet showing below the combinations. He was almost indecent, and it would be easy enough to accept Cobleigh's estimation of him. But he wasn't going to let Cobleigh win this round. Blue had thought on paying out any debt, and had made his choice. He was little more than the worth of his word, and it galled him but he needed to stand and make good on the dead horse.

"Cobleigh, you take that buckskin of mine in trade for the black. You knew when you got the horse, you knew how he'd be and you tried to make a killing off me and him fighting it out." He paused, finding the words thick and bitter; "You set us both up and you know it. That horse had no chance; he should have been turned loose and left to run wild. I owe you only 'cause I was fool enough to try riding that black. Me, I always pay my debts."

He heard nothing from the man; Blue looked up, which took some considerable doing 'cause his neck hurt almost as much as his head. Cobleigh's face was white, his smooth hands reaching for each other. "I'll take that buckskin, Mitchell. It's a fair trade." Blue waved a hand in front of him, palm toward Cobleigh as if to erase the man's face. "Yeah, a fair trade."

It surprised him that the massive black horse had not destroyed his gear. He picked the saddle up, rested the cantle above his knee, pulled hard on the horn and nothing gave so the tree wasn't splintered. He'd spent one of those long winters to the eastern plains of Colorado making this saddle, and he'd hoped the tree could stand up to 'most anything.

He would pack what gear he could on the brown gelding. First he needed to go over everything to check for damage. At times his fingers would touch a deep gouge on the saddle skirting and he'd remember that black falling on him, the cracking fence, and know that the saddle hadn't received the worst of that battle.

The brown seemed glad for the activity. Getting going was what this horse did best. And Blue was ready to move on. Good sense would have had him walk away from trying to ride the black horse, common sense that had other men betting on him, or the horse, but knowing themselves not to try riding the outsized bronc.

But common sense was a wrong-labeled idea that didn't fit, Blue decided. He'd know that a long time ago, when he turned twenty-one in a barnyard in Tucson, lying on his back having just won a lop-sided fight.

Cobleigh tried to get Blue to pay the doc's bill but the old man refused Blue's dollars and turned to the livery owner, angry clear through. "You thought to make a pretty penny on this man, you pay his bill or I ain't letting you through the door ever again when one of your own sorry horses gives you a good kick." Quite a mouthful but the doc won out and Cobleigh paid.

Horses had their own sense of things; the buckskin wouldn't care who rode him as long as he got fed. The loss of the horse meant little to Blue other than the memory of a good man who'd put the first training on the handsome animal.

The brown mustang would let Blue catch and saddle him and no one else. He had to keep the horse by default, and here too a debt was owed; the horse had won him good money on most races. He'd be a fool to pick the buckskin's beauty over the practicality of the shaggy brown.

He rode out a week after waking up, even with Cobleigh suddenly deciding that he and Blue could still work a deal, Blue could break some of the range stock ranchers wanted to sell him but weren't biddable for common folk. Blue thanked Cobleigh, said no, he was done with bronc-riding. They didn't speak of death or dying.

Cobleigh nodded as if it made sense to him; Blue was getting slow to stand, stiff in the cold mornings, a limp left over from a badly healed leg break and an ancient bullet wound deep in the thigh. Cobleigh never asked but it was obvious to the livery owner that past wounds were aging the man. Cobleigh was better off taking the buckskin and get himself shed of any obligation as to what might happen next.

The buckskin would get left behind, and there was a few surprising coins in Blue's saddlebags, a bedroll and a new slicker tied on. The gifts seemed out of place coming from

Cobleigh, but Blue guessed the gesture was to settle the man's uneasy conscience.

 Before he rode out from the small town, Blue spent a few of those coins on a shave, haircut, and a spring bath. Seeing his own face too close in the mirror unhinged him; lines at the eyes and mouth, eyes no longer that deep blue-green that had always gotten him in so much trouble but paler now, the whites more red, blood vessels broken from rough rides and worried sleep.

Blue told the barber to shear the uneven hair, which left blond strands piled on the floor. What remained on Blue's head had more than its share of gray. He pushed the mirror away, told the man he'd done a good job with the poor material to hand.

All the time the barber wanted to talk, about watching that black monster in the corral and knowing it was too dangerous for any man. Blue wouldn't listen, gave no answers, said nothing even when the man asked him to his face wasn't he glad the black was dead and didn't that death keep the horse out of his dreams. The man had no idea, no sense of a horseman's life; cutting hair and watching the rough stock didn't make for excitement but it kept a man alive and moving straight, not twisted and broken.

He took a bath after the shearing, and while it made him smell better, or not stink quite so bad, being naked made him relive the damage done to weak flesh and he remembered each fight. He was nothing but flesh leaned down from a bad year, each rib and hip looking like a winter-starved bronc, which in a way he guessed was as good a description of Blue Mitchell as any ever given.

Warm water was a pleasure but it weakened a man, made him light-headed and soft, fingers wrinkled, toes curled up. Given a choice Blue would choose to swim in cold water high in the mountains, and not be among folks curious about him, wanting to stop him in town and talk about that black horse or any horse. He'd had enough of humans and their picking at him. Just curious, they always said, wanting to know is all.

It felt good to be outside in the chilled air and sun, wind again on his face, no stink of wet straw and frozen waste, only distance and grasses and once in a while, too damned often for him, fences of that damnable wire. Blue thought on life and living as he rode the mustang, headed north still, but the days were warmer, and the nights almost bearable.

It was all around him, mankind claiming what had once been wild. Blue understood the need for fencing, since he'd already experienced the terrible consequences when cattle drifted ahead of a storm. The fence lines made year-round riding jobs for cowhands, using a team and sledge to pull hay out to the herds, keep them close in, no drifting to pile up at the fences and freeze. No more need to skin stinking flesh in the new spring warmth, leaving thawing mounds to rot under the summer heat.

The hunting was still decent enough in these plains, and there were herbs and wild greens that Blue knew to eat. It'd be hard for him to starve unless he gave up on himself and didn't try. Riding out helped during the first hours; feeling the good mustang's stride took away much of his sadness. Until he began thinking again and that was poison enough to interrupt even the best spring day.

When he listened to his private thoughts, not spoken out loud to the restless mustang but ringing inside his head like old church bells, he knew he was feeling sorry for himself so he did what came to mind, put his heels to the brown's sides and let the rank horse run. The footing was good, a nice slow road with no great turns or bends, no trees to jump, no deep gullies to catch a hoof and pull horse and rider down.

The brown took the challenge; it was his life, his whole being, to run carrying this particular rider who often seemed to be confused except when it was time to race.

That first day and night of traveling, horse and rider covered maybe thirty miles, and when Blue unsaddled in the dark, close to a bent pine and not too far from a noiseless stream, he felt the brown's frame, backbone too sharp, lungs breathing hard. Thick foam had soaked through the bright wool saddle blanket, and Blue served his punishment by sleeping under its salty weight. He woke shivering, while the brown was dozing maybe ten feet away, eyes closed, ears loose, lower lip hanging. The brown too looked old and tired, yet when Blue spoke the brown's name, 'Hey, Keno', the horse lifted his head and nickered.

He made enough effort to build a fire and boil coffee in the morning, set out a trap for a rabbit rather than eat beans, but when it came time to saddle and ride, Blue lay back down, rested an arm over his eyes. The thumping of a hobbled horse searching out better graze was a gentle music that put Blue back to sleep.

Somewhere in the second week of traveling Blue recognized that his strength and the mustang's endurance had improved. He saddled up one morning and got a hump in the mustang's back, a grunt and a wicked look in the brown's eye. Blue grinned; he'd been waiting for this moment.

It wasn't much of a show, the fight was more for their pleasure than to dislodge a rider or settle a horse, and for that Blue was thankful, as his head told him he could be in trouble. He got the brown lined straight to a distant ridge and had enough breath to whoop and holler as the mustang flattened into a decent run.

Two nights later he bedded down near a spring. Giving in to temptation, and conscious now of his own stink since he'd had the luxury of that town bath, he shucked out of his clothes and boots, even hung his hat on a nearby bush and splashed water where it was most needed, yelled with the chill, laughed at the brown's distressed whinny, and sat a moment bare-assed on a slab of rock. It held some of the sun's heat and kept him warm as he dried off.

Camp was simple; another bagged rabbit slow-roasted over a fire, meat chewed, marrow sucked from the bones. The brown mustang grazed, hobbled of course, but tearing into good grass and rarely stopping except to rub his nose on a front leg, ridding himself of a pesky fly.

Blue came out of a deep sleep to early daylight and a noisy quarrel. He sat up reaching for his rifle set close by, the brown was headed towards camp with hobbled leaps, eyes showing white, tail flipped over his back in agitation. The noise was ungodly; a deep guttural call that rose to a squawk combined with the yips and rolls of a coyote howl.

Blue looked for the sound, and laughed. A coyote ran low to the ground, hair around its neck standing straight up. It held a bone in its teeth, a thighbone from last night's supper. Above him a grandfather raven, black as the night and wings wide enough to scare the devil, was diving against the coyote's run, scraping the coyote's back with his talons, screeching and scolding as if the coyote had stolen the raven's last meal.

When Blue quit laughing, he pulled out his clothes from the bedroll and climbed into them, sat down to pull on his boots, and by then the coyote was long gone. The raven found a perch in a stunted piñon tree and was gently scolding Blue as if the entire ruckus had been of his making.

Blue nodded to the raven as he tightened the cinch on the brown; "Grandfather, you've earned whatever's left of that old rabbit. He didn't give up much flesh, but there's the lights if you want them, in the bush over there. Us humans don't eat those parts less we're starving." The raven cocked his head and watched as Blue swung up on the brown. When horse and rider were safely out of range, the raven slipped down from his perch and hopped to where Blue had thrown the grisly entrails.

They traveled the rolling land north and west, moving easily in the same pattern; a day's hard ride, a day's rest. Hunting brought down a pronghorn, a few rabbits, once a mule deer that he gorged on, then smoked and dried great strips of meat. The brown put on muscle and stamina, and his old cantankerous attitude returned; Blue added muscle and found a rare peace. The black horse's ghost was gone, left behind in long miles and quiet evenings.

There were too many towns, and too few ranches. When it was necessary, to eat or use tools to reset a shoe on the mustang, Blue would work with a scared bronc on the ground, no more strange saddles for him, or do some shoeing, repair gear, mend fence, anything for a meal and a night's rest. He'd become a saddle bum, a grub-line rider, and for the moment it was enough.

The land was uniform; reddish soil, scrub grasses, nothing to look at while dreaming about herds of fine horses racing over the endless hills, but enough to raise decent cattle. He'd find small groups of white-faced cows and their babies standing around the well-trampled water holes, or a windmill that hissed in the wind and pumped water through a long pipe to a dirt tank or metal pond.

Windmills and Blue were old friends; he'd taken advantage of the underground water to wash off too many killings. Now he figured to ride from one to the next; they stood tall and flashing and were a good guide to keep headed west. Wire fences often barred the way but a pair of wire cutters and a simple repair made passage easy.

A few years back carrying wire cutters on a man's saddle could get him hung for a cattle thief. Heated they could free-draw the wrong brand. Blue kept his cutters deep in a saddlebag and wished he had a packhorse.

A passing rider told him he was in Nebraska territory and the wild town of Scott's Bluff was ahead if he dropped down a mile or two. The rider winked and grinned and said you could find a good time there, you had the coin and the need. Blue nodded and reined the brown west, toward Wyoming where he'd come from so many years ago. He'd been a kid, almost a man at fifteen, tired of beatings and doing hard work for no pay. It must have been 1880, maybe earlier – it didn't matter except that the years had passed with him doing the same work and now doing nothing, still for no pay.

He was souring again, so he picked the brown up into a lope and when they crested a ridge, there were three horses, a deep bay, a buckskin, and a dark dun. One looked to be maybe a two-year-old, one a mare heavy in foal. And a stallion wearing no brand Blue could see; from blooded stock though, that was easy to judge. This escaped stallion looked to be one of those horses bred for speed; thin clean legs, strong hindquarters, a natural arrogance in those dark eyes.

Blue reined the brown toward the three horses. He guessed he was taking a risk again, for a stallion with one mare could think up almost any reason to challenge a new enemy.

The stallion turned and raised his head, snorted loud enough that the brown hesitated; the buckskin mare walked in a ponderous circle, the dark dun colt took several steps forward and then stood sideways in front of what had to be his mama as if protecting her.

The mare was an unbranded escapee and it'd been years since a curry or harness had touched her, but the white marks against her withers, and the signs of a poor-fitting collar told him she'd once pulled a plow that stirred up dust in this godforsaken land, while the mindless destruction grew few crops and folks left, turning loose their unwanted stock.

The colt was well built for a two-year old; he carried a good lean neck, high withers and a short back, strong quarters. His papa'd been something more than a throwback mustang.

Then Blue patted the brown mustang and considered how he could drop a rope over the wild colt's neck. The mustang pinned his ears as if he could hear Blue's thoughts.

He reined the brown sideways, knowing the stallion would challenge their presence to protect his small band. So Blue waited. The horse was a dark bay with no white, carrying too much weight and it was obvious he hadn't been long in the wild. He wasn't particularly threatened by one horse and rider, which meant he was used to other horses around him.

Blue moved the brown forward slowly as he laid out his rope, fashioned a loop, threw a houlihan and that soft loop slipped itself over the stallion's neck like nothing more than catching out a good cowpony for a day's circle to check fence.

What came then wasn't quite what Blue expected; the bay stallion felt the squeeze and pull, and reared, pawed at the rope while Blue dallied. Then the stallion charged. No setting back, no more fight, no head shaking and squealing and trying to run backwards but a charge straight at the saddled mustang and Blue.

Blue reacted almost as quick as the brown; together they turned and ran. Blue felt the pull of the rope over his thigh then it loosened which wasn't good for it meant the stallion was catching up. He clamped his legs to the mustang's sides, dug in his spurless boots and cursed being too lazy to buckle them on each morning. He could hear their chatter, the jinglebobs hitting each other tucked in his saddlebags. They weren't doing much good packed away.

"Damn it, Keno. Run." After a half mile he felt the rope again, high against his hip, taut and painful. This time it meant the stallion was slowing from the mustang's gallop. So he eased up on the brown, let him settle to a lope and took the risk of looking back. The stallion was sweated out, white lather on his neck and chest, nostrils wide, slowing on his own to a trot, then a walk, head down, strides short. Not until he could hear the labored breathing of the stallion against Keno's light huffing did Blue take up a loop or two in the rope and tugged gently, eased the brown to a short walk and the stallion came along like a lady-broke saddler.

Now that the chase had settled into a lead and follow, Blue could confirm his quick early judgments. The crested neck, heavily-padded ribs, tail and mane unknotted, forelock hanging clean and straight down between the wide-set eyes, all those clues accounted for the stallion's lack of condition. The brown mustang must look like an underfed child's pony next to the fancy horse.

Slowly, each step heavy and raising dust, the mare walked faster to catch up. Once she broke into a trot and it was painful to see; her heavy belly went sideways, the mare raised her tail and broke wind, then came to a coughing walk. She was about due to drop and Blue knew she was distressed with all the hooraying, so he led the stallion toward her, hoping she wouldn't try running again. The two-year-old colt got anxious, circling his mama while staying back from Blue's presence.

Finally the horses settled, and Blue gently encouraged the stallion to walk quietly next to Keno. Finding a mare alone, with only her own two-year-old for company, was unusual. Maybe a mountain lion, a bad winter, a broke leg got the sire of her foal and left the mare unprotected. Whatever it had been, the mare had been quick to find a stallion to ensure her safety. It would have been recent for it sure wasn't this stud's colt about to get born. The horse hadn't been running loose long enough to service a mare and sire a colt.

He reined in the brown, let the stallion come up close and the horse seemed grateful when Blue leaned over and rubbed the sweat-soaked neck from the poll down to the withers. When the stallion made to bite at the brown, Blue slapped his nose with the flat of his hand and the horse looked away as if he hadn't meant to bite the mustang after all.

They managed a few miles in single file, Blue on Keno, the stallion held close to Blue's knee, the buckskin mare coming along slowly, and her youngster to the back, afraid to leave his mama yet uncertain of the new leader of the small band. Eventually Blue found the right place for the night's camp, good grass, a few trees, even a small stream maybe ten yards away.

After Blue had Keno unsaddled and hobbled, he fashioned a halter for the stallion, and ran his hands all over the horse, rubbing the sweat, scratching where the tired horse itched. Only then did the mare and her two year old come in close to camp.

The mare whinnied a sweet endearment to her protector, and the stallion responded in kind, arching his neck, whickering to her in quick puffs while letting down his organ, and prancing in place. The two-year-old made a wild dash between his mama and the stallion, who tried to spin and kick out. Blue slapped the bay horse, yelled at the dun and the mare dropped her head to graze.

CHAPTER THREE

It was a lively night but Blue wasn't willing to admit he might have roped and tied up more livestock than he could handle. The stallion stood for the hobbles made with short ropes and soft leather, and Blue side-lined him for good measure. The buckskin mare wasn't leaving her new love but wouldn't come in to him, which meant a chorus of girlish squeals and a stud's deep whinny. The two-year-old, the dun colt Blue already called Charley, dashed around avoiding Blue and generally got in the way but didn't seem to be frightened of Blue or the brown mustang.

The stallion belonged to a gentleman, an Army officer Blue decided, since the shoes were standard issue and marked USA. Picking up a front hoof, he'd read the mark branded into the heel. He was glad too when he let the hoof drop for the stallion leaned his bulk against Blue, not holding himself like a gentleman's horse should have been taught to do.

More than likely the big horse had gotten loose but hadn't gone far before settling in with the mare. Returning him might bring Blue a reward. He leaned back against the pitiful excuse for a tree, in the dark, far enough from the fire that he could still see each horse, and thought about a few extra dollars for delivering this ole boy to the right owner.

That cowpoke he'd traded lies with had spoken about a fort to the north and west in the Nebraska territory. Blue figured, from all the signs, it was likely that this high-bred, fancy thoroughbred came from that Fort. He'd ride north and west for a while, to see if he found the bay's home.

Then before false dawn, the horses quit bickering and dozed and Blue got maybe ninety minutes of sleep. He lay on top of his bedroll, barefoot with a hat over his face, head resting on the saddle, more like taking a nap than really sleeping, He needed to hear if the dun colt tried chasing Keno a second time.

A variety of calls, whinnies and squeals woke him too quickly and he came awake tangled in his boots, stinking of horse and worried who'd gotten kicked, who'd been fighting, who'd tried to escape this time. He opened his eyes to early light and the barrel of a pistol held five inches from his head. "Mister, you stay down right there and keep quiet." Blue rolled back on the blanket and figured this one time he might do what the soldier told him.

No one knew the truth. And Joshua Snow wasn't going to tell. One hostler, with only six months in the Army, had been given time in the stockade for letting the stallion run off, which wasn't so bad and didn't prick Josh's conscience enough to confess. No one would dare confess such a sin to his father, Colonel Snow; the Colonel held everyone and everything to his own high standards and when challenged became a stern dictator.

When Josh's conscience woke him in the middle of the night, and he couldn't risk moving around his room or heaven forbid creeping down the long stairway and going outside to sit on the front verandah and look at the loose collection of buildings known as Fort Robinson, Josh admitted to himself that his description of his father was too easy, and vaguely wrong. The man was a commanding officer and had earned the necessary reputation for being strict and fair.

Josh was Army like his papa, and his mama had been the daughter of a general so she too accepted Army life and helped her son deal with the constant changes and endless orders. Still his world was not bound by the same rules and regulations that soldiers and non-commissioned officers and even the Colonel's aides had to follow. But he would not venture out of the upstairs room in their brick house, the tall house newly built on the Fort, to sit in the night air and think about his actions and what he might do now to remedy his mistake.

He had been allowed on occasion to ride out with the designated troops hunting for the bay stallion. The escaped animal, named Comet for his supposed speed, was Papa's particular favorite. It was the Colonel's highest accolade, to saddle Comet and stand in the drill field, overseeing the troops as they performed at their very best.

Papa had a track built around the edge of the drill field and on occasional Saturdays, men from different companies would place bets and race their special mounts. The horses were assigned to specific troopers and the care and conditioning of these individuals became more than simple survival. Rivalry and boasting about the horses were common elements of almost any conversation on the Post.

No one ever offered to race the Colonel on his fancy Thoroughbred. The Colonel felt this oversight was a silent acknowledgement of Comet's speed and breeding, and Josh was a wise-enough son not to tell his father the truth, that Comet's prowess was a fiction, which only the Colonel whole-heartedly believed. Not one man on the Post wanted to be the winner in any race with the Colonel.

At sixteen, Josh longed to ride in these races but was held back by his father's stern comments, that he wasn't strong enough or rode well enough to not cause a problem with a number of horses going at speed. It took strength and knowledge that he did not yet possess to compete. Josh always wanted to ask how he would learn such a skill if he was not allowed to compete but he knew instinctively that such a return question to one of his father's orders would result in the punishment of no riding at all.

Josh knew his size made the racing more difficult; unlike his father's compact height, Joshua was close to six feet and mostly arms and legs, which at impossible times did not do his bidding. But he could feel a horse, know its fears and how to ride it. Just not well enough for his father, not correctly enough in the military style for Colonel Harlan Snow.

He'd known Corporal Sutter and several troopers were going out for another search; perhaps this time they would again allow Josh to accompany them. School was on hold; the Post teacher had the mumps like half the troops, and the girls were having classes in deportment, whatever that was, and sewing, but the boys had been turned loose to get into their own trouble. It was late enough in the school year no one bothered to get a new teacher. Papa had threatened them with serious consequences if pranks or troubles arose out of this freedom, so if Josh volunteered for a military duty, there was a chance he would be allowed to ride along.

He asked his mother first, needing her agreement before he proposed anything to the Colonel. It was always that way, not that his mother interfered, but if she agreed, they could usually win over the Colonel to whatever it was Josh wanted.

That next morning, far too early, Sutter brought out the dark bay son of Comet, the horse Josh was allowed to ride as it was another private mount belong to the Colonel. Jupiter was saddled with the dreaded Army split-seat wooden McClellan rig, but it meant that Josh was invited along for the hunt.

He never expected that Sutter and his soldiers would actually find Comet; in fact it seemed that no one expected to find the horse, so when they rode over a low ridge and there was a camp, a bedroll with a body sprawled on it, the remains *of a fire, and a group of four horses, everyone went for their pistols and rode down at a moderate speed, with Sutter using hand-gestures to keep them in formation.*

Jupiter tried to whinny at his papa but Josh turned the bay's head and touched the damp muzzle, which silenced the horse. He envied some of the men riding lean military mounts; Jupiter was heavy and hard-footed, unlike his sire, and he always made Josh feel like a kid riding a fat pony.

It was the military, bless them, acting on orders and grouped together in a tight bunch as if there was safety that way. They made it downright tempting for a hard-minded drifter to pick them off damned quick and neat. Soldiers were meant to know better, to spread out and keep an eye on him from several points as an unknown in their home territory, but Blue wasn't going to mention that flaw in their maneuvers. Instead and for once, Blue did as he was told.

Slowly, keeping each movement distinct and not a threat, he came to his knees on the blanket, looked at his boots and one of the men, setting to a nasty-eyed bay, said 'all right' and Blue struggled into the boots, shrugged on a damp shirt. Then he stood, always conscious of the pistol pointed at him, and others like it held in sweating, nervous hands.

His own hands hovered slightly above his waist, palms out, quiet, hoping no one challenged him; he turned slowly to keep an eye on the rider of the weedy bay. The slight man with a squinty face and corporal stripes led the opposition. Blue had been here too often, threatened over nothing at all.

It would be the horses, the telltale hobbles and sideline on the stallion, the grazing mustang, the unbranded mare and her two-year-old. Not one of them was an Army remount but he was betting someone had to pay for the stallion's disappearance. He resisted lifting his head to stare at the corporal; it was often that one gesture that stirred tempers and started a brawl. A glance seen as a threat, a turn of the

223

head read as an attack. Blue was careful not to look straight into any of the faces.

These boys didn't give any sense of being soldiers or hunters, just city kids in poor-fitted blue wool uniforms, perched on those wood saddles, riding stiff-legged and hard-fisted on a bunch of uninterested geldings. Two were non-descript troopers, whey-faced and bony, trading bitter childhoods for Army promises. Their corporal rode a slightly better-looking horse, but the son was bench-kneed and toed out in the left front and had that mean eye. The bronc wouldn't hold up on a long march but no one seemed to care. Generally the horses looked good enough, all were shiny and well fed, the mark of an Army too long in one place. The Indians were quieted now, frozen and starved and buried in a mass grave, and those damned fences divided ranches and towns, leaving little need for the Army at the moment.

There was a kid along, not a soldier but still military. On a stout dark bay gelding that looked something like the lost stud. It seemed odd to have a child riding along; the boy looked to be fifteen or so, Blue didn't know much about kids to be sure of his guess. The boy was tall and lean, with his legs drawn up on the round sides of the bay gelding; an awkward child growing into himself. A boy like this riding with these paid hunters didn't make sense to Blue. It was beginning to be personal and too familiar.

He made the mistake of looking up at the kid, who jumped away from Blue's stare and the corporal took offense. "You leave the Colonel's son out of this, mister. You got a rope on the Colonel's horse so that's why you're being taken in as a horse thief." It was a battle Blue would always lose; he'd done nothing but catch up a wandering horse and was taking him back, no call to brand him a horse thief. And that corporal with the big mouth, he made the coward's choice of resting his hand on a holstered pistol.

Blue lowered his hands and waved at the rifle leaned against the tree, his sidearm hanging from a branch; both of them out of reach. "All of you, you that afraid of me? I'm standing here surrounded, doing nothing but try to sleep and you want to arrest me?" He lowered his head briefly, wiped his mouth, then looked up straight into the man's watery eyes and laughed.

It was foolish and stupid but it was also a clear day, the air smelled good except near the troopers and now the mare and her two-year-old were coming in to inspect the new arrivals, causing a fuss around the troopers' mounts. The stallion was particularly taken with the gelding that boy rode. Like father, like son was Blue's thinking; the boy's mount was sturdier, perhaps a mustang dam, not a purebred like his sire and better suited for an even-tempered cavalry mount.

Then he got back to paying attention to these fools who'd interrupted his morning nap. "You boys going to ask me 'bout what you see or just tell me I'm a thief." Too close to a pleading for the nothing he'd done wrong. The words, the need to speak them, got into Blue's belly and raised his already uncertain temper. Then the homely corporal nudged his horse too close to Blue; "You got a bad mouth, mister, for a man facing a rope." Blue shook his head and grinned; he knew he ought to not do this but the foolishness of the man's statement pressed his temper.

"Corporal, I've done nothing wrong, I found a horse obviously saddle-broke and valuable, hell he's wearing US shoes and they're still tight. So I roped and caught him and now we're headed to that almighty Fort where you gentlemen obviously reside and I plan to return this here son, maybe keep the mare and her two babies for my payment." He wiped his mouth again, finding anger creeping into his words; "Hell, if I was a decent horse thief I'd have these three branded last night and already be gone from this godforsaken place."

It all became too much talk, too much challenge and now Blue saw into the blue eyes of the corporal and he thought, ah hell. He'd already had enough when the corporal pushed his bay forward to bluff Blue into backing that one step to show the corporal was in power. The scrawny rider was an easy target, as the soldier was intent on impressing Blue and instead Blue grabbed the booted foot, careful around the low spurs, and shoved hard, sending the military man backwards off his horse. The whey-eyed bay took it in his head and bolted, tail over his back, eyes rolling, reins flying as the horse headed straight for the safety of the fort.

The buckskin mare lifted her head from grazing and watched, the stallion roared and the dun colt ran a hundred yards with the escapee before sliding to a halt as he realized his mama wasn't with him. The troopers' horses threw their heads, swung around and one whinnied, but they were seasoned veterans, more so than their confused riders, and finally the horses settled. Blue's mustang barely raised his head from a clump of grass.

One of the troopers dismounted to grab the corporal's hand and help him stand; the corporal managed despite the help to hold on to his pistol and now he pulled back on the trigger. That single click stopped everything; Blue was careful even breathing, and the trooper moved far away as he could from the angry corporal.

It was the boy, on that stolid dark bay, who pushed forward. For a kid his voice and manner were calm and Blue found himself studying the boy's face as the youngster spoke his mind. "Sutter, the man's done nothing wrong, at least nothing that warrants a shooting. I don't think the Colonel would approve if harm came to this man before we hear his story."

They were simple words, well spoken and cautious, with a faint warning stressed in those almighty important words 'the Colonel.' Blue had a feeling the boy might have saved his life or at the least rescued him from a good beating.

Sutter kept the pistol pointed at Blue just long enough to show his troops that he was not under the boy's command. Then he grunted and eased back on the trigger, returned the *pistol to its holster. Each man let out a sigh, and one of the horses squealed.*

It was almost worth the dust-up to watch the corporal struggle with the brown mustang, who wasn't fond of most people riding him and especially not a soldier boy wearing spurs. It was common sense to the troopers and the boy, and the dirtied and sore corporal, that Sutter ride the mustang with Blue's rig. And that left Blue to walk, or ride the stallion without a saddle, no bridle, just a rope looped around the clean head, over the nose and up close to the ears. The big horse jigged and bounced in the beginning, back humped, tail swishing at the indignity of a human seated directly on his well-bred hide.

About every half mile, Blue found a new excuse to stop or turn the stallion, which broke up the short march and added to the corporal's hatred. The stops became a source of devilment for Blue, taxing him to be creative. He'd gig the stallion while turning the neck, or poke one of the trooper's horses in the ribs with a boot toe. At one point, Sutter pulled out his pistol and again threatened to kill Blue, who quietly pointed out that he might well miss and kill the Colonel's valuable stallion. That ended the threats, and eventually Blue quit disrupting the march, as soon as he saw the first chimney rising from the Fort housing.

Blue talked to the stallion between skirmishes with Sutter; he scratched gently in front of the withers, stroked the crested neck and let his legs hang soft and quiet near the bay hide, not asking but using his body to tell the horse he wanted quiet. Eventually, when the stallion lowered his head and let out a huge sigh, Blue grinned at the kid riding next to him as he leaned back and patted the stallion on the rump with his elbow, in kind of a sideways twist.

On occasion Blue caught the bruised and miserable corporal staring at him, and knew there would be a reckoning. Hell, he thought, life never quite seemed to be different no *matter where he chose to ride. The brown mustang sensed the corporal's weakness and jigged, threw his head, spooked, tried to rear. Blue would have laughed but that would have been even more stupid than the mess he was already in.*

It turned out the boy's pa did own the stallion, and 'the Colonel' was going to be pleased that the horse was returned in such good shape. Blue nodded to keep the kid happy, but there was more going on that just a horse that went missing. There would be a few days or longer in jail for Blue, which wasn't much of an imposition. Any thanks would go to the corporal for his injury in the line of duty. No pity would be shown to Blue for catching the escapee.

Eventually the boy introduced himself; "I'm Joshua Snow" and he was mighty polite with his manners. His arm made a motion as if to offer a handshake then retreated in light of Blue's hands being bound together in front, so he could ride, but not so he could escape. No one thought to figure that he was riding a Thoroughbred and a stallion, and with bound hands he could be bounced off by the stallion's excessive energy and that would mean a loose horse on the grassland again, probably headed straight back to the buckskin mare, who was still trailing the group of horses but far to the back.

Blue grinned as he spoke his own name in return to the boy's formal introduction; "Blue Mitchell." There was a silent beat when the boy digested the name and Blue kept to his invisible task. The ropes around his wrists were loosening, giving him room to slide his hands; someone hadn't paid attention when rope tying was taught in soldier school.

"Thanks to you, Joshua Snow, for asking since no one else was interested in any name I would give them. Guess they wouldn't mind hanging a nameless horse thief but then I didn't steal this horse, he was running with the mare, plumb in love with her. It's nice to make your acquaintance, Mr. Snow." The boy's eyes widened as if it hadn't occurred to him that such a rough-looking man would know his manners. Blue grinned; "My mama taught me, like your mama taught you. Be a worse

mess in this world if there weren't mamas like ours." The boy smiled and his face became a man's, no more a foolish child but a hint of what he would be.

"Who named you Blue? Do you have another name, beside Mitchell I mean?" Most folks didn't ask, just looked at him and the color of his eyes and got mad or forgot him. Either way there weren't many questions about his past. "Guess my ma saw me when my eyes opened and they weren't that light blue of most babies." He was uncomfortable; he'd never talked on the subject before since no one ever asked.

He couldn't even look at the kid. Then the corporal barked out an order to one of his men, demanding that the prisoner not speak with the escort. Josh Snow reined his blocky mount around and slammed its bulk into the mustang who took that moment to buck and the corporal had quite a battle to occupy his attention and challenge his less stellar skills as a horseman.

While Sutter kicked and hauled on the reins, he lost his temper completely; his voice squeaked as the brown mustang stood on his hind legs. "Your father. . ." Josh interrupted; "This man is not a formal prisoner and I can talk with him if I choose. There isn't much else to do, riding with you and the escort." To the point, Blue thought, and fighting words but the boy wasn't thinking about what the corporal might do to his 'prisoner' once out of sight.

The brown came down, bounced on rigid front legs and the corporal was close to sliding off. The order was given to proceed at the trot and Blue laughed even as the kid, Josh, looked over at him in alarm. The stallion had a smooth trot and Blue sat it easy enough, knees drawn up and legs swung forward to touch the bay's shoulders. The horse was uneven in his gait but simple enough to ride. In payment for his own discomfort, Blue knew the corporal was being tortured between the mustang's trot and the high swell of the unfamiliar saddle. The brown would not glide into his easy pace, not with the military's hand rigid on the bridle.

There was another reason Blue appreciated the order to move out; no one bothered to look closely at him, they were busy with their own inabilities to ride, which made it easy for Blue to twist and rub and pull until the ropes were opened enough to let his hands slip out any time he chose.

Josh kept his own bay close in stride to his father's stallion and the man they had unexpectedly captured; he'd never seen anyone sit a trot by allowing his lean body to move with the animal's stride.

Then on careful examination, he saw that the rider was working his hands against each other, and when the rope finally gave way, those long fingers held to the strands, kept them wound over the bony wrists as the rider's eyes caught Josh's stare and they widened the slightest bit, looked down at the hands and then back at Josh and there was careless humor in their peculiar color.

Josh nodded, almost embarrassed by the glance, and those odd eyes reflected back pleasure in Josh's silent understanding. It was a rare moment when each man had been right about a stranger, followed their instinct and perhaps had made a friend.

Dorothy Snow had been against her husband allowing their only son to ride with Corporal Sutter and the two troopers. They might be tracking down Colonel Snow's favorite horse, who being entire was more than likely out courting a few ladies for after all it was early spring, but still she felt it unsafe, and perhaps too earthy, too intimate with the facts of life, for their son to be in such poor company while on a fool's errand.

To herself she admitted it was mostly the company Josh rode with; she did not approve of anything that Corporal Sutter might suggest. The man was detestable, not that he had harmed her in any manner or ever really spoke to her other than on formal occasions, and always with the utmost respect in his words, but behind those shiny eyes and weak mouth was a man who despised himself and therefore would dislike all others, causing trouble wherever he could. She did not want her son at the mercy of such a man's poor judgment.

Harlan Snow was many years her senior, this was her second marriage and Joshua the result of that first brief contract; this single fact, of Joshua's actual fathering, and the knowledge that she had been taken by a previous male, had become an irritant between husband and wife.

Intimate issues were rarely mentioned, but Dorothy was experienced enough to know that her military husband was less enamored with her in the bedroom than he was of her fine manner and elegance while being escorted to all military functions. He was the Post Commander and of necessity needed a wife of refinement and good will. Dorothy had agreed to the marriage on those terms, a matter of convenience for them both. One of the first promises Harlan had extracted from her was that Josh would never know that Harlan was not his physical parent.

She sometimes wondered if Harlan truly thought the boy would never look at his father and see a different person than the features reflected in his own face and build. Harlan was short and well muscled, with rather delicate hands for such a strong body. His eyes were a deep brown, his hair almost black, only recently streaked with gray. He made a fine figure on a horse, a true Commander of the troops both physically and mentally.

It was Harlan's biggest disappointment after moving in to the grand new Post Commander's home, that the local uprisings of Indians had been subdued during his time on the Post but not while the troops were under his command. As a consequence, he could only send out men under younger officers while he was held to the Fort for his duties. This inability to hunt the enemy after rising to such an elevated rank frustrated her husband, and there were times when he took out this frustration on her and the boy. She might understand but she did not accept his drinking or his unintended cruelties on those occasions.

Joshua's father had been tall and fair with blue eyes, which his son had inherited along with his father's thoughtful temperament. It wouldn't be long before the child became a man and would study in college and learn that these anomalies in his physical being were not a product of these two particular parents mating. She had often considered what she might say when the time came, and had as yet not come to any brilliant conclusion, except, perhaps, to tell the truth.

Dorothy felt herself blush; that a son might think of his mother in terms of mating and its byproduct was an unhealthy and unchristian concept. She bowed her head, rested her fingers across her mouth. It would not do for her to ever mention these ideas or ramblings to anyone of her immediate acquaintance.

In matters concerning their son, her son although Harlan had legally adopted the boy, in these matters Dorothy had first refusal. Unusually, this time, on this particular situation, Harlan had stood firmly with Josh and their combined force so startled her that Dorothy allowed her child to ride out with the disreputable Corporal Sutter. Harlan insisted the man was a more than adequate tracker, and she often thought to challenge him with asking why, if Sutter were so talented in his tracking abilities, was Comet still out on the range, running free and doing as he pleased.

However common sense kept her mouth closed, and she had touched her fingers lightly to Josh's arm as he sat on the bay gelding, dear Jupiter who Dorothy had ridden on several occasions, offering by her touch a wordless reminder that those at home waited and worried.

Still, watching the boy ride with the soldiers, on a horse the Colonel had bred and raised, had her experiencing pride and mixed fears. Her son was no longer a child. And he'd recently told her he intended to try for the Academy when it was time. But would she please not tell his father in case he *didn't get in. Dorothy sighed; there were times when the single word pricked her heart.*

After a late lunch and a sit under the huge oak at the front of their house, Dorothy was ready to return indoors and begin preparation of the evening meal. Although the Post was formal, with a large mess hall, Harlan often chose to dine at home, to maintain the family unit, he once told her, and to enjoy peace and quiet after the endless daily demands of the Army Post.

There had been an earlier interruption to her quiet repose when a riderless horse charged down the track toward the stables, jumping and bucking around those soldiers who came out to attempt its capture. There were several men involved in the failed exercise and ensuing discussions, and initially their excited language had frightened Dorothy, since the horse was one of many bays assigned to the Fort. She eventually had recognized the animal's build and size and knew that it wasn't the horse Josh rode. Nor, since it was saddled and bridled, could it be Harlan's beloved Comet.

Now, as she was opening the door to the house, intending to begin her meal-time chores, unexpectedly and with little formal announcement, a collection of horses pranced and cavorted down the wide road leading past the Post Commander's house and guard shack and on toward the stables.

Dorothy picked up her skirts and ran, for Josh was with them, and a stranger rode Comet. The insufferable Corporal Sutter rode a smaller brown horse who seemed intent on removing Sutter from his perch in the non-military saddle, and slowly, with great dignity, a mare most obviously ready to give birth followed the mismatch of men and horses. An oddly colored horse, who seemed the most anxious and could possibly be a wild horse, ran between the ponderous mare and back toward the plains and sandy ridges where freedom waited.

Dorothy abruptly slowed when her son glanced back and the stricken look to his face told her she was being over-protective. So it was a quiet walk, dropping her skirts, fingers gently patting her hair and face to lessen the blush of exertion.

It was the rider on Comet who confused her. No one except for her husband ever rode the great stallion, and yet here was a nondescript range rider of absolutely no consequence setting on Comet's back without benefit of saddle, controlling the spoiled horse with only a rope wrapped around the finely chiseled head. Oh how Harlan rhapsodized about the bloodlines of the horse, how far back his pedigree could be traced, what fine offspring he had produced.

There the discussion inevitably stopped, as it was unseemly for any man to discuss such crude matters with a woman. Even if that woman had her own offspring, and in fact would like to bring more children into the world.

To his wife's dismay, Harlan Snow wasn't particularly interested in the human aspect of breeding.

Blue scrubbed at the stallion's withers with his loosely-bound hands and the short ears came back, the horse snorted, shook unexpectedly and Blue laughed as he clung to the slippery hide. There were folks showing up from all direction; he guessed they'd come in as a parade and Blue's first thought was for the mare and her rowdy offspring who might bolt and take the mare with him. A fast escape could kill both the mare and her unborn foal

A woman approached, one of those prim and slender ladies who married captains and colonels. She hurried to the boy and their relationship was easy to see. Blue nodded to her as the boy looked down; "Ma'am, that's a good boy you're raising. It's been a pleasure riding with him for company."

Then he leaned forward, slid off the bay, moved quickly through the milling horses and confusion of uniformed soldiers, and asked a youngster if he had a good rope. While the boy looked for the gear, Blue slipped his hands free of the corporal's restraints. The boy returned with a long tangle of rope and leather.

Behind him he could hear that corporal yelling but no one seemed to take much notice or chase after him so Blue fashioned a crude loop as he walk quietly toward the pregnant mare. Thankfully the mare was absolutely uninterested in Blue and whatever notion he had in mind. Her head was almost to the ground, she grunted once in a while and she had that telltale drop on both sides of her quarters as a trickle of milk made its way down the inside of her hind legs. She'd foal out in a day, maybe less. Blue vaguely thought to worry about her in all the yelling.

He stayed near the mare, not too close to bother her, and when the dun colt made another circle of his mama, Blue slid the rope over the frantic dun's head to settle deep on the neck.

There was a sturdy tree close to him, one of a long row, and he headed there on the run with the squalling colt fighting and tearing at the rope. Blue ran the rope around the trunk, held hard to his end while leaning back, using his weight to hold the colt.

It was the Colonel's boy who recognized what Blue was doing; he slid off the fat bay and came running to take the rope and hold it across his back, snug to the tree that was bending some but not close to breaking. Blue swung in behind the dun and picked up small rocks, tossed them at the colt's hindquarters to skid the dun forward while yelling at the kid to get around the tree, take up more slack and tie off, not let the colt get loose.

Only then, as the colt was securely tied, did something slam into Blue and he went down too fast to stop his fall. Gravel scraped his forehead, got into his eyes and filled his mouth; he groaned with the weight driving him deeper into the earth. Then he inched his face sideways, snorting blood, spitting out stones, and heard a voice whisper into his ears;

"You son of a bitch, you've insulted me enough and now this in front of my men and the Commander. I'll make you pay."

Ah hell.

Blue didn't get to catch up the mare. Instead he went to jail.

CHAPTER FOUR

It was difficult to sort out the varying stories, so Colonel Snow started with what was most important. Comet was safely secured in a pen, looking fit and uninjured from his one-month vacation. The bay's coat needed a good brushing, and there were a few scars of negligible severity that would eventually disappear with the correct ointment applied daily. Sutter had promised the Colonel he would tend to the horse personally.

The Colonel did not fully understand the details of Comet's capture. He had yet to interrogate the blond-haired cowboy who had ridden Comet with his hands tied in front of him. That the man had managed to escape both his guard and bondage, then roped and tied off a wild mustang while almost the entire Fort population watched, was unnerving. When the escapade ended with the man being yanked out from under Corporal Sutter, who insisted that the man was trying to get away, the ensuing arguments did not offer sufficient balance to restore the Colonel's faith in the training of his men.

Unwilling to hear the stranger's excuses, the Colonel had the man placed in the guardhouse, with orders to feed him and provide enough water and some salve to treat the facial wounds from Sutter's precipitous capture. Dorothy had promised brisket and fresh vegetables for supper, and the Colonel wanted to hear the boy's account of the situation before listening to Sutter's bravado recitation.

He had no illusions as to Sutter's intelligence; however the corporal had managed to bring Comet home without

236

injury. It had been interesting to note that it had not been Sutter either leading or riding Comet. It still amazed Harlan Snow that a complete stranger was able to ride the stallion without benefit of saddle or proper bridle. He would closely question Josh as to the parameters of the situation, under the guise of family dining.

Later he would review Sutter's report. And he needed to insure that the Post veterinarian wrote up a detailed account after he examined Comet at length. What to do about the mare and her vagrant companion was another question that could wait until after the anticipated evening meal.

At some point, he conceded that he must hear out the explanation of the man he'd just placed under guard in a cell. Harlan sighed, being the Commander wasn't always about military matters and he did not like the chaos of the civilian world.

As jails went, this one wasn't bad. There was light from a high, barred window that looked onto the parade ground, and the two men in front of the guardhouse weren't that reluctant to talk when they had the mind to, so Blue entertained himself by making up questions. They even provided a bucket of water, some reasonably clean cloths, and a tar salve that Blue used on a multitude of horses, and himself, on far too many occasions.

He thanked the guards, and asked for a bit of a mirror so he could see the damage. One of the men obliged, going back to his quarters to retrieve a piece of shiny metal, with a hole so it could be hung on a nail in the wall. It took Blue a good half hour of washing and picking out gravel before he got to the salve and when it was applied, he stood and laughed. He looked like some kid's drawing of an animal with spots.

These pinpricks in his face and hands were a minor nuisance, and the meal he was served made up for the inconvenience. He'd ridden too long out of Tom Cobleigh's livery on rabbit and venison, and dried strips of mule deer. This was food; green things he couldn't name, slices of meat drenched in a pepper gravy, a potato mashed and also peppered, no chile but it all tasted good and he wished the younger of the two guards would come asking if he wanted more.

Eventually one of them opened the heavy iron-strapped door and while the other soldier stood guard, he came in and picked up the plate, the mirror, the wet cloths and the water bucket. When these items were put outside, the young guard asked if Blue needed to use the outhouse. After such a meal, Blue was exceedingly eager to get to the small building behind the jail. He thanked the young man for being that quick to pick up on what a prisoner might need. The kid turned red on the words.

Later, when Blue was safely locked back inside his cell, that same young guard slid two blankets and the bedroll with Blue's meager gear through the bars. It wasn't proper, the guard said, but then there were no formal charges on Blue. Not yet.

He wadded up his clothes out of the saddlebags and rolled up in the blankets. The clothes smelled and that made him grin; 'bout time he did a wash or had a bath again, something he bet the Army would provide once they got a good whiff of him while he stood before the Commander and gave his unvarnished version of the recent events.

The evening meal was late, mainly because Josh needed to bathe and change before he was allowed to sit at the table, and he fought this unnecessary restriction, eager to tell his tale of the past two days. But it was important he understand a gentleman's priorities and the proprieties of etiquette. When they sat down, Josh was still too excited to eat but his father reminded him that his mother had worked hard to prepare the meal and it was a courtesy to her to take a bite of each item of food.

The boy turned away from his father and spoke to his mother, chewing quickly between the words. "He rode Comet as if the horse was a child's pony. He sat there while the troopers, they bounced and jounced along and he talked to me as if nothing unusual was happening. He didn't fight us at all, just when Sutter. . . ." There her son stopped abruptly, hesitating as if in the back of his mind he knew that too much information would not be in the man's best interest.

Then he became a child again, for Josh was just barely turned sixteen and while tall enough was not yet a man. "Corporal Sutter he tried to run Blue down with his troop horse and Blue grabbed him and pushed him over backwards off the horse who ran away. That's the one that came back to the stable, Papa, and Private Kyrsynski told me the horse came in without a scratch but that's why Sutter was riding the mustang because he didn't think he dared ride Comet."

Here Josh slowed, turned to his father and smiled, quite a charming gesture. "I think Sutter was uncertain that you would want him riding Comet, sir, and he certainly wasn't going to put Blue's. . . Mr. Mitchell's gear on Comet. His solution seemed the most logical at the time, for Sutter hurt himself in the fall. Not badly though, he didn't seem to have a problem tackling Blue when he caught and tied that dun colt."

Dorothy watched her husband's face and would guess that Harlan was disturbed with Josh's use of the man's name too often and on quite familiar terms. He would feel the need to pursue inquiries as to why the boy was allowed to ride close enough to speak with the prisoner.

For the Colonel, as he took a second helping of the pot roast, he considered how interesting it would be in the morning, to hear Sutter's version of today's occurrences.

Blue woke quickly, uncertain where he was and panicked about the mare. He went to the barred jail door. "Guard, guard!" His voice cracked, then strengthened. It wasn't the kindly face from the early evening but an even younger trooper, in fact it was the kid who'd brought him the rope earlier. He had a chance with this one, already used to doing what Blue said. "Mister, I need to use the outhouse. Quick."

It was a plea most anyone understood and so the unlocking routine was repeated, an almost invisible guard stood with rifle at the ready while the boy cranked around the key and opened the cell door, stepped back to let Blue out. He walked quickly around the edge of the adobe jail, knowing exactly where he needed to be. The young guard followed too close, Blue quickened his step as if in distress and the boy hurried to keep up. Out of sight of the older, wiser guard, Blue spun and clobbered the kid on the jaw, catching him as he dropped, gently supporting the limp body to help it lie peaceably on the ground. He rolled the kid's hat under his head, and stacked the rifle and pistol against the jail wall, offered as evidence of his peaceable intent.

He hesitated, expecting the second guard to appear but there was no sound, no heel clicks on stone, no voice raised in concern. The guard must have gone back inside, convinced the boy could handle their prisoner.

Blue ran past the outhouse where he wanted to stop but he needed to hurry into the shadows, toward where he could hear and smell horses. Then he stopped, stood motionless, hardly breathing, close to a fence line. He let his eyes become used to the dark, turned his head to sense what he knew had to be happening.

A grunt, a sharp nicker, the harsh snap of teeth; he walked quickly toward a solitary pen some distance from the main stables, where any sensible Commander would isolate two range horses away from the Army stock.

The mare was down, groaning softly now; protruding from her quarters were the head and one hoof of her foal. Fluid drenched the ground, dark enough in the shadows to be blood but it was only liquid from the interrupted birth. The dun colt stood alone in the far corner of the pen; eyes wide, nostrils flaring at the strange scents.

Blue climbed through the railings, approached the mare at her shoulder, placed a hand on her neck and she tried to reach around and bite him but he touched her jowl, patted between her eyes and told her what he intended to do and how she could help him. She let out a sigh, and rested her muzzle in the sand. She was calm now, but her sides heaved and her coat was dark with sweat. He moved carefully around to her hindquarters, squatted and touched the nose and soft hoof still encased in the birth sac. One hoof was doubled back; without help both mare and foal would die.

He shrugged out of his shirt, threw it toward the fence before he unbuttoned the combinations and half-shrugged out of them. Then he reached his arm into the birth canal beside the foal. He strained to grab that bent leg, the mare grunted, banged her head on the ground, then tried to stand and Blue stood with her, feeling at his fingertips the small doubled hoof. He dug through the membrane and grabbed the hoof, brought it up alongside the foal's nose and hoof just as the mare kicked him on the meat of his thigh. He dropped to his knees as his arm, slick with fluid and blood, was yanked from the birth canal by the force of the kick.

The mare went down again. Blue knelt with her, put both hands on the two delicate, softened hooves and pulled; she grunted again, pushed, strained, and the foal slipped into Blue's arms before it hit the ground. The mare lay quiet a moment, the foal stirred, hooves breaking through the restricting membrane, nostrils wide, ears flat, hair lying in damp curls from the months of pressure.

Intent in retrieving his shirt, Blue stood as the mare came up and was too slow to get out of the way. She nailed him with another kick, the upper left arm this time. He heard the bone break and cursed the mare, got the hell out of the pen by painfully climbing through the rails. Some night's work he'd done, some smart move tugging a foal out of a wild mare. He sure enough got what he deserved; he took in a deep breath and gasped.

Then he heard voices and saw lights and there were horses whinnying and leather soles on packed ground, orders yelled out he couldn't understand and it occurred to him they'd found the young guard and hadn't been clever enough to figure out what a rifle and a pistol laid against the jail wall meant. He hoped the kid didn't get too bad a cursing out, or literally put on shit detail, but he wasn't ready to go back to the jail and explain.

Blue moved toward where he'd seen the Commander of the Post disappear through the fancy door of a handsome two-story brick house, a verandah across the front, bigger than the surrounding buildings, obviously the boss's home. He doubted the soldiers would look for him here.

He went up the steps, amazed that the running, yelling soldiers didn't see him, and found a chair placed conveniently close to the formal front door. When he heard a horse whinny and turned to stare into the night where the corral would be, the chilled dark air showed him exactly where he'd left his last decent shirt, in the dirt of the corral. Little more than a pale glow crumpled on the ground, right now the shirt was probably being pawed at by the restless and upset dun colt, who would stop and whinny, then tear at the shirt as if it held all the unknown enemies inside its wrinkles and stains.

Blue sat in stages, careful not to jar the arm. He could feel the bone, and the blood, and cursed the buckskin mare but didn't blame her. Surprisingly enough he wasn't cold; despite the air hard on the exposed bone, his body carried its own heat magnified by the flapping combination top sticking to his flesh. It was a bad situation to figure.

His brain wasn't working right. He knew it, had been hurt enough times to sense the body's try at regaining normalcy. He was blasted with thoughts going in wrong directions, voices, promises, cold relief. Then he realized it was a real woman speaking to him and he half-tried to stand but couldn't keep his legs steady enough to finish the attempt. The chair moved back and forward under his sad tries and that set up the hurt in his broke arm. He'd seen men go into shock, sweaty, cold, eyes losing focus. He could feel his own flesh betraying him as he sat down and held his arm close, motionless, defeated by a moving chair.

She had been resting her eyes, needlepoint pattern and thread lying in her lap, when a knock at the door and her husband's hurried response told her once again that the Army had entered their quiet house with one of its endless crises. Harlan was quickly agitated by the man's unintelligible words, and left with barely a nod in her direction and certainly without any meaningful explanation. She expected nothing from her husband when it was a military matter, and it was always a military matter.

She had deliberately picked up the canvas as Harlan left with the corporal sent to retrieve him, and finished off an inch of the petit point, a griffin she was told, a mythological beast, facing a lion. The griffin pleased her the most, in soft blues with a flaming red crest; the lion was turned away from the griffin's power, subdued in golden yellows and brown, much less magnificent than the slightly outrageous mythological griffin.

A peculiar sound outside on the verandah stopped her hand in mid-air, thread pulled through the needle by the distraction. It was not Josh, for he was in his room upstairs at the back, exhausted he said by the past two days of adventure. Despite his height and the flickers of maturity she witnessed at odd moments, he was a boy and needed his sleep.

Since there were no further steps, no one opening the front door to tell her bad news, or her husband returning from an easily rearranged situation, she assumed it was a one-time noise, wind perhaps that moved the rocking chair, a nocturnal animal checking the house for possible scraps, something of that sort.

Still she rested her hands in her lap, willing herself to breathe slowly, hear what was happening outside her door.

243

There was an occasional distant yell but no horses yet so it remained an on-post problem. Then that noise was repeated; a boot scrape on wood, the distinctive sound of the rocker Harlan had brought with them from Kansas when he was transferred to Fort Robinson.

When she stood, careful to slide the needle twice through the unstitched fabric where it would remain until she had the time to work again, she found her heart beating too fast and it was difficult to breathe correctly. Fear did that to her, and it always made her quite angry that something unseen and invisible could so charge her body. She was of the belief that it was possible to control every aspect of one's life through thought, deliberation, and knowledge.

Well, she said to herself, you need to go find outside and find what it is that makes such noises so you no longer have to be afraid. It sounded odd to be talking to herself in this manner, and if Harlan were here, or Josh were awake, she would never indulge in such a peculiar and non-productive habit.

She opened the front door, stepped out onto the verandah, and let the door close. She held in her breath, recognizing that her entrance into this dark and unknown world would startle and therefore expose whatever force it was that upset her.

There was no answer to the turn of her head, her silent question; the air was stilled, as if nothing could move or breathe or think. She held herself erect, refusing to feel the pulse in her throat, the banging in her chest. Any reasonable beast of the night could hear and possibly smell her presence and run away, and yet the silence continued.

Until that one word; "Ma'am." Spoken very cautiously and coming from the left side of the verandah, where the rocker was positioned. She had been correct in her assumption that the noise was produced by the infernal chair, which she had asked Harlan several times to have corrected and his response had always been to tell Josh to do the work, a Post

Commander had more serious matters that needed his attention.

Josh of course had no idea how to fix such a problem, for his father had never taught him such mundane things nor was there anyone with the time or skill to teach him on Post. Still Harlan insisted it was Josh's role to be the handyman. This backwards thinking led Dorothy to shake her head and put up with the rocker's irritating noise those rare times when it was in use.

The voice was insistent; "Ma'am." And she could hear attempts to stand; that creak again, a softened grunt, then a weight setting back into the defective rocker. This time she turned and looked into the dark cave under the slanted roof; there was light slicing through the shadows from inside the front room, where she had been sitting doing her petit point. She had felt secure then, not knowing that outside on their verandah a stranger waited.

She took two steps closer to the chair, where a man sat, his head bowed and she could see the streaked blond hair that was too shaggy. The same light glistened across his chest, illuminating no dark shirt or blouse but the dim weave of half-worn combinations.

There, at his feet in dusty boots, long tan pants with leather lining the inside of the legs, a more southern habit or mode of dressing she had learned, there at his feet was a shining object. One more step and Dorothy Snow realized the slowly expanding shape was blood.

CHAPTER FIVE

He could smell it from long memory; that hot too-sweet scent of blood, his own blood, running a chilled track down his left arm and belly, staining the already gruesome combinations before soaking into the fabric of his pants and leaking onto the floor. It was his blood that shimmered in the thinned light.

Now the woman stood in front of him and her scream would bring in the troops. There was nothing he could do to defend himself. Any explanation was more than he could manage; hell he couldn't even get out of the rocking chair. He tried his best; "Ma'am. Don't. I can't hurt you, I can't even get up. I could use a bandage and a splint, some help setting this arm before I bleed to death on your front verandah. I don't want to make more of a mess. Please ma'am, I won't hurt you."

The few sounds were all he had left; words, clear thinking, all that had disappeared into the pain. He hope the foal was standing now, nursing on his mama, she sure would take good care of her colt, take the best care possible, protect her baby from anything tried to hurt him. He could use a female like that right now; no questions, no fuss just doing what needed to be done. And right quick. He could feel himself going. Blue shook his head and that wasn't a good idea. He needed to talk to the woman, to keep her from screaming; "Ma'am, can you help?"

She heard his plea and there was a place in her mind where the voice was familiar. Then it came to her, a few words spoken when her son rode in with the captured stallion and a non-military rider on his back. That absurd escape in front of the entire Fort, when Josh and this man roped a wild horse who had unaccountably followed the assortment of men and horses.

She remembered him; he had told her she was to be commended for raising a fine boy. An odd comment, she had thought at the time, from a man tied up and escorted by the cavalry for stealing and who knows what else. Still, few of the Fort's inhabitants took the time to see into Josh and realize he was indeed a fine young man. It was that same voice. The blond hair and its shaggy growth were odd enough she should have known from the first glimpse who and what he was. But how had he gotten here? And then it came to her that he was Harlan's mysterious night crisis.

She had only a moment in which to make a choice, and as she spoke, she could hear Harlan's fury chastising her for interfering in Army matters. But this man had befriended Josh, and for that she owed him some kindness. "I will call Josh and boil water for you, mister." She did not ask but waited politely. He had that much left in him; "Blue Mitchell, ma'am. Blue."

"Well yes, Mr. Mitchell, I can see that you've been gravely wounded." He shook his head, and again it hurt him and she couldn't possibly see the gesture but he wanted to make his point clear. "I'm injured, ma'am. Not shot trying to escape or nothing. I got to the back pen to help that mare birth out, the youngster had a leg folded wrong and they both would have died."

The words were shaky; he would be in shock from whatever caused the bleeding, she needed to get him into the house quickly. She almost smiled at his delicacy when he realized he'd spoken incorrectly. That such a rough man had these sensibilities was a surprise.

"But you were put in the guard house, the Colonel told me. For safekeeping until your story could be verified. He told me he wanted to hear Corporal Sutter's version first." She hesitated, but the rules didn't seem to apply here. "I don't like that man." Her visitor actually laughed, a brief sound but she recognized its intent. "I ain't too fond of the gentleman myself." She smiled, put a hand to her mouth to cover her mistake and then realized he couldn't see either gesture.

"Let's get that arm tended to, I gather it is broken?" "Yes ma'am, that mare didn't take much to my help and kicked me for my efforts." "Oh dear, that must be painful." A foolish comment; really, Dorothy chided herself, the man was more clever than she had been led to believe and she was babbling nonsense.

He watched her turn to leave him and his body protested. Embarrassed, safer in the dark where he sat, he had to tell her one more thing. "Ma'am, I was, the guard was taking me to. . . ." He couldn't say the exact words. She stopped in a shaft of light, nodded her head once. "Mr. Mitchell, our facility is attached to the house at the back. Let me bring you a cloth so we may wrap your arm before you enter the house. I prefer that you not bleed on the carpet or floors; Harlan can be quite particular about these household matters. But I will have Joshua escort you."

Here was a practical woman who remained a lady at the same time. It was a becoming trait Blue thought. She opened the front door and was gone, leaving Blue sweating, chilled and shaking. It seemed forever but he knew it was less than five minutes when she returned, with the boy behind her buttoning his shirt, his hair standing on end. She handed Blue a thick wad of white rolled cloth and then asked him if he needed help. He nodded, realized again how foolish that was but words took effort; "Yes, ma'am. Help."

The boy steadied Blue's forearm while his mother wrapped the thick white fabric around the upper arm, tugging gently at each turn of the material, causing Blue to wince. She knew; she glanced at his face so close to hers, and with her free hand touched the side of his head. The wild yellow hair was damp with sweat. She tried to comfort him with a promise; "Only a few more wraps, Mr. Mitchell."

Her mouth was close to him, words whispered into his ear, against his skin. He shuddered as she tied his arm to his chest with a short sling, making him as comfortable as possible before the next crisis. Then Josh simply picked Blue up, both hands under his good arm, leaning back so Blue could steady himself. The boy was smart and obviously learned it from his ma. It was a long unsteady trip through the house to a dark hallway and a door that opened into a narrow hall then a small room with a seat and a tin-lined hole.

A few minutes later, he emerged from the cramped room and the boy had waited for him; "Mother wants you in the kitchen. Here." His hand was a comfort, steadying and turning Blue so all he had to do was focus on getting one foot to move and land, then wait for the other foot to follow. It was a bright room, a big tin sink with a pump handle, a polished and blackened cook stove, water bubbling in an iron pot. A small table with one chair pulled back, more of that thick white cloth and scissors, two flat sticks of wood, a needle and thread. Light came from a kerosene lantern set on a smaller table.

Blue sat, almost passed out letting her lift and place his arm where she wanted it. He could feel the trembling in her hands; they had no calluses and only one small burn scar. It looked fresh, like she'd been baking earlier this morning. He appreciated her efforts and felt an urge to comfort her but he couldn't find words. "Here," she said, and handed him a glass half-full of amber liquid. He could smell the taste, not harsh or oily but smooth and seductive and he drank most of the brandy in three gulps, stopping briefly before finishing the portion.

Dorothy directed her son to get her scissors out of the sewing room and asked him then to cut away the filthy underwear as gently as possible, allowing her full access to the wounded arm. She was fascinated to watch her son's hand, fingers too big now for the feminine scissors, as he snipped through half-rotten cloth. A shiver went across Mr. Mitchell's chest, she could hear his quick intake of air but he said nothing, did nothing except to close his eyes.

She gave him another large dose of brandy, and the following ministrations became a dance he barely registered; the pain was distant, renewing itself in waves. The woman's sympathetic cries were soft, muted by small grunts of effort as she tried to set the break. When the boy left to vomit outside the back door, Blue was remotely amused. There was one bad moment when the placing of the splints and the pull of cloth to set the bone in place drew a gasp that seemed to come from all three of them.

He wanted to rest his head on his good arm and pass out but it would be a hardship for his nurse and an admitted weakness.

Dorothy Snow carefully re-examined the fractured bone and torn flesh around it and decided that stitching such a wound was more than her neat hand could manage. There were nerves or at least small vessels showing and she did not wish to cause further damage by sewing the wrong things together.

She was fully impressed with the man's stoic attitude, his eyes flashed their unpredictable color, a most amazing glistening blue, and he often smiled or grimaced when she spoke to him, telling of her intent to move one part of the injury, touch a nerve, press edges together. The brandy seemed to help, as it usually did in such circumstances, so she continued to offer a half-full glass and he continued to drink its renewed contents, not getting drunk but she could feel him relax in shivering inches beneath her unsteady touch.

When she forced Josh to hold one of the splints, after dousing the open wound and bone with more of that brandy, and told Mr. Mitchell to hold the other splint in place, he did as she directed, staring at the depth of his separated parts. It wasn't fear in his eyes but curiosity.

She too was fascinated by what lay exposed in her hands; not white like the bleached remains of a cow or coyote, but thick with blood and flesh and filled in the exposed center with a thickened matter of small circles. Blood that seeped from the break created more interest than any panic.

When she tied off the white thick cloth, of necessity using some force of pressure, Blue laid his head on the table, letting out a brief sigh, either unconscious or drunk.

His mother was amazing; she accepted a half-dressed man into their house and doctored what to Josh was a vicious wound and yet her face was quiet, her eyes concerned like those few times when Josh himself was taken with a cold or bad cough, but she was not flustered and she didn't order him about with any harshness. She remained herself, asking him to bring more hot water to the table, suggesting that he help her rinse most of the dirt from the open wound while Blue, Mr. Mitchell, turned his face away but not once during the trying ordeal did the man curse or complain. Nor did his mother betray any nerve or shyness but continued her work quite gently.

Josh even saw his mother touch Mr. Mitchell's face and the man's responding smile looked sad. Mother then patted her own hair back into place, careful that nothing shaded her eyes so that she might see exactly what needed to be done with the exposed bone.

He understood the effect of brandy for Josh had seen his father, the Colonel, drink almost an entire bottle one evening after a skirmish with a few renegade Indians in which four of his men had been murdered. That's what he called it, murder, despite the Indians clearly wanting to avoid the conflict, and the fact of these four men enlisted in an army with the intent and purpose to fight.

The Colonel had fallen asleep in the chair, so drunk he came close to sliding onto the floor, and Josh and his mother knew such a display would be an embarrassment to the Colonel when he woke, so between them they carried his body to the spare room at the back, where a cot was kept for Joshua to use when the family had visitors.

Basically the officers' quarters were identical halves along a common wall; they lined up under planted shade trees set a respectful distance apart. On the distant edge of the parade ground, the new Post Commander's resident had been built in the late 1880s. The building was a two-story, unadorned Victorian with extra rooms and a front parlor designed for formal entertaining.

There were four bedrooms upstairs, and a small room downstairs connected to the kitchen, for a serving girl Dorothy supposed. She preferred to use the Post non-commissioned officers' wives for help during parties or when guest descended on the Snow household. When there were family visitors, Josh by necessity lived in that back room on the cot. Dorothy also used the room for her mending and sewing.

As the guestroom beds were stripped, their mattresses rolled up and waiting, and the thought of dragging a drunken Colonel up the stairs was impossible, they had laid the Post Commander out on the cot and his mother told Josh to leave, she would undress her husband and make him as comfortable as possible.

That one time it had been three days before the Colonel could look at either of them square in the eye. He rarely drank like that again. At least as far as Josh knew; that his parents had lives separate from his began to be a reality he studied and wished to understand, but neither parent would tell him of any private matters. There were secrets between them, secrets he would never learn from their lips.

Mitchell proved to be quite different from a drunken Colonel Snow; after ten minutes of noisy sleep with his head on the kitchen table, Mr. Mitchell woke and called out to Josh, who was in the living room with his mother; "Boy, any chance for a cup of coffee?" Mother started to rise but Josh waved his hand; he knew how to boil the coffee his parents preferred, he could do this small chore for Mitchell himself.

As he came into the kitchen, Josh considered the full effect of Blue Mitchell; injured, half-naked, those eyes looked straight at Josh and he wanted to turn and run. He'd never had anyone stare into him like this, the eyes and their vivid color, the long browned face in contrast to the white skin of his chest, the already blood-stained bandage around his upper arm.

"That was hell, boy, your ma's something to marvel at, isn't she. You're a lucky son to grow up with such a mama, most folks'd faint at what she just did for me." There was that sad smile again, from too far in the past for Josh to understand.

With a few comments and knowledgeable suggestions from their patient, Josh got the stove heated up again and the coffee boiling. When he turned to look at Mitchell, the man was leaned back in the chair, legs stretched out in front of him, chair sideways to the table, arm rested on a pile of the white cloth Mother always kept in abundance for these rare emergencies.

The man looked too alive for the situation; no reddish haze in his eyes from the quantity of brandy he'd consumed, no squinting, soured look from what had to be a painful injury. His face was open, the eyes startling in their color, the mouth wide, seeming ready but not quite smiling. Josh wondered what beginning in life created such an ability to accept danger.

On Mitchell's chest, too near the heart, was a thickened scar. Yet when Mitchell's eyes caught Josh's directed stare, there was no whine or spoiled complaint; "Yeah, the man had poor intentions toward me but I'd guess he wasn't too successful." He laughed. The man laughed at the possibility of his own death. Josh stood motionless until he smelled burned coffee and had to move quickly.

Mitchell leaned forward as Josh poured coffee into a tin cup and handed it to the man. Mitchell lifted the cup gingerly, holding the rim to his mouth a moment. Only then did he take a sip, look up at Josh and grin; "Ain't bad, could let the grinds set a bit, or put in an eggshell, a dollop of cold water. But it ain't bad. Thanks, boy."

His mother came in from the living room. Her hair had been pulled back clearly from her face, and the waist she'd worn through the doctoring was replaced by a fresh one despite it being almost time for her to retire. It would not do to appear disheveled in front of company, if a wounded escapee possible horse thief could be considered company. It came to Josh then that Mr. Mitchell wore no shirt and only part of his torn combinations, which normally would upset his mother. Josh slid around her and went to his room.

He heard their voices and it was a pleasant sound, no quarrel, no sharp command, just questions and easy answers and even a laugh from his mother, a snort that had to come from Mr. Mitchell.

She sat down at the table and their guest made a half-rise she knew was quite difficult for him; that he made the attempt impressed her. He had been taught manners despite some of his speech being almost illiterate. At least he did not curse, although she suspected that out of earshot he would use profanity liberally and with an inventive flare.

It was impossible not to see that the man was half-naked, and at one point in his rather short life had been badly shot. He shrugged and raised his good hand across his chest. "Ma'am, your son wanted to know too; this was a long time ago." She pulled back slightly, unused to having what she was thinking understood without speaking in great detail. For Harlan, each thought and emotion had to be clearly delineated.

She could not stifle her curiosity and the man seemed amenable to questions; "How indeed were you able to get out of the guardhouse to assist with the mare?" He grinned, actually grinned and shook his head and she did not understand such a man. "I tricked one of the guards into thinking I had an emergency, then I knocked him out." He raised his good hand at the look that must have crossed her face.

"No worry, ma'am, I caught him on the way down, and made sure he had something under his head to keep him comfortable." His face turned sober and she almost asked why. But he was ahead of her and offered his explanation; "I made

a point of putting his rifle and handgun against the wall, so the soldier boys finding him would know I meant no harm." Then Josh returned and her chance to ask anything more personal disappeared.

The boy appeared with a shirt she had meant to mend; he'd already cut off the left sleeve and split the seam, and he helped their guest gently pull the opened edge over the white padding and then as Mitchell leaned forward, Josh slipped his good arm in the full sleeve. With the shirt buttoned, by Josh as it was impossible or highly difficult to button a shirt one-handed, their guest looked more normal and much less of a threat.

The bleached whiteness of the linen shirt contrasted with the strong face and heightened the brightly-colored eyes. The hands were bony and scarred also. All of this man was damaged; Dorothy's first husband had been smooth, massaged, softened with lotions, and Harlan had only one small bullet hole, against his ribs, where rifle fire had entered and exited taking with it very little flesh. This had occurred during his one encounter with a band of Indians. When he was in need of sympathy, Harlan managed to use that wound to soften her, make her more approachable. After seeing what this man had endured, Harlan's sad ploy would no longer be effective.

Dorothy studied their patient, noting a gentleness quite out of character with his raw appearance when he spoke to Josh, teasing him about the coffee as he pushed the cup forward with his one good hand, letting the wounded arm stay resting on the white cotton pad. With effort, their patient looked directly her; "And maybe a splash of that brandy, ma'am?" He lowered his gaze and her skin quivered.

Josh poured his mother a half-cup of coffee, then made a decision and poured a cup for himself. She mentioned that there was a tin of milk, and a bowl of sugar, if either of them would enjoy such a luxury. Mitchell's face opened in a shy smile, and the eyes had a different glow, as if the thought of sugar and tinned milk could mitigate the pain he must be experiencing. "Ma'am, it's been a long ride with cold camps so milk and sweetening would be a treat. Thank you."

He was a charmer. Partly dressed, hair sticking up in damp curls, face relaxed with that ever-present hint of a smile, Mr. Mitchell was almost handsome. Dorothy nodded to Josh; "Please get the brandy from your father's study, our guest would appreciate a generous shot poured into his coffee as well as the milk and sugar." She smiled graciously at Mr. Mitchell, and he inclined his head in return.

While Josh was retrieving Harlan's 'secret' bottle, she took the opportunity to ask another disquieting question; "How did you find Comet, Mr. Mitchell? Corporal Sutter had been out several times with troops following tracks but they never even saw the horse. At least that's what they told Harlan." Her husband's given name sounded peculiar inside the warm kitchen.

Blue shook his head, wanted to rub his face, lord he was tired and hurt all over but the woman's questions deserved an answer and he liked talking with her. "I rode up a ridge and they were in a small valley with good grass and a stream. A kind of a horse heaven I guess. My mustang, well he's not too scary for a horse of Comet's quality. So I rode down and dropped a loop over the stallion's neck and we had a tug of war that Keno and I won."

Josh returned, the bottle in one hand, and had his own question; "What about the mare? How could you think to bring in a wild mare?" Mitchell's reply was studied and intelligent, and so very obvious. "She's an escapee, boy, or let loose. Look at her close tomorrow; mind the new colt, though, a nice little dun, which tells me she's been out there at least three years. The new colt looks to have the same father as that two-year-old colt following her."

He rubbed his face, took a gulp of the brandied coffee and put the cup down. "She's saddle and harness-galled, got some draft in her from the width of her chest and all that hair to her legs. *She throws good colts though, have to say that. And she sure can kick."*

He hesitated again and Dorothy could see the lines of exhaustion in his face, around his mouth and eyes as he tried to answer Josh's curiosity. *"She knows people and they don't frighten her. She came with us since we had her stallion and she intends to stay with him. I sure as. . .sure didn't bring her anywhere, sure enough wouldn't wish an Army Post, pardon me, ma'am, but it's the truth, I wouldn't put a horse in the Army 'less I had no choice."*

Dorothy jumped, startled by an intruding voice; *"Those are good answers, Mr. Mitchell, although I don't appreciate your view of our Army Post. You've invented a story that is almost plausible."* It was the Colonel, standing at the back kitchen door. Head uncovered, hair displaced and exhibiting his bald spot, which was usually hidden by his hat, his evening whiskers white along his jaw line, exhaustion deep in his dark eyes.

"I applaud your imagination, Mr. Mitchell. Now it is time for you to be returned to your cell."

Dorothy had considered this moment, having studied the options and various scenes and had made a decision, lined up the words with which to tell her husband what would and would not occur concerning their unusual visitor. Despite his injuries, Mr. Mitchell had been nothing but polite, and treated her son as if he were a man full-grown and worthy of respect.

She didn't stand, that would give Harlan a physical edge for he was imposing despite his short stature; strong across the chest, vivid dark eyes that could intimidate, and a sense of commanding her even when he attempted politeness or, more rarely, affection. What she intended to say would not suit the Colonel but her husband would not be allowed to bully Mr. Mitchell.

"Sir, this man is a guest, on the Post and in our house, and he is not trying out a story on us. Go to the pens and see

the mare and foal for yourself. You might notice that our guest is wearing one of the shirts I made for Josh, since Mr. Mitchell left his own shirt in the corral while helping the mare. It should have been easily seen, since if I remembered he rode in wearing a light-colored garment. He most obviously has made no attempt to escape, either from the Post itself or from your own house."

The Colonel sputtered, as she knew he would. She stubbornly continued; "We have made up fresh linens in the back room, and Mr. Mitchell will remain here until the doctor sees to that arm in the morning and the accompanying fever goes down. I would have sent Joshua for the doctor tonight, but I know he's been up late tending to those in the hospital. Mr. Mitchell is incapable of walking unaided, Harlan. He is no threat to anyone except perhaps to himself in trying to help that mare and her foal."

She nodded then to Josh, who smiled back at his mother, rose from the table and disappeared into the back of the house. He would be finding the patched sheets and a light blanket and the boy knew well enough how to make up a bed, with or without tight Army corners. Her son was growing into a good man.

Harlan's face showed every bit of the annoyance and anger she had anticipated. Dorothy smiled at him, patted her hair and now she stood and went to him, rested a hand on his forearm. "Dear, we are all under a great strain. But Comet has been returned without harm, and Mr. Mitchell has spoken highly of Josh and his exemplary behavior with Corporal Sutter and the troops."

She had noticed that Mr. Mitchell had forced himself to stand, making a momentary liar out of her. Knowing what the effort cost him, she admired him even more; he would not sit and let a woman speak for him, and the rare exhibition of chivalry was pleasing.

Mitchell took a few unsteady steps, then rested his good hand on a chair back, quite literally holding himself up for the

Colonel's inspection. Surrounded by flapping shirt tails, wild eyes carrying a hard challenge, too-long hair still damp with curls, the man typified everything Colonel Snow disliked about the civilian population, yet he met the Colonel's stare.

Mitchell nodded; "Sir." Then he took a long breath and his entire body shivered as he held the Colonel's autocratic attention with those heated eyes, deliberately not looking away. Dorothy was privileged to witness two occurrences; her husband actually backed off from another man's stare, and while Mitchell staggered and grabbed the chair back so hard that his uninjured hand went white, he kept to his feet and the discipline behind this simple act was impressive.

"Sir, your wife's been kind to a stranger who's messed up her pretty house, and she's done a good job tending to me. Your son's a strong boy who has the makings of a good man. I don't think I could walk to the guardhouse right now, but with your son's help I can most likely make the back room Mrs. Snow speaks about." She was situated so that the trembling in Mr. Mitchell was again evident, his arm shook and the supporting hand was bloodless but she doubted that her husband would take note of such minutiae.

She interceded on Mr. Mitchell's behalf; This is enough, Harlan. Help me guide Mr. Mitchell to his room." There was no recourse but for the Post Commander to do as his wife requested. It would be an embarrassment for Harlan to refuse her request in front of an injured civilian.

Blue wasn't too steady but they made progress down the back hall. A colonel on one side, a lady on the other; damn he was going up in the world.

CHAPTER SIX

Before he began inquiries into the entire episode, Harlan sent a messenger to find the Post doctor. He promised

Dorothy that there would be care offered to the man but that he would of necessity be returned to the guardhouse when practical.

His first concern was Corporal Sutter, who entered the office and stood at attention, and was as neatly polished as the Colonel had ever seen the man. There wasn't much to Sutter, a loose chin, watery eyes, thinning hair, but he could when pressed track quite well, and had a way of binding the men to him so they worked as a unit.

However he was less than excellent with horses, having a destructive tendency to rough up his mounts. Consequently Sutter was given the less desirable mounts, and the man was well aware of the slight to his reputation. That this slight might reflect on his own horsemanship did not seem to occur to him.

"Has the mare foaled out?" Sutter drew himself to stricter attention; "Yes sir. She has a dun colt." "Was there a shirt in the corral?" He detected a hesitation, a pause to find the needed words. The weedy corporal cleared his throat; "Yes sir, a blue shirt with several patches." "Was it the shirt our, rather your, prisoner had been wearing earlier?" "Yes sir." Good, no prevarications yet, no attempts at denial of what was known to be true.

The Colonel looked at the papers on his desk. Sutter quickly rubbed his leaking eyes. He could not quite find a pattern to the questions, or any sense of fury in the normally quick-tempered colonel. "Was the guard hurt last night?" Here at last was a question with meat to it; "Yes sir, he had a bad bruise from being attacked." "Is he on the injured list at the moment?" Damn, that didn't last long. "No sir, the doctor sent him back to the barracks on regular duty."

Harlan Snow hesitated; this next question came through his wife, who'd spoken to him in quiet tones as they readied for bed. She explained in detail what the patient had told her and Josh, and insisted that he question Sutter about the specifics, and watch his face and eyes as he answered.

Dorothy was quite astute about the men under his command, picking out those who were reckless or cruel on the basis of a few comments, an action he himself might not have seen. Harlan learned early to trust his wife's instincts, so once again he couched the question in her words.

"Where were the guard's weapons when you found him unconscious?" It was not a question he would have thought to ask, for when the guard had been found and news brought to the Colonel, the rifle and pistol were already back in the barracks under lock and key. However Dorothy had forced him to believe that there was importance attached to the question, and the actual truth of Sutter's answer.

Sutter was immediately uneasy despite his stance, that much was obvious. His hands wiped each other, then fell to his sides. He couldn't quite meet Harlan's eyes and that was all the answer needed. "The rifle was thrown quite a distance, sir, and the pistol was tossed in another direction." Snow shook his head slowly; this was as he feared, a lie that made sense unless the truth was known. And the facts concerning the rest of the man's actions did not support such abandonment of the weapons. Dorothy insisted that their guest, as she called him, told her exactly where he'd left the weapons, and why, down to folding the man's hat under his head to make him comfortable.

"Mr. Sutter, report to the barracks and remain there until this matter has been decided."

So the horse thief got to the pretty wife and now Sutter was a nothing to be excused until sometime when it was more convenient to deal with him. The Colonel would listen to that damned spoiled brat of a son, the drifter too, on the say-so of his wife.

The woman was pretty in a tight way but Sutter had no illusions about him and women. The whores in Crawford took care of him. A decent woman wanted no truck with a bony Army corporal who could barely talk. The other kind of women kept him from having to make any effort, just hand over the money and be done.

The Army wasn't much of a life but better than the rats and freezing cities and riding drag on a cattle drive, helping the coosie, being the butt of jokes and intentional cruelties. The Army gave him something, a title and a rank and those under him thought he actually knew his job.

Sutter saluted best he could, turned and left the office. He had him a mind to check on the horses, first that damnable stallion, then the mare and her new babe and that two-year-old whose capture shamed him, and last, the evil brown mustang who'd made his life misery on the ride in.

He wiped his mouth, spat out what tasted like pure fury. It was a bitter gall and an edge of shame that goaded him. He knew enough to recognize the need to be careful; he was stirred up and agitated and could make a fatal mistake.

There had been several moments during the night when Dorothy had awakened to a groan, even a cry, from the downstairs sewing room, but lying next to Harlan, she had debated the wisdom of getting up to check on their visitor and knew immediately that Harlan would disapprove. If it came to a battle on the rightness of keeping Mr. Mitchell in their home, she wanted Harlan to have as little ammunition as possible. Mr. Mitchell's continued residence would necessitate a balance between the return of Comet and the smallest intrusion into the family routine. She lay in bed, rigid next to her sleeping husband, and endured those few minutes of crying, another deep groan, then it was quiet again and she drifted back into sleep.

As she prepared breakfast that morning, Dorothy sent Josh in to wake Mr. Mitchell, for she had reason to believe that their patient might be in need of assistance.

Josh returned from his mercy errand and upon questioning said that Mitchell seemed in good spirits but that his eyes had a peculiar glaze. She thanked her son, pleased that the boy was this observant, and proceeded to make up a cup of coffee the way she had noted Mitchell enjoyed his coffee last night; heavy on the tinned milk, and with two spoonfuls of sugar, another generous dollop of Harlan's fine brandy. She considered these tastes rarified for a drifting cowhand.

The boy had roused him from a fretful sleep. And that damnable trip to the back facility had been torture. Now Blue lay still, trying to remember where he was and how he'd gotten here. And here was different this time; no hay, no stable smells, a clean bed with white sheets, softness when he rolled his head on the pillow.

He stared at an oddity, a flat surface with a shiny machine on it, letters and wheels, bright gold against black. He studied the shape until he knew what it was. He'd seen one in a ranch house in Cimarron. It was a sewing machine.

He fingered the sheet draped across his chest, lacey edges, stitches that rolled gently under his fingers. He glanced at the machine, touched the sheet rolled up against his chest, a fine set of stitches forming a pattern. This work was done by hand, he figured. The stitches weren't regular enough yet they were neat-set and delicate and when he pulled the sheet edge to his face, the smell was a clean soap, a hint of something flowery that he almost knew.

This was the room of a clever woman, surrounded by a richness of color and feel. There were spools, tall shapes holding a variety of color. Thick wool thread, that was the wrong word but he didn't know what the long strands were called, beautiful in their different colors, shaded within each twist, almost begging for hands to touch them.

Lying in the bed, staring at the surprise of his new surroundings, Blue had a sense the woman held more in her than being an army officer's wife. He could close his eyes and see her face, inhale her scent as she leaned in to him, tugging on the broke arm, apologizing with a determined smile as she hurt him.

The boy was a lucky kid. He had a good heart, and a secret that needing telling to someone who'd listen and not judge and it wouldn't be the boy's father. Blue would wait, and then make an offer. It might be enough to pry loose what bothered the boy.

Once again he'd landed in the middle of folks' lives and all he did was escape from a jail to help a wild mare birth out her foal. While his eyes were closed, he let himself go back to sleep briefly, then somewhere he heard footsteps and the door knob rattled and moved. He came awake fully, grimaced with shocking pain as he struggled to sit up, drawing the figured sheet to his chin, ashamed of the grayed remnants of the combinations he still wore. The stench in this private room was of his sickness, and his time on the trail. A lady would be offended; his visitor was a lady, but her smile over the cup of coffee she handed him was polite and genuine, with no distaste or social judgment.

The man was decidedly ill; his tanned face was gray, with an odd tinge around his mouth. Those eyes had intensified in color to the point where she could become frightened, and had the vague understanding of why the soldiers spoke of this man in hushed tones. His breakout from the jail, the efforts he had put into helping the mare and then managing to get to the front porch of the Post Command without being seen were already a legend throughout the ranks. Most of the new recruits had not seen battle, and the few older soldiers were the only long-time survivors. Word had gone out of Mitchell's actions, and in truth the man seemed more a ghost than a viable human being.

However, with a few sips of the doctored coffee, he recovered enough to offer that grin from last night, but without attempting to move from the bed. He nodded his head in a brief jerk and his eyes shut briefly; "Ma'am, thanks for this." He raised the cup and smiled. "You had the right to send me back to jail. I sure 'preciate you defending me." Then he sagged back into the pillow and his eyes closed.

She salvaged the cup from his trembling fingers and told him the doctor would see him as soon as possible. Mitchell only grunted

Dr. Hager opened the door, guided by the hand of Mrs. Snow placed on the doorknob. She left him with his patient, and Dr. Hager noted that although the man had originally arrived on Post as a prisoner, there was neither guard nor restraints to contain him. Interesting situation, he thought, as he stood a moment and studied his new patient. The young man was obviously not of any military training. He was sprawled on the bed at an odd angle and quite disheveled, the blond hair streaked by the sun and including gray hair, to give the doctor an idea of his age. He wore a shirt missing one sleeve, hard wool pants, feet bare, boots and socks neatly tucked under a chair by a window. He suspected the Snow boy of that particular gesture.

When the patient became aware that the doctor had indeed entered the room, he simply opened his eyes, making no effort to sit up or in any manner acknowledge the doctor's presence except with a blank stare that showed both pain and exhaustion. There emanated from his breath the distinct odor of brandy.

It appeared that Mrs. Snow had done an admirable job in her repair of the break; there was no bulging of separated bone under the neat binding. Still the arm needed to be unwrapped and sutured, with a limited prognosis since the torn flesh would have already begun to die away; however, from his years of experience with battlefield surgical repairs, he recognized that the wound would close badly, and take much longer to heal, if left in this state.

He helped Mr. Mitchell sit precariously on the edge of the bed, and then went searching for Mrs. Snow to ask for assistance from her son. He would not expose the woman to the horror of the wounded man again.

The boy entered and quickly knelt to pull socks and the disreputable boots onto Mr. Mitchell's feet, thereby confirming Hager's original assumption. Between them, with the doctor talking more than being of much physical help, they guided Mitchell into the kitchen and sat him at the hard table, on a straight-backed chair, resting his arm on a mound of slightly stained white fabric.

The Colonel's wife had used the time from the doctor's arrival to his escorting of Mitchell into the kitchen to fill a number of kettles with water, which now bubbled and simmered on the cook stove. The heat generated from the water made the room a steam bath but it was only proper that the wound and bone be cleansed before stitching. Dr. Hager was considered fussy in the Army medical circles and he took pride in that description, for he lost few patients to sepsis.

He cut away the bandaging, complimented Mrs. Snow on her efforts, and proceeded to clean the wound.

Laudanum was a step above brandy, Blue decided. While the brandy tasted better, it didn't remove the pain, only helped the owner of whatever wound or disaster to simply not give a damn.

Laudanum, on the other hand, removed all sensation, no care, no fear, no jerking away when the stitches went through live flesh and were tugged close together. Laudanum and brandy combined was decent medicine; right now he didn't feel a thing. The funny little man who said he was a doctor kept apologizing for the stitching not being his best, that it would leave an ugly scar and perhaps might not even take hold since the edges had deteriorated overnight.

He apologized for not coming immediately to the Snow home but there were all those young men in the hospital who were quite ill, and then the boy at the guardhouse. After he spoke that one lethal word, the doc seemed to flush, bit, pulled *his mouth in a thin line as if having crossed a line in his mutterings. Blue listened to the words over again in his mind and figured out the doc had shocked himself, putting the guardhouse boy and Blue's injury together. There must be quite a story circulating the Post grounds.*

Blue finally grinned at the man, who looked up in some distress as Blue spoke; "I surely don't want you worried on my 'count, doc. You do what you can, I'll heal just fine."

He was acting like a fool but he felt the heat inside him, knowing the signs, hating the weakness. Going back to the guardhouse would like to kill him, he knew that, but he couldn't ask to stay here, and no one seemed to think about putting him in the Post hospital.

He supposed if they dumped him in the hospital, there would have to be round-the-clock guards and his reputation with guards on the Post was already bad. He surely hoped that kid was all right. So he asked, since the doc never finished his version of the story, and the surprise to the doc's face was worth the effort of finding the energy to ask.

"The boy is back on duty. You barely left a mark on him, Mr. Mitchell. If that was your intent, you were quite successful." Blue responded, wanting to keep everything clear; "I wasn't escaping, though it's a mighty miserable place to be locked in, sorry, ma'am. I mostly didn't want to hurt that kid. But I could tell the mare was in trouble." The statement seemed to fascinate the doc, so between stitches and applying some kind of cold liquid that hurt and then numbed, he asked Blue to tell him; "Just how did you know that a horse, in the dark, about a hundred yards away and behind a stone barn, was in trouble? How do you explain such a thing, Mr. Mitchell?" The doc's unwillingness to believe whatever Blue might tell him was in the tone and words.

It wasn't ever easy to explain, he'd tried before with not much success and he was doubtful that this particular doc would understand but he'd try again; since the doc was doing his best in his line of work, Blue owed him the same courtesy.

"Horses got souls, doc, like humans only different. They tell each other, and anyone who'll listen, what's going on without using words. That mare, she came with us slow and heavy and I kept causing trouble so we had to stop and she could catch up at her own speed." He grinned at the memory of Sutter's frustration and the doc shook his head.

"She was close to birth then, there's a line along the hindquarters that gets deeper, and her teats, they leaked milk." Mrs. Snow was listening and Blue felt his mouth thicken around his own words but he was speaking the truth and there was no other way to call it.

"All the signs was there if you took the time to look and with no one wanting to talk to me 'cept the boy here on the ride in, I had time to study her." He ducked his head; this was the tough part of the talk. "Last night I could hear her, inside the guard house. Not a whinny, not even a nicker, but she was in trouble. When I got outside I could smell blood mixed with that fluid they carry around the baby, and I heard her grunts, so I knew. I surely didn't want to hurt the boy but it would have taken time to explain and anyway he wouldn't have believed me."

Blue stopped, hesitated, then gave it his best shot; "I figured if I stacked the rifle and the pistol up against the wall, in clear view and reach of the boy, then anyone finding him would have to know I'd meant no harm." Blue was telling was the truth, the doc didn't look to believe him.

This was a man of unusual perceptions, and quite resilient, for he tolerated the resetting and stitching with a minimum of fuss, and the sips of laudanum weren't the strongest doses Hager could choose to administer.

He studied the face closely, noting the vivid eyes and their deep intelligence. Asa Hager had once been clear out on the ocean to a series of small islands, and there the water was the same color, unusual and quite restorative when he found his nerve to enter the ocean and try swimming.

He would not have thought a man's eyes could be that color. Nor could a man know so much about horses and yet care so little for the travail of his own flesh. The myriad scars had not escaped Hager's notation, and he knew, as did most men who practiced in the west, that horses and making a living working with them was a young men's game that did not allow for the practitioner to attain more than thirty years. He'd guess, his knowledge based on science and some intuition, and the stare in those eyes, that this one was quickly reaching his limit.

"Mr. Mitchell, you are running a fever, and that arm will bother you for some time. I have asked permission for you to remain here, where if there is a problem you will receive immediate assistance." Mitchell was quick; "Why not the Post hospital, doc? I'm a nuisance to these good folk."

Hager smiled, he liked this rough man, willing to speak out even against his own best interests. He cared about the inconvenience of those around him. Dr. Hager shook his head; "There is an epidemic of mumps on the Post and I don't think your body could deal with such an illness at this point. So it has to be private nursing, and Mrs. Mitchell has indicated that she and her son are willing to accept that duty. I will discuss the matter with Colonel Snow."

"One more question, doc. You know what they did with that brown horse of mine? He's tough and ornery but a good 'un and I don't want him inducted into the Army. He'd make a bad soldier, kinda like trying to put me in uniform."

The grin and the peculiar statement were engaging, and Dr. Hager found himself laughing as he neatly finished bandaging the wound.

Corporal Sutter knew the brown devil was tucked into a small pen usually reserved for sick horses or ones the Army intended to kill, which was exactly what was on Sutter's mind. That first night he'd thrown the cowboy's gear in the back of the blacksmith's building, figuring a little smoke and dust wouldn't hurt the rig. He stood over the gear, considered removing the saddle blanket from the rest of the junk; it was finely woven, with bright colors, something an Army man would never use but the feel of the wool was soothing, the color patterns deep blues and a tan, a dark brown, some reds, its beauty more than a drifter deserved.

Hiding it would be impossible, and the man would ask about its disappearance. So Sutter kicked the damned thing into a heap of bent shoes, cut nails, grease from the coal fire; a good enough place for anything belonging to the maverick ruining Sutter's life.

No one had said a word yet about the brown mustang, and the colonel hadn't bothered to ask for the reasons connected to Sutter riding in on a civilian horse when his own mount had come flying back to the stables without its rider.

It wasn't that the questions would not be asked; it was a matter of straightening out the escape and injury to the guard, the rider's broken arm. Then would come that moment when Sutter would see the Colonel's anger as he asked why Joker had come in alone. The Colonel never let up on what was proper and military. Sutter was truly in trouble this time, worse than when the stallion had originally escaped and he'd had no answer and couldn't find the horse fast enough. None of this was good for any possible advancement of his miserable career.

As he headed around the back of the shop, he actually ran into a trooper, a Private Engel if he remembered right, who was holding a pitchfork and was unacceptably filthy. Sutter barked at him; "Private, you are a disgrace." The man's voice trembled; "Sir, it's that horse. . .he. . .came after me while I was cleaning his pen. I ain't going near him again, no sir."

Here was his chance, given to him flat out with good cause. Sutter had to hide his pleasure; "I'll deal with the horse, you get cleaned up."

He had a moment's doubt when he got to the pen and discovered that not only was the brown mustang watching him with those big eyes, snorting, ears pinned back, but the loose dun colt, an animal whose appearance still had no reasonable explanation, was in the pen with the brown. The dun stood in a corner, covered with what Sutter assumed were bite and kick marks from the mustang. The colt held one foreleg off the ground and Sutter felt a growing fury. That mustang needed to be ridden by a real horseman and taught Army obedience.

Sutter returned to the stables and ordered Private Davenport to rope out the mustang and saddle him with correct military gear, including an officer's double bridle.

He'd slept through the morning, helped once by the boy to that back facility within the house. He still didn't understand why no smell or how it didn't fill up, but he also didn't care.

She brought in soup at noon and he sat up to drink most of it but nodded off holding the mug and woke only when spilled soup burned his leg. The woman let out a gasp and called her son to bring in a pan of water and a cloth but this time Blue wasn't going to let her do the washing. That hot spot was too close to private places for a lady to be doing the clean-up and no man 'cepting a doc was going to touch him there.

He found sitting up and actually moving around felt pretty good; he cleaned the soup off his leg and out of his combinations, which were beginning to smell much like a proper outhouse ought to smell. He needed fresh clothes and a good wash. Maybe he could ask the boy; the Army must have ready supplies.

Meanwhile he struggled back into the one-armed shirt the boy brought for him, and got both boots on without the socks, there wasn't much left of them anyway, more hole than wool. Another necessary item he could ask the boy about, maybe the Army provided socks too.

Standing on his own wasn't bad, so he carried the stained pan of water out to the kitchen, and she was surprised to see him, and if he was any judge of such matters, she was also pleased. He took the liberty of sitting down as she gestured to a chair and said, 'please sit, let me make you some tea.' "Thank you, ma'am. That'd be a treat." He'd never had tea, but the woman was easy to watch, neatly dressed, even in an apron of her own embroidery he would guess. She looked the type; there would be help in the household chores although he'd seen no one yet, and there would be other ladies of almost equal standing who would gather to do these dainty stitches and discuss Army life, never complaining, just hinting at small dissatisfactions.

He'd barely met the Colonel but from watching this woman, she was younger than her husband, and there was life in her hands, her eyes, the smallest movement of her lips when she was pleased. Her presentation to him of the hot beverage with two spoonfuls of sugar was a small and pleasurable gift.

Remembering his earlier performance with the soup, he was extra careful to lean over the table and draw the container to his mouth with his fingers tightly holding the foolish half-ring where he was meant to put a finger. Not even the tip of his finger would fit and Blue laughed.

It tasted like dried leaves with sugar; he took another sip, burned the inside of his mouth and swallowed hard. His gut rumbled and he knew to respect the warning. "Ma'am. Please excuse me. " He rose and as quickly as was polite got into the back hall and through that too-familiar door. It was only when he got settled that he realized he'd managed on his own this time.

He left her breathing hard, her palms sweating and her mouth slightly opened. She could not imagine what was happening to her, nothing had prepared her for the riot of feeling that made it necessary to sit down suddenly, her knees weakened by an outside force. The man had bolted from her presence, with the poor excuse of obviously heading to that unmentionable facility. She was certain he fled from her, her notions and sudden fantasies.

Josh came in, having been rough-housing with friends, trying to be somewhat quiet so that Mr. Mitchell was not disturbed. His appearance reminded her of life inside this large and cavernous house, her duties and her regrets. The boy looked at his mother strangely and she threw back her head, then settled her gaze on her son's sweet face. "Mr. Mitchell seems to be feeling better, Josh. Would you like a glass of water?"

Davenport quickly saddled the brown mustang as Sutter had requested. Other than a continuous fussing with the bits, the brown seemed amenable to standing next to the trooper, ears forward, tail quiet, as if curious as to what came next.

Sutter had the horse brought into the fenced school, where young horses were started and new troops evaluated as to their possibilities. The mustang walked quietly next to his handler. The offensive animal did regrettably snap at Davenport's arm and received a slap across his muzzle. The horse barely jerked back from the blow, as if he'd been expecting the response.

Sutter had Davenport hold the bridle as he mounted. The mustang shivered once, fussed briefly with the bits, and for the moment Sutter was content to sit on the animal. He was much more comfortable in regulation Army gear.

Eventually, Sutter shrugged and pricked his spurs against the brown's side and the horse leaped forward into a gallop. Three turns around the school and Sutter discovered that double bits and a tightened curb chain had no effect on the mustang at all.

Blue found the back door open, with the sunlight a pleasant offering, and figured why the hell not so he stepped through, closed the door quietly and found he was standing on green grass cut to a single length like nothing he'd seen before.

He was tiring but pulled toward the stables. He had worried some about the mare and her foal, the dun two-year-old colt, but had few concerns about the mustang. That son could take care of himself. At least he'd always figured until dust and noise turned him toward a fenced area, hurrying him as fast as he could manage.

It had to be Keno tearing around out of control with a terrified rider swaying loosely in the saddle. Blue leaned on the fence and saw the white face of a soldier and it was a face he recognized and instantly hated. Damn fool trying out another man's horse. He yelled, barely a sorrowful croak; "Keno!" and the brown circled, jarring to a stop in front of Blue.

He stared at the rider; "Mister, if I weren't half-dead I'd kill you. Get off that horse, he's no member of your Army."

CHAPTER SEVEN

He didn't approve of the injured man billeted in their spare room but the doctor had explained the conditions in the Post hospital and Colonel Snow recognized that the enmity between the patient and Sutter could escalate if the man was confined to the guardhouse. Sutter held too much influence over some of the younger troops.

He sat in his chair, let out his breath; this entire matter had to be resolved quickly, yet he couldn't, in good conscience, simply send the injured man on his way. Then there was the matter of the unbroken dun mustang, and the mare and her foal. He recognized that he was deliberately straying from the simple fact that Sutter had lied to him about the injured guard and the deliberate placement of the weapons.

The initial question had yet to be answered; who was responsible for letting Comet out of his paddock. The trooper *who languished in the stockade continued to protest his innocence. Now that it was clear Sutter would lie, Harlan Snow no longer valued the man's insistence that this particular trooper was at fault.*

And it must be resolved about the patient's escape, the rigor with which he would be judged for what appeared to be an act of kindness to a wild creature. There was far too much of the incomprehensible and illogical in the situation to confound the Colonel.

He had the orderly send for Corporal Sutter. There was a rumor going through the Post that Sutter had attempted to ride Mitchell's horse and the two men got into a fight. That would have been most odd since Mitchell was bed-ridden with a badly broken arm. According to Dr. Hager, the man had been given enough laudanum to knock out a horse. The Colonel leaned back in his chair; perhaps that particular analogy had not been a correct choice, given the present circumstances. He smiled, then forced his mouth into a stern line.

Josh found Mr. Mitchell seated on a tree stump some ten feet from the house, seemingly unable to walk those last few steps. He had to wonder how the man had gotten out on his own. Mitchell looked up, and amazingly he grinned; "Well, boy, guess it's time to rescue me again." The words were choppy and harsh, as if every breath needed to speak them was a knife through the belly.

The wrapped arm was dusty and there were some greenish stains on the bandage, a bruise high on Mitchell's right cheek, a few drops of blood on the front of his shirt. If Mother saw the man in such disarray she would surely be upset. Josh offered his hand; Mitchell took it with his good one and they pulled him up. Standing this close, Josh realized how tall the man was. The muscle and pull in that one good hand impressed Josh, and he could see more muscle in the arm underneath the tightness of his old shirt, muscle that moved across the shoulders and back.

275

The voice trembled, then cleared; "Josh, thanks, boy. I'm getting a lot of use out of you and I do 'preciate it."

She watched them, her beloved son who was becoming a man too quickly, and a stranger like no one she had ever known. Even now, ill and off-balance, he walked differently than Josh. There was an ease within his own body that was not common in the Army where men were taught to march in step, to turn and drill and move as a single unit.

This man seemed to keep his length and height together for the express purpose of being on a horse. His one hand hung lightly at his side, his torso swung easily over his hips, and then she blushed and turned away from the window. They were entering the house at the back; she would call down the hallway to offer hot coffee and a bowl of soup at the kitchen table.

Josh bounced in and unexpectedly gave his mother a quick kiss; behind him Mr. Mitchell was slower to enter, and when she studied his face, she knew why. "Mr. Mitchell you are not healthy enough to go out fighting. Who were you defending this time?"

He blushed and it was as usual quite charming; "My horse, ma'am." She could not believe his answer. So she attacked; "And why would a range mustang needed defending, Mr. Mitchell?" The man was seemingly reluctant to answer and Josh elected himself to tell the tale.

"Corporal Sutter decided to ride Keno and Keno didn't think much of Sutter's riding skills so I guess Blue came to the rescue, of his horse, not Sutter, and the corporal took exception to some of the names he received as Keno bucked him off and Blue here removed the Army gear."

Josh was grinning now, remembering what Blue told him. How he'd dumped Sutter with the mustang's help, then stripped the saddle one-handed and in pulling off the saddle hit himself in the face with the cinch ring. He'd thrown the saddle and bridle on top of Sutter, who'd stayed down in

276

defeat. Then Blue'd rested his good arm on Keno's neck, and they walked out of the arena to the pen where the dun colt nickered to his new buddy. Josh couldn't keep those images out of his mind, and his mother stared at him so he tried not to smile and sort of pulled out a chair where Blue might sit. His mother quickly understood the half-gesture.

"Right there, Mr. Mitchell, you sit down and let me wash away some of the evidence. Your arm isn't meant to take any such abuse so you must not wander off again, even to see to your horse. I'm sure Josh here can accompany you if you feel another such venture is warranted."

She didn't understand why her speech became stilted and awkward when she was near this man. It was easier to boil more water and set out clean cloths than to understand what confused her. There was nothing in her life, no childhood happening or young lady vapors, that were comparable to her current fluster.

This time as she wiped his mouth and nose where there were blood traces, she could smell him; a strong odor comprised of old sweat and fever, all the miles traveled plus something sweet hidden beneath the typical male scent. She became quite uncomfortable, especially when she had to lean down and gently tap the rapidly swelling bruise under his eye with the dampened cloth. More cold water would be needed after removing the seeping blood; he would have a black eye soon, swollen and more than likely painful.

There was more laudanum, and Dorothy knew that despite the small grin, the lack of complaint, the man was hurting and needed sleep. He finally looked at her, those beautiful eyes a deeper color, sweat forming droplets under the mat of blond hair. "Ma'am, it's rare anyone taking care of me like this. Thank you." She was not used to being appreciated, and his words startled her so she had to dismiss them.

"It's nothing, Mr. Mitchell. My husband is involved with this matter, in a small way of course. I will do whatever I may

to assist Harlan. . . ." *She hesitated, saw a wince cross Mr. Mitchell's face and remembered that he and Harlan were not exactly fond of each other. Although both were polite around her, they were on opposing sides, and she was certain Mr. Mitchell was not used to living in the house of his opponent. Still, she had to try.*

"The Colonel will see that justice is done to all concerned, Mr. Mitchell. I have full faith in him. And you must also."

He drank what he could of the soup, ate a slice of fresh bread with butter, something he hadn't enjoyed in a long time. No corndodger or tortillas, not in this home. The lecture on her husband's virtues was more a warning to him than any attempt to make the two men become friends. Blue saw her fretting and tried to busy himself with eating, something that seemed to please her.

His hand trembled as he put the last bite of bread in his mouth. The taste was lost in a cold sweat, a bitter smell; time to get out of here. He stood and almost fell, looked at the boy who got a hand under Blue's good arm and they managed the door, the hall, even onto the spare bed. Blue was asleep as Josh laid him down.

He woke briefly as Josh let the door close, and called out to the boy. Josh came back, standing at the bedside. "Yes?" It took Blue a moment to find his voice again but it was in his mind and had to be said; "You check on Keno, the colt too." He rolled his head, trying to see clear up to the boy's shaded eyes. "Feed 'em, water too. Me, I'm betting on Sutter told his men not to bother."

That was enough.

His dreams were part illness, part wishful; he'd been blinded once, by a single blow to his head from a hot-tempered horse, and he remembered but could not see the woman's hands that touched and held, soothed, washed and fed him. He'd barely seen her face, she had not been beautiful like Mrs. Snow, but she had shown him love and compassion and he'd never forgotten her.

Mrs. Colonel Snow's hands were softer, her voice educated, yet there were these two women miles apart, one killed by a monster, one married to the Army, and they came to him in his dreams offering rare solace.

He fought back, striking out, finding one arm bound to his chest, rolled away and used his good hand to half-untie himself, groaning as a deeper pain flared through his arm and chest and stopped his heart, gagged him, forced a cry out of him he couldn't hear, tormenting him with flashes of old and new shadows.

Dorothy ran to the room while calling for her son but he was not in the house. There were no troopers nearby; her husband was at the Post Command office. She ran and bit the side of her mouth as she pulled up her damnable skirts to keep from tripping. She froze when she yanked the door open; Mr. Mitchell was tangled on the bed, crying and she could not understand his words.

He'd torn through the bandage, blood soaked the sheet and pillow, his eyes were open but he didn't see her. She pushed down on his chest and murmured to him and he hesitated; she could feel nothing in his chest, then a thump, a beat that found a rhythm and he let himself sag back into the bed, his head rolling off the doubled pillow, eyes still wide open. Tears flooded his face.

She leaned over his quieting body, and lightly, so gently that it wasn't real, she kissed his forehead, tasted the salt of old dirt and a tantalizing sweetness; then she moved to his mouth, which lay dry under her lips until she pressed down, feeling her breasts touch his chest as her mouth moved on his. In jerking stages, his one good hand rose to touch the side of her face, then her neck, and rested just at the edge of her high shirtwaist and she did not want him to stop there.

"Ma'am."

That one word returned her senses. It was all in the single word; dismay, question, pain, and grief, when she thought about it later. At this moment she was mortified and ashamed of what she had done while wanting more of him, a sensation missing in her married life. She tried to calm him with words when all she wanted was more of his touch.

"Mr. Mitchell, you were fighting something in your sleep, it was the only way I knew. . . ." It wasn't possible to complete her thought. "Ma'am, best be I move on to the guardhouse." She placed her hand back on his chest, slightly to the left and felt the thump and roll, lacking syncopation, irregular is what a doctor would say. "Mr. Mitchell, you have done nothing wrong to be locked up in a jail. I am the one who overstepped a boundary we both acknowledge. It is my poor discipline that has so distressed you. Please forgive me."

Then he spoke the terrible words; "Ma'am, I wanted that kiss. I could see you in my dream. It's what I was fighting. You were there with me." Only then did they both look at his arm, bleeding through torn stitches. "I need to find Dr. Hager." "Yes. Ma'am." She didn't like the blurred response.

She poured out double the amount of laudanum than the doctor recommended, and forced it into Blue's mouth, which she then kissed, and licked her lips to share the medicine, to share with him some of the wounding. His mouth under hers was smiling, then she felt it loosen. As she pulled back, his eyes closed and she panicked, then put her hand inside his shirt, to rest on his heart where the veins and arteries and the heart itself still kept a ragged time.

Later, after Dr. Hager left, she made sure that household duties and Harlan's concerns kept her away from the sick room and its beguiling patient. She asked Josh to attend to the man's needs, especially to accompany him on any of his wanderings concerning the horses and their treatment. It was the welfare of these animals that seemed to occupy most of Mr. Mitchell's lucid time.

She refused to remember kissing him.

As he began to heal, the arm ached and then itched, and when he tried scratching, the kid, Josh, would shake his head and tell him again that Dr. Hager said not to risk infection in any manner, that he was in a critical phase of recovery and when that warning didn't have any effect on Blue's digging at the arm, Josh simply grabbed the hand and pulled it away. It was a lesson for both of them; that Blue was still weak, and that Josh was growing into his height, for the boy easily pulled the hand from its task and Blue had no strength to fight back.

He gave in; "All right, kid, I won't try scratching again." Blue tried a grin, the boy swatted at his good shoulder; "You make that a promise, Mr. Mitchell. I see you grin and talk in a different direction and I'm not inclined to believe you unless it's a promise made. I've learned I can trust your given word"

Blue studied the boy; childish features, bare shadow of a beard, yet a brightness and sense that would make him a good man. "I promise. I won't scratch. Can't guarantee that in my sleep mind you, but I'll do best I can when I'm awake."

Josh returned the lesson with what he'd learned from the man, he grinned and said; "Let's go see to the horses."

Walking with Mitchell was difficult; the man's weakened state made him stumble and lose direction, but he would not allow Josh to steady him nor would he use a cane. So it took twice as long to get to the stables and behind them to where the dun and the brown mustang were quartered. An order from the Colonel had come to put the mare and her foal in a paddock where there was shelter, and to insure that they received daily water and hay. The two mustangs were less well tended, and Josh had taken on their care, with Blue leaning against the fence to keep the brown from attacking as the boy shoveled.

It was a small daily ritual of necessity and Josh found he enjoyed the work, the lift and swing of the manure fork, even carrying the water bucket on several trips from the Army well had a good feel to it. He was doing something needed, unlike his friends who, let out of school early, were hunting or fighting or doing chores assigned by a parent or military guardian.

A day came when Blue entered the paddock with Josh, who thought to turn him back but read a strange determination in the drawn face and kept his concerns to himself.

The dun colt continued to favor the front leg even though he and the brown no longer chased each other. The brown seemed to have mellowed for whatever reason; now Blue wanted to deal with the colt. He went to a corner of the paddock, near where the boy had thrown out two piles of hay. The brown cocked an ear as Blue settled himself against a fence post; it was an act of compassion for truthfully it hurt to lower himself down, one armed, sore through his body, but it needed to be done.

The colt whirled away from his hay pile and ran a few yards, stopped and turned, snorted at Blue, lowered his head and stared. Blue calmly pulled out a blade of grass and chewed on it. The brown went over and pushed through the dun's scattered hay for the better stalks.

Josh stopped cleaning to stare at Blue, who shook his head and looked away, so the boy went back to his work. Josh had learned this much, Blue Mitchell knew what he was doing if it was about horses. Slowly, at times holding one front hoof in the air, the dun returned to his pile of hay, flattening his ears at the brown, who casually walked back to his own meal. The dun kept an eye on Blue, sitting against the fence post, doing nothing but chewing on a blade of grass.

With hay hanging from his teeth, the dun took a step toward Blue. Another step, a halt to chew on the dangling hay, Blue looked at the ground as he pulled out a few more stalks of grass from around the post.

They faced each other, the colt's head low, eye-level with Blue, who looked past the colt, watched Josh as he worked. Then he studied the grass stalks laid across his good hand. The colt took another step and stood over Blue.

Josh stopped work to lean on the pitchfork. Blue had no defenses if the colt were to attack him. Josh had to anticipate any trouble or his mother would be furious at him. He studied the man's behavior and was impressed.

The dun's nose rested on Blue's head; he felt lips take some of the hair and tug. No biting, nothing else, just a simple tug. Blue studied the infected wound on the leg, a slice from the brown's too accurate kick. It had filled with pus and needed to be cleaned. The colt worried more of Blue's hair. Blue reached out with his good hand and laid it firmly against the colt's knee on the healthy leg. The colt dropped Blue's hair and lowered his nose to touch the back of Blue's hand. Teeth grazed Blue's knuckles and he clucked. The colt withdrew the bite and rested his muzzle on Blue's face.

A moment of breathing, each into the other's face, no motion, no worry. Then the colt went back to his hay pile and continued eating breakfast.

Blue called out, his voice barely above a whisper; "I need help getting up, boy, and help back to the house, if you're done cleaning."

He spoke only a few times on the return; orders to Josh, brief, no room for questions. Two buckets of clean water, cloths, find a tin of that black salve. Then minutes of no words, the walk taking all of Blue's energies.

Almost at the back door, Blue sat abruptly on the stump of the oak tree. When Josh saw Blue's face, he understood. The skin was white, the mouth thinned. Mitchell's eyes were that outrageous color that meant he was feverish again. The voice was clear, outlining exactly what he needed; "A soft rope, not that Army hemp but soft, thick, with an easy-sliding hondo, pair of gloves, 'bout this size." And he held out both hands, the bound arm trembling with effort. Josh started to shake his head. "Boy, I ain't asking for now but when I tell you." He hesitated, Josh watched the struggle; "That leg's got to be cleaned, you want to do it?"

Blue slept heavily; Josh tried on his mother's advice to wake him several times and got a push, then a groan and a slap. Josh told Mother about Blue's refusal to wake and she turned away from him, busied herself at the stove, stirring something in a pot that hadn't begun to boil.

He went outside and sat on the stump, tried to figure out adults and to reconsider the value of his own sins. Supper was with the Colonel in attendance this evening, and Josh tried to explain between his parents' more obvious conversations what he had seen in the paddock behind the stables where the misfit horses had been abandoned. He had become part of these horses and their existence, both when the dun and his mama came reluctantly along with the recaptured stallion, and when Blue sat in the paddock and paid no attention to the wild colt, who then walked over and tested this strange person. A wild horse chewing on a man's hair, allowing that man to touch him, the two of them sniffing each other; Josh truly did not understand what he had witnessed.

It was when he mentioned the sniffing, or breathing, that Mother turned away from serving another slice of the Colonel's favored pot roast, and said that such terms were not to be used at the dinner table. Papa spoke of interviewing more of the troopers involved with the capturing of Comet, and the guardhouse escape, and he had come to the conclusion that while Sutter had tried to embellish his role in the return of Comet, he had acted in good faith upon finding the unconscious guard. Yes there was a discrepancy as to where the weapons had been found, but in the confusion of the night, and in view of the wound that disabled Mr. Mitchell, there would be no further investigation or allegations, or any charges brought against the man.

The Colonel then stared at his son, whose face turned red under his father's gaze but the eyes did not move away or blink. Snow hardened his voice, delivering a flat statement; "It is yet to be determined just how and why Comet escaped, but for now Mr. Mitchell is no longer considered involved in any aspect of the rescued horses."

The Colonel wasn't certain there was a flicker in Josh's eyes, a shift of something that couldn't be given a name but he had witnessed this expression in men allowed an innocent verdict in court marshal cases. Perhaps it was simply relief for Mr. Mitchell, since the boy seemed greatly taken with the man's odd personage.

He cut into a center slice of the pot roast and then packed mashed potatoes and some of the gravy onto the meat, put it in his mouth and chewed with great pleasure. When it was possible to swallow, he looked at his boy again. "That's very interesting, what you told me about Mr. Mitchell and that wild horse. He might be of some use on the Post, to repay his room and board when he is healed."

There was so much that offended Josh in his father's complacent words that he choked and almost spat out what suddenly expanded into impossible dimensions in his mouth. His father proceeded to cut another slice of the beef, and treat it exactly as he had the first slice. The pleasure on the man's face angered Josh, made him want to stand and throw something at his father.

"Mother, I'm not hungry. Let me fix a plate for Blue. . .Mr. Mitchell." His mother's face turned pink, and she looked down. "Yes, Joshua, that's a good idea. Harlan, may I get you more roast?" He'd been dismissed.

The following day Josh expected great things yet it was the same slowed walk to the paddock, more cleaning while Blue sat against the fence post and this time the colt came over quickly, tugged on Blue's sleeve, allow Blue to touch the flat jowl of his face, his forearm, slide a hand down the forearm and knee to just above the infection. When the colt pulled his leg away, Blue talked to the horse but in such a gentle tone that Josh heard nothing except the gasps between words.

The colt eventually dropped his head and Blue stroked the muzzle. Once again the colt used his teeth to grab Blue's hand and got that clicking sound that made him release his hold. When the chores were done, Blue stood very slowly, and walked to the brown mustang, who seemed to curve his head and neck around Blue and they were quiet, no movement, nothing but Blue stroking the mustang's muzzle, playing with the long lips, tugging on both ears and then looking up at Josh, nodding toward the gate and they walked out, leaving both horses staring at the strange humans before returning to the more important matters of eating up every wisp of hay and taking a long drink of fresh water.

Blue walked past the stump and opened the back door. He'd said nothing on the return trip and Josh found himself studying the man, wondering what happened inside that brain to sense how to reach an unbroken wild horse.

That evening Blue walked outside, down the long road in front of the house, restless and not needing Josh's assistance. The boy spoke to his mother, asking if Blue could join them at supper and she turned away, busied herself pounding at well-kneaded bread and suggested that perhaps a plate brought into his room would be more comfortable for Mr. Mitchell. And more pleasant for the Colonel, who was ill at ease with a civilian billeted in his quarters.

As Josh suspected, Blue left early the next morning without waiting for him to tag along. Last night, Josh had taken in the plate of food and Blue told him to put out the supplies, have them ready near the fence. It had been awkward, for Josh had to lie to his father to get out of the house and do the promised chore. Now Blue was gone, and Josh ran toward the paddock, knowing enough to slow to a walk and whistle, make some noises before he came around the corner.

Blue had the dun colt caught with the soft rope he'd requested, and there was a slip noose around the colt's nose as well. Horse and human watched each other. Then Blue tugged on the rope, the colt reared, Blue waited until the colt came down and tugged again. Blue didn't move but kept talking that nonsense to the dun while he waited.

Josh watched for ten minutes, the give and pull, release, a few words, asking again, until he got bored and sat down, and his quick change of place spooked the dun who pulled back, almost toppling Blue. But the man steadied himself, spoke to the horse and didn't bother with Josh who went hot with shame.

Another five minutes and Blue walked to where the buckets sat inside the fence line. White cloths were soaking in the water.

The dun colt followed with a tug on the soft rope. Blue knelt and wrung out one of the cloths with his good hand, turned on his knees and placed the damp cloth on the infection. The colt jerked back once, Blue only clicked his tongue and touched the soft rope and the colt stood while Blue washed out the stained cloth and reapplied it to the wound and finally removed most of the pus and opened the cut to clean air. Only them did it occur to Josh that Blue was occasionally using his injured arm.

Then Blue told Josh, in that quiet voice, to stand slowly, walk to them. He was needed to wrap the leg; Blue would hold the colt and convince him to allow the doctoring. Within ten minutes and a few snorts, a light hand on the rope, the colt had a leg smeared with tar salve and tied with a bandage.

Blue fell back against the fence and used the railings to hold himself until he could stand on his own, breathing hard, face blanched of color but he grinned at Josh. "That wasn't so bad, you take it slow most things'll get done." He stepped in close to the dun, put the end of the rope over the arched neck and removed the rope from the head. The colt thought to pull free, Blue caught the rope end and tugged until the colt stood. Then Blue let the rope slide off the neck as he walked away. He barely had enough breath for the words; "Don't let him think he can run away from you. Leave while you're the boss."

The next day Papa rode out with several squads of troopers, responding to an anxious rancher's concerns. Only a year ago there had been a slaughter and burial of the last of the rebellious Indians, Bigfoot and the families trying to escape. But still ranchers and even townsfolk would panic if they saw a lone Indian, and now Papa chose to ride at the head of these expeditions, to provide comfort and safety to the frantic civilians.

CHAPTER EIGHT

She had pleaded with Harlan to allow a junior officer to take this command; there were several good men assigned to him that had scant experience in the field. They could benefit from these expeditions where commanding the troops was an exercise rather than having to contend with any possible danger.

Harlan smiled and patted her hand and said that he was getting restless under the constraints of peace time and needed to at least follow the formalities of chasing an enemy. So he would ride out in the morning, and would leave her safely with Josh, reminding her that she lived in the middle of a military post and had no reason to fear being without her husband for a few days.

Harlan went on, warming to the subject at hand; Mr. Mitchell seemed to be healing nicely, and while Dr. Hager said it was not yet safe to quarter the man in the hospital, he had proven himself to be a moral individual and seemed to have a stabilizing effect on Josh's impetuous tendencies.

There were no further arguments Dorothy could muster to convince her husband that leaving her with a boy, and the strange man inhabiting the downstairs sewing room, was in any manner a good idea. Despite her concerns, however, supper was a pleasant affair. She had found live chickens at the commissary and when Josh brought the struggling fowl home, Mr. Mitchell had shown the boy how to quickly and painlessly wring a neck so that the intended main course did not suffer. And Blue Mitchell was once again their guest, invited to the table by Harlan in a grand gesture. Dorothy knew better; Harlan wanted a larger audience.

It was however an older fowl so they had stewed hen with dumplings, and lettuce that Dorothy planted in their back yard. The dark green leaves lay rather plainly on the plate next to the richness of the chicken chunks and the lightest of dumplings in gravy, but she persevered, and finally Mr. Mitchell said he'd eat the lettuce if she doused it with something so he wouldn't feel like a rabbit nibbling at its supper.

Dorothy laughed, for Mr. Mitchell's few words conjured up quite an image. She rose quite self-consciously from the table, in the kitchen of course, the dining room was for family and the company of friends. There had been a suggestion from one of the ladies who had friends still in the east, when at a sewing circle Dorothy mentioned she had planted the exotic leafy green called lettuce and she wasn't certain how to serve it. The woman had been direct and rather superior in describing how the edible was dressed in the east as to give it a certain flavor.

This one time Dorothy listened to the pompous woman's recipe and had prepared a mixture of oil and vinegar, with salt and pepper, bottled in a small jar. She brought it to the table and told the skeptics to shake the bottle, then quickly pour a small amount of the liquid on the lettuce.

They followed her directions, chewed and swallowed and the dual expressions told her the experiment was not an unqualified success. Harlan of course abstained from the adventure, stating that he preferred his vegetables cooked and well salted.

It was extremely difficult to sleep that night. Josh was snoring lightly in the room down the hall and with the door open she could hear him. Dorothy was unaccountably restless, turning over, lying still, listening, not once thinking about her husband and his safety on tomorrow's brave and foolhardy expedition.

She heard Mr. Mitchell get up in the middle of the night and use the inside facility, yet there was no sound of a return trip and it must be that he'd gone outside. She got up and put on her wrapper, went very softly down the back stairway and into the kitchen where she could look through the larger window and there he was, barefoot and shirtless, in those odd leather-seated pants he preferred, standing, turning his head as if listening and she remembered Josh's explanation, confirmed by Harlan's recital, of why the man broke out of the guardhouse; that he could sense and hear things that most people did not understand, especially anything to do with horses and their wellbeing.

Only when Mr. Mitchell was back inside did she return to her own room, where she removed the wrapper and lay down, desperate to sleep and escape her dreams.

They were all gone in the morning when she woke late; she'd felt Harlan leave the bed much earlier, and then a bugle played a different call as she rolled over and went back to sleep. Eventually she woke remembering her responsibilities, and ventured down the stairs after spending a long time dressing.

In the kitchen a pot of coffee simmered on a back burner, thickened to the consistency of molasses. There was a note on the table saying Josh had gone with Mr. Mitchell to the paddock, to check on the injured horse. She was not to worry, he promised they wouldn't do anything foolish.

"That leg's looking better, can you get me my gear, think ole Sutter dumped it inside that blacksmith shop." Blue was different, changing, no longer in need of Josh's assistance yet he had allowed the boy to accompanying him.

When Josh found the gear it was black and greasy, the beautifully woven saddle blanket coated with ash. He wiped off what he could and put the gear down near Blue. The man glanced over and grinned and Josh couldn't believe it. 'Man's got a small soul, ain't he', was all Mitchell said.

Then, "Here, hold Charley, light now on the rope, no leaning or pulling." And Josh had a mustang on the other end of a short rope. He looked at the dun and the horse swung his head, pawed at the ground. "Don't stare at him, kid, he's thinking you might be getting ready to have him for dinner." Josh looked down and away and the horse immediately quieted. Blue smoothed the blanket over the high withers and the dun turned his head, snorting at the peculiar sensation. Blue spoke very softly, watching the dun but focused also on Josh; "This might get wild, boy, you hang on."

He set the saddle gently on the blanket, the colt humped his back and Blue eased up near his face, rubbed the flat jowl, then cupped the muzzle. It was when he bent down, awkward with the bound arm, and retrieved the cinch, threaded the latigo and quickly formed the slipknot that the colt exploded. "Let him go, boy, get the hell out of the way."

The two men watched, safe against the fence and in a corner, while the colt bucked and the brown mustang kept eating. Finally the colt got tired or bored, the saddle still sat on his back, and he joined the brown for the morning hay.

"Let's leave 'em a bit, he'll figure it out given time." Blue found a big enough tree outside the fence line where two men could set against it and watch without getting in each other's way.

"I was the one who let Comet escape." Josh's voice shook. Blue's answer confounded him; "Figured that, first time we

met, saw it in your face." The man had no mercy; Josh rubbed his upper arms with his hands and wished for a cup of coffee. Mitchell didn't quit; "It's up to you when you tell your pa, that man sent to the guardhouse, he only did a few days. But they was your days, not his. He needs an apology from you more'n anyone in this mess. It's up to you, boy. To set it straight." The voice was muted; the man stared out at the horses, carefully not looking at Josh.

Then Blue shoved himself to standing; "Set, boy, what gets done now needs only one of us." He walked into the paddock, up alongside the brown mustang who quit eating long enough to sniff at Blue as he reached under the brown neck and picked up the rope still on the dun's head. The colt spooked then stood quiet.

Blue walked around the front of the older mustang, who bumped Blue's bad arm with his nose, then went back to the hay, and the dun was merely curious as Blue checked the cinch, tugged another few inches and the colt humped backwards. The brown continued to eat.

Then Blue stepped into the saddle with an easy move and the colt shook, looked around, sniffed at Blue's foot and stood quiet alongside his friend. Blue sat there for a few moments, then toed the brown who moved away, and the colt moved with him. The brown walked over to the water buckets, the colt went along, Blue sitting quiet. From his place at the tree, Josh could see that most of Blue's weight was held on his thighs, as if he were floating above the saddle.

The brown stopped to itch his leg, the colt wanted to stop but Blue sort of put his legs on the colt who humped and took a step forward on his own, then another step until he walked the whole paddock and then Blue dismounted, stripped the gear one-handed and let the colt go.

He called to Josh; "I'm done."

Josh tried asking questions but when he got no answers he glanced at Blue and saw that look and he remembered the man was injured and still healing. But what he'd seen was impossible and he wanted to know how to make the same miracle happen.

"When I get enough breath, boy, I'll try and show you. It's feel mostly, you got to listen to what the horse's telling you." They were at the back door; Blue's hand on the wood frame was white and shaking. "Thanks for the help. Good to know you were there." Mitchell went straight to the back room and Josh hesitated long enough to know the man had laid himself down on the bed and was most likely already asleep.

His mother was seated in the kitchen, sipping out of a white cup, holding it with both hands and staring as if she didn't see Josh. When he made enough noise to attract her attention, she smiled and looked tired and told him two of the boys had come looking for him, they were gone rabbit hunting, he would know where, and they had taken a lunch with them. She had a bag ready for him on the table.

Josh grabbed the food and ran out the back door and across the parade ground, wildly going over in his head what he'd seen, pretty certain these boys wouldn't believe him but it would be fun to chase a few rabbits, maybe bring home supper. He wanted time to set what he'd witnessed that morning and think about Blue's promise to teach him how.

She watched her son from the kitchen window and smiled; Josh and those two boys wouldn't be home until well after dark. He needed that free time, his father out on a mission, no school, he needed to be with those his own age. He was spending too much time with Mr. Mitchell. Soon enough he would go to college and then all the innocence of these last months would be gone. She sighed and refilled the white teacup with the smallest amount of sherry.

Two hours later Dorothy looked in on their visitor. Mr. Mitchell was still sleeping, sprawled across the bed and not having removed his boots. She went in to do for him, to loosen his collar and slide off the heeled boots, for she'd had experience and knew exactly how to do this without waking *the man. Harlan drank more than was good for him on many occasions other than the one time Josh helped put his father into bed.*

She allowed to herself that the sherry had given her a boldness she did not normally possess and she put her hand to her mouth to suppress a giggle. The boots came easily, then she proceeded to unbutton his shirt. Each button was a challenge; her fingers were awkward, her mind racing with the sherry's assistance.

There was no wasted, sagging flesh on this body, no belly spread along his ribs, no pouched jowls that waggled when he made a pronouncement. That hair was a color women sighed over, the thick curls begging to be touched. And his hands, their long fingers and enlarged knuckles held small scars of a life fully lived.

Her own hand reached out to touch his naked chest, grateful that Josh had procured fresh undergarments for the man and he'd shed those ruined combinations. And of course he opened his eyes; "Yes, ma'am." His voice, gentle and knowing, gave her permission so she lay down beside him. At first she was careful but he smiled and breathed into her ear that she could move closer, and his good arm supported her head while she shifted, bound by her heavy clothes, all the foolish undergarments women must wear to maintain respectability.

For this moment outside of daily life, she did not care. She was no longer a well-mannered and well-married lady but a woman so badly taken by a man that she had shed her shame as quickly as she allowed him to undo her clothing. The feel of skin on skin was so much more than she expected

He wasn't much assistance in removing much of the strangling material within which a decent woman hid her shape and cloaked her desires. However, he could work the buttons with his strong fingers, she discovered, an unlikely one-handed skill and especially those buttons at her throat, her neck, the slowly emerging swell of her bosom.

The lightest of touches there made it impossible to continue her disrobing, it became even more difficult when he supported himself on his one good arm and slid across her breast to kiss her, beginning at her throat.

It had never occurred to Dorothy that such intimacies could provide this indecent, encompassing pleasure. She reached for him, having learned in marriage that certain places on a man made for a quick finish to the act itself. Then she stopped, not out of shyness for a stranger's body, but the thought of all this being over with too quickly.

He was gone in the early morning, taking the brown mustang and the dun colt, leaving the mare and her week-old foal. There was no one to order troops after him, no reason to return him to Fort Robinson. The Colonel had given his decision that Mitchell was not to be charged, so the few men who noticed his departure did so more with relief than any concern.

Joshua Snow woke late, burned by yesterday's hunt with his friends. He'd been quickly bored with their nonsense teasing and childish games, but he'd stayed out of loyalty into the evening, when they lit a fire and cook the day's catch on sticks held over the flame. He'd come home in the dark, expecting to find his mother doing her needlepoint and Blue asleep.

The door to the sewing room was closed, but a light showed underneath the imperfect frame. Josh almost knocked, but it was late and he wasn't sure enough of Blue's recovery to bother him. Mother was in the living room, seated quietly near the window, her project was draped over her lap, her hands unmoving. She barely looked at him as he entered, and when he spoke; "Mother," she jumped and turned and he thought how beautiful she was. And how strange that he'd never noticed her beauty before.

When she told him that Mr. Mitchell had ridden out, taking the two horses, Josh went after him on foot. He wasn't foolish enough to think he could find Blue or catch up to him, but he wanted to see which way Mitchell was headed, to say a goodbye in solitude. He was gone several hours, following the civilian-shod prints so easy to pick out from the Army mounts who also used this trail. It was a trick that Blue had taught him, like seeing the buckskin mare and reading the marred hide for her history.

The man was headed north into the Dakotas or Montana and not west into Wyoming. When Josh got to the top of a ridge, he sat for an hour, chewing on a stalk of grass as Blue had done in the pen, waiting for the dun gelding to approach him. He could see into the distance and almost taste the lingering dust of Mitchell's horses. The scene was high yellow grass, the bare tips of rocks to the north and west; strange beauty hidden in a harsh land.

Then he stood up, dusted himself clean, and walked back to the noisy Fort and the familiar security of home without his father in it.

Harlan Snow rode in three days later and accepted his son's sullen temper, and his wife's reluctance in their marriage bed during their perfunctory intimacy, as signs of her continued misunderstanding of his need for adventure and the boy's disappointment at not being allowed to ride along.

1897

CHAPTER NINE

It was luck and a loose shoe that gave Blue a home the fall of '91 and unexpectedly lasted into winter and spring and now it was six years he'd worked for Con Norris in the Nebraska sand hills.

Riding vaguely north from the Fort, bruised in heart and body, Blue had paid little attention to the horses' condition and his lack of good judgment caught up with him. Five slow weeks out and Keno threw the shoe, bent it first, nails tearing through the hoof wall, horse lamed and it was all for Blue not noticing as he saddled up each morning. His mind was occupied with other matters.

He knew better; it just didn't seem important. And of course it wasn't simply Keno taking a bad step and overreaching, but a wild spook from the unexpected that caused the trouble.

They came around a corner on the edge of a series of low hills thick with grasses held by sandy soil that offered slick going and there was a wolf, then two of them that scared Keno who whirled, half-reared and skidded down the hill edge, taking the dun colt and Blue along for the ride.

The colt flipped over, slammed into Keno who sat down, slid ten feet more then tried to turn and charge up hill. Blue came off sideways, rolling and holding to the dun's lead. When the dust settled, the horses were standing and Blue still had the colt's line. It was only when he went to step into the saddle that he realized Keno was holding that off front hoof from the ground. Blue knelt and held the leg and there was no heat or swelling, just a twisted shoe hanging by one nail with a large section of the damaged and scarred hoof wall still attached.

Well damn was Blue's first thought. Then he tied the colt to Keno's saddle horn, pulled out a blunt hammer he always carried and pried the last nail out. When he looked at what he held in his hand, he was disgusted. Keno lowered his head to graze, doubling over on that front hoof, reluctant to put his weight down on the torn wall. Blue shook his head, all for two wolves probably as scared by them as the horses were terrified of the wolves. He sat down, felt the bent grass beneath him and let his fingers dig into the earth. He released wet roots, thick and tangled together, holding topsoil against wind and rain.

Finally he raised his head and took note of where he was, stranded and afoot unless he tried riding the colt again. The sun was low, he and the horses were surrounded by miles of low smooth hills. The reopened ache in his arm reminded Blue he wasn't whole yet.

And way in the distance, if he stood tall and stared at the edge of the land, he could see a windmill, and what appeared to be fences, maybe even a chimney. With the endless miles of smooth land, any bump or hollow stood out.

Tomorrow he'd ride straight toward the windmill; at least he'd have fresh water.

Saddling the colt was a slow repetition of what he'd done at the Fort. The dun was curious but not particularly worried, until Blue tightened the cinch and Charley kicked out. It got rough trying to hold his temper; another broke arm would be the end to him. Blue let the colt kick but pushed him in a circle off a long rein, keeping the colt going forward and slowly tiring him.

When it felt right he redid the cinch and got nothing more than a nose against his arm, so he patted the colt's neck, stepped up into the saddle and let the colt figure out what'd happened as Blue tugged on Keno's lead.

Blue glanced back once and saw the wandering bent grass left by each horse's path. All over the place, from right to left, halfway up a small hill, straight down, then maybe ten feet in a line. Blue laughed and the dun colt's ears came back. Blue patted the damp neck and the colt bobbed his head.

The land folded into a low series of hills ringed around a set of corrals and that windmill he'd seen from last night's camp. Grass was trampled down, muddied at the edges of the windmill's water supply. A thin pipe emptied a steady stream into a dirt tank. The whirr of the blades set the colt to bucking, a few crow hops in a line away from the windmill itself. Blue got the horses turned around and made them stand; he could hear the colt taking in deep breaths, Blue did the same and the scent of water was overwhelming.

He pushed the colt forward, right up to the muddy edge, and when Keno shoved his head in up to his eyes, the dun took a quick sniff of the water surface, licked it, then drank greedily.

It was easy enough following a trail from the water; headed south and east through a series of low valleys banded with more hills. Around one more corner past a single bent tree and there was a ranch house, barns, a good set of corrals, a man walking across the yard toward a house set back and up on one of those hills flattened to hold a building. He let the dun colt rest, stood in the stirrups and hollered; the man stopped, looked up and seemed to nod so Blue guided the colt and Keno down the last hill.

A red-headed man came out of what looked like a bunkhouse and this time the colt knew it was a wolf and went to serious bucking. Blue let the lead go, put spurs lightly to the dun and rode out a pretty fair display. It wasn't a bad way to come into a ranch, he figured, long as he didn't come off or pull leather and disgrace himself.

The colt slipped and sat down, Blue leaned forward, patted the colt's neck, and stepped off. Keno had drifted on three legs to a corral and was fussing with a penned-up bronc that held a differing opinion on Keno's arrival. The man at the bunkhouse door scowled, obviously not impressed. Blue barely glanced at him, for he'd seen a door open out of the main house and that would be the boss. A tall man, bent some to one side, gray hair with a dented hat slapped on it. Blue held the colt, let Keno keep at his conversation, and waited.

"What'd you want, mister?" Right to the point and not too friendly; Blue understood. He nodded; "I've got a horse threw a shoe, would be obliged to use your blacksmithing tools or pay your smith for the work. Ain't got much cash but I can work a horse or two." It was his usual bargain, and sometimes

he got a good deal, but the frown on this man's face didn't give him much hope.

Connor Norris wasn't old by his reckoning but this morning he felt ninety. In three days' time he'd lost a good smith worked for him twenty years to a colt kicked up and sideways, got the man in the skull and he went down hard, the colt got loose and raised hell running through the yard, wanting back in his pen, wanting hay and water and nothing to do with some strange being tried to pick up a hind leg.

Another man rode out the next morning, never even waited to bury the smith. Con had thought the man would stay but the rider simply disappeared. Now some wild-eyed drifter comes bucking and sliding into the ranch yard asking to pick up a job or two riding broncs while doing some shoeing on his own. The man's arrival was almost too good to be possible, so Con figured he'd have to study on the man doing the talking.

He knew from years of experience that the best way to judge was to study the man's horses and gear. He nodded to the man, took a second look and had his doubts. The colt was too young to be ridden hard, the man was injured, holding his left arm tight to his side. Con saw red stains on the shirt, the thickness of a bandage under the sleeve. Not a good beginning for a smithy or a horse breaker. Then the man looked straight at Con. They were strange eyes but clear, in a long, homely face. The man was no drinker, no lazy son of a bitch. Con said yes, for now, take a few days of work, some rest for the horses and then they'd talk.

The drifter was polite if nothing else; "Thanks. Can you show me a place I can put the colt, I don't want to wear him down, he's too young for hard riding but I didn't have much choice." The man waved at the three-legged brown and that was almost enough for Con to hire him on the spot. But the arm bothered him; he didn't need a single-winged smithy. There were enough cripples to the spread, with him at the top of the list.

Con grunted; "Use the back pen, take what hay you need." The drifter turned away and headed to pick up the brown mustang now dozing near the pens. He spoke soft to the horse who woke, waited until the man picked up the lead and then turned willingly enough. Damned lame all right; Con saw the ruined hoof wall, shook his head, be goddamn lucky the horse could ever be ridden again.

That afternoon the drifter, said his name was Mitchell, added the peculiar first name and Con nodded, grunted again, said he'd heard of him. Mitchell shrugged, countered with he figured what Norris heard wasn't all bad or they'd not be standing here talking to each other. Con laughed; he liked it when a man didn't take it too serious that a rancher in the middle of the sand hills had heard his name and was still willing to give him a try.

Anyway the son worked on his brown horse, pure mustang far as Con could read, a crude brand belonging to no outfit he'd ever heard tell of, a big head, lean neck, good back and strong hind end but a hard look to the eye when Con thought to touch the horse.

Mitchell only swung his head and didn't look up at Con with those goddamn eyes but said that Keno wasn't partial to most folk. Con took the hint and backed off, but he was determined to stay and watch. The bad arm obviously was a bother to Mitchell as he picked up the damaged hoof. His face tightened, eyes narrowed, still he settled the hoof on his thigh, used a paring knife gently, cutting careful around the chipped wall. He spoke once; "Damn." Con nodded agreement.

Mitchell let the hoof down gently and the brown grunted. "Mister, I need to make a deal with you, a winter here working horses or I'll turn this son loose. He can't be ridden, or led, with a foot like that." Con nodded; "Let's see what happens, Mitchell. I got an empty line shack not too far from here, with good corrals, a decent wood stove and enough trees to keep a man warm all winter. That ought to do you."

Right Taylor didn't think much of the sidewinder who came slamming into the Norris yard. The man was showing off, swinging his legs on a good dun colt and hooraying like the mustang was a whirlwind bucking straight into hell.

Right was always leery of a man started out saying he was the best there was. It might be that Mitchell didn't say those words but he sure rode the dun like he was advertising. And Right was surprised Con bought it. Until Con explained later that he'd heard Mitchell's name and reputation and what he could do with a riled-up bronc, so it was his choice to give the man a winter to heal, get him food and a few horses and see what happened come spring. The man would owe Con a few broke horses by then.

That first week Right led two horses to the line camp along with the loaded pack mule. Mitchell didn't seem much interested in Right's company; he accepted the supplies and told Right to take the unbroken stock back to Con, he couldn't do nothing yet. Raised his arm, busted bad, any fool could see that, raised that bad wing and shrugged and let Right explain to Con that the man was eating and sleeping and not doing nothing. Having to tell Con the truth near to ruined Right's mostly even temper.

Con laughed and told Right that the arm looked bad and he sure didn't want the responsibility of a man healing poorly. Mitchell would ride the young stock when he could. It took Con time spent explaining all this to Right; Mitchell's reputation said he kept to his given promise so Con could feel easy feeding the man and letting him be.

In the spring Right learned a whole lot about the size of Blue Mitchell and came to respect the man. Con had a well, dug maybe twenty years past, hand dug to twenty-five feet Con said. Some son of a bitch after the War thought to make him a claim but after digging at the well, the man disappeared. Indians, it was thought.

Con bought the land and got the half-dug well with it. Took him a year, he once said, thinking back, took him a year of hand-digging to get to that depth. Goddamn good well it was too. Right had noticed the boss swore a lot, mostly 'goddamn' but he didn't let it bother him, although Right himself didn't swear much.

The well served the big pasture Con used in late summer for the mares before he took their colts off them. Con bred up a good herd of maybe ten mares and he was proud of what the herd produced. His favorite mare, a sturdy bay with little white, a good eye and clean hindquarters, papered even as a Thoroughbred, was carrying this year to a racing stallion a man north of Valentine owned. Con was figuring to put new blood into the herd.

The mare birthed out a nice bay colt, clean like his mama, with a hint of speed and height. Her wise eye set right in the youngster's head, short cannon bone and a good forearm. Con was tickled when she gave him the colt, then another mare, a sorrel with a small snip, she foaled out a second colt half brother to the bay. Double win on the gamble, Con said, and sent the boys to bring in the two mares for a few days so he could study on them.

It was Right who brought Con the news; the mares were fine, staying together and lonesome 'cause the two colts had plumb disappeared. Right tried letting the mares move on without herding them, hoping they would take him to wherever the colts were asleep. The mares drifted some, nickered quietly and when nothing answered, the mares put their heads back down to graze.

He was upset and wary of Con when he came in to tell him. Con didn't do much but stare at Right, told him to ride a careful search of the whole damned pasture, camp out if he got to the far end, but find those two colts. Right was gone two days and found nothing, no tracks, no nested colts, not even two half-eaten bodies or a few fresh bones. He was cautious returning to the ranch but Con took the news quiet, nodded his *head once and went back into the house. Slammed the door hard, but that was it.*

Blue Mitchell saddled a stout roan, took the bronc up into the unused fall pasture through a break in the fence line, for some miles and wet saddle blankets. The colt had a tendency to spook and buck and Blue figured he could ride out that idea, replace it with the thought of trotting a long line in any direction Blue chose, nevermind what else might catch the colt's attention. He'd tell Con about the busted fence when he put the colt up for the night.

The hand-dug well was on a hill, and a low pipe drew the water out into a dirt tank. When there weren't horses in the pasture, the water was used by pronghorn, coyote and deer. Their tracks crowded the edge of the tank, but to Blue's eyes the tracks were old, covered in with blown dirt and spattered with rain.

He stepped off the colt and stood a moment, hearing only the colt's explosive breathing, and tasting a sweet smell on the air. He walked the colt a bit, loosened the cinch before allowing the roan to drink from the well water. The colt stuck his nose deep into the water, then bolted backwards, hauling Blue along with him. Blue got the colt settled, spent time crooning to him, touching his muzzle and then his neck, until he felt the colt let out a breath.

A too-familiar stench alerted Blue, and he drew the colt with him, knelt at the edge of the water and scooped out a handful, brought it to his face and pulled back, wanting to run like the sensible colt had done. Something had died in the well.

He tied the colt to a stout tree and started climbing. Sure enough one rock slipped underfoot and the colt scrambled back, tried to fight the tree and the good rope Blue'd used to snug him. The battle went on about five minutes before the colt quit. That was one lesson learned.

Blue climbed up to the mouth of the well, five feet across, water shimmering below the pipe. The water appeared oily, with a swirled surface, and the stench quickly sickened Blue. He stared, leaning over the edge, cursing that the top hadn't been covered. Neat timbers lined the four sides but it was too easy to pick out the bay and sorrel hides, black tail, long blond mane, a separated hoof, strands of loose blond and black hair wrapped around stick-size legs.

He pulled back, leaned over and retched, spat out bile and the stench and wiped his mouth.

Con took the news hard at first, the dark blue eyes blazing, face going white, then deep red and he started coughing until Blue thought the man would die right then. The hands gathered as Blue talked, and for once there were no whispers or shoving; the men stood quiet, their faces stern and uncomfortable.

"Mr. Norris." Blue had to get the boss's attention. "You've got to clean out that well, the water's rotten, nothing's drinking from the tank. You put horses in there and they'll all die." Norris's head came up, the look to those eyes deeper'n the well hole. "You and Right, you deal with it. I can't. . .won't, ah goddamn, Mitchell. Those were good colts." Norris turned and walked to the back door of the house as Blue felt a man come up next to him.

It was Right Taylor, as Blue expected; hearing the boss, the man came to do his job. Right was straight on; "We'll need a pack horse, take up a bucket and line and drag those. . . ." Here Right got stuck and Blue turned to study the man. There was a catch to his words; "We'll haul 'em out, it won't be easy but it's got to be done."

Blue watched the weathered face crowned with that red hair and knew the man disliked him yet he was allowing Blue a look into his private being. Right surprised him; "It's waste, Mitchell, and pure bad luck. Them colts were Con's future. Damn whatever broke the fence, damn we needed to cover that well and didn't think of it. Just damn."

There was nothing to do but agree. Blue nodded; "Let's get going now and we can make camp tonight, be at work by sun-up." Right agreed.

Right said they'd draw straws for who went down the shaft and who got to lower the bucket and haul out the mess. From the look on Right's face, Blue figured the man would drown from the stench.

Blue grinned and dragged out the short straw, threw it to the ground and pushed at it with his boot toe. "Hell, Right, you do the hauling, I don't think my arm's ready for that kind of work." They were silent, watchful, each man uncomfortable with the other's presence. Right finally nodded.

The work was terrible; Blue climbed down on the exposed timbers, gripping hard, afraid he would fall in and drown in the refuse. Bits and pieces floated on the surface, larger sections of mostly bone jabbed through the top of the water, then swirled and disappeared. The stink masked Blue's face, making his hands slippery with oil; he coughed, spat, nothing helped. The rope tied around his middle was his only safety.

He had to let his bare feet and legs slide into the muck so he could reach the pieces, toss them into the bucket that came down with him. It was quick to fill, hoof, ribs, an ear. Blue gagged and spat again, then tugged on the bucket line and called up to Right. He heard a grunt, the bucket rose, began to swing, hit the well sides and pieces spilled over the bucket rim. Blue ducked but not in time and he was drenched with liquid flesh.

Five buckets filled with remains, five stinking baths as the buckets got hauled up; Blue was shivering, hands too slippery to catch and pull out bone but he got the lights, the innards that even the ravens wouldn't want.

He couldn't reach two leg bones, each time his fingers touched them they bobbed and sank and he wasn't diving in. Finally he had to laugh; stuck down a hole in living flesh, soaked, dripping, smelling like a bone yard and it seemed clear to him he wasn't getting on in the world. One more grab and he caught the knob end of a bone, dropped it in the empty bucket and heard the metal sing. When he caught the second bone plumb in the middle, it made the same sound when he pushed it into the bucket. It was music he never wanted to hear again.

Right yelled down, "You want the bucket pulled up?" and Blue answered; "Pull it up, then get me the hell out of here, this work stinks." By the time Blue got to the top, clawing his way as he was pulled, using fingers and toes, Right had a peculiar expression on his usually sour face.

"You're okay, Mitchell. I don't know many fools'd do such work and laugh about it."

That was six years ago; after the episode with the polluted well it was settled that Blue worked for the Rafter Bar T and Con Norris. Con bought the Thoroughbred stallion from his friend and bred the mares back, got two colts again, and more over the years. There were mares on the ranch, all of a similar color and build, solid working mares that bred to the new stallion gave out a sturdy offspring capable of hard work and long miles. Still Con kept his fondness for the racehorses.

When he set up a herd to travel south, Con bought the best geldings from his neighbors. They liked the profit, and Con didn't mind the drive. The government paid well for using horses. The boys working for Con drove horses south five times to sell to the military, and always Con tried to order Blue to ride along but it didn't work. Blue said flat out he'd pack up and leave before he'd go back to Fort Robinson.

This time though, with Con sick, getting old mostly he said, Blue was needed and he gave in. She'd have forgotten him, he told himself. He hadn't forgotten about her but she would have long since put him out of her thoughts.

His mount for the drive this year was the dun colt, who'd turned into a fine working horse with a steady handle and a good sense of moving stock; horses or cattle, it didn't matter to Charley 'cepting that they went where he and Blue wanted them to go.

Blue agreed to trail with the remounts headed toward Fort Robinson. He couldn't refuse Con, not after all these years, the man letting him stay on, giving Blue good horses to work. It was what he owed his boss.

CHAPTER TEN

The dun whirled and went after the escaping bay with a vengeance. Blue let the horse make his move, trusting the dun's better instincts. Out of the twenty horses being delivered to the Fort, only this one bay, a decent size, good bone, solid and well-trained, insisted on quitting the bunch. Lord help the non-com or officer who got assigned to the rogue bronc.

Blue discovered this trailing horses wasn't bad work for an old man in a young man's game. Blue carried enough years working rough stock to where most punchers quit the wild ones and found a riding job more suited to their broke bones and bent legs. Blue had no such thoughts; he'd ride till that one horse killed him. But he sure as hell hadn't planned on riding back to Fort Robinson.

This time when the Post Commander gave Josh his orders, it wasn't his old man barking out this and that, but the recently-appointed officer, Colonel Radcliff, issuing orders to his brand-new second lieutenant; Lt. Joshua Snow, graduated from West Point and through Army mistake and miscommunication posted to his old home in the northwest corner of Nebraska.

Now that the Indians were contained, Snow's time would be spent working with the new stock. Radcliff had read the reports and knew that at West Point Joshua Snow received excellent remarks on his equestrian abilities, but had several

308

reports of unusual methods of training or retraining horses. The side notes did not condemn the young lieutenant, except perhaps for one bitter exclamation of a captain who had been challenged by Snow over treatment of that officer's mount. From reading the notes of the other officers, it would appear that Snow had refused the brutal actions that this one captain preferred. No charges on either man had been filed. The horse in question had been reassigned.

Sergeant Sutter had been ordered to ride out and meet with the herd; the sergeant was good at handling the men but hard on the horses, and Colonel Radcliff intended to carefully select which mounts went to Sutter. He would not have another good horse destroyed by the man's indifference and lack of sense when it came to what a horse could and could not be expected to perform.

Harlan Snow's decline and then resignation from the Post command, and from the Army, had precipitated a number of difficulties, among them the unexpected and unwanted elevation of Sutter from corporal to sergeant. If Radcliff had his way, he would remove Sutter from the active field and put him behind a desk until his twenty years were finished. Or transfer him east, as far east as possible, where the man and his small arrogance could do little damage.

However, he did not have that luxury of choice, so he'd sent Sutter with a small number of troops to oversee bringing in this newest herd of remounts. In some cases they received their horses by train, but this batch was from a hundred plus miles north and to the east and it was a simple matter for a few hands to drive them.

Radcliff realized he'd been thinking too long while the brand-new second lieutenant had remained at attention. He forced himself to be congenial, for it was young Snow's father who had held the Post command previously. He would try to find the line between welcoming the boy home and treating him as a newly commissioned officer.

Then it occurred to him; "Snow, since you know this area, ride out and meet with the incoming herd. Sutter might need some backup in his dealings with the wranglers." Radcliff laughed to himself as the boy saluted and made an abrupt turn. His greeting had lacked a degree of warmth or tact but it seemed to suit the new lieutenant, for a quick grin had briefly changed his young face.

It had surprised Josh when he saw the dun gelding in a corral. Usually the Army used solid colored horse, never paints and rarely grays except for officers' parade mounts, but he guessed a dark dun was close enough. Then he took another look at the horse and smiled; it had to be that foal, born six years ago right here on the Post. He wondered who rode the horse now, for there were those telltale signs that Mitchell had taught him to watch for; white marks on both sides of the high withers, none on the neck, a few white hairs along the rib where a harsh rider wearing spurs could injudiciously leave scars.

He asked a private who laid claim to the dun and shook his head at the answer. Sergeant Sutter, elevated now in rank, and consequently spoiling a better class of horses, he was the non-com solely responsible for the dun's training. Josh got the distinct feeling the private did not approve of the sergeant's methods.

Josh was given a good sorrel mount, not fancy to look at, an orange color with a tufted forelock and heavy bone but it had a fine long trot and covered ground with ease. He had a general idea of where the horse herd would be coming from, so he lined out the sorrel, finally letting the horse have a short run. He knew where the trails went, he remembered running to this particular trail on foot when he'd learned that Mitchell had left the Post. He'd been a boy then, now he was an officer and supposedly a gentleman, and he'd already forgotten much about the horseman except for his unusual name.

Josh guided the sorrel along the trail, which inevitably took them to the ridge top, where it was needed to stop and *give the horse a breather. As he let the sorrel blow, the new Lt. Snow looked down onto a loosely-herded band of horses. Three wranglers kept to the herd's side and there was Sutter with his small troop, busy riding too close in the back, yelling and making noise until without warning the horse herd burst into a run and Josh found himself on the receiving end of a mild stampede.*

He ran the sorrel headlong down the steepest part of the ridge, yelling and waving his hat, effectively startling the front runners who swerved and began to slow out of confusion. In back of the herd he saw Sergeant Sutter get bucked off his horse and Josh laughed. Then he searched for the head wrangler, wanting to apologize and offer his credentials.

The voice hadn't changed and it spun Josh around, the sorrel willing to swap directions real quick by the twist of Josh's shoulders. "Boy, you look good in that uniform. Guess you told your old man what you'd done and he came to forgive you." That voice, the comment, from a man who seemed to look into Josh and know everything about him, brought back the past too quickly.

Blue Mitchell rode a dark dun gelding that looked a whole lot like the dun left back at the Fort. Josh grinned, kneed his sorrel up close to the rider. "Like your horse, mister. This bunch got any good ones to it?" Josh surprised himself; the anger at Sutter's incompetence was gone, dissolved in seeing his old friend. Both men stuck out a hand while they studied the other. Each thought back six years, to a boy and an injured man and their unlikely partnership.

In Blue's judgment, Josh Snow wore his youth easily, a clean expression to his eyes, looking straight at Blue without reservation. Blue held back, knowing he'd quit on the boy all those years ago, but he finally made a try; "I see you're a new lieutenant. Had to be West Point, how's your. . .pa?" It was rough being polite.

Josh was keen on studying Blue, noting the awkward tilt to the left arm, deeper lines on the face, more gray showing in the blond hair. It was too obvious that Blue's years had been no kinder than when Josh met him. Josh opened his mouth to answer his friend's awkward question.

Sutter interrupted; remounted and grass stained, he pushed his light bay between Josh and Mitchell, turned his horse so he could stare at the boy. "You know better than to ride suddenly into a group of horses. Report to the barracks." Josh smiled, shrugged his shoulders deliberately; "You forget, sergeant, I'm a lieutenant and not one of your troops. If you wish to make a complaint to Colonel Radcliff, I will be glad to offer my side of what just happened here." He added the twist, unable to hold back; "And I believe I have a number of witnesses."

There was no testiness or threat in the boy's words, only a simple truth that shifted the fury in Sutter's eyes. The man turned his attention to Blue as his three troopers rode up to make a line at their sergeant's back.

"You!" Blue had to laugh. Sutter fussed with the new whiskers on his upper lip as he continued; "You are not to set foot on the Fort, your business here was never settled." Blue rested his hands on the saddle horn and stared at the soldier, noting fresh stripes sewn badly to the sleeve; a sergeant now and too bad for those under his command. He finally decided he couldn't let the challenge go unnoticed. Those boys behind Sutter, they were beginning to rest their hands on their close pistols. None of this was what Blue wanted to see at the particular moment.

"Mister Sutter, you got no say in me or what I do. I got paid to deliver these horses to the Fort and that's what I'm doing. Your hee-hawing and yelling back there when that kid's pony you ride took to bucking started the stampede. Josh here rode in to turn the herd." Blue figured the kid could handle himself with this fool so he spoke his mind.

312

"Get out of my way, Sutter, or get run over. It ain't far if I remember right, and maybe if you're careful you can stay mounted for the next few miles." These were words guaranteed to make a full-time enemy but Blue didn't give a damn. The past few years hadn't softened his temper or improved his opinion of humanity, and this sergeant with the fancied mustache and slicked hair certainly didn't change his mind. Now the Snow youngster, the new lieutenant with the shiny bars and a set to his hat, a gleam in his eyes, this boy was worth whatever pleasure Blue still found in the human species.

It was a simple matter to get the horses moving again, with Sutter and his kind going in ahead to 'report the herd's immediate appearance' as the sergeant put it. The boys Connor Norris hired from the sand hills to work his horses knew their job and guided each side lightly; the ponies were lazy now, as if their short run had been enough. Without the Army fools at their back, Blue figured they'd come in quiet and respectful to their new quarters.

Blue glanced over at the boy; the lieutenant rode light with his hands and seat, legs quiet on the sorrel's ribs. Blue nodded approval and the boy surprised him with an answer to his thoughts; "I watched you ride that dun when you were half-dead and one-armed, without any fuss, and I never forgot what you did, how you got to him. You don't ever get hard with a horse and I've seen you. . .well what they tried to teach me at the Point, I kept my own ideas and got a few commendations for it." Blue grinned; "And some trouble too I bet." The boy laughed.

Then he went silent, stared ahead and his hands tightened on the reins; Blue guessed at the reason, not knowing how wrong he was. "Your pa had a fit when you told him." "Yeah." "How bad?" "I spent the rest of that summer mucking out stalls and the paddocks. Got to know the mare and foal, damn shame there." Blue studied the boy; "Sutter got him." Josh's face tightened; "I'd forgotten you could do that."

*"What?" "Know what I was thinking. That's how you knew I'd
been the one. . . ." Blue grinned; "It's common sense, kid, just
common sense and watching the eyes and hands." Josh
grunted and his grip on the reins loosened enough the sorrel
could stretch its neck.*

*A flurry of whinnies and kicks, and it was that bay
gelding trying to bolt until Blue got back to his work, letting
Charley bring in the bay and when it was all settled again,
Josh Snow was riding ahead. The new officer on his steady
horse got to another ridge and raised his hand in a backward
salute. Blue was pleased; the boy'd turned out all right, for a
military man. He sat a horse fine, like he'd once been taught.*

*They brought the horses in at a trot, straight into the
holding pens where the Army took over. It was Sutter again,
not in charge but there, setting a fine dun gelding that looked
just like his older brother. Blue touched Charley's neck and
cursed that he'd left the mare and foal to Sutter's care.*

*The arm never did heal up too well, a bought woman in
Deadwood told him it was rough on her skin but it didn't seem
to slow the proceedings. Still the scarred flesh left a physical
memory that seeing the kid and being at Fort Robinson dug in
to where nothing had ever healed.*

*Connor Norris sent Blue with the horses and a note
giving permission for the quartermaster to pay him the
amount owed. Blue's instructions were to present himself to
the Post Commander, who would sign and legalize the
contract and authorize payment. He didn't want to do this,
didn't want to face Colonel Snow, couldn't do it after all this
time. But Con had asked and Blue had no right to refuse.*

*He unsaddled and rubbed down the dun, and a trooper
offered to lead the horse to a back paddock but Blue said he
already knew where a visitor's horse went and led the dun
around the stone barn, to a small paddock that now held a
water trough filled to the brim. It was a pleasure to turn
Charley loose, and he wondered if the dun gelding had any*

memory of his capture here, his first saddling and the brown mustang who was his enemy and then became his friend.

Charley'd grown to almost sixteen hands, a height Blue liked for his own length of leg but usually that size wasn't the making of a good working horse. Charley proved him wrong and Blue was glad to learn the lesson.

Charley also turned up with speed, and when the brown choked from bad hay, it had been Blue's sorry chore to shoot his old friend. The dun was four then, and Blue worked the colt sparingly, between riding out Con's rough stock, putting on serious manners so anyone could ride the sale horses, including ladies and raw Army recruits.

He had to stop brushing the dun and face what put an edge to him. He had to meet with Colonel, which meant the wife would be close by – ah hell, he thought, I'll get the check, sign the contract in Con's name, and get out of here. This is wrong.

It felt like his jaw dropped when he walked into the Post Commander's office and it wasn't the boy's father. This new one was a tall, lean man, obviously a horseman, and he exhibited his preference with pictures, photographs actually, of horses on the wall behind his desk. Blue'd see a few pictures like this, hadn't believe the picture-making was real but he'd learned, seen more of them and still didn't understand how they got done but it told him a few things about the new Commander. Radcliff was a man who knew horses.

"I watched you come in with the herd, Mr. Mitchell. That's a fine lot Con sent us. I've been buying stock from him a long time. Are there any specific problem horses in the bunch?" This was a direct question meant to catch Blue off balance. He stuttered a few sounds, rubbed his jaw. The Colonel tried to make talk easy for Blue. He didn't know it was the long-born problem of an isolated man.

"Please, Mr. Mitchell, sit down, I know you've been on the trail a few days." Five days, Blue thought, and truly he

appreciated the seat and the offer of coffee and brandy if he wanted it. He sat, and then tried to answer the man's concerns.

"No thanks on the brandy. As for the mounts, there's a couple in there that could be difficult. One bay in particular, off hind sock, whirled hair on his forehead, small ears – he's got his own mind. Somebody rough gets him, there'll be hell coming out the window." The soldier smiled, nodded, acted as if he could understand what Blue was feeling as he continued his report. "There's a sorrel with a snip nose but he's just young, needs some miles on him is all. Con thought he'd do, but if you want to turn him back, that's all right. He said to tell you."

Mitchell looked almighty uncomfortable giving his report and Radcliff felt pity for the man. Out of his element yet Con trusted him, said to listen to him, so Radcliff thought he'd try making the man feel at ease.

He spoke softly; "That young officer new to the Fort, he knows about horses so he'll get the bay. I'm willing to bet he already knows which horse is the troublemaker." The Colonel made a deep sound; "See, Mr. Mitchell, I listen to Post stories and I know your direct effect on Joshua Snow. It will be a pleasure to have him with us. His recommendations from the Point have been sterling, although he was not always receptive to the Army manual of horsemanship and training. I would guess that small blemish on his record could be attributed to your influence also. But it must be added to his record that you gave him a fine hand on any horse."

It was a new notion, that he had helped someone's life. Mostly it was ruination or fights, but not being useful. Not with people leastways, horses he understood, people he mostly angered. Blue nodded back to the Colonel, his face determinedly neutral.

"Sign here, Mr. Mitchell. Con certainly trusts you, for that is a big check you will be returning." Blue grunted and was slow with putting down his name, used Blue Mitchell, all *he really knew to sign. Right next to ole Con's name printed out by some clerk in the Colonel's office.*

He left Con's letter giving him the say-so to do this on the polished wood desk and stood up, uneasy with the military formality, the officer himself and the high-ceiling room, the shining windows, even the bare wood floor with a fancy patterned rug in front of the desk. Blue didn't want to walk on its thickness, too aware his boots would leave clumps of manure on the fine wool. He'd learned that much from staying with the Snows. And the memory snagged him, slowed his response.

Radcliff saw something change in the horseman's face and spoke out thoughtlessly, thinking he knew the nature of the man's distress; "Son, you're getting old for breaking horses. It's a young man's game, we all know that."

It became a moment of tight anger; still Blue had answered this particular insult before. "Colonel, that's none of your business."

One glance at the check amount and Blue's stomach lurched. He needed to saddle up and ride; Right and Haney, they were ready and waiting. It struck Blue odd that it wasn't one of the old hands Norris would trust with the check. Man was getting soured by his age and picked on Blue to be his rep even though others on the crew'd been to the Rafter Bar T more years. Damn. He needed protection with this thing riding in his pocket. First, though, he intended to say good-bye to the boy. He wasn't going to run like that again.

He naturally headed back to the pen of horses where a sergeant was ordering men to separate the stock. And it would be the damnable Sutter of course, getting it all wrong. Blue noted that the wily bay managed twice to escape being penned with a particular group. Then he retreated, bothered by the constant yelling, dust, and the frightened horses, all of it unnecessary. It was smart to separate the horses into groups, but it was better done without the fear. And secretly he was pleased that the bay would have none of the sectioned captivity.

A hand landed high up on Blue's left forearm and he turned and struck without thought, barely missing the chinless jaw, the dumb grin visible through the weedy moustache. It was Sutter of course and the man had been wise enough to know exactly what he was doing, and what Blue's reaction would be, for he'd already pulled out of reach.

"I see you haven't changed in the years, Mr. Mitchell, far too willing to fight. All I wished to do was to draw your attention to some of these horses that are not up to military specifications."

If it had been purely a personal attack, Blue would walk away, but running down Con's horses, that was plain wrong. His voice cracked; "These are good horses, there ain't one that will be trouble to a decent rider." Sutter shook his head; "I understand our new Colonel and Mr. Norris have bought and sold together for years. So any complaints will have to be kept quiet. However now I must put proper manners on a few of the new remounts, thanks to you."

The disgust was mutual. Blue walked away.

This place was angering him, sons a bitches telling him what and who and where and demanding how. None of their business what he did and how he did it so he wanted nothing more than to get on a horse and ride out.

Then a voice called and all anger disappeared; "Hey mister horse wrangler, you got time for a cup a coffee?" It was Josh Snow, his voice a startling mix for Blue, a confusion of good memories and that terrible beckoning hole. He turned and nodded. The boy was all right, educated and seen the big cities and still he knew his friends.

Blue met up with Josh at the doorway to the mess. Josh grinned; "I got an in here, I've known the cook most of my life." They sat at one of the long tables, and the cook brought out coffee, and canned milk, and sugar, as Josh laughed. "See, I remember. You don't get this much on the trail I bet."

He eyed the boy, grown into what Blue'd seen possible in him six years back. Filled out, muscled, tall and moving easy. He wanted to ask without having the words or the right to know.

The boy told him some of it piecemeal and without the question ever asked; "My father retired, Blue. He went back east to die, basically. He's got a cancer." Blue started, clenched his hands around the hot cup. Josh nodded at his surprise; "I learned that from you, to watch, I could see you thinking and the only question you'd have would be about my folks."

But it wasn't all the answer he needed. And that answer still depended on a question he couldn't or wouldn't ask. So he talked over what he knew while hoping the boy would hear beneath the words. "You watch out on the bay the Colonel, Colonel Radcliff, he's going to set on you. He's quick and smart, don't like no one pulling on him but he's fast and can do his job. You soldiers still having your horse races?" The boy laughed; "Yes, and it sounds like I finally got me a racer. Sutter brags on that dun, you know." Blue laughed. "If he's like his older brother, he'll be damned fast even with Sutter aboard. I've won some good change on Charley."

They looked at each other and laughed. Josh said it first; "It'd be kind of interesting for me to take on you and Sutter in a race. Given that I don't know the bay, that you're some older, and that Sutter's still a fool, we'd be evenly matched for handicapping."

Blue put down the heavy cup and looked at the surroundings; high windows, a narrow board floor, too many tables to count, all with matched chairs. Brick walls, Army pennants hung on blank spaces. "Where you went to college, it was like this?" Josh nodded, sighed; "A bit fancier but yeah, barracks and buildings and long lines." "You learn much?" "How to fight mostly, and a lot of reading."

Blue laughed; "Sounds like the life I've been living, mostly the fighting." "You read much?" "Some, when I can find a book. Ain't many out here." Silence hung a moment, Blue could sense the boy trying to hide his surprise. Then they got back to what mattered. "What about the race, Blue?" Blue countered with; "I'm supposed to get this check back to Mr. Norris and that's a good many miles. Don't know." He pushed back from the table.

It had been five easy days to trail the horses in, so it was maybe three, four days going back, time at Norris's spread up near Valentine, another few days coming in. "Give me three weeks, and we'll make it a race." The words felt good saying them; racing against the boy on one of Con's horses out of that bay mare had a lot of twists and turns that appealed to Blue.

As they separated at the mess hall door, Blue tugged on his hat and nodded to the boy. There'd been no word about Josh's mother, but at least he knew she wasn't on the Fort grounds. He didn't know if he felt relief or sorrow for her being gone.

CHAPTER ELEVEN

Mid afternoon Sutter came by the paddock, checking on the visitors' horses, and the dun horse was there, sleeping over the remnants of good Army hay. He studied the animal, wanting to compare the dun to his own favored mount. The colt was willing enough and had speed; one time he bucked Sutter off and none of the troops could catch up to the colt. Sutter laughed and his men acted as if their sergeant had lost his mind. But it was a joke none of the fools could see; finally Sutter had his racehorse.

Mitchell's dun was two years older, had a non-military brand and some extra muscling on the hindquarters, a longer neck with a clean arch to it. Sutter's mount was branded USA of course, and seemed leaner in the neck and ribs. Fitter, and faster was his determination; not carrying so much weight, which would made him the better racehorse. Sutter was pleased.

"You get away from that horse, mister." The devil-eyed cowboy again, not a polite word ever came out of his mouth. Not to him anyway. Sutter turned around; "Just studying on this mount, admiring how alike he is to his younger brother."

Mitchell didn't give an inch; "You ain't studied hard enough, Sutter. Guess you can't see that well. You ride the bit and your horse carries his head too high, that's why you depend on the tie down." Sutter defended himself; "All military horses are required to carry a tie down." "Your fella leans on it. A good wreck and that poor son'll break leather and run out from under you. I've seen it happen with those who ride a hard hand and a harsh bit."

Sutter almost didn't want to speak the words, to savor them for their effect; "Your men left, it was unexpected." Mitchell shrugged; "I'll catch up to them come morning, it's a straight easy ride back, and I've got a fast horse."

It wasn't what Sutter wanted in a reaction. The son of a bitch had to dig it in. Sutter forced a smile; "Before you ride out, be sure to stop in the commissary. I'll leave orders you are to be given supplies." Even that got an undeserved response; "You that eager to get me gone, Sutter? Guess I don't blame you." Then a moment, another surprise; "Thanks, though." As an afterthought, the man turned and actually looked at Sutter. "What happened to their mama?" Sutter grinned; he'd been waiting for this question. "She broke a leg and I shot her." That finally left Mitchell with nothing to say.

Blue didn't like his gut feeling that Sutter would harm the dun gelding for revenge. He kept watch and the dun came nosing over, lipping at Blue's hair and generally making a nuisance of himself. It was a good way to spend an hour; sunshine, a light wind, quiet company.

Then he leaned away from the fence. First he needed food, then a chance to speak with the boy. The Colonel had told him he could take meals at the company mess. It wasn't Blue's choice but he set himself square and walked in the front door.

The long tables, where he and the boy'd sat and drank coffee earlier, were filled with men. The hard wood floors echoed his boot heels. Faces turned to him, uniform in their short hair, shaded eyes. He nodded blankly, wanting to run; there were too damned many people in one place and all were looking at him.

One man stood and spoke his name; "Mr. Mitchell. Here, sir." Blue couldn't tell if he was insulted or amused at being called like a dog. But it was food and an escape.

His savior was a man name of Rhynes he told Blue. "I'm from the east, sir, and am only now getting used to the space out here, and the horses. I'd never ridden but the cavalry promised me training and a new life." He laughed, sour and bitter maybe but it was a laugh. "They certainly didn't lie, this's nothing like Cleveland."

Blue jerked and stared at the man, who now seemed to be talking to himself, not caring if Blue was listening. Kind of lost sight of how Blue was here, what he was needing. Blue had to stop him. "Mr. ah. . .Rhynes, how do I get to the food?" It was a decent question, and Rhynes ceased his talk long enough to raise a hand and a man leaning against a wall came over, bent to Rhynes as he spoke, and returned with a plate heaped with food. It tasted good, better than trail grub, and there was enough of it that Blue didn't mind when Rhynes kept talking.

It was after enjoying seconds, and a cup of bitter coffee, that he went looking for the boy. Rhynes told him where the kid was quartered; the man was stopped for a good breath and Blue quickly got in his chance to thank him before he got up and left the hall.

Sutter watched the man come in the mess hall. That miserable bad-tempered side-winder pushed through the doors and stood, arms to his side, legs wide, head tilted and those eyes staring around the room as if looking for a victim. Sutter wanted to rise up and shout Mitchell's name as a curse, wanted to strike the man, send him away without feeding. It was in fact a waste of the half-decent Army chow.

He kept to his seat, didn't join with those other fools who watched Mitchell and muttered among themselves, talking about him; horses, the bay gelding that Lt. Snow had been assigned to ride, vague murmurs of Mitchell's superior skills with the rough string.

Each word, each mention was a slur to Sutter. He looked at his hands, one on each side of the plate heaped with food. His gut rolled over and if he put one spoonful of the stinking mound into his mouth he'd disgrace himself. He withdrew his hands, folded them in his lap, felt his fingers clench into his palms. Rage roared through him and he barely looked up when a familiar voice spoke the hated name and Sutter heard Mitchell walk across the mess hall floor, boots and spurs ringing. The man was illiterate and ill-mannered and didn't know enough to take off his spurs before entering a dining room.

Hate tasted raw and burning in Sutter's dry mouth.

Josh Snow was outside a small house; it had two front doors side by side. The boy was enjoying free time in the evening when Blue found him setting under a tree, studying something in a book. Blue grunted; Josh looked up and grinned. "I'd hoped you'd come visiting, Mr. Mitchell, for it surely didn't feel like we'd said enough at noon."

He hadn't been training the boy right; "The name's Blue, there's no mister inside me. And when we're alone, you're Josh, for I ain't too fond of lieutenant's bars."

"That's fair enough. Set down." There was the slightest stop, a breath, then; "Blue." There was a second chair, a

splintered seat, stained arms, legs nailed to shrunken rockers. Blue touched its wood-slat back. "It seems to me I've sat here before." Josh nodded. "I remember. Papa left it when he returned to his family home. I asked him once he decided to retire if he wanted the rocker and he declined, so for now it's useful, well sort of"

There hadn't been a word about the mother and Blue still wasn't going to ask. The boy kept talking; "Although I really need to do some repairs. Papa kept asking me, demanding that I fix the thing, it always squeaked. . . ." He stopped there, too abruptly and Blue could see the boy's mama come through their front door. She'd heard the squeal of the dry wood, moved by Blue's restless body as he fought the searing pain in that busted arm.

He needed something to drive out the memory; "Boy, did you check on that bay I told you about?" It was a good practical question. "Yes sir, he's what you said. Came up to me, sniffed my hand and tried to bite me, then walked away and nothing I could do brought him back." Blue added his opinion; "He's one stubborn son." Josh nodded; "But I bet he can run."

Blue let the rocker glide back and forward, same squeak, maybe drier now but there. He agreed silently with the boy, then told a truth; "I let him out a few times, he can cover ground." "Faster than your brown?" There it was, a question he didn't want. He ducked around the talk then, didn't tell Josh what'd happened to the brown but went in a different direction knowing he could trap the kid. "How can we get Sutter into a race, boy?"

Josh sidetracked on him, Blue hadn't guessed the kid'd grown up this much; "I hadn't been east since I was a baby, it was new to me but I found out real quick folks were much the same. And a horseman with a good horse will always want to try him."

Blue sat, considered what they couldn't talk about, and let the rocker take him forward and back. Josh's voice was easy on the ear. "I'll start riding that bay, set up a training schedule for him and make sure it's done when Sutter is around. He'll be begging me pretty soon, and I'll hold off till you show up. I know you've got to get that payment back to Mr. Norris."

He studied the boy, with his clean face, no sideburns like the sports were wearing. The boy smiled, Blue nodded. "It's a plan, lieutenant. You're turning out to be a mighty good horseman. I got faith in you, and the bay, to give Sutter a run. Might be Charley and me, we'll be running neck and neck with you."

They were silent then, only the slight noise of the chairs, a few animals whispering in the dark. Leaves rattling, a wind blowing warm air past Blue's mouth. He licked his lips, wanting to know more but the words were stuck. He might be crude but he knew not to ask 'bout the mother.

Blue stood up slowly, hearing one last squeal from the rocker. There were no more words, no thoughts he'd share with Josh Snow. He nodded, knowing the boy couldn't see his face but would understand. Then he went to the pen and the dun's company, where he was safe and alone.

Blue left before the false dawn without stopping for the promised supplies. He'd eaten all he could last night, and carried his own grub so he didn't need to beg food. The dun was rested and eager, bored with the days of slow trailing. They slipped into an easy lope and the air freshened away from the Post, reminding Blue why he scorned most towns. Humans smelled terrible when they gathered in one place. He wasn't going to remember how good she had smelled; close to him, soft skin and sweet breath and a feeling he'd never known. He waved a hand into the air as if to break up the memory.

Eventually he had to let the dun take a breather at the second ridge; it was beautiful standing here, the long expanse of grassland, shielded to the left by those sand towers, looked like giant toys that children had destroyed. The dun was eager but breathing hard, so Blue made him wait. They'd catch up soon enough to Right and Haney, maybe before they got home to Norris's spread.

As they slid down the ridge, the dun hit something chest high and went over sideways, sliding to the flat grassland. Blue pushed himself clear of the saddle and falling horse, knew he was free until a stirrup jumped up and hit him.

Sutter sat on his reliable bay and watched the accident; he was surprised when the dun got up so easily, shook, took a few steps, then gave a mighty buck and leaped off running east toward that distant ranch in Valentine, eager to leave Mitchell behind.

The dun's rider lay sprawled out on the slide, head turned toward Sutter, mouth open. Even at this distance, Sutter swore he could hear the flies as they circled their prey and landed; on his closed eyes, the open mouth, even the back of one exposed hand. The vision made Sutter laugh. It was sweet revenge. Then it occurred to Sutter that a huge check was pocketed somewhere on Mitchell's person, there for the taking as long as the man stayed down.

Sutter stopped first to untie the thin rope he'd put up tight between the two strongest bushes hanging on to the ridge's sides. 'Less a man looked hard, he wouldn't find the marks. It'd been easy guessing this was where Mitchell would come; his two riding buddies made homebound tracks through here just last night. Then he angled the bay downhill, coming dangerously close to Mitchell's body.

He studied some on the problems and choices facing him. The thought of having Mitchell wake while Sutter was going through his clothes was enough for Sutter to decide that despite the check's size, it wouldn't do him no good since he couldn't cash it. Couldn't get himself far enough out of Army range to sign Connor Norris's name.

He rode back to camp, his decision not to take the check making him feel superior as he ordered one of the troops to put

326

up his sweaty horse. He wanted to get to the mess before all breakfast was gone.

It came to him he hadn't bothered to check a pulse, see if the man lived or died. Then he grinned, rubbed his fingers through his mustache and decided that life or death in this case didn't matter. It was an accident, and if Mitchell woke and could stand, he had a miserable walk ahead of him, whatever direction he chose. Sutter grinned as he sucked in his first gulp of coffee.

It was Charley's lips tugging at Blue that woke him. The colt never did outgrow his interest in Blue's hair and for once he was grateful. He rubbed the side of his head; no blood, barely a bump. Ah hell, he thought, and sat up.

First thing he saw was Charley's wide chest. The dun snorted, backed up then came forward again. It was strange, setting deep in loose sand, face almost against Charley's chest, looking through the four legs and past the tail end to the rest of the sandy ridge where it met up with the grassland. What the hell had happened to bring Charley down?

Next thing Blue saw was the line across the dun-colored chest, more a burn than a cut, with hide scoured, a few droplets of blood but no real damage. Blue stood, had to grab for the dun's mane and then the saddle horn. He could smell the settling dust and his temper wanted to ride to the Fort fast as Charley could go. It would be Sutter who did this. The coward would get to the stables fast, away from any danger and all the time he'd pretend he hadn't tried to hurt or kill a man.

Blue patted his chest pocket, felt the outlines of folded paper. He owed Mr. Norris first, and he knew exactly where Sutter would be for at least the next few months.

The fractious bay gelding was exactly as Blue had described, so Josh went about dealing with the horse in Blue's peculiar way. First he received permission from Colonel Radcliff to use the back pen for a week. The request was met only after Josh explained how Blue would go about working with the rebellious horse. Radcliff responded by stating that he intended to come down and watch. Josh didn't know if he was pleased or terrified. If it didn't work, if he couldn't convince the bay that Army life wasn't that bad, then he'd be in a poor place with his commanding officer.

He positioned himself inside the pen and up against the fence where he did nothing but watch the bay for a few hours, and noticed the horse was uninterested in the fact that he was separated from the other mounts. The bay didn't call out or run the fence, but ate his hay, drank the water, lay down to rest as if he'd been raised right here.

The second day, after a placid hour where the bay didn't bother with Josh at all, Josh picked up the halter and lead and the horse barely turned to look, then went back to eating. Josh slipped the line over the bay's neck and tugged, the horse reluctantly came up from the hay and Josh fitted the halter to his fine head.

The bay's big eye watched Josh calmly and it felt like inspection from the senior cadet at the Point. The notion made Josh laugh and the bay nodded his head. Josh picked up the non-military bridle, a simple headstall with a broken-mouthed bit; no curb, no chains to rattle or any tie-down, not even a nose band.

Saddle and bridle were no trouble; the bay watched, snorting occasionally as Josh went about his business. When he stepped into the stirrup, the horse flinched, raised his head, tense through his whole body. Josh settled lightly, touched the bay's neck and ignored the temptation of the reins. The horse brought his head around and stared directly at Josh

Then Josh picked up the reins and the horse walked off, a big-striding walk that quickly toured the paddock until Josh asked for a trot and immediately learned that the bay gelding could trot out. Josh took up light contact and the bay bowed his neck, chewed the bit and Josh laughed, steadied the horse and aimed him to the paddock fence. Horse and rider cleared the four-foot barrier as if it'd been a shallow ditch.

Sutter watched the performance from the doorway of the non-commissioned officers' barn and cursed lightly, then forced a smile as the young man rode past him; "Nice-going horse you got there, lieutenant." Neither man was fooled by the compliment. Snow took the horse to the officers' barn, dismounted and fixed his stirrups, waved aside an offer of help from the waiting private. If a man took care of his own horse, he'd know every new bump and sore spot. It only made good sense to know the mount your life depended on. Word would get back to the Colonel that the new lieutenant took care of his own.

Connor Norris was surprised when the boys rode in without Mitchell. They dismounted, saw to their broncs and only then did they approach the house. Norris met them at the verandah. Right Taylor spoke up before Con could open his mouth; "One of them soldiers told us Blue'd said to go along. He never did catch up on the trail and we didn't hurry." It took Con a moment to digest that simple fact. He felt his heart quicken, then slow; goddamn. Right spoke his mind and eased Con some. "You want us to rope up fresh horses and ride back?"

Norris studied Right. There never was nothing off about Right and his talk. "Ain't like him, Mr. Norris, ain't like Blue to order us to come ahead. And that dun he rides, that horse is dependable. Something bad's happened."

Connor Norris was a powerful man when he got bothered so Right Taylor stepped back, pushing against Haney; sometimes you needed a clear path of escape when Connor got going. The boss this time surprised him; "You boys get a meal under your belt, rope out fresh horses, and yeah, ride back a ways. It ain't like Blue at all." Right nodded then got the hell off the verandah; that was too easy and he wasn't going to wait for the explosion.

Halfway back to the bar, he could hear Connor swearing more, 'godamning' this and that, mostly at Blue Mitchell. Right was grinning; the man'd be along soon as he could. He'd ridden with Blue time enough to know that much. Even if he had to walk the width of Nebraska, the man would come along when he could.

Right refused any other possibility. To his way of thinking, Mitchell was close to immortal.

They ran into each other about five miles from Norris's spread. Right and Haney set their broncs to a stop and waited while Blue got close enough they could figure out a few things.

Mitchell had a fierce bruise on the side of his head. Right was the one to ask; if Haney tried asking, there'd be a war 'tween him and Blue. "That dun finally unload you?" Right was grinning, knew Haney was wisely staying back. Mitchell wasn't bad hurt, not like when he showed up that first time. There was that grin all right, and the eyes weren't changed. Haney had often tried to slap that grin off the long face or change the color of at least one eye, but then Right acted as the law and usually the fight was done.

Blue reined in Charley close enough the cow ponies all touched noses and there was the usual squealing and snorting. Blue tapped the dun on the shoulder, and Haney backed his clumsy buckskin. "Nope, you look, there's a burn across his chest. Some fool at the Fort had it in for me. Damned lucky he didn't take the check. I think he figured Charley here would leave me, like any sensible renegade rode by that particular man would do."

Right wiped his mouth; "That scrawny gent with the serious thicket 'round his mouth hiding the truth 'bout his chin? That little feller, hell he ain't never gonna be man enough to face you." Blue nodded, "He ain't worth fretting on, Right. That's the bare truth."

The horses swung around, the three riders chatted on what they'd seen and how much they appreciated that the Army wouldn't have nothing to do with the likes of them.

Norris had a young roan he wanted started, so Blue spent time with the three-year-old, working in the pen first, to ease the colt's worries. He rode out on the dun, doing short hard gallops and some long trotting, and Right Taylor came up to him going into the cook shack one night, mentioned he'd like to put a bet on the dun, whatever the race was. "Charley's running pretty fast, Blue. It would seem to me you got an idea." Blue rubbed at his jaw and agreed.

"I'm going back to challenge that fool at the Fort. And the kid wants to find out how fast the bay is. It ought to be a good race however it runs." Right rubbed the side of his face, picked off a piece of hay and chewed on it. "Now I might ask Mr. Norris real polite if me and Haney, that is if you've got no objections, if we can ride along. From the look to that bruise, the man's got himself a big hate."

"We best talk to Norris one at a time but I'll be glad for the company, Right." The next words said Mitchell had changed. "And Haney too, long as he keeps his opinions to himself." It was agreed and two weeks later Blue rode out on the eager dun, Right and Haney trailing along at their own pace.

CHAPTER TWELVE

He'd meant to keep up the bay's training regime but a Miss Lizbeth Thurman came to visit her great uncle, Colonel Radcliff, and Josh had been ordered to ride with the young woman daily, as she was quite an accomplished equestrienne and wanted to explore the countryside. There was to be no galloping despite the young woman's wishes, and only easy cantering, as Miss Lizbeth rode side-saddle and was still a child despite her sighs and protestations.

Josh had intended to keep up the training even when Blue did not return in the three weeks he'd said. That last week with Miss Lizbeth it was hard to remember what else was going on other than her requests and Colonel Radcliff's repeated orders that Josh accompany his grand niece, for protection and as a guide for her curiosity. Josh wouldn't think of ignoring such orders.

To Josh's young eyes she wasn't a child; she was eighteen and blond with dark brown eyes and a manner of looking at him while she listened to his explanations that distracted and pleased him. Here at the Fort, and then at the Point, his interaction with young ladies had been extremely limited. The bay grew lazy with this slacking off, willing to graze next to the young lady's experienced cavalry mount while Lizbeth talked and Josh mainly listened. He loved the sound of her voice.

She had been gone three days, with a tearful promise to write, when Blue reappeared. He tied up in front of the Post Command and asked the corporal guarding the door permission to speak with Colonel Radcliff.

Once ushered inside, Blue sat unmoving, content to study the floor and pay little attention to the voices, words, sounds of too many people in one place going about their important business. The Colonel would be busy, and Blue wasn't here this time on military matters, so he settled in for a long wait.

Outside the Post headquarters, on his way to the stables, Josh recognized the dun, noted the hard muscle, sleek coat, trimmed hooves. It was almost a starting flag to the race, having the dun tied outside the Colonel's office, and Josh smiled to himself, wishing he could hear that conversation.

The invite to speak his piece came after a long hour's wait and Blue was losing what little patience he ever had. His words were close and direct; "Colonel, you asked me when I brought in your remounts and I told you then it was none of your business what I was going to do after I got too old. Probably go to raising horses rather than racing 'em but there's time still for racing. Right now I got me a good horse, you might know about him but it was on Colonel Snow's time." He took in a deep breath and watched the smallest smile move the new colonel's mouth.

"I want to challenge that young lieutenant and your Sergeant Sutter to a race. It's a sweet track you've got here and I'd like to run a horse on it. I ain't raced on a real track before." He might be overplaying the ignorance of his talk, but he was curious about Radcliff, what kind of sense ran the man's decisions.

In turn it was Colonel Radcliff's delight to study this oddity as he spoke about racing. The man was tall enough, and lean, yes, but too beaten to be an effective jockey in any match race. He'd be encumbered by riding in one of the heavy saddles used out here, Radcliff would guess. He bore the visible bruises, nicks and scratches of his rough life. His left arm was bent, held as if it didn't work correctly. Ah yes, he remembered the story, told to him by the smithy who'd retired a month after Radcliff arrived.

The gentleman who stood before him, for despite his demeanor and the crudeness of his dress there was an air of confidence and compassion that Radcliff admired, this young man, he was young still according to Radcliff's almost fifty-five years, was of a kind to give his word and keep it. He was suspicious of others' motives while straightforward in his own dealings; a true western type that Radcliff appreciated.

Radcliff found his thinking upset as Mitchell continued; the voice was lazy, the words erratic but clear in their intent. He would enjoy having more time to deal with Mitchell but the duties of Post Commander forced him to be abrupt.

"I may not look like much to your eyes, Radcliff, but I've been around horses a long time and done a lot of racing. It

ain't only a young man's game. Just need your word is all." So, Mitchell wouldn't use the correct title, wouldn't call him 'sir' despite asking for a favor. Mitchell was pure maverick, and the military didn't like such individuals involved in their regimented life. Radcliff's smile was genuine; *"Mr. Mitchell, what allows you to think you have a chance against a lightweight boy on a horse you yourself said was fast, and an even less beefy sergeant on a younger version of your own mount?"* It really was of no consequence to Radcliff who rode in or won the race, but he was curious as to Mitchell's thought process.

Then Mitchell grinned and Radcliff had the fleeting thought that he'd like to punch that smile off the angular face. Now he understood what Sutter had tried to tell him. The eventual brief explanation was vague but reasonable, which in a way made the man's natural arrogance harder to bear. Still Radcliff found himself admiring Mitchell's confidence as he listened to the man's thought process; *"It's what I know, Colonel, about those three horses, and the riders, that gives me a good chance to win. A man like me, he's got to have an edge in a race like this one's setting up to be."*

There was that grin again, and the flash of those odd eyes he'd been warned about, and John Radcliff felt his blood rise with the prospect of a good horse race despite his concerns about Mitchell and his behavior, his possible influence on the new lieutenant.

"It's fine with me, Mr. Mitchell. What day're you planning on this event?" Soldiering in peacetime, even with a war looming, often took away the men's edge to fight. A good race could be the perfect antidote to boredom.

Mitchell had all the answers, everything worked out to make it easy for Radcliff to say yes. *"You let me stable the dun in that back pen and a week from this Sunday'll be fine, less you got restrictions on racing on a church-going afternoon."* The man was too quick, too smart, asking for just enough to keep him ahead of the others. Snow and Sutter had their duties, Mitchell would train over the unfamiliar track and relax, eat well at the Army's expense. It would be impossible to deny the man access to the mess hall although Radcliff briefly considered it as a way in which he could offer an advantage to his own men.

Upon studying Mitchell, the Colonel recognized that the man was pared down to bone, and more poor cooking amidst the company of other rough men would be cruel. He nodded agreement to all of Mitchell's requests. Eventually the man summed up their entire discussion; "Fine, Colonel, we got us a race a week from this Sunday."

Blue walked out of the office pleased with the Colonel's quick approval. Across the open parade ground, he could see that damnable sergeant perched stiffly on the younger dun. The man was directing chaos, troops riding into each other, horses squealing, their distress drifting the length of the flat ground.

He would do nothing to directly torment Sutter until after the race. Still, he knew enough of human nature to recognize that watching Sutter, frowning each time their eyes connected, was its own punishment. Sutter's non-existent conscience wouldn't bother the man, but the implied threat of violence from Blue, at any time, in any manner, had to prey on Sutter's confidence. This alone would be payment for the failed assassination.

Radcliff called in the other two participants in the upcoming race, to confirm with them that they wished to enter the contest.

Sutter naturally protested Mitchell's staying at the Post, and then asked for time off to finish his own dun's training. Radcliff refused the request, amused to watch Sutter's face go through its predictable contortions before asking permission to leave and then, as if his reluctant demeanor would punish his superior officer, saluted with muted enthusiasm.

The boy in turn grinned and tipped his head and asked permission that Mitchell share his rooms since he was for the moment billeted alone in the older officer's quarters.

Permission granted.

"I'll sleep near the horse, thank you boy." Josh studied Blue's face, saw the eyes narrowed, the mouth thinned as if tasting something rotten. He thought a moment and came to the same conclusion. "Oh." Blue nodded; "I'll come by when I can." Josh nodded in return, feeling like a conspirator; "You can clean up at my quarters and take meals with me." Blue agreed and walked away. Josh watched him leave, noting the tight swing on that left arm, the slightest of limps. Despite the handicap, the man was willing to bet on himself in a horse race.

Blue still hadn't asked, didn't have the courage, or the right. The boy was too much like his ma, being around him kept that hole in Blue's gut opened. Then Josh called out to him; "You all right, Blue?" The boy's voice still held a touch of his mama's talk. Blue could only nod mutely and keep on walking.

Sutter's expectations had been filled; it was officers against the enlisted using an outsider as a decoy. The boy didn't stand a chance, and that stock saddle and Mitchell's various injuries would slow the man. Sutter decided to speed up his training despite how the Colonel worked him.

It worried Sutter that Mitchell had seen him, walked past him leading his own dun and had not made any threats except to stare, then looked away and nodded his head. The man could not be so thick that Sutter's ambush was forgotten or forgiven. There would remain the stubborn knowledge of Sutter's attack, and having seen the man over these past years, Sutter recognized there would be a high price to his ill-planned brutality. He worried; face to face, Sutter could not handle Mitchell without resorting to a pistol.

336

Still, Sutter laid out his daily schedule to prepare for the race; he would begin with early morning gallops, so he could wake that damned cowpuncher and let him see the dun's speed. He would glory in the running, then let one of his troops walk the horse out while Sutter got himself a good breakfast. Mitchell was always near the dun, excepting when he sat with the young lieutenant at meals.

Smart feller, thought Sutter, taking the trouble to protect his mount. Then those two cowhands came in, pastured their mounts with the dun and there were three of them keeping guard. Sutter chose to vary his routine and sometimes circled their camp, letting his dun walk past to cool off and stir up dust. He studied the men, stared at the older dun, hoping to make them nervous.

The men in his squad offered their help; they were more willing to cool out the dun, time him on short runs, groom and offer extra hay. Their money was on the sergeant's horse. They'd seen the colt run and win too many times. None of them had much faith in the lieutenant's bay; it was a horse new to the Fort, new to its rider, with an obvious temper and so the men talked among themselves and offered their assistance to Sutter.

The sergeant knew better than to think the men were supporting him; they were looking out for their betting money. Still it made life easier, not having to order and watch to be certain the orders were carried out. It was a false sense of having the men like him. Sutter was no fool in that department, but working together would bring a sweeter victory.

Davenport had the idea and brought the other two in on it; they couldn't touch Mitchell's dun, but they could act on the new lieutenant's horse. Davenport had grown up in New York City and he'd learned from the bookmakers and men at the track out at Coney Island just how to slow a horse. He didn't give away his secret, only made the others promise when it was time they would be ready to do exactly as he told them.

"It won't be hurting the lieutenant, we wouldn't want to do that. Just to slow that bay 'cause I seen him run and he's damned fast. We ain't got nothing to worry about with the cowboy, he's too old." His recruits only nodded; they were in awe of all the important details that Corporal Davenport seemed to know.

Davenport gave the secret orders; for now they were to give the bay extra grain, several pounds of it morning and night. And they weren't to let anyone know what they were doing.

Mitchell did move in to the officer's quarters with Josh Snow and there was talk around the Fort until the Colonel's aide told them all it was with the Colonel's approval. Josh heard the bevy of rumors and actually laughed when the aide told him. Consorting with the enemy, making alliances. Nothing would hold Blue Mitchell back in a horse race, the man would ride to win, the same way Josh Snow would ride.

As a boy of sixteen, Josh had thought Corporeal Sutter was a good horseman. It hadn't taken Josh long upon his return as a commissioned officer to figure out that Sutter was mostly posturing and words but very little actual doing. The man was a fool on horseback and a fool on the ground.

Blue bunked in the other room. The man had changed from Josh's memory; his blond hair was thinned, his body was crooked but those eyes were the same. Mitchell was reluctant to talk much, said he needed his sleep, as he inevitably got up for his first ride in the cool dawn.

Where Sutter and Josh used the track, trying to stay away from each other yet ride before their military day started, Mitchell took the dun out into the ridges and hills; sometimes they could see him charging up one of the steep sandy grades, almost able to hear the horse grunt with the effort. Mitchell rode in that infernal stock saddle, while Josh used his father's long-neglected flat saddle brought over from England. It weighed pounds less than the military or stock saddles, and Josh knew the lack of extra weight would give him an advantage. He'd gone to Ireland once, to fox hunt with his father and an old friend, with the Kilkenny Hunt. He had been amazed at how fast the men rode to their fences and banks or ditches, secure enough in their lightweight, barely padded hunting saddles.

His father rode as madly as their host, undone by a potent whiskey shared from his friend's silver flask, and the pair of them had attacked fences, hills, ditches and banks as if they were tied to their horses. Now Josh owned that saddle, and knew its slight weight and secure knee rolls were his edge.

The bay was putting on good muscle; the horse seemed to delight in the running, and was easier to ride in any parade-ground maneuvers after a hard gallop. Sutter had managed to get his dun released from all military exercise on the excuse that the colt was the youngest of the three and needed rest between training exercises.

Mitchell rode at odd hours, short hard burst of energy in the early morning, then again at mid-day, in the worst of the heat.

It was late, dark and quiet, few stars, the rocking chair empty beside Josh's chair under the ramada. Then it registered, the smallest movement, a soft step, a light cough, Blue's voice; "All right I set a spell?" Josh nodded, laughed at himself; "Been waiting on you since the evening meal." He heard the nerve in his own voice, hoped Blue didn't catch it. He was in over his head, not knowing much about getting a horse ready to race. And Blue had become remote, uneven in his temper so Josh had tried to stay out of his way. Now Blue approached him and Josh found himself fighting the urge to stand and salute.

Instead Blue settled quickly on the edge of the rocker, letting his weight move the fragile chair back and forth. "I've been studying you on the bay. He's looking good." Blue

339

stopped, Josh cocked his head. "You mind a few words, boy?" Josh laughed; "If you're willing to help your opponent, that's fine by me." Blue shrugged; "You need to shorten your stirrup leathers and get off his back." Josh snorted. "That's helping the enemy?" Blue answered, choosing his words; "It's a horse race and nothing more. I've won enough races, will win a few more before I'm done. Don't get cocky 'cause I'm past you in years. That dun makes up for a lot of my mistakes." Blue hesitated, wiped his mouth; "Shortening the length puts you up and off the horse's back. A black man's been winning races riding this way, on horses no one thought could run worth a damn. Just a word of advice."

Josh was shamed, and quiet for a moment, then; "How'd you learn all this, Blue? The horses I mean, how to get so much from them." There was a long silence. "My pa sold me to the local ranchers when I was a kid, light-weight and already in trouble, thrown out of what schooling I'd had; him and then his brother, they hired me to men wanting broke horses or a good race."

There was a lot behind that statement. Josh wanted facts more than memories, wanted to know what those rough hands felt on the reins, touching the horse. How one man accepted what others never bothered to notice.

"But how did you learn? I've watched you, been right close and seen your hands, they find places and ask things no other man I've seen can get from a horse." There was a pause, long enough that Josh knew he'd hit something in Blue's past that still hurt.

His voice was oddly soft, without rancor; "They were the only thing that didn't beat me. Horses I mean. I spent a lot of time hiding in the corrals, watching, listening, seeing what other, older men did to the horses that scared them. So I tried my own way and it worked. For me at least." Then he laughed, as if a laugh could break up the seriousness of the discussion.

Josh wouldn't let go; "It's how, how can you feel and sense like you do?" Blue shook his head; "Seems like you *learned quick enough and what you have works for you. Just get off the bay's back when you run him." Blue coughed, trying to finish up what he was saying; "Not when you're working out where Sutter can see you. Alone, away from any of these men." Josh heard the finality of those last comments and knew it was all he would get, tonight at least.*

"Blue, I, well I want to beat you, and Sutter of course, but I don't want you to think it's. . . ." "Boy, a horse race ain't personal, it's speed and there's nothing like it." Then the man stood, and once again Josh was made aware of his height, his spare frame, and the odd angle of that badly healed arm.

"You ever raced, Josh?" Josh sighed, "No sir." Then he laughed, "I take back the sir."

Josh stood, Blue was grinning and in the dark there were only patches and outlines of shapes suggesting his manner, his light hair, the startling eyes, the shoulder of a dusty shirt; "Let's us race each other, a short run so we don't really know what each horse can do. Get you used to what's going to come at you almighty fast."

"Now boy, my age is getting me. See you before dawn tomorrow." Once again, Mitchell walked away, one step up into the quarters' doorway, then to the right, to the smaller bedroom. Josh knew, if he sat and listened, he would hear the thump of dropped boots, and then light snoring.

Blue's dun carried that heavy saddle, and Blue was all grin and laughter as they met at the other side of the sand ridges in the half light before reveille. Blue waved casually at the steep sides and thick sand. "Riding these builds up a horse's wind, and legs. These three horses are rugged, they've led hard lives, they don't need special footing or fancy tracks. It's just that it's going to be a pleasure running where the footing won't reach up and bite back." There was a look on Blue's face that told Josh the man was reliving something in his past. He wanted to ask but knew better. Not now.

341

Blue moved his horse to stand near Josh and the bay, even as he kept talking; "Hold a steady line, watch the other horses, keep your horse straight. GO!" The dun was gone, Josh's bay half-rearing on too short a rein, throwing Josh back then forward as the horse plunged into a gallop. He couldn't get enough air, his hat was blown off, and dirt clods from Blue's horse kicked into his face. Then he remember the advice, bent his knees and leaned over the bay's neck, mouth opened to the strands of black mane but he could breathe and then Blue's dun slowed and he let his bay roar past.

It was a struggle to pull up; Josh leaned back and the bay ran through the bridle, mouth jawing open. The runaway went on for fifty feet before the bay gave in to Josh pulling on one rein. Blue waited while Josh got the bay turned around. Blue's voice was patient; "Now, stand here next to me, yeah, settle him, ease up on the bit, pat his neck. Get him quiet." The older dun stood almost square, breathing easily.

"I'll 'one two three' and you'll walk that horse out past me, walk mind you. Quick as you can off three." They practiced; halt, stand, walk, then on occasion halt, stand and gallop, until Josh could hear the change in Blue's voice as he came to the command; GO!"

"You can win it all on the start, kid." Then he turned the dun and leaned forward and was laughing as he let the horse run. Josh came after the pair, asking more and more of the bay until he thought he'd lost and then they flew past the dun and Blue was sitting up, still laughing. He could hear the few words; "Nothing like it, Josh. There's not much in this world like a good horse running his heart for you." Blue heard the echo of his own words and looked away from the boy.

It was only that evening, late and in the complete dark, sitting outside listening, taking in cool air and comfortable with the man in the rocker, hearing it squeak, when Josh Snow had time to fit together all that Blue'd been telling him.

That ride in the hills, almost ten hours ago but still fresh, had given him a new perspective on horses, and the knowledge was a gift from Mitchell. The words were clear in Josh's mind; the man deserved to know.

Blue's voice was quiet as he spoke before Josh could open his mouth; "We've got two more days, Josh. Right and Huney, they've said no one's tried anything on the dun. You need to keep an eye on your bay. Check the hay every day. I don't trust Sutter. Don't trust any of the soldiers, one of them might have his own bet in mind. Hell boy, there ain't no such thing as an honest horse race."

Josh protested; "We're doing nothing wrong." Blue snorted; "We spent the morning teaching each other how to run the starting line. Somehow we didn't manage to include Sutter. You want to teach him what you learned today? You really want to be that much of a fool?"

It was time; "I got a letter from my father today. I wrote him that you'd promised to come back and told him about the horse race." Blue dug in, held himself to figuring what started the boy talking about family things. Blue studied the young face, highlighted by long evening shadows. "He ain't doing well, you're worried." Josh didn't question Blue's concern; "He says the doctors tell him another month to six weeks. I can't get leave, can't get there in time. I've only been here a month, since the day before you delivered the horses."

Again there was no mention of the boy's mother. Blue choked, spat, from his own cowardly silence. The boy's sadness was a deepening hurt. He could hear unsaid words pushing through the boy's breathing. Blue tried; "Josh, I'm no good 'bout family, never had one for love, just for work and getting hit. You ask Colonel Radcliff, give him a chance." Then he took a risk. "Your ma'll need you."

Josh took in a deep breath and as he spoke, Blue didn't see the blow that tried to knock him out of his chair onto the dusty ground. Already half-killed by the first words, he sat, rocked, held his breath.

"They divorced and I have a half-brother. I know because I heard two of the Post wives talking. Of course they wouldn't tell me the truth for I don't think either of them would say a harsh word against Mother." Josh's voice was suddenly exhausted.

Blue's ribs hurt, he shuddered too hard, held on to the rocker arms, back and forth trying to slow the pace and keep himself quiet so the boy would not see any reaction. It was unbearable; Josh kept talking. "Papa said the baby wasn't his. I heard him say that to her just after the baby was born. They thought I was out of the house." Blue gagged, hands clenched. The boy wouldn't stop.

"It wasn't long after you left, I'd quit getting into trouble and decided on the Point and Papa was pleased, then he got quiet and Mama, well she swelled up and I was too young to be sensible and asked and she hushed me, told me she wasn't well. Then she had a baby and I barely got to see him before Mama was sent away and Papa told me not to speak of her again."

The words drew Josh back into childhood; "I asked him in a letter just recently, I wanted to know the truth. He responded by telling me he was dying, but nothing about Mother." The calm voice continued as Blue stood up. "I'm sorry, boy." Josh turned to the words but Blue was already gone.

She wouldn't have, she wouldn't risk it, it wasn't possible, bearing a child not belonging to Harlan Snow. He tried to remember; he could see her face still, her hands soft on his body, but the Colonel had made no impression.

Then he knew without thinking, could feel her at the end of his fingers, could almost see the child as it first look up to its mother. His own mother, in a rare moment of remembrance, had told him of the startling effects of his eyes the first time she held him. Blue shook his head, felt that damned blond hair slap his neck; he'd done what he swore he'd never do. He'd created

344

a child and left it and its mother alone. A wedded woman not his wife, and no chance to be his wife; he'd sired a bastard son, damn his giving in to need for creating the misery.

Walking helped and Blue walked for hours, stalking the Fort grounds, tracing the racetrack where they'd run too soon and not soon enough. The race didn't matter now, nothing mattered but to keep walking until he was exhausted.

He finally stumbled into the back pen, spooking the dun and waking Right, who sat up in his bedding and put a hand out to his rifle held close by. It was a good response even though Blue glared at him and Right glared back.

CHAPTER THIRTEEN

Sutter overheard a few words at Snow's quarters. Earlier he'd settled himself near a tree to watch the two men outside, talking, laughing even. Until those words he didn't hear forced Mitchell to rise and walk away and for a brief moment Sutter delighted in believing that the two were now separated.

He could not understand loyalty or friendship. He had no friends; he did not have words or thoughts that anyone wanted to hear. He tried to blame it on his face, small and round, lacking any resemblance of a chin, but he'd grown up some since that blame had worked. He'd met homelier men who had friends and laughed with companions and he still didn't understand how it was done.

Giving orders helped drive away his doubts, and now Corporals Davenport, Rhynes and McCoy were friendly, helping without being told, making suggestions, spying on Mitchell's dun and the lieutenant's bay. They were almost friends, wanting Sutter to win, careful when asking at times how the sergeant felt, was he eating right, was the dun's workout a good one that day. It would last to the end of the race, but for now Sutter intended to enjoy the recognition that he was about to do something special. Finally his training and riding of the dun gelding would receive its withheld merit.

He'd thought about this, pondered on the unfairness of his life. He'd watched Mitchell, studied the man as he insulted the Army, ignored those who wished to congregate near him and talk horses, and yet the men spoke highly of him, including Colonel Radcliff who often mentioned Mitchell's fine hand with a fractious horse.

Sutter wanted to state that he too could ride, that he had taken a wild-bred colt and made it a good Army mount, but he hesitated, knowing deep inside a truth that would never leave him. Whatever gift Mitchell had and didn't care about, it was the knowledge and touch that Martin Sutter yearned for and knew he could never own. But this once, only for himself, he would win the race by honest means.

He spoke his vow to his new cohorts and they nudged each other and agreed and said 'yes sir' and grinned at him and he was lost again, knowing they were up to something, unable to stop it, friendless again after a few days of agreeable company.

It occurred to Sutter that if he never knew what these men were setting in place, then his winning the race would be done fairly on his part, with no knowledge of anything underhanded or downright dishonest. This, he thought, was a fair trade for Mitchell's skill and the boy's youth. It was an edge that he deserved.

Corporal Davenport had done his studying on the race that soon enough would be run. He'd been spreading out his bets, using money he'd saved, hidden away for a time just like this. No one thought to figure it out that the heavy betting was all from one source

He knew exactly what to do. He instructed Rhynes, who he almost trusted, and didn't bother with McCoy who was a lightweight with a conscience. He already had them over-graining the bay, now he'd change tactics for a guaranteed *win. It was simple and impossible to detect and Davenport once again silently thanked his buddy at the track for teaching him how to make a bundle on a close race.*

He sent Rhynes, with his baby-face and calm manner, to help with the boy's new racer. And he sent Rhynes with specific instructions, telling the man he wasn't doing nothing real wrong, just changing the bay's schedule. Rhynes was from a city, he didn't know nothing about the nags.

He laid out the rules; water the bay real light, don't let him fill up at the trough, put only a quarter of a bucket's worth in his stall, pull him away from any extra water. Let the lieutenant run him, bring the horse back. Rhynes could offer to walk out the horse, cool him down, wash him clean and not let the horse drink.

That all-important night before the race, there would be no water. That next morning; no water until an hour before the race, when Rhynes could give the bay all the water he wanted. It worked, always did, nothing showed, no wound or poison, just water on top of a deadly week of heavy graining and never enough to drink.

Davenport figured it was best he and his buddies keep away from Sutter and each other. They didn't hang around and jabber but did their work, followed their orders. No one would see them jawing and wonder what they was talking about. They weren't doing much, just keeping a bay gelding from drinking his fill until before the race.

Right Taylor had ridden for different brands, worked under bad bosses and those who knew their business. He'd signed on to the Rafter Bar T almost seven years ago and stayed, first time in his life he didn't move on when the need came to him.

Right was thirty, maybe a few years younger than Mitchell but there were times when he felt ages older. Mitchell had that lone ability to anger every man woman and child he met, while taming their horses without fear or brutality.

Still Right got along with Mitchell and might have called him a friend but they rarely rode together, mostly it was Right delivering supplies, or bringing in new broncs. Blue would set outside rather than inside the line shack, a fire, a pan of stew, a few words, stories about past mavericks and horse races and very little about Blue himself.

That one time cleaning out the well, it was different then, a horror Right lost sleep over that didn't seem to get to Mitchell. Still Right felt comfortable around the man and knew to trust him. The man was proven steady and reliable after all the years.

Mitchell's steadiness had shifted; the man stalked the fence line and woke Right from a good sleep. He was spooking the dun and the two Norris broncs away from their evening hay courtesy of the US Army. Right had checked through each pile, feeling for stickers, anything that might get into a racehorse's belly and give him the collywobbles. No one had to tell him, he did this on his own. He knew better than to trust those Army boys not to try something mean.

He sat up and studied Mitchell, who had come to stand over Right's bedroll. The man should have been asleep inside that officers' quarters, not here driving the horses, and Right, into a worried frenzy. He'd known Mitchell long enough to see panic in the odd eyes, tension pull at the mouth.

"Blue." The man started, hands raised in front as if set for murder. Right talked to the man like he was a green bronc; "It ain't me, Blue, whatever got you riled it ain't me and Haney hell he ain't been out of my sight. He couldn't of done it this time." The struggle was so obvious that Right let out a breath, knew he could trust Mitchell again. The man's voice shook then quickly steadied; "Sure, Right, it ain't you, it's me. Keep an eye on the dun, don't trust no one comes near you."

Right nodded; "Listen to me. For once do what you're getting told to do that's plain common sense. You get yourself in a blanket and lie down. Running the fence line all night'll lose you the race and all my hard-earned wages are bet on you and Charley. You quit fussing at whatever's stuck in your craw and at least let me and Haney and your race horse sleep."

He couldn't deal with himself; his hands ached, his gut turned, his eyes blurred. He'd been a damned fool for a woman one time and now there was a child meant to be part of him and he'd never known, never had the chance to know.

    He knew Right was saying what needed saying. Lying down on his blanket, Blue rested his head on his saddle, smelled the old sweat, dirt, the stink of hard work and long miles, and he couldn't stop his mind from going over what he'd just learned.

    There was no point in hunting down Josh Snow, no reason to ask, to talk again, hear words from the child's family. The boy didn't know more than he'd said and it would be cruel to let him think of his mama coming to a stranger, of a night that meant too much to Blue, linking him with Josh Snow in a manner he or the boy, the baby too, didn't ask for and couldn't believe. And speaking of a woman crudely to another man, especially her own son, was to dishonor her.

    Blue didn't have time to sit up before he had to vomit. He swallowed, spat out bile, anger turned in his own belly. He had to race, had to ride, no time now to quit on Josh. He lay back down, hands clenched into fists, wanting something or someone to hit.

One day before the race, Colonel Radcliff called the three participants to the office. He stood near the window and stared out as the men entered. Josh saluted with perfection, Sutter snapped with some agility, while Mitchell leaned against the doorframe.

    Radcliff spoke without turning from the window; his voice rang strong and clear and there could be no mistaking his orders or his temper. "There will be no trouble between the three of you. If I hear of any wrongdoing, those under my command will be punished and you, Mr. Mitchell, will be banned from the Post and I will speak to Con about your continued employment."

Josh glanced at his two opponents; Sutter was still-faced, unmoving, staring past the Commander while drawn up in a crisp military manner. There was nothing on Blue's face; without moving from his posture against the door, the man drawled out his opinion.

"I don't give a fiddler's damn about your rules, Colonel. There ain't nothing you can say to Con that'll change his knowing me. And I don't cheat in a race, don't need to. I've been beat before, and will lose again but not this time."

Blue slowly pulled away from the wood frame supporting him, turning to stare at Josh and Sutter. His eyes intensified in color until Josh thought the man would catch fire. Sutter stepped back as if to put the Colonel's desk between him and his opponent.

Mitchell's gaze settled on Josh and the boy was immediately on guard; Mitchell did not look as if he recognized him. "You soldiers try cheating and I'll outrace you then give you the beating you deserve. These horses'll run their hearts out and no one's going to do what could hurt them. That's my comment on this meeting you called, Colonel." With a brief nod to Josh, the man was gone. Josh Snow knew his mouth hung open and he closed it, bit his tongue, heard a deep intake and watched the Colonel's back stiffen. Nothing was said, nothing was left to be said; Josh and Sutter filed out and quickly split away from each other.

Josh studied the parade ground, the vast open expanse of tended grass; Blue was halfway across, not waiting, no allowing Josh near him. There was no wide grin and swift apology, nothing but an unexpected bitterness.

Blue saddled the dun and climbed on, let the horse walk out toward the ridges, beyond the confinement of the Post and its endless regulations. He let the horse's stride ease him, sat careful in the saddle, back straight, hands light on the loose rein. *No struggling bursts of a hard run today, instead they walked up the ridges, stood looking out to the hills, then Blue found a circular way down, only to go up the next ridge; more sun, heat, sweat, even the churned ground released a sweet scent. Blue stopped briefly to water Charley out of his canteen, but took none of the water for himself. Punishment for a sin he hadn't known he'd committed.*

He let the dun gallop briefly so he entered the Fort on a sweaty, steaming horse. He wanted to laugh at the faces, men watching without looking, turning quickly as he rode by, assessing the dun's condition, revising their expectations for tomorrow's race. Blue noted that neither the bay nor Sutter's dun had gone out, saving their energy for the challenge.

Sutter's callous attempt to hurt Blue no longer mattered; the man was worried and lacked any skill as a horseman. He wasn't worth the bother; Blue had other concerns.

When Blue'd unsaddled and put up the dun, the restlessness hadn't left him – he needed a fight, a face to punch, a rank horse to ride. He'd insulted the boy on no cause but his own and it galled him. So he made a resolution and tried to carry it out.

After a long pained afternoon spent waiting until evening, Blue approached the small officer's quarters. He was fully embarrassed and shamed by what he'd done, hell his whole being burned and shook. He had to apologize. He'd have to be careful though, he couldn't tell the boy outright the why of his words, only that he'd treated Josh badly and needed to make his amends.

This time he knocked on the door and caught a glimpse of the boy tucking in his shirt, straightening a tie, grabbing for a hat. "Yes?" The boy was tight, drawn hard, not interested in forgiveness. In that he was his father's son.

Blue choked, spat to one side. The words weren't there, wouldn't come through. Josh Snow studied him; "You made yourself quite clear this morning, Mr. Mitchell, to the Colonel as well as me. That you would suspect I might even considering cheating is an insult. I will see you tomorrow at the race. Good night."

Right Taylor had some kind of meat simmering in pot liquor over a fire and it smelled almost decent until Blue shoveled it toward his mouth and his belly retched. He made himself chew and swallow, recognizing the need for fuel. Right watched him and had little to say. "If you was a drinking man, my friend, I'd sure as hell buy you a bottle. But since you don't partake that often, I won't suggest nothing like it." Right watched Blue's face, saw only anger without agreement so he quit talking. Haney wisely stayed across the fire, ducking whenever Blue looked his way.

Right held back any questions; he recognized that whatever went on between Blue and the new lieutenant, it was none of his, or Haney's, business. Asking any questions might open up a real war. He studied Blue, saw the trembling hands and how little he'd eaten and felt a surprising sadness. Whatever had gone on, it wasn't about a horse race.

This time sleep came as an escape, rolled up in a blanket smelling of horse and dust, a second blanket under his head, reminding him of places he'd ridden, places he still wanted to see. All the empty land he had yet to ride. Right now, these few hours, Blue could focus on nothing except winning another horse race. His conscience had to move aside; the sense of a loss he did not understand could not interfere. He slept, waking at odd hours, turned restless, hands clenched, choking at times from a nameless fear.

In the morning, Blue groomed the dun, checked the legs for any swelling, watered the horse lightly and swung up on the dun's back, He rode out and around the Post at a walk, letting the dun amble along, no hurry, nothing fancy, walking to loosen muscles while doing as little as possible.

The race was early afternoon, to allow for church services and the Sunday noon meal, all the daily habits necessary to an orderly and reasonable life. Two troopers were leading Sutter's dun outside the barns; one man on each side as if the quiet gelding would bolt at any moment. Blue patted Charley's neck. There was no sign of Josh's bay.

The formalities of life; church and Sunday dinner, comradeship and good manners, a prayer or two, a lecture from an unknowing preacher, delivered to men expected and trained to kill. Blue never could grasp that conduct, a man of god blessing soldiers trained and willing to shoot, maim, murder, destroy. He'd killed a few times, and he'd shot more horses than men, horses maimed or ruined by another man's carelessness. He hated the shot, the trusting look from eyes he understood; both acceptance and relief, what he rarely found in human company.

He had to push aside all those fool thoughts. The dun felt good, light even against the leather halter and woven lead. It was time now to put the horse up for a few hours, then saddle for the race. There was no excitement inside him, no eagerness waiting for the run. Blue turned Charley back into the pen, made sure he had some hay but not much. Charley'd been watered early and that would be enough for now. He knew never to race a horse on a full belly.

He could smell the noon meal, hear the raised voices and his belly rumbled. He needed to eat, even if it was in the unwilling company of soldiers and sergeants. Blue forced himself to walk the parade ground to the mess where he pushed open the door and stood a moment, uncertain in front of all the glaring faces.

Josh had stopped to pick up his mail on the way to mess at noon and it was already damp from his hand. He'd been too busy, and too scared, to go look all week. There was never mail for him except bad news from his father, and now there was an envelope, an address written in a lady's hand that had to be hers, Miss Lizbeth, the only one who would write him from back east in a feminine hand.

He'd had one letter from his mother, sent to him at West Point from the city of New York with no return address. He'd reread the letter until its carefully penned words had dissolved, the tissue beneath them powdered into fine dust. He remembered each word, asking about his health, how he liked the Point, whether he had met any nice young women.

He wished he could tell his mother about Lizbeth, how beautiful she was, how he delighted in her smile, her words of poetry and drama and what fun it was to ride a horse again in the Nebraska hills with Lizbeth as company. But there was no way he could write that letter, no place it could be sent.

Josh sat outside on the long wood verandah, in one of the identical rockers that were allocated to the men of this mess. He forced himself to open the letter, read the words slowly, reminding himself that these were not words from his mother but from a young woman he found quite appealing.

She missed him; riding wasn't the same without him, had he seen the full moon last week. She liked dreaming of him standing under the same moon, how tall and straight he would be, handsome in his uniform. There were parties now, dances and formal gatherings to introduce the young ladies to society and she wished he were in attendance, for she would choose to dance every dance with him.

The light words and sweet thoughts gave him time. He was at war now, troubled about Blue, the horse race, his papa, and this girl. Josh regretted his cruelty to Blue, about the bastard child who had torn Josh's life apart, and then his churlish refusal to listen to the man. While Josh had made no accusations, such information tossed out to a drifter like Mitchell had to cause great harm; he could still see the pain in those eyes and the sight haunted him.

Josh knew he needed to keep his mind on the race. When it was over, he would talk with Blue, try to explain his own feelings when he came to understand the confusion of that time. He'd forgotten what he had seen; his mother's unexplained fondness for the wounded man, her sadness after he left, and a growing bitterness from his father. As a boy none of the events made sense; as a young man Josh thought he understood.

He folded Miss Lizbeth's letter neatly in his back pocket and went inside to join his companions for Sunday dinner. There was a seat for him at the head table. Resting on his plate lay a pair of polished spurs, meant for a gentleman rather than a soldier. For this one day he would consider himself both; he'd never felt a gentleman before, not even upon his graduation from the Point when he was pinned with his lieutenant's bars.

The men stood and clapped, a friend waited behind the chair ready to pull it out for him. Josh stared at the spurs, then looked up and all his friends, his new military comrades, were cheering. He had only a few words; "I haven't ridden the race yet." One of the men he did know well answered for him; "You're doing what we'd all like to do, riding a good horse against fair competition. Now an officer can beat Sutter and it's about time."

The race had shaped itself into a grudge match between commissioned and the non-commissioned officers, with no mention of the outsider. The mass of cheering soldiers had no idea what they would see this afternoon.

Josh picked up his glass and filled it with the mess's poor wine. "To my father, Colonel Snow, who gave me this opportunity." Cheers and hurrahs erupted in the mess hall, only to cease amidst the scraping of chairs and the instant quiet as hungry men sat down to eat.

Blue chose the noncommissioned officers mess out of practicality. He'd find that man again, Rhynes, and eat a meal, drink more water, maybe have a cup of coffee. He hadn't stayed to share breakfast with Right and Haney, he couldn't look anyone he knew in the face. Even these bland middling soldiers were too much for him but he needed to eat.

As he entered the mess hall he quickly found Rhynes and the man saw him, abruptly stood and walked out, passing Blue without even a nod. The man must have a lot on his mind, Blue thought. But Rhynes' leaving opened a space where Blue sat down, a man brought him a plate so he could pick, eat some, swallow hard, drink bitter coffee and wipe his mouth. It was a meal eaten in silence, surrounded by too many men watching him.

He stood, gave a general nod as he stepped out of the mess hall, hearing that dammed quiet explode as he went down the few stone steps to the parade grounds.

Martin Sutter had finished his meal quickly and gone to tend to the dun. The horse was fit and instantly restless as he heard the noise. The dun would be expecting a parade, a charge, not simply one man in too much of a hurry.

Haltered and tied, the dun settled; this was a routine he knew. Brush, curry, a hay wisp to polish his coat, feet picked clean and oiled to a high gloss, for it was a parade of sorts, a victory march before the win. The dun nipped at Sutter when his hands were rough with the brush and Sutter slapped the colt's neck. The dun pinned his ears back and raised a hind foot in warning; the animal would not accept being treated badly.

Sutter looked at his hands, saw their stretched skin, knuckles rigid around the brush's wooden handle. Perhaps he had been rough; he exhaled and swept the brush lightly over the dun's hide, the horse twitched his upper lip. That was better.

He was extra careful smoothing the drab saddle blanket on the muscled back, and could almost feel the sweet wool of that colorful blanket he'd thrown on the trash heap years ago. Nothing had ever been said about the act, but if it had been Sutter's blanket, he would still be carrying a grudge. The thought went quickly through his mind that he owed debts to

Mitchell; his treatment of the man's gear, the attempt to bring Mitchell and the horse down. Even his humbling ride on the mustang when Mitchell was injured; none of these incidents had yet had an accounting. Slowly it dawned on Sutter that the race was not a good idea, that Mitchell could use his horsemanship to ruin Sutter in front of the entire Post.

Sutter was fully aware that if the situation was reversed, he would have a plan by which he could humiliate Mitchell.

The McClellan saddle fitted snug against the withers, the horsehair cinch was pulled up gently, tucked in its proper knot. This one time he chose a simple snaffle, one set of reins, no tie-down, nothing for show. He'd already stripped his own uniform; a horse race didn't need a pistol or knife. At least Sutter hoped it wouldn't come to fighting.

He would allow the dun a sip of water, then make his way out to the race course.

A mass of people lined the track; carriages and ladies with parasols, children running, men standing, talking too loud in their small groups. The manicured flat plain with its center of green grass, its dirt track smoothed over, almost free of stones, held no prairie dog holes, no dips or valleys, and behind all this civilization and planned course were the high ridges and sand sculpted by wind and rain.

In the back pen, Blue felt the weight of the crowd, people along the track edge, expecting him and two others to ride out and give them an exciting spectacle. He was extra careful settling the plain wool blanket on Charley's back, keeping it well ahead of the high withers, rolling it to rise above the bone itself. Then he folded and pinned back the corners, put a leather strap across the dun's back, meant only to hold the blanket in place.

He laughed as he did this, his fingers knowing exactly how the corners needed to be held, where the leather went, and when he did up the crude cinch and the dun grunted, turned his head and pushed at Blue's arm, Blue knew they were ready to race. Charley recognized the rigging, and a shiver went through the horse, who lifted his head and arched his neck.

The bit slipped in easily, a simple bridle pulled over the swiveling ears; a soft leather headstall and rope reins that would grip Blue's palms despite sweat or dirt. He led Charley out of the paddock, and only then did he notice that Right and Haney were saddled and mounted, waiting for him. He fussed with the rigging, then slipped up onto the dun's back, grunting as he settled on the blanket. He was getting too old to ride like this.

Right had thought it through and knew his business, which he told to Blue in straight terms. "We're your escort, Blue, we'll make our own parade. It seems fitting since I still don't trust these Army boys." Blue nodded in agreement, then remembered what he had finally learned; "Thanks." He stuttered, wiped his mouth; "I feel safer with you two riding along." Right grinned at him, nodded at the eager dun. "That crowd out there and those two boys'll have a fit once they see your rigging." Blue agreed; "No one put down rules on gear, and I'm betting that the boy, their new lieutenant, has himself a flat saddle and it ain't no bet that Sutter will ride cavalry. It's miserable gear but it don't weigh much."

He recognized he was talking too fast and the nerves in his voice made the dun anxious until the black-tipped ears flicked back then went forward to focus on the crowds. They did make a small parade marching to the track, drawing a few latecomers alongside them, questions asked about Blue setting that blanket, the dun prancing some, then finally walking. Blue's legs hung loose, his hands played lightly with the reins, talking to Charley, telling him to wait, hold his eagerness, getting them both ready to run.

Josh couldn't find enough air and was smart enough to let some of his new friends clean and saddle up the bay. He wasn't going to trust one of the troops. He always preferred to take *care of his own mount but not this time. Today he couldn't get his hands quiet enough to touch the bay so he let Lt. Shumway and Lt. Nix do the saddling, see to the tightened girth on his father's old saddle. He'd been cleaning and oiling it all week, checking the billets, the stuffing, testing the buckle stitching, the strength of the girth itself.*

When Shumway and Nix shoved him up on the bay, it took Josh three or four strides to wonder what was wrong. The rebellious horse had no fire; his walk was flat, his head low. He could hear the belly-rumble sounds that meant the horse wasn't bound up or colicking, but the animal felt peculiar, unresponsive to his hands on the bit. Josh tugged sharply with the reins and still got no reaction. Then he looked at his fingers resting on the leather reins and saw how white they were, felt his own belly rumble and complain and he decided it was nerves, his nerves, that made the horse sense something was wrong.

Sutter came out on his shiny dun with his group of followers, men walking beside him, in front and behind, laughing and setting the dun to prancing and allowing Sutter to ride with the cheering, taking his moment of fame early. Josh encouraged the bay, who started jigging sideways as the Sutter entourage collided with Josh's small party and it became a confusion of loud voices. Sutter's dun kicked out until the men scattered, leaving the two horses to walk side by side headed toward the gathering crowd.

To his extreme right, Josh saw the other dun, the blond hair of its rider glowing among the hats and uniforms. Then Josh laughed as Blue looked over and nodded in return to Josh's recognition. Now he understood; Mitchell rode a simple rolled blanket, strapped on with leather, no stirrups, a plain bridle, no extra pounds to the rigging. That was why he'd trained with all that extra saddle weight; the man knew what he was doing all right. The horse would run almost fifty pounds lighter. Josh grinned to himself; the courage to ride basically with nothing more than a blanket spoke to the man's belief in his abilities. Josh Snow was impressed, and suddenly truly worried. Not about his own riding, but that the chance of his winning was already gone.

Close by he heard Sutter's laugh rise above the sudden noise of the crowds and he knew it was the sight of Blue and his odd gear that set off the sergeant and his friends. It wasn't a pleasing sound.

CHAPTER FOURTEEN

Colonel Radcliff was the official starter. He sat on a fine gray gelding of some height and bulk, white mane and tail picked out and flowing, dapples shining, a true horse for the Post Commander, lifting him above the yelling spectators and giving him a good view of the entire track.

It was once around the oval, approximately a mile more or less, an unofficial distance of no significance. It was all speed, full out, no strategy, no playing with the leader. The line-up was chosen by lots, the riders' representatives drew the bits of paper; Sutter's man was a Private Davenport, whose oily grin displeased the Colonel but this was all in good sport so he nodded to the well-known troublemaker, and vowed to speak with Sutter about his choice of associates when it was appropriate.

Sutter drew the inside to the cheers from his cohorts. Then it was Lt. Snow's man, another second lieutenant by the name of Nix, only recently posted to the Fort; Lt. Nix pulled out number three, putting the boy to the outside. Too bad, thought Radcliff, that set the inexperienced boy in an awkward place.

Mitchell's representative, a disreputable cowhand, only shrugged and looked at Radcliff. "There ain't no point in making the effort." He grinned, tipped his head; "Sir." Radcliff thought to take offense, then studied the man's eyes and they looked back steadily at him, showing no ill humor or disrespect. He nodded in turn; "That's right." The man laughed, Radcliff wasn't certain why.

Mitchell's dun stood quietly between the rather lethargic bay and the restless, fretting younger horse. Sutter looked pressed to stay in the saddle. Lt. Snow's horse was calm, a product no doubt of Mitchell's training and the boy's innate feel for the animal. Squeezed between these two, Mitchell's appearance was all the more inappropriate; that yellow hair long enough to club with leather, a striped shirt with no collar, those tan pants with the leather-lined legs and seat. There, thought Radcliff, that was a good idea.

He'd tried once to sell it to the Army Quartermaster Corps, procurement division, but it was not deemed effective enough to warrant the price. The quartermaster insisted that sewing extra wool inside the seat and upper leg was enough protection for the wearer. Damn the fools, Radcliff had thought then, and now, as he watched Mitchell sit his horse relaxed and secure, legs close to the dun's sweaty sides. Radcliff wanted to shout 'watch this man ride and tell me that leather on the seat and legs of slippery wool britches doesn't make a difference.'

He settled his own mount and ordered the riders to bring their horses up to the mark. He would give a 'one two three go' call, he instructed them, but only when their horses stood calmly, their noses as even as possible. Radcliff was adamant and his voice seemed to quiet the cheering crowd. "No tricks mind you, for I will call you back and penalize you if it is apparent that you have willfully jumped the mark."

He studied each man, seeing what he expected. Both Sutter and the boy had tight faces, hands gripped to the reins, which made their horses nervy. Sutter's horse was throwing its head, sweat dark on its neck and loins, while Sutter complained in a low voice. Lt. Snow's mount was unexpectedly quiet, except for a thrashing tail. More like a cat than a horse, Radcliff decided, which was peculiar indeed.

Mitchell, well the man was as nature fashioned him. Face calm, eyes bright, those damnable eyes that looked into and through a man, challenging him to behave with utter stupidity. The man sat loose, almost collapsed on his peculiar rig; only the drawing up of his legs, so that his knees rested on the forward roll of that blanket, gave away that he intended to make this a race. Radcliff knew about this radical positioning of the jockey, although with the few professionals using the seat, it was done with shortening the stirrup leathers and riding on what was barely a leather seat and a place to tighten a girth.

There was a moment, not perfect or set in stone, but that one moment when from Radcliff's line of sight the horses stood with front legs on the ground, noses tucked, heads placed in their riders hand – on that moment he gave the signal. "Go!"

Sutter's dun jumped high then was propelled forward by spurs dug into his sides. The bay stumbled, tossing Josh forward; as the horse leaped up the boy slid back into the saddle and clung there, body crouched over the bay's neck. Only then did Radcliff note that the boy, too, rode with awkwardly-shortened leathers.

Mitchell's horse plunged easily into a long gallop, taking leaps that pushed him past the other horses. Mitchell leaned forward off of those raised legs and clamped thighs, his body moving with the dun's quickening stride, then he slowed the dun with a light hand as the others sorted themselves out.

Watching the race, Radcliff hated to admit that Mitchell was by far the better rider, and his horse moved so much in stride with its rider, their connection beyond what the military could teach, that Radcliff regretted his insulting words of the day before.

The bay moved raggedly and Josh wanted to pull up but when he tested the bay's mouth there was no response. The horse was running blindly, rough and out of Josh's control so he took up what rein he could and got off the horse's back, feeling the unsteady rhythm and trying to help, to offer a rhythm of his own that might ease the bay's laboring stride. He worked his arms and hands against the tight mouth, swung his legs along the bay's sides, pushing for a steady gait.

It seemed to work, for an opening showed up behind Mitchell's dun in front of Sutter, and Josh was able to steer his horse to the inside, missing Blue's horse, nosing in front of Sutter, gaining good footing and extra lengths. He eased up on his demands and the bay let out a gulping sigh. Josh took the chance and looked to his left; Blue's dun ran easily ahead of him, not by much but enough. Sutter's colt was fighting, pulling wildly until Sutter landed on the colt's neck and lost his reins. His hands grabbing frantically as Sutter and his horse bolted down the track, veering across the dirt, headed toward the crowd, finally steered back onto the course by the frantic yells and waving arms of the eager spectators.

Blue let his dun drift out to the left, wide around Sutter's careening mount. Josh followed two strides behind Blue's horse, far away from the panicked cavalry mount. Josh could hear a low thread of sound competing with the wind and his horse's labored breathing. He kept an eye on Blue, moved with him, letting the bay drift in behind the dun. They left the rail to Sutter and his troubles, where the unbalanced colt finally found his stride as if comforted by the close line of grass and the wall of people.

The bay's stride seemed to even out until Josh felt a response in his hands, a tug at the bit, asking for more rein, wanting more speed. He smiled and answered, closing his fingers, telling the bay to wait. Blue seemed to do nothing but his dun was one length, then three lengths in the lead, Sutter's colt galloping wildly, Josh restraining the bay.

They came around the far turn, beginning to hear the spectators again, each man eyeing what had to be the finish line, people leaning into the track, posted guards pushing them back. *Sutter's dun leaped forward in an erratic bolt, coming up close to Josh and the bay. On the outside, Blue let out more rein, his horse responding with lengthened strides. Josh had to kick his bay, the horse seemed to falter, slow, then speed up again until Sutter's horse slammed the bay's shoulder and Josh yelled, felt the bay stagger and roll under him, down and thrashing, rolling again, tangled in reins and leather, flattening Josh to the ground.*

It registered slowly in Blue that the bay had stuttered and spun around, then tumbled over; Blue used his weight and drew Charley up in four strides, yanked him around to get to the boy. The bay was standing alone, reins looped under a front leg, head pulled to the left, eyes rolling, his entire body trembling.

Blue came off Charley and let the horse go as he slid in next to the boy. Josh was still, one arm raised over his head, eyes closed, hips twisted. There was no visible blood but the face was harsh white, lips turned blue, a hard pulse visible at the neck, and a slowed beat when Blue placed his hand on the boy's chest.

There was silence, not a bird call or even a light wind; the spectators disappeared, there was no one but Joshua Snow as Blue raised the boy's head, cradled it against his arm, breathed with the boy's breathing, trying to keep the rhythm alive.

Josh's eyes opened, staring up, his voice a cracked whisper; "He didn't feel right, Blue. I tried to pull him up. . .we got hit." More silence, then "She lived in Philadelphia, New York now. She remarried. Happy." The glazed eyes studied Blue; "Your son is with her." Then life ended with a terrible breath.

The loss came through Blue as he held the boy's head. There was a blessed moment when nothing moved; then Blue heard the soft words again, repeated inside his mind, saw the boy's eyes watch him as the words were refused; death was refused. Refusal didn't matter, Josh Snow died and with two gentle fingers, Blue closed the staring eyes.

Blue's eyes were muddied when the Colonel and the Army ambulance arrived. He stood back slowly, reluctant to let go but the soldiers needed to do their job. The Colonel sputtered and gave orders, repeating what had to be done; the ambulance corpsmen were silent in their careful handling of the body. The boy who died as his ruined horse rolled over him. Blue had been this witness before. Here he did not understand why or how; the bay was strong, clever, careful, even a slam from that crazed dun would not be enough to bring the bay down.

He moved through the growing crowd, seeking Charley and the bay. The horses had come together, standing side by side, reins trailing; Charley was breathing easily, sweat quickly dried. The bay had a thick lather on his neck and loins, and when Blue touched the bay's hide, spoke softly, then bent his head to listen to the bay's gut, the horse twitched and shivered, and there were too many gut sounds; it was all wrong.

His fingers scooped off lather, thick like soap suds, stinking when he held it to his nose. Then he was conscious of Sutter riding up on his horse, the man smiling, calling out 'What happened? I didn't know there'd been trouble till I crossed the finish line. Did I win?" Blue rubbed his fingers together, watched the thickened sweat dry and crumble. He studied Sutter's face, filled with high pleasure beginning to fade as four men shifted a body onto a canvas stretcher and slid the burden into the covered ambulance. These facts were slow to penetrate Sutter's mind.

At that moment, Blue lunged. Catching Sutter's knee and arm, he dragged the man off his horse. The dun spun, kicked out and bolted. Charley took a few steps, then stayed in place. The bay only shivered.

Blue's fingers circled Sutter's throat as the man struggled, kicking, arms flailing, doing little damage in his frantic protest. Blue felt hands on him and he pulled back, throwing his head, hearing that thump, a cry, cursing. More hands pulled at him but he gripped Sutter and wouldn't let go. It was only Radcliff's voice, Radcliff's face near his that allowed Blue to release his grip, and Sutter dropped away, puffing up stirred dirt, careful to lie still, watching Blue out of terrified eyes.

Radcliff placed a hand on Blue's shoulder, stared into him so close Blue could see the man's anger; "Mitchell, I appreciate your pain at the loss of a friend, we have all lost a good man, but we must not make judgments before knowing the facts. There will be an inquiry. Believe me." Radcliff's fingers dug into Blue's shoulder and Blue allowed the gesture, unable to move, unable to see anything except the absent body, to feel anything except that last breath.

Then Charley's nose pushed at his arm and Blue jumped, the Colonel stepped back. Blue's voice was ragged, uneven but determined; "I'll look after the horses, something was done to the bay." Colonel Radcliff touched Blue again and this time the hand remained only briefly on Blue's arm as it reached for the bay's reins. The Colonel's command gave Blue no room.

"I will have the horse escorted to our veterinarian who will do a complete check. This is a military concern, Mr. Mitchell." Blue shook his head, looking at the ground; "It's a matter of a killing, Radcliff. I'll go along with that escort and the horse. I ain't doubting your man, just want to be sure." He was finding himself again, steady on his feet, temper easing into practical grief; the death became real as the Colonel made sense.

A trooper brought Sutter his horse, another trooper under command from the Colonel took the bay's reins and started walking toward the stables. Blue slid up on Charley, sat a moment taking deep breaths, then he wiped his mouth, his eyes, and let the dun horse follow the slow procession. The *bay was exhausted, stopping several times, trying to urinate, straining and producing nothing.*

It took the Army vet five minutes of listening, touching, walking around the horse, watching that same straining, to make his pronouncement. "The horse has been fed too much rich grains and not enough water. His kidneys are failing; he needs to be put down. I will tend to it."

Blue had his own thoughts about the vet's cold pronouncement. "I'll take him, there's things that can be done." The vet was willing to argue; "No, the Army cannot simply give up a horse to a civilian and this horse will never be fit for duty again." There was no sense bothering with words. One good punch knocked the veterinarian down and Blue ached for more of a fight; the man wisely stayed put as Blue led the shivering bay out of the stable. When the horse stopped, Blue let him, waiting patiently until the bay nudged his arm as if saying they could take a few more steps now.

It was Colonel Radcliff who came to the paddock, in a plain uniform, no medals, no colors, a straw hat shading his face. He leaned on the gate, watched Blue as he covered the bay's back and hindquarters in his one good blanket. Radcliff's voice was soft; "Prescott will have a sore jaw for a few days. However he will not file a complaint. Here, I've written an order giving you the horse." He held out the paper, Blue acted as if he hadn't heard the offer. Radcliff opened the gate and went inside and was instantly confronted with a dun gelding, wide-eyed and anxious. He patted the horse, then pushed beyond him.

Mitchell was pouring something down the bay's throat, amber liquid with a familiar smell. Radcliff waited while the man administered the unusual drench. "What is that?" Finally Mitchell acknowledged Radcliff's presence. "Cider vinegar cut with water. You can bill me for it. I took a bottle from the mess kitchen." He kicked at an emptied container.

"Why, what does it do?" Mitchell kept at the drenching, the bay's jaw resting on Blue's shoulder, the long head held up by one arm, the other keeping a bottle inside the bay's mouth. *"It can help heal the muscles attacked by the body's poison. Your vet was right, but he don't know how to treat the problem."*

Blue turned his back to the Colonel. His hands shook, his arm ached, he wanted to curse and kick and pound but he kept pouring the vinegar/water mix and talking to the bay, telling him it would be fine, just a few more swallows. Damn and hell to the Colonel who thought a bill of sale and a kind word made up for the tear in Blue's heart.

The boy'd known all along about his mama and Blue. He'd held that secret and welcomed Blue, offered friendship and company to a man who'd dishonored his family, split it in half. She was remarried, not that he would try to find her and the child but he hoped she was happy, he wanted to ask Josh how he knew, had he seen her, talked with her. Back east, ah yes, the four years in college and she would know where her son was.

Radcliff left the bill of sale for the bay tucked into Blue's old saddle and bridle. Right Taylor and Haney themselves were careful entering the pen and watching Blue work on that bay gelding. Right stepped up first, leaving Haney to keep hold of their broncs. Right was still in shock; he'd been a close witness, he and Haney, near that spot when the bay went down and flipped over on the boy.

He made a noise but Blue didn't flinch or turn around just kept working on the bay, stroking the extended throat to help the animal swallow, holding that big head on his shoulder and steadying the horse, using his voice and hands to support the bay. Mitchell would kill a man come troubling him now. Right watched the scarred hands, remembered their strength and figured he and Haney best keep their own company.

As they led the horses out of the pen, over to their camp spot, Right thought he saw a shiver run through Mitchell, and knew he'd made a good choice. Right and Haney, they didn't want to fight the man, not over a death like this.

Blue was drunk late at night when the guards found him, drunk on wine he'd taken from the mess, a poor substitute for the whiskey he'd craved but enough of it got him drunk so that he fought the whole goddamn Army and ended up bloodied and locked in the guard house. Jails didn't matter to Blue and he'd been in this one before.

CHAPTER FIFTEEN

No one had seen the child except Dr. Hager. He had carefully placed the damp body on her breast and when those baby eyes looked up at her and she touched the soft blond hair, she knew, irrevocably, that life had to change. It took Harlan perhaps a minute to actually recognize the child as his hands went out to touch her and the baby. He froze and his hands hung in mid air while the child cried and stared at his new world and the man who should have been his father.

Harlan turned his back without speaking and left the room, rigid and unforgiving as she knew he would be. There was nothing to be said, explained, begged or forgiven. She had strayed and here was proof of that infidelity and it had occurred in his house, under his command; there could be no compromise.

Later she heard Dr. Hager suggest to Harlan that if the baby were given away, and he as the attending doctor, signed a form saying it died in childbirth, that perhaps the marriage could remain intact for the sake of the Colonel's son. Hager had forgotten, or perhaps never knew, that Joshua was her child and not Harlan's.

The suggestion was brushed aside without explanation, and Dorothy knew that when she was able, in a month or less, she would be leaving Fort Robinson. There would be no choice given, and she suspected Harlan would take over Joshua, demand that the boy remain with him as proof he could sire a child, with no one to know, not even Josh, that Harlan was not a true father.

She lay there with the child snuggled close to her, hands reaching out, touching her skin, not yet ready to suckle but opening and closing those eyes that weren't a baby's opaque blue but the color of the ocean or that stone used in native adornment.

It was her choice; she knew from her earlier bereavement, the loss of her first husband, that she herself could decide what came next; to love this child who was the constant memory of her loss and infidelity, or she could push him away, give him up to a family wanting a beautiful son. From knowing the father, even briefly, she believed that their son would become an extraordinary man. She knew, without logic or sense, that she would keep her child and damn Harlan, damn him for withholding from their marriage what she had found with Blue Mitchell.

She brought the baby to her breast and offered up her flesh, watched the small pursed mouth open and close, coming nearer and nearer, her one finger stroking his cheek, helping him want to suckle, stimulating that first essential response until he found her offering and his mouth closed on her breast. At first it hurt, more as an irritation, then as her milk flowed, she sighed and relaxed and her son opened those eyes again, to stare up at his mother while he drank. A twist of his mouth around her nipple looked to her like his father's smile.

His father. She had not ever forgotten the one time in her life where passion overrode common sense and the intelligence born and bred into her. Both her marriages had been made from practicality and not passion, marriage to strong men who would take care of a wife in return for her services, both as housekeeper and in the bedroom. She in turn received security and status.

Then there was one time, with a man so out of her social class that in ordinary day-to-day living she would not ever *have known he existed, except for her Josh and his enthusiastic championing of a stranger.*

Flesh on flesh, with him and now with his son. A feeling below her belly, both times, of deep fulfillment and pleasure; what it meant to fully love as a physical woman, to give birth as a mother. She and her new son were connected with an undercurrent of enjoyment she had rarely experienced. Even Josh's birth and his first suckle had not carried with it this extraordinary sensation.

She was given sufficient funds to travel east with her child and a nurse-companion. The woman's salary was paid for a year, and Harlan had settled a decent sum on his wife to ensure that she did not starve while raising the child. She would need to find employment of course, a respectable position as perhaps tutor or seamstress to a family of quality.

Once settled on the east coast, Dorothy remarried within two years, pleading widowhood with no one interested in disputing her solitary status. The child was bright and barely obedient, yet charming to those men who showed an interest in him and his mother. Her third husband was from the business class, a step down from the Colonel, and a greater step down from the gentleman who was Josh's father.

However middle-class her beloved Alfred was, with his men's shop and deference to those above him, inquiring as to their choice in clothing, they indeed would look quite splendid in the newest fashion, Alfred Marquardt loved her, and their activities in the bedroom were definitely an improvement from the Colonel, while she barely remembered the fumblings of Josh's father. It was an aspect of married life no one had spoken about with Dorothy, she had not known what to expect, or what to give, and now she thanked her peculiar stranger, her lover of one night, who showed her that physical love held aspects within it of trust and adoration.

Eventually Alfred moved his business from the fine city of Philadelphia to outside New York. He had become interested in the racing world, telling her that those gentlemen who gathered to wager and earn honors from their fastest horses had large amounts of money to spend, and he wished to branch out and become their tailor. He pleaded with her, his beloved wife, that in making this move they would ensure the best schools and a rich background for their children.

She bore him two daughters, and then there was Robert, the blond-haired son whose father had so tragically died in the Indian wars out west. Dorothy only admitted the truth to herself, about love and loving. She had his child, beloved, unspoiled, always willful but growing into his promise as a young man.

Right and Haney were gone and Blue had the vaguest memory of Right calling to him through the high-barred guardhouse window, asking if he was alive, then telling him they was movin' on. Blue said it was fine by him, to tell Norris he'd show up to the ranch come winter and the boss best have some new colts for Blue to work.

Haney stepped up to the window to speak Blue's name, nothing else. Then Right said his piece; "Damn shame about that boy, knowed he was a friend to you. We don't get friends too often, not drifters like us. Real sorry, Blue, real sorry."

One guard came around the corner; Blue heard the ring of footsteps on the stone walk and he backed down from the window, heard the soldier tell Right and Haney to get along, what they was doing was against military law. Blue could almost see Right's face, his eyes furious, hand sliding to a pistol, the click of the guard's weapon as he brought it to the firing position.

Right called out; "I'll give your message to Norris." Then both men were gone. The guard came to the window and told Blue he could not have visitors. Blue answered that he didn't think any of the rest of the Fort would bother with him. And he was right.

They let him out for the burial so it was only a day in the guardhouse. His head still ached, more from the brawl than the sour wine. Radcliff gave him permission to use Josh's quarters to clean up for the services.

It was promising to be all the reasons Blue disliked the military; music and flags and a draped coffin, solemn words, white faces and pitiful glares. Marching in step, the hearse pulled by matched blacks. A color guard, that damned bugle, words meaning nothing against the weight and sound of the lowered coffin.

He'd buried men, some just bones, others rotting flesh; men of his own type, loners, horse-breakers, cowhands headed someplace else. Most had been brought down by accident or a rifle shot, some old, a few young like Josh Snow. Rarely had they been friends, none close like this boy, who was part of a family Blue didn't know he had.

This morning, fresh from the guardhouse and its stench, he had washed at the boy's quarters, bathing from a pan, which was just barely better than a chilled stream. But it made him look at himself; some ten years older than Josh Snow and little to show for a life lived to his terms. No one to mourn if he'd died instead, his flesh peppered with insults, wounds, breaks, monuments to hatred and failing skills.

He had shaved, staring into a mirror that in itself was meant to be a luxury but he did not like the face staring back. His hand was unsteady with the sharpened straight razor, borrowed from the boy's military kit. Even that hand, holding the razor, it was ugly, distanced from his arms, belonging to a stranger as he scraped and tugged at harsh whiskers and gave a false blood color to the revealed skin.

He took his knife, not the scissors or a more suitable tool but the knife he'd used too many times for different purposes. He remembered holding that same knife to a man's testicles, then pointing it into neck flesh, pricking blood, backing up a threat. Today he used the knife's sharpened blade to hack off the tangled hair It was an uneven shearing but hell, Blue thought, it was as close to military as he could get in time for the funeral.

There were two non-Army shirts hung off a peg in the boy's room; he tried one, the sleeves were too long and it was tight through the shoulders but the shirt didn't smell of sweat, wine, vomit, and confinement. It was the best he could do and good enough for him.

Then, as a last gesture, he sat on the outside verandah, really just a few boards nailed together, room for a chair, a roof covering the small setting area, and he cleaned off his boots, used a bit of saddle oil he'd lifted from the stables and polished away what he could of the years and miles in the faded, patched leather.

He stood up, feeling different, awkward and very much in the wrong place. He went back to Josh's room, wanting one small thing he could take that wouldn't be missed.

There was a book, signed from Dorothy Snow to her beloved son on his twenty-first birthday. It was a text translated from the Greek, The Iliad by Homer it said. Blue read a few pages and it seemed a story about a noble warrior fighting for a cause. Blue took it for her name as well as knowing the boy had treasured it. They'd had contact or the book wouldn't be in Josh's room. He bundled up his dirty clothes with the book inside and left them at his camp outside the paddock. No intelligent soldier following orders would bother to paw through the stench of these clothes and discover Blue's theft.

He marched to his own time, moving easily, head lifted to take in the fresh air, belly rumbling with unappeased hunger, meaning to be at the grave before the mournful pageant began. He wanted a few moments alone over an empty hole, the scent of freshly released earth, worms wiggling through their disturbed home, small birds flying down for a meal, a light wind and sunshine. Then the squall of military music started and Blue stepped back to let the boy go.

Ten minutes after the ceremony was done, the men marched in proper file back into the Fort grounds, the women returned to their houses for private mourning, a cup of tea and some gossip about one woman wearing brown instead of black, another's child behaving improperly. Empty small words to cover the fear that someday it would be their son or husband laid into the waiting grave.

Blue saddled Charley, packed gear on the recovering bay. Charley had put back on the weight he'd lost in racing, the bay's eyes were brighter, he moved easier, stiff some behind but willing to travel. It would be a slow trip to Valentine and Con Norris's Rafter Bar T, but Blue had all the time needed for the journey.

That night he lit a small fire, cooked something from a tin to ease his belly, and sat near the dim light, holding to the leather-bound book that contained too many lives.

To read reviews of William Luckey's other books, and to learn about Joe Evans' trip from Pennsylvania to Nebraska leading a horse, please go to www.waluckey-west.com